TERROR IN THE WITCH CITY

TERROR IN THE WITCH CITY

KEVIN GILLAN

This book is dedicated to all the men and woman of the Armed Forces of the United States of America who put their lives on the line and family on hold to defend the nation against all enemies. It is also dedicated to the men and women of law enforcement who keep their communities safe against those who wish harm upon others.

"No weapon formed against us shall prosper"

ISA 54:17

I would like to personally thank my family for their support, time and patience while this book was written over the years. I also want to thank friends and colleagues who provided facts, support, data, feedback, and criticism which helped me make this possible.

Chapter 1

Smoking and Joking

April 2003

Southern Iraq

The vehicles were all lined in columns, four to be exact. The columns were about 10-deep. The drivers and passengers were crowded in front, in the rear and along the sides of the trucks. They were smoking and joking, as it was referred to. Some were checking the loads on their vehicles making sure the straps and chains were secure. Some were laying around waiting for the order to move out. Others were thinking of whom they left behind and what the immediate future was going to bring. The temperature had struck 100 degrees and only now with the sun setting had seemed bearable. Even during the cooler months, the temperature would hit 90 degrees during the day.

It was a sea of bodies in between the vehicles. He was looking aimlessly to find members of his group. He was looking for a certain truck in a sea of vehicles. There were many in this group that ranged from the normal to the absurd. They were old and new, single colors and multi-colored, some were plain others were extravagant. Some had lights and others were dark. Some resembled circus cars with the different colored lights on the outside, and others were the serious type.

The vehicles were parked on and along the side of the road. The worn black road tore through the tan, brown background that filled everything. The road was empty ahead and behind, the vehicles were clumped together. The only movement was the blowing sand that passed over the weather-beaten asphalt. They were in the middle of a flat desert void of anything. There were no buildings, people, vegetation, nothing; just an endless sea of sand that rose on one side and spread for miles on the other. They were just north of the border that separated the two nations.

TERROR IN THE WITCH CITY

The platoon sergeant who was also the convoy commander hustled quickly in and around the vehicles. He was looking for his marines. These marines were embarking on a journey that they were becoming accustomed to, a journey that they have been preparing for their whole careers. They were currently on a mission to deliver supplies and materials to a specific unit. The platoon sergeant was Staff Sergeant Kevin Blake, who had been in the United States Marine Corps for about 16 years.

The first five years of Blake's enlistment were spent as a tank crewman on active duty. The years of active duty took him around the world from the Far East to the Middle East. It was an interesting life for a young, single man. A far cry from his boring life in Massachusetts. Blake served one more year than the four he was supposed to then left after his deployment to Saudi Arabia and Kuwait. It was a short, but action-packed war, the first Gulf War, as it was being called now.

After a few years spent away from the Marines Corps he missed it. He reenlisted and joined the reserve component in Providence, Rhode Island. While on active duty Blake had thought the reserve requirement of 1 weekend a month and 2 weeks a year was a joke. While in Saudi Arabia after viewing the reservist in action he changed his mind. He adapted to the reservist ways while teaching his men the active duty tricks of the trade. Promotions were steady, and he met many good marines. Now, twelve years after the first Gulf War, he was standing in the same desert. As much as he quietly bitched about the Corps, he loved it and had known it for half his life.

His goal now was to locate his vehicle. The vehicles were moved into their appropriate groups according to their loads and depending on their size. A convoy could be broken apart for manageability purposes which they referred to as a stick. The sticks would provide easier maneuverability through any given terrain especially a hostile area. The convoy would also be easier to defend against attackers, bigger wasn't always better in the military. The load on the vehicle was minor in nature, but important to the thousands of marines that would be dependent to the cargo.

After bullshitting with one of the guys in the unit, Blake, finally spotted the truck. The vehicle was red with a white hand painted "77" on the side which made Blake laugh as he entered the truck. The vehicle was the Arab version of an American tractor-trailer, a red cab attached to a flatbed body. The seats were luxurious in comparison to the military vehicles that he preferred to be riding in. This model had a sleeper bed just behind the seats. If anyone was tired, they never had to leave the vehicle and in a combat zone that meant a lot. For now, the back was filled with the packs, food, and precious belongings of the two marines who called this vehicle their home.

The cabs of the trucks were all different. When a driver entered a vehicle, the controls were never the same. If you didn't know Arabic, German, or a host of other foreign languages you were on your own. This usually meant a lot of gear grinding and whiplash until you figured out how to operate it. The drivers held on to their vehicles until it broke down after which they would check out a different one. The lucky drivers had a stereo system installed.

This convoy was the first time that Blake was a passenger. Up to this point he had his own vehicle, which had become a problem. Loading and driving the vehicle was enough, but trying to organize, monitor and keep track of 10 to 15 other vehicles was impossible. This time Blake was in the convoy commander, not the role that he was accustomed to back in the states. His actual title was Motor Transport Chief which entailed knowing everything about motor vehicle operations. Being the convoy commander usually meant he was responsible for the convoy from beginning to end. That included receiving the mission, the routes that would be taken, communications, security and vehicle and driver assignments - which he knew well.

Now his job had been watered down to monitoring the vehicles and more importantly the marines assigned to them. The Marine Corps in its infinite wisdom had taken the role of the convoy commander and outsourced it to a third party. The new group responsible for his previous duties was made up of marines from various occupations. Their occupations ranged from cook to administrative clerk. None of these occupations involved motor vehicle operations. They were marines whose jobs were not really needed at the time or already filled by others. They were dubbed, "Convoy Control Company", a company of marines who had no real knowledge of their new occupations. The drivers on the other hand were school-trained and capable of operating many highly complex pieces of machinery. They were also knowledgeable about tactics, assignments, routes, security, maintenance and a host of other important details. However, the new-formed unit was etched in stone, for the time being. They would be responsible for moving vehicles from one point to the other, safely and on time. Blake and his fellow platoon sergeants were responsible for the loads, operation, and limits of the machines and marines aboard them.

"You all set Staff Sergeant?" The driver asked.

"Yes, I am," Blake responded.

The driver, Timothy Carr, was a resourceful marine from Worcester, Massachusetts. Carr becoming his driver, was not intentional, but Blake became fond of the young man, so they stayed together. He had not been the poster boy the marines sought after. He had been absent for the past few months and was marked as a potential "problem".

Unauthorized absence had been his forte for a few months prior to the activation. When Carr learned through other marines that the unit was getting activated, he reported in with all the necessary gear. He was brought to the first sergeants office where a determination was made as to whether he should stay or discharge him out. After some begging and pleading and a reduction in rank, Private First Class Carr could stay and serve his nation. That would be the last problem he would pose to the Marine Corps. Carr was very competent at his job and never questioned his orders.

Blake did not intend to have him as his driver; he merely picked the first vehicle in line in which Carr was the operator. After that Blake decided Carr was his driver. The two got along well considering the difference in age and rank. Blake felt that Carr should have been a Corporal because he had more faith in Carr's decision-making capabilities than those of higher ranks.

Blake slid over a bottle of cold water to Carr which was a small slice of heaven in a place like this. The convoy was moving out. It would still be a few minutes before truck "77" would move. All the necessary equipment would be set into place. As a staff non-commissioned officer,

TERROR IN THE WITCH CITY

Blake was issued a 9mm Beretta Pistol for his duty weapon, unlike Carr who carried the standard M-16 service rifle. Since the driver could not utilize his weapon properly while driving, Blake let him use his pistol for the ride just in case someone got to close to the vehicle. It also served the passenger best to arm himself with a long-range weapon like the rifle. Blake handed his pistol to Carr, then he grabbed the rifle and placed it between his legs. Helmets were put on and adjusted and the night vision goggles were placed close by. In the setting sun the vehicle started rolling along the barren highway.

It didn't take the marines long to realize how extensive the road network was in Southern and Central Iraq. The highway they were traveling on was an abandoned project of the recently deposed regime. The modern roadway stretched for hundreds of miles. It went through villages, towns and cities that either sprouted up because of it or survived by the rivers that flowed close by. There were three lanes, the middle lane was the safest. Getting too close to the far-right lane might entice a militiaman or guerilla to carry out an attack and the left lanes were known to be booby trapped. The bridges and intersections were always dangerous. Underneath the bridge was a perfect nesting spot for the enemy to spring an ambush. In fact, some overpasses had been previously used as bunkers. The brick, stone, and sandbagged bunkers still had the firing holes where their army had maintained them as checkpoints. The old regime never doubted that it was going to be invaded; by 2001, security was tight around most major cities with curfews imposed between midnight and 5.a.m. All vehicles and persons traveling in or out of the capital during those times were searched. Movement was halted at strategic and sensitive area including certain sections of Baghdad.

The highway signs along the way were blue and hung lifeless on the eerie road. The words were in Arabic with English underneath and used kilometers instead of miles. The names were famous and scary to the foreigners. A picture of the sign would make a nice addition in a scrap book, to show the grandkids when you were old and gray. The driver and the passenger placed their gear close enough to grab when all hell broke loose, the hell that they expected and knew would occur. Carr lit up a Marlboro Light before the wheels of the vehicle started rolling. He reasoned that it would settle his nerves down before the long and dangerous drive to the new camp. It would be his last cigarette until tomorrow morning. Light discipline had to be maintained constantly. That meant no smoking at night; no headlights or marker lights were to be used after dusk. Instead drivers used night vision goggles. Flashlights had to have red or blue lenses which made map reading almost impossible. Sometimes this made no sense when a large convoy was on the move, drawing enough attention from the noise it, but it was procedure.

The first checkpoint was reached before nightfall as the convoy snaked through the first village. They drove past small grey and stone colored homes. Some were simply baked mud huts while others were large gated and stone colored walled compounds. Some had bars and grates on the window and others were literally holes in the walls. Some places looked like they were destroyed years' prior and were a pile of rubble left to decay. The peddlers and beggars were already there to greet the convoy. The young men and boys lined the sides of the unpaved roads. Their clothing ranged from the traditional Arab clothing to t-shirts and jeans. Most wore sandals, but some had bare feet which Blake thought would be painful on the rocks and stones.

The peddlers sold cigarettes and anything else they could to make a dollar as the convoy chugged past them. An old man off in the distance tipped his hand back by his mouth, a sign that he wanted water, not just any water, but the bottled water that was free of the filth and disease that surrounded him.

On the other side of the road was a young boy who sold Iraqi currency, an item that was worthless to anyone at this point, but another memento. The notes were from the Bank of Iraq and adorned with the face of Saddam Hussein. The money was worthless though, literally not even worth the paper it was printed on. The boy only wanted a dollar from the strangers, a small amount to them, but would allow him to provide food for his family. Not all the vendors and beggars were innocent. Some were militia dressed as civilians and insurgents gathering Intel against the Americans. As the months progressed, they would also be responsible for the numerous improvised explosive device attacks.

TERROR IN THE WITCH CITY

As the convoy started through the farmland, the passengers and drivers needed to pay close attention. Dusk turned into darkness and the NVG's were activated. No one in Blake's unit had been attacked yet, but it was only a matter of time. Palm groves and orchards broke up the connected houses. Even with all the room in the middle of the desert, the Iraqi people lived near each other. While people in America craved their space, a village here was a close-knit community.

The palm groves and orchards were also a perfect hiding place since the trees were thick and the leaves were large. The remnants of the army or the militia would move into the groves and orchards before the convoys arrived. Men with weapons would hide until the convoy arrived. They would use small arms, mortars and rifle propelled grenades in their assault. Most of the fire was inaccurate, but effective in disrupting the troop and vehicle movement. The insurgents would attack and leave before the Americans could respond. It also became a painstaking place to search for the enemy as well. Blake was not aware of how many vehicles were in this convoy but knew that each vehicle played an integral part. Each dependent on one another in case they broke down or were attacked.

The vehicle in front slowed down before speeding up again. The vehicles were trying to gain speed to cross a rickety bridge above rapid canal. The Saddam Canal would later be responsible for the deaths of a few young marines that never took into consideration the strength of the powerful and fast moving current. Blake watched the old bridge sway as the vehicle in front crossed over. The bridge was made of steel, but hardy enough for the weight of the equipment that they were hauling. The bridge was wide enough for one vehicle at a time. Local traffic consisted of either small cars or a donkey and cart; at least that was all they had seen so far. The bridge was now supporting vehicles that weighted more than 25 tons. Some were towing heavy machinery to include graders and bulldozers.

The light armored reconnaissance vehicles and armored assault amphibious vehicles also played hell on the bridge. It was only a matter a time before it would collapse, and Blake prayed that it would not be while they crossed it. The scene reminded him of the video taken of a car swaying on the Golden Gate Bridge during an earthquake. Knowing they were next, Blake and Carr exchanged looks as the vehicle ahead moved off the bridge. Carr floored the truck in hopes that if the bridge did collapse momentum would carry it to the other side. They held their breath as the vehicle crossed feeling the sway underneath them. Finally making it across, the marines had no time to enjoy the moment as once they had crossed, they saw a white flare explode in the distance.

"I never seen that color before" was the only thing Carr could get out before they saw tracer rounds ripping over their vehicle.

Blake and Carr watched as both vehicles in front of them stop next to each other whether it be panic or the road ahead. The road was blocked. There was nowhere to go. One of the first things that motor vehicle operators are taught is to drive through an ambush, never stop the vehicle.

Salem Police Department, Salem, MA

The Lieutenant entered the office of special investigations. The office was located on the 1st floor of the building at 95 Margin Street. William Hayes was a guy who grew up, worked and lived in Salem. He was in his 40's, single, and never had any children. His longtime girlfriend had finally given up on trying to convince him to get married. They had finally moved in together which he knew kept her happy.

He carried with him a fresh cup of his favorite coffee and two newspapers. The local paper would report the politics he had to deal with. The other paper would tell him what was really going on in the world. Both papers were placed on the desk as the computer was turned on. A check of the e-mail would cover one of his jobs. He handled the complaints, concerns and gripes of the local populace, a painstaking and necessary part of his job.

"Quality of life issues" as they were called were mundane in nature, but a boiling point for the residents who had to endure them daily. Parking complaints, barking dogs and the loud obnoxious neighbor were some just to name a few. The complainants, as they were legally called, e-mailed the police department in hopes that their problem would be dealt with swiftly and quietly. The last thing these people wanted was the police at their door. They were scared themselves of knocking on a neighbor's door to ask them to lower the music or take care of their wild kids. So, the e-mails were discreet and anonymous.

TERROR IN THE WITCH CITY

One of the e-mail's caught the commander's attention. As he read the e-mail address, he realized it was an officer of the department. The patrolman was responsible for a small, but surprisingly active area of the city. The beat, as they were called, was a hot bed of criminal activity, especially in the summer. The calls now were far tamer than the multiple stabbings and shooting of years past when he patrolled the same area, but still a serious crime generator. The lieutenant was familiar with the patrolman and his work. Besides dealing with special investigations which covered a host of jobs and responsibilities, media officer was another title that the job carried. In the morning, especially after a busy night of policing, the local reporters would call and try to get more information than the police report carried. The lieutenant would then have to put on another hat of his, mediator.

He would try to keep the reporter or radio talk host happy and not give to much information that would hinder prosecution. The patrolman had generated some interesting reports in his pursuit of cleaning up the "point" area. Among the incidents were car breaks, drug transactions, chases, drunk drivers, wife beaters and the raging alcoholics that kept the officers employed. Occasionally, Lieutenant William Hayes was also the damage control officer. When any officer swayed in his judgment or the lack thereof, he had to make things right. Some people were always unhappy with the police no matter what they did or failed to do. The lieutenant was happy telling the media or victim that the officers found, captured, and arrested the defendant for their crimes against society. Mostly importantly, was the happiness of the man in the corner office down the hall with what he heard about his officers on the local radio station or in the paper.

The commander sipped the coffee as he read the subject line: "Greetings from Iraq". He read the letter and would post it, so the other police officers could read it. The e-mail gave a short description of the typical day's activity in Iraq. This letter would be posted in the muster room.

Southern Iraq

Carr and Blake both jumped out of the vehicle as it rolled to a halt. Their escape route was sealed so they took up a defensive position on the passenger' side of the vehicle. The white flare was a signal from the enemy to attack the convoy from the opposite side. The militia or remnants of the Army had used the bridge as a choke point for attack. The plan was simple, let some of the convoy through so it would appear as if everything was normal, and then attack at the heart of the convoy. The rounds were coming from the palm groves on the right side as well as in front of the truck. The date and palm groves that once covered large areas of Southern Iraq were decimated due to the fighting in the Iraq-Iran war from 1980 to 1988. They were further destroyed when Saddam Hussein bulldozed trees and drained the marshes to make room for roads and deny his opponents the ability to hide.

The marines quickly abandoned their vehicles and set up a hasty defense in the brush. Hasty was the quick, down and dirty version of a defensive perimeter; two and four-man squads dismounted their vehicles and meticulously set up their weapons. The awesome firepower began as 100 plus marines of the detachment poured 5.56 and 7.62-millimeter rounds at the hidden enemy. In the dark of the night all that could be seen was the red and green streaks caused by the tracers as they cut into the thick palms.

The fight was short lived, only a few minutes. The small group had either fled into the night or died a quiet death. The marines were lucky in the firefight, no injured or dead to report. The ambush consisted of small arms fire, mainly soviet AK-47 rounds. The ambush was to disrupt the flow of supplies, just harassment for now. The mission had only been delayed by a few minutes. Blake and Carr were impressed by the shock and awe of the concentrated firepower. They brushed the dirt off their uniforms and mounted the vehicle. The excitement had passed and now it was time to reflect on what had happened and their reaction in the battle. All the other marines in the convoy were doing the same. They carefully reloaded their weapons and checked their gear for the next time. They would make it a point to clean their weapons when they stopped. The Marine Corps had it drilled in their head to have a clean weapon, so it performs to its fullest capabilities.

TERROR IN THE WITCH CITY

According to the global positioning unit, Camp Chesty was 65 miles south of the Capital, Baghdad. The camp was formed by the remnants of a previously used staging area and airstrip. Several-paved roads connected to a small runway. There were no houses or shacks near, and the closest town was several miles away. Carr moved the truck through the rusty, dilapidated gates of the abandoned area. The only thing they encountered was a barking dog.

The dog was thin like all the other animals Blake had seen there. Dogs were all over the place, left to fend for themselves, foraging for the meager scraps that were left behind. Blake chased the dog off on foot as he led the vehicle to the staging area. The marines of Combat Service Support Detachment-10 would stage their vehicles and sleep for the night. The guards were set and the drivers winded down for the evening. The marines bunched up in small groups to spin their tales of what had taken place. Most of the young troops could not wait to tell the rest of the platoon of their heroics the next day.

Chapter 2

Camp Life

April

Camp Chesty, Iraq

The next morning several vehicles assigned to Blake took their place along the road. Their purpose was to deliver the necessary equipment they had carried for an engineering battalion to purify water. Camp Chesty was not only picked for its paved road system and airstrip, but its proximity to water. After gassing up at a bulk fuel point the vehicles were driven to a remote area of the camp. The load delivered consisted of pumps and other equipment that was used to purify water. One by one, each truck was unloaded and the marines of 6th Engineer Battalion went to work. The pumps were placed in a small river that ran around the edge of the camp. The water that was originally brown and muddy was turned into clear drinkable water. After several hours the trucks were finally unloaded and waiting to move out. A sampling of the water and its processes revealed that the water was purer and safer to drink than bottled water that had been given out earlier in Kuwait. The men filled anything that could contain liquid and the convoy headed for the next destination.

Life had sprung up all over the camp as the motor vehicle operators of Heavy Company 1st Transport Support Group made their way back to the staging area. Marines from a helicopter squadron were piecing together a helipad for their transport and attack helicopters along the newly acquired runway. Maintenance tents and portable hangers were being erected. A patriot missile battery was poised in its position to counter any scud or other missile attack.

Less than two weeks ago during the opening volleys of the war, the marines were awakened by the sounds of whistles and alarms when incoming scud missiles were detected in Kuwait. The alarm would sound and a few seconds later the rumble of the patriot missile battery could be felt. Blake and the others would scramble out of their racks; grab their weapons and gas masks and head to their assigned bunkers. The bunkers consisted of deep holes in the ground with plywood on top for a roof and hundreds of sandbags created the walls. They housed 20 to 30 marines and each tent had their own assigned bunker. Most of the guys bitched when the attack came in the middle of the night when they were woken from sleep. In the day though, it broke up the monotony of waiting for the war to begin. The attacks would usually come in the middle of the night or early in the morning and last for 30 minutes to an hour.

In another section of the camp closer to their position, dozers and other construction vehicles were digging massive pits. Constantine wire was encircling them, and a tower was being erected. It was a temporary prison to hold the prisoners of war, or "detainees" as the liberal media was calling them. Blake saw the letters "TSG" newly painted on the vehicles. 1st Transportation Support Group, which had been formed less than a month ago, had consisted of four companies that had their own purposes.

Headquarters and Service Company consisted of the mechanics, cooks, supply men and all the other enlisted and commissioned officers that were needed to support the other companies. General Support Company consisted of marines who mostly transported fuel and water. They drove vehicles specially designed for hauling large amounts of each to replenish the front-line troops. Light Company hauled troops and cargo. The vehicles were either the new 7-ton truck or older 5-ton trucks that transported troops and all sorts of cargo and marines. The last was Heavy Company, 165 marines made up from all the 6th motor transports seven sites. These sites covered from Las Vegas to Texas and to Rhode Island. Heavy Company's main assets were the LVS. Logistical Vehicle System was the name given to the versatile hauler.

The LVS was like a tractor-trailer, but the vehicle articulated which meant that the front could move independently of the rear. The vehicle was extremely versatile and could move in a tight spot. The vehicle was referred to as a system because the rear unit had several variants. Each variant had its own designation and purpose from flatbed trailer to 5th wheel and a unit that can retrieve cargo containers. Due to shortages of the LVS and the extreme demand of the vehicle, the military acquired many Arab tractor trailers in their place. They were commonly referred to as "hajji" trucks or the politically correct "third world nationals' vehicle".

Heavy Company was tasked with mounting a fleet of the hajji vehicles to use alongside the few military vehicles they had at the time. The tractor trailers would be used until they either broke down or were replaced with a military vehicle. The problem as the marines saw it was not just about driving the vehicle, it was about reliability, maintenance, and capabilities. Anyone could drive a truck, but the load was crucial to the troops who needed the supplies. If the vehicle broke down no one knew how to fix them. They did not have the proper tools to work on them, nor the parts to fix or the experience to work on them. Blake even had an argument with a Captain over his refusal to have those vehicles move his unit's equipment. Blake had told him that there were no more military vehicles available and the vehicles he requested would be used for another mission. He was also informed that a Marine Corps general had made the decision about using the "hajji" trucks not himself. Blake gave the officer time to change his mind before he left the area. The captain reluctantly decided to use the assets of Heavy Company.

As the vehicles arrived in the staging area the faces in the crowd were marines from his and other platoons. 1st platoon consisted of 54 marines from his unit in Providence, Rhode Island and six marines from the sister unit in Orlando, Florida. A marine was cutting hair on the back of the 870 and a line had formed. The 870 was a special trailer used to haul heavy equipment. A dozer was chained on the back and was going to an engineer battalion. The marines were waiting for a night run back to Camp Anderson. Anderson was not actually a camp, but a place to take on fuel, food and ammo, referred to as a rapid resupply point. Anderson was just a grid point on a map, which was located on the MSR (Main Supply Route). The route was a straight shot from southern Iraq to Baghdad. The only problem was parts of the route passed over the Tigris and Euphrates rivers. Some did not have bridges in place, or they had been destroyed to slow down the advancing forces. Engineers were placing bridging equipment to solve the problem. The convoy would leave at night and probably be back in a day or so.

TERROR IN THE WITCH CITY

The marines in the platoon and company were spread-out all-over
Iraq and Kuwait. Keeping track of them was nearly impossible especially
while Blake was on the road. The names and faces of the marines would
change as the convoys went out on missions. The senior man on the
convoy would take charge of the vehicles and drivers while they were on
the road. Blake did not like the way the marines were spread out all the
time. While he was a tank crewman back on active duty that never
happened. At most, one tank company would be assigned to another unit
for a certain purpose or mission like a task force. This constant moving
around of marines and vehicles was frustrating. Units trained as a group
and the marines were accustomed to each other in the unit. They knew
how the other would perform, their capabilities, reliability and friendships
that formed.

Carr stopped the vehicle in the dirt parking spot and hopped out to
join his buddies. The marines gathered in groups and swapped stories,
joked around, and exchanged stuff they received from friends or families
back home. Blake would look for his own rank at these gatherings.

He spotted Staff Sergeant William Hall. Blake called him Billie
which pissed him off more than anything. While first names were not to be
used in the Marine Corps, the formalities ceased within the confines of the
groups. Blake had known Hall for 12 years now. Since his first drill as a
corporal with the unit Hall had made his presence known. Blake had never
forgotten when he approached him as he was doing maintenance on a
vehicle and Hall made a smart-ass comment about one of the other "new"
guys that Blake checked in with him. Blake thought Hall was a punk at
first, but their friendship grew as they stayed in the unit and were
promoted through the ranks. The two would always wind up in the same
platoon or overlapped as the SNCOIC (staff non-commissioned officer in
charge).

The two marines raised glasses in unison at many military social
functions in local bars after weekend drill. They toasted to the promotional
"wet downs" and the goodbye and farewell receptions that accompanied
the reservists. Hall was assigned to General Support Company due to his
job specialty which were water trucks and fuel. The two proceeded to
discuss who was going where, and how screwed up things were. They

loved to bitch about how disorganized the unit and command was. They knew a thing or two about motor vehicle operations though, and how things were to be performed by the book. The combined experience between the two marines was over 28 years of experience in their field.

William Hall stood a little taller than Blake, 75 inches is what his military identification card stated. His camouflage utilities hung on the thin marine. He wore military issued glasses that were affectionately referred to as "birth control glasses". That was since no one would fuck you with those glasses on. Blake knew that Hall was neither married or had kids. Blake thought that as a little odd for a man in his late 30's or maybe he was just jealous, he had been dating the same woman for a while. Blake knew that Hall wanted to be a Rhode Island State Trooper but had not fared too well on the exam. He worked as a correctional officer at the adult correctional institute in Rhode Island (ACI). He was assigned to the maximum-security facility. Blake considered Hall a good friend and would have hung out with him more if they lived closer and if he wasn't married with kids. Once a month was good though and they did manage to go out to dinner and have some drinks usually on a Saturday night unless they were on a field operation.

Their reunion was short lived though. Convoy control was gathering a convoy to return to Anderson. The convoy would depart within the hour and certain vehicles were excluded. Blake's convoy had not made the manifest list in time, so they would spend another night in camp awaiting their turn. While this did not make the marines, who were being left behind happy, they would get some well needed sleep.

Salem City Hall, Salem, MA

The office of the mayor was on the second floor of city hall. The building was situated in the middle of downtown. The entrance to the building were large, gothic, dark wooden doors with metal buttons on the outside; the doors looked intimidating while they were closed. It was rumored that the more buttons on the door represented the more prestige that was given to the occupants of the building, at least back in the days of early Salem village. This city hall was the second oldest in the United States, dating back to 1817. The city itself was first settled in 1626.

TERROR IN THE WITCH CITY

The mayor who was in his office studied the traffic as it crawled outside his large window. Vehicles would stop occasionally for a pedestrian in the crosswalk, people going about their business. The crosswalk looked like a white ladder in the road from his vantage point. The ladder that he was ascending one rung at a time; the same ladder he would continue to his higher political aspirations. Not this little piss ant city. Jacob Parker wanted a real city, like Boston, New York, or Los Angeles, but since he was an outsider in those communities he would never get elected. Instead, he would settle for state congress.

As he stared down from his perch, the mayor peeled himself away to the task at hand. He had studied the proposals of the city councilmen, police chief, and fire chief, head of the public works, parking, and every other city department that had a stake at this event. The council members would be meeting with him at 10 this morning, an hour to go. The meeting would be no big deal, only preliminary, but the closer they got to that night the more prepared they would need to be. He could not afford any real problems at least not any that could be foreseen. The election would be in November and he did not need any bad memories fresh in the mind of his constituents especially not while they were at the ballot box. Parker opened the folder and reviewed the figures that were penciled in the columns of each commodity. Something was going to have to be cut from the budget. They simply could not afford all the expenditures and he did not want to have to rob from Peter to pay Paul.

In less than seven months Halloween night would be upon them. That meant tourism money for the businesses, shopkeepers, and revenue for the city. The drawback would be the cost for overtime: police, fire, and public works. The mayor knew that they were all needed though.

Halloween festivities were not always like this he knew. Halloween night had grown over the years in the 1990's after parts of a Halloween movie were filmed in the city. Salem pushed advertisement of their museums and tourist traps then added some Halloween activities for the children. The billboards, radio spots and ads had all paid off. Now the problem was that it was starting to get out of control. A rowdy crowd had replaced the family friendly and children events that it was intended for. Near riots and stabbings had broken out when the police shut down the vendors and started moving the crowd along. The police chief had told the

TERROR IN THE WITCH CITY

Mayor that it was only matter of time before all hell broke loose with 60,000 tourists all contained within a six-block area. The mayor, city council members, and department heads would hold their breath until the night was over. The mayor knew that sooner or later something terrible would happen on Halloween night, but only so much could be done to stop the crowd. People were coming whether he liked it or not. He would pitch his plan to the council members and heads. The proposed budget would go back and forth for a while, but an agreement would be reached.

The residents had grown tired of Halloween in their quiet city. In fact, most grew to hate it. Tourism really picked up at the beginning of the month and increased rapidly until Halloween night. During this time the residents could count on several things: total gridlock while driving anywhere in the downtown area, no parking, and long lines at their favorite shops most of which occurred on the weekends. After working all week long, they had to endure the annoying visitors on their precious time off. If they lived downtown, they were really screwed. This meant they could not move their cars because if they did a tourist would snatch their parking spot in a second, regardless of the resident-only parking signs or tow zones. The police were only allowed to ticket the vehicles, and unless the vehicles were blocking a driveway or fire hydrant, they wouldn't tow it.

The tourists were a burden to the police as well. Vandalism was usually reserved for Halloween night. The local thugs looked for the chaos of the night to mask their revenge with thousands of drunk youths converged in the downtown area. The geniuses who ran the school system made it easier for the punks to stay out late and cause problems by cancelling school the next day. Smashed windows and vandalized vehicles were inevitable during the witching hours. The day after Halloween the police were bogged down with reports of vandalism and they were sympathetic to the complainants. The police would explain that residents could thank the city for pushing the event like it had. The residents would complain to their city councilor, who then would complain to the mayor. Sometimes a letter to the editor might make the Salem Evening News. Someone would then promise a solution "next year" and that would be the end of that.

Chapter 3

Mail Call

April

Heavy Company 1ˢᵗ TSG, Camp Chesty, Iraq

Mail call was a treasured event in the marines' day. Since there was nothing to look forward to except leaving, mail call was the next best thing. There were no stores, recreation or entertainment available to escape the stresses of living in a combat zone. It could drive some over the edge if one let it. Whatever the mail contained could make or break the man or woman who received it. The marines in each platoon milled around in front of the tent that was the company office. They were hoping and praying to get some news from their family or friends. If they were lucky a package would be waiting for them. A package was like a Christmas gift and you never knew what it contained. Cigarettes, magazines, drink powder; DVDs and porn magazines were all worth their weight in gold in Iraq. Letters were just as precious though, especially from the right person.

Lance Corporal Richard Powers read the name on the envelope. The name of the sender was the girl he would call his wife after the deployment ended. Richard and Amy had been together for several years. The couple met in high school and continued dating through her college years and his military service. Now she would soon be graduating from Brown University and he would be wrapping up his six years of service. They planned on living in Warwick, R.I. not too far from his folks. They would eventually buy a house and have some children. Powers remembered saying goodbye to her in the dark parking lot in Rhode Island on a very cold and early January morning.

Powers was now brought back to reality by the thud he felt on the side of his chest, punched by the marine next to him.

"Now that I have your attention," stated Troy Ward in his deep voice," go to chow and be ready if anything comes in later. Clean your weapon and there is no guard tonight."

The marines liked Sgt. Ward and would follow him even if it meant their death. He was a fair and demanding man that expected the marines to carry out his orders without question. In return they knew that Ward had their back. He would never have them do anything that he would not do himself, a true leader by example. His motto, "work hard and play harder." The men respected him for his leadership. Blake had made it a point to teach Ward everything that he knew as he progressed in rank. Blake had told him what needed to be done, but let Ward carry out the task by his own means.

Powers stood 5'11 and weighed 180 lbs. The 24-year-old reservist had blond hair, blue eyes and had an athletic build to him. He joined the military to help pay for college. He also reasoned it would open doors and look great on a resume. He was a business major at the University of Rhode Island and wanted to pursue a career in politics at some point. He knew he would have to practice law to make that desire more attainable. He had the charm for the lawyering and politics as well as the intelligence and business smarts. He worked security, which allowed him the time to study for classes.

Powers could smell the sweet perfume that emanated from the envelope. He opened the letter carefully, inhaling the nectars of her beauty. He remembered that last night they spent together. Powers had walked in the bedroom to gather some items that he needed to pack. There she was in the dim glow of the candles. She was lying naked, half of her under the soft satin sheets covered in rose pedals. Normally he would have been the one to set up the night, but he was lost with what he needed to do before he left. He had been told 48 hours prior and was trying to tie up his life before deployment. Her body glistened in the flickering light and was now his for the taking. The stone in her belly button reflecting the light. Her sumptuous breasts and erect nipples looked perfect. The red sheet just barely concealed the place where he wanted to be the most. He studied her for a minute mapping out what he wanted to do first, then took off his clothes and slid under the sheets. Without a word she climbed on his body and passionately kissed him, starting at his lips and working her way down. Powers knew that he better enjoy himself and her tonight. Formation was in nine hours and then his ass belonged to the Corps for as long as they needed him.

Powers was hoping that a picture would accompany the letter, but he could not complain. Even though the mail had been slow, the letter had made it. He was excited as soon as he started reading the letter.

"Dear Sweetie, it has been a long time since we were together."

He thought of that night, all the time. The last thought he had before he went to sleep at night.

"I cannot stop thinking about the passion and love I felt between us and what you did to me."

Powers had felt the same way; he knew she was right for him.

"I miss talking to you and hearing your voice, I wish you would call me!"

It had been nearly impossible to call because the lack of satellite phones and when it was possible security was an issue. Only recently did it seem like calling home would be easier.

"The night we shared was incredible, the way you touched me, held me and made me feel, words cannot describe my feelings for you."

It was a remarkable night.

"You took my breath away and captured my heart on Valentine's Day!"

He thought, "wait a minute I was fucking here on Valentine's Day." He almost yelled out loud. Then it happened, the pain that every man feels at least once in his life. The nausea and sickness that encompasses you and the wretched feeling. He almost fell back in the sand as he read the letter. He could not believe what he was reading. It was a love letter all right, but not for him. The envelope was for him; the name was his, even the fucking address, but the letter was not his. "That fucking bitch, she cheated on me," is all he could think of. He could not believe what was happening and did not want to read the rest of the letter, but he had to. He had to know what was going on.

"You going to chow Powers?"

"Huh?" Replied the shocked marine.

"It must be a good letter, are you going to eat, man?" One of his buddies asked.

"No, I'll catch up later," he said.

"Well you have a good time reading that letter, I am sure she is worth it," his friend said as he walked away.

"She was," he said to himself.

Powers finished reading the rest of the letter. He stood as he scanned over the words that would change his life. He would read the envelope and letter over and over just to ensure that he had not read the wrong thing, but he knew he hadn't. He would have to call her to hear it in her voice. The distinct silence that he would hear when he told her about the letter. He would have to think of what he was going to say so as not to give her a way out. At least he could prepare himself for the inevitable, he knew that finding out now was better than after he was married, but he was still heart broken. How could she cheat on him after he had put her on a fucking pedestal and treated her like a queen? He would never do that again. Now he'd treat them all like shit, just like the others guy did. He had to find a phone, but there weren't any to be found. He had to get on a convoy and maybe then he could find one.

Blake had returned from the evening meal with his buddies, Staff Sergeant Hall and newly promoted Staff Sergeant Burton who had worn the rank for only a month. Robert Burton had been treated like the higher rank for quite some time though. The lack of promotions was not his fault, but a problem created by headquarters Marine Corps and the way promotions were given. Burton had met requirements needed for promotion, but the field was frozen. Even the officers and senior staff treated him differently because of his seniority and experience. Burton had spent 12 years in the Marine Corps reserve so far and had every intention of doing at least 20 years.

When they got back from chow Blake was given a package from one of the marines in the platoon. The package was from his employer, The Salem Police Department. Blake missed being a police officer and would have liked to be patrolling the streets of Salem instead of this place. He would not even mind working the midnight shift which he hated. Blake opened the package and found candy, magazines, music CD's, and a few other odds and ends. In a letter from one of the lieutenants was a decal. The decal was the actual sticker that went on the door of the patrol car; the same as the patch on his uniform which was a witch on a broom stick with the moon in the background. The Salem Police logo was the most sought-after patch in the policing world. Patch collectors had called from as far away as France for the actual patch that was copyrighted by law.

Since Blake was never in the same vehicle on convoys, he decided that he would mount the decal on a piece of cardboard and place it in the window of the vehicle that he traveled in. A copy of a police report was found in the box as well. The report stated that a vehicle was stopped for a minor traffic offense in the point area where he patrolled. After the driver made some furtive movements, legalese for moving around, the driver was told to get out of the vehicle and he reluctantly complied. After a knife was found in the driver's door pocket, a search of the vehicle revealed a large rock of almost pure cocaine in the glove compartment. The rock was weighed in at an alarming ¾ of a pound. Blake read the report and chuckled, the job never escaped him.

"I am sure the driver is going to pay dearly for that fuck up," Blake said as he handed the report to Hall.

Chapter 4

Rainy day fund

April

Staging Area 1st TSG, Camp Chesty, Iraq

All the vehicles that were going on the convoy were parked in the company's staging area. The drivers were waiting for the order to move out for their next mission. No personnel, however, could leave the area at this time due to the bombing run that was taking place several miles away. Components of the 3rd Marine Air Wing were flying missions against the local militia. The continued ambushes on the marine convoys had annoyed enough of the command structure to generate a serious attack against the villages on the convoy route. Blake, who was settled in the passenger seat of the truck, was reading the words of his favorite author and had just reached a key part in his book, the counter-assault on the amusement park. The book was long, but the best part had begun. It had been a while since Blake found time to lose himself in the book since he arrived in this shithole. As he turned the page, he was interrupted by one of the marines. Blake who was resting his feet on the dashboard took his boots off and sat up in the seat; He was clearly annoyed. Carr who was writing a letter looked up, Blake assumed it was to his girlfriend. For the past few weeks both marines had shared their pasts with each other, but Carr was tight lipped about his girlfriend.

"Hey, staff sergeant, there is an American reporter looking for American cigarettes," the marine said.

"Well I am an American marine who wants an American phone," Blake said as he opened the door to the cab and hopped down on the sand.

The reporter stood between the two vehicles and had heard what Blake said. The man, outfitted in a tan vest, tan pants and hat spun around and told them that he would be right back. Did this guy really have a phone, a satellite phone? Blake had been carrying an emergency stash of cigarettes in case a situation like this developed. Blake climbed back in the truck to the back seat of the vehicle and grabbed the .50 caliber ammo can that he was carrying around. The can that held this type of ammo at one time now held approximately 48 packs of cigarettes, not just any kind, but American cigarettes.

Blake realized when he was deployed to Saudi Arabia in the first "gulf war" that when there was nothing available one of the most precious commodity was a pack of cigarettes. There were no stores to buy anything, so money became useless; so instead of money he had cigarettes. He was not going to black market them but wanted to have them just in case. He stocked up while they were in California and in Kuwait. If the marines needed them, he would take care of them.

Carr asked, "Are you going to give them all away?"

"No, just the foreign ones," Blake said.

American cigarettes were sold all over the world, but in foreign countries the tobacco was different than the tobacco grown in United States, which changed the taste. A desperate smoker who ran out wouldn't even care. Blake removed 10 packs from the stash that had the Arab writing on the side and went to the back of the vehicle to wait for the reporter. The reporter came back with what appeared to be a satellite phone and a smile.

"Hello, my name is Brennen, and this is my assistant, Scott" Brennen said as they all shook hand.

"Nice to meet you guys, these are the marines" Blake said.

"The mail hasn't come to us yet. We ran out of cigarettes and someone said you were the man," Brennen said.

Blake began the bartering, "okay then how much for a call?" He asked as he laid out the 10 packs on the bed of the truck.

A group of marines started to gather around the truck.

"One call, one pack," Brennen said as he slid one pack away from the pile, "you mind" He said to Blake.

"Of course not. They are yours now." Blake replied.

He opened the pack and pulled a cigarette out.

"Hold on," Blake said as he went back to the cab of the truck.

He returned with eight more packs and threw them in the pile.

Brennen explained that he was working for a newspaper in New Jersey.

TERROR IN THE WITCH CITY

He looked at the pile and said, "Listen I don't want to take all your cigarettes."

"The problem is that there are 17 marines here and I am the senior man. I cannot make a call-in good faith without them calling first. It's the way it is in the Marine Corps," Blake explained.

Brennen thought about it for a minute. He counted 14 packs from the pile and pushed the rest back to Blake.

"Okay they have 5 to 10 minutes; you have 15 to 20."

"What about the phone bill?" Blake asked.

"I am not paying, and the boss isn't here is he?" Brennen said.

"And anyway, you can give me a story about the trucks you are driving, they will like that."

The interview lasted about an hour long. Blake explained to the reporter and his assistant the logistical reasons for the vehicles and their role in the war. The three smoked and drank cold bottles of water that had been given by one of the marines.

It was evident by his mannerisms that something was eating Powers. He stood by the vehicle and waited his turn to call. When it was his turn, Powers moved on the other side of the vehicle to speak in private. He waited as the phone rang and rang. He had thought about what he would say and when he would say it.

What he did not expect was the answering machine to pick-up, "Hi, you have reached Amy, please leave your name, number and short message and I will get back to you, bye!"

"Hi, it's me, we had a chance to call and I was hoping you were home. I love you." Powers was trying his best to sound like nothing was wrong.

The fact that she was not home started eating him alive almost immediately. With the time difference she had probably already left for work already but considering his mental state it didn't really matter. After almost two hours of waiting, it was Blake's turn to call home. It had been six weeks since he talked to his wife and that call had been rushed.

At that time Blake had learned only hours earlier that he and his men would be leaving their assignment at the airport and head back to Camp Coyote, which was located 33 miles south of the Iraq border in Kuwait. Now he waited patiently as the phone rang in his house some

12,000 miles away. All the time and effort to make this call and now he got the answering machine.

"Dammit!" he said out loud.

The sound of the answering machine engaging deflated his hope. He listened to his wife give instructions and the annoying beep that followed.

Then he heard a sweet "Hello" from his little 5-year-old daughter, Erin.

"Hi baby," Blake said to her.

"Daddy, daddy, daddy," Erin said excitedly.

"I miss you and love you so much."

"Me too, honey."

"When are you coming home?" she asked him.

He hated that question but had to say something even though she did not understand. Blake remembered the last night he spent with her and when he put her to bed. He did his best to explain why he was leaving, and he wanted her to know that he was going to miss her a lot. He kissed her goodnight and he stayed with her for a while, holding her hand watching her breathing. The room was dark except for the dim of the nightlight. He stayed with her until she fell asleep. He was heartbroken and knew he would not see her for at least six months if not a year.

"I don't know honey. They still need us here to help out," Blake explained.

"But I want you home with me" she said.

This was going to be tough. Then the line went dead.

"What the fuck is wrong with this thing?" Blake said as there was silence.

"Try again staff sergeant, the signal was probably interrupted, maybe the weather somewhere," replied one of the marines.

He dialed the number again, this time his wife answered. She told him that she was in the attic when the call came in. Erin was upset and was missing him a lot. The couple then proceeded to talk about what was going on. He prepared her for the fact that the phone call would cut out any time, but he would be able to call more frequently in a few weeks. She asked where he was.

"About 200 miles south of Baghdad," Blake said.

TERROR IN THE WITCH CITY

As he said it someone held a GPS unit in front of Blake's face as he spoke. Baghdad was a mere 65 miles to the north. He figured that his wife had enough on her plate with two small kids, a new house and everything in between and he did not want her to worry some more. The conversation lasted about 10 minutes before the phone died. The battery was running low and needed to be charged up now. Blake returned the phone to the reporter and thanked him for everything. Well at least the morale of the men had improved over the last two hours. 20 marines in all had called home and spoke to someone. The men were smiling again.

Chapter 5

More Than a Mouthful

April

Cranston, R. I.

The young man noticed there was a new message on the answering machine.

"Hey Dan, sorry I grabbed your mail by accident, it's on the table, Later."

The letter was on the kitchen table and he examined it, making note of the return address. Dan Allen had just come home from work, he stood in the kitchen reading the letter. He was mechanic by trade and content with life working Monday through Friday and partying on the weekends. He had graduated from Cranston High School west and joined the Marine Corps reserve shortly after. He had finished his six-year enlistment and only now started thinking of what he was going to do in life. He looked down at the letter with a smile on his face. What a night they had together, "Happy Valentine's Day" had a new meaning to him. He detected the sweet aroma of her perfume on the letter and eagerly opened and it.

"Dear Sweetheart, I miss and love you so much."

Well she was a bit overwhelmed in her feelings, but he could deal with that.

"It has been such a long time since we've been together, but the memory of our last night stays fresh in my mind."

It was that not long ago, but whatever, hopefully there would be more.

"You are the first thought in the morning and last thought at night."

That's sweet.

"I cannot image how hard life is out there."

Where? What is she talking about, things aren't that bad here?

TERROR IN THE WITCH CITY

"I watch and listen to the news every chance I get, hoping and praying that you are fine."

It took him a second, before he realized this letter wasn't for him.

"That stupid bitch!" He yelled to no one.

He would have to contact her as soon as possible to give her heads up. She might not even realize what she had done. He looked around for his phone to try to find her phone number.

Dan thought about her boyfriend. He had known Powers and had been good friends for a few years. The two had met together while attending heavy equipment operator's school in Missouri as part of their Marine Corps training. They bonded together in part because they were both from Rhode Island and reservists. After the pair completed their several weeks of training they checked into their unit, 6th Motor Transport Company, 6th Motor Transport Battalion Providence, Rhode Island. Since they were both new to the unit and had no friends there, they maintained their relationship during the drill weekends and two weeks of training every year. Several months had passed when Powers introduced his girlfriend Amy to him at a military family day event.

Over the years Dan became friendlier with her. He would occasionally see Amy when he was over Powers apartment. A friendship evolved between the two after a while. The more he saw her the more his feelings grew. Feeling a sense of shame over his thoughts, he started to distance himself from his friendship with Powers. He was going to leave the military soon, which provided the excuse that he needed. Still, when he saw her, his attention became aroused which led to a little crush. Soon Dan ended all contact with Powers and the problem solved itself, so he thought.

One night, Dan and his friends were celebrating the weekend over some wings and beer at a local eatery. The lovely young waitresses, dressed scantily clad, made the food and drink taste much better than it was.

Amy was on the other side of the spectrum. She was pissed off because she had a terrible day in school by nearly failing a test in a core class. To top it all off her car decided that it was going to break down. The "idiot light" on the dashboard came on indicating a battery problem. The light was now flickering. She knew it was going to die soon. She rounded the corner on Airport Road in Warwick, R.I. The radio cut off then came the sound of the vehicle and the powerlessness of the steering wheel. She did manage to get the vehicle into a parking lot. Her car, a black Mercury Capri, was old, but had been reliable and dependable. Her father had bought it used and made sure it was in good working order.

She managed to wrestle the wheel into an abandoned part of the lot. Her first inclination was to call Richard, but he was deployed. She would have to call her father instead. As she thought about grabbing her cell phone, she realized where she left it in her jacket pocket. The only problem was that her jacket was right where she left it last, in the kitchen of her apartment. The restaurant might have a pay phone which was becoming a rarity due to cell phones. As she walked toward the building, she was amazed that some guys took their families to this place. Their wives and children would have to watch as the waitresses walked around in tight shorts and tank tops nearly exposing themselves. She understood it was a "guys' place", but taking the family? "I hope he never pulls that shit with me," she thought. She would kill him if he ever even thought about it. She wanted to be the one that teased him with her boobs falling out of her shirt, not some bimbo who whored herself for tip money. She would have to buy one of those outfits and surprise him at home one night. She knew she could fill it out a lot better than some of the ones in there. To her relief the payphone was by the front door.

Dan had raised his glass to the toast when the woman on the phone caught his eye. He saw her long flowing brown hair. He moved to the other side of the table to get a better glimpse of her. She was attractive all right and somewhat familiar, he thought. Probably too much booze already, he figured, but he knew her from somewhere.

As Amy dialed the number, she looked up to see a muscular guy with black hair and a beer in his hand, he was staring at her. "What an ass," she thought; she couldn't even use the phone in peace. The phone rang and rang. She knew that there was no answering machine or call waiting on the other side. Her father and mother believed that if someone wanted to get a hold of them, they would either wait or take care of the matter themselves. Unfortunately, Amy would be waiting or calling for a cab.

TERROR IN THE WITCH CITY

As she placed the receiver back in the cradle, she realized that she knew the person watching her. She looked at him then remembered it was Powers friend Dan from the Marine Corps.

"Uh-oh," Dan said to himself watching the woman look at him then walk to the front door. "She must be pissed off from me starring at her," he thought to himself. He continued to stand there as she approached him.

"Hi, you remember me?" She said with her beautiful smile.

"Of course, Amy, right?" He said. "How is it going? I haven't seen you in a while."

"My car broke down and I rolled to a stop in the parking lot," she grumbled. "I came here to use the phone; my cell phone is missing in action."

"We're here just having a few drinks and some laughs, want to join us?"

"I can't. I have to get a ride home and then try to get the car going."

Dan thought for a minute, "I'll tell you what, have a drink with us, I'll look at the car myself, and if I can't fix it, I will give you a ride home." Amy gave him a suspicious look.

"I am a mechanic, that's what I do all day," he replied.

"No, you don't have to do that," she protested, but what else was she going to do? Waiting for her father that was going to take a while, and that was if he came home. The other option was to pay for a ride in a gross cab with some creep. "Okay, one drink, because I've had a shitty day and need to relax a little."

Dan nodded, then continued their conversation, "How's Richard? I haven't seen him since I got out?"

"He was activated and sent to Iraq with the rest of the unit," she said.

"Wow, I had no idea sorry."

"Yeah"

"I haven't kept in touch with anyone there. I hope they stay safe." Dan said with genuine concern, "Let him know I send my best and if I can get his address, I'll send him some things."

TERROR IN THE WITCH CITY

"Thanks, they're waiting for something to start right now. No Happy Valentine's Day this year for them?"

"Sorry," is all Dan could think to say.

Dan then made the proper introductions to the group and he poured her a beer from the pitcher. "How about a toast to Valentine's day," he said, holding up his glass.

"To Valentine's Day," his friends replied, not in unison.

Dan looked at her with a smile.

"To Valentine's Day," she said with a dutiful smile.

The two engaged themselves in a conversation about school, work, and life in general. Amy was feeling better and forgot about her shitty day after a few drinks. Dan realized that he better look at the car and drive her home if necessary before he was too drunk to drive. It only took a few turns of the key and a few minutes to realize that he was not fixing this vehicle tonight.

He shut the hood and turned to her, "I don't know yet, but you need a tow. Need some tests, but nothing that will happen tonight."

"Great more money and running around," she muttered.

"Well I can fix it for you tomorrow if you'd like. I'm parked over there and fine to drive," he explained.

"Okay, thank you," she said.

Amy grabbed her book bag and a few things that she needed from Capri. The two drove to her apartment still chatting up a storm. What started out to be a nightmare had turned out pretty good she thought. Dan was interesting and a good-looking guy too. Amy was being polite when she invited him upstairs. Deep down inside and with the help of the alcohol, she was intrigued. Amy asked if he wanted anything to drink or eat as they entered her apartment. She went into the kitchen to discard her belongings. She appeared a short time later displaying the cell phone.

"Here it is," she said triumphantly.

She invited him into the living room, and they sat down on the couch, like they were in high school and her parents were out for the night. She turned on the radio to her favorite soft rock station. Dan glanced around the room to look at the pictures and displays on the tables. Pictures of she and Richard were scattered around the room. He tried not thinking too deeply about what was happening or what was about too. If he did

33

think, he would have leapt off the couch; now it was holding him down like a magnet. He was not like this, moving in on someone's girl: especially friend's girl. Dan hated those guys, despised them, and would preach that he would never do that, yet he was.

She sat next to him with a glass of wine and asked if he wanted any. He shook his head no, knowing that he already had enough to drink. Dan's heartbeat started to race, and his throat went dry as she sat next to him. He knew that something was going to happen. She moved her face a little closer to his as she questioned him in a cute, flirtatious way. He moved his face a little closer to hear hers. They both stopped inches away, as they studied each other's eyes in the dim glow of the apartment. The soft music playing in the background.

She stared into his hazel eyes. He started kissing her soft, wet lips. He did not hesitate for a second as he moved his arm around to her body. The foreplay only lasted a short time before it gave way to their desire. The flames of lust and passion had been ignited and were well past the point of extinguishment.

Chapter 6

Happy Birthday to Me

April

Camp Anderson, Iraq

The convoy was a few miles away from Camp Anderson. The mission was to retrieve ammunition from the makeshift ammo dump and bring it forward to Camp Chesty. From there it would make it to units in the field or a re-supply point in the north or west. Some of the marines on the convoy were excited about going to the ammo dump. Blake knew there must have been a female around there because no one got excited about going there. In all his 16 years in the corps he did not have a lot of interactions with his female counterparts.

There were no females allowed to serve in the combat arms field when Blake was on active duty assigned to tank battalion. The only other time females in the Marine Corps could be spotted were on the rare trips to Main Side section of Camp Pendleton. Main Side was where the headquarters of the division was located and all the pleasantries of life; a movie theater, stores, restaurants, and recreational facilities. All of which were over 20 miles away from tank battalion. In boot camp at Parris Island, South Carolina the genders were separated geographically. There was a rumor that a male recruit was caught banging a female recruit in a trash dumpster, desperate times lead to desperate measures. Only in the reserve did Blake have any real dealings with female marines and they worked mostly in administrative billets.

"Hot" female marines were somewhat of an oxymoron. Blake could count those numbers on one hand. If they were "hot" they were either married or surrounded by a bunch of horny guys who would cut each other throats to hook up with her. Was she "hot" in the real world or just in Iraq? Here in Iraq, they were operating on the desert scale. That meant you had to take into consideration several factors; the lack of women in the Marine Corps and in Iraq, the scenery, which in this case was an empty desert void of normal life, and the lack of women especially in a region of the world where the culture and religion forbid women in mainstream society.

The convoy pulled in to the secure area a little after sunset. The marines were disappointed to learn that they would have to wait until morning to see if the rumor was true. They did take advantage of the secure environment to relax and enjoy the peace. Blake had a package that he had saved to open. The box was sent within another box and instructed him to only open the package on today's date.

"What's in the box, Staff Sergeant?" Carr asked.

"I don't know maybe my birthday gift."

"Happy Birthday, Staff Sergeant!" Lance Corporal Black chimed in who was standing on the platform outside of Carr's door.

Of all the marines in the company, Blake kept a watchful eye over Black. He was not a standout marine, but he was dedicated, loyal and very hard working. If Philippe Black did not know how to work a weapon or piece of machinery, he would figure it out on his own and then teach everyone else. Black went by Phil, so no one thought he was Spanish which he wasn't. The name was French, and he apparently had taken a lot of shit for it.

Black was a member of the platoon who could be counted on to get things done with little or no supervision. He volunteered on several occasions where most would have walked away. He was comfortable with the junior ranks and experienced enough for the senior ranks to seek his knowledge. He was loyal to Blake and because of that, Blake kept an eye out for him. Blake tried hard not to play favorites and sometimes had to remind himself of this. He knew little of Blacks' personal life, only that he was a tall, muscular, hardworking 20 something year old guy who grew up in Rhode Island.

"Thanks, some birthday, huh? Never thought I'd spend my birthday in an ammo dump in Iraq at war," Blake rambled.

He opened the package and started pulling out the goodies that his wife had sent him. The candy had melted then reformed into a blob but was still edible. One of the gifts was a small robot-like dog. After reading the directions, he placed it on a board they had in the truck. Blake gave some commands out loud and the "dog" preformed his tricks. The guys laughed out loud as "Jake" barked and moved about. Blake passed out some candy to Carr and Black before they left the vehicle for the night.

They wanted to sleep outside under the stars. Now with some quiet and privacy, Blake removed the pictures and cassette that were enclosed in the box. He gazed at the photos and wished that he could be there. In the picture the snow was high around the back deck and swing set where the kids posed. The kids had made a happy birthday picture for him in crayon and marker. He read the card and a letter his wife had written.

Blake prepared his sleeping area for the night, making sure his pistol and gas mask were close at hand. He rummaged into his pack for his beat-up Walkman that he had saved for years. The radio was useless since most of the music or talk was in Arabic. There was one American station, Armed Forces Radio that played the same 10 songs over and over. After he was situated for the night he lay in the dark and pressed the play button on the cassette player. It sounded like he was right there with them and in the darkness, he could make out their faces as they spoke.

He heard his wife explain what was going on and how they were all doing. His daughter was singing, and his son was cooing. Blake drifted to where he dreamed of being, more than any other place on earth. To be home lying on the carpet with his daughter jumping on him, and his son crawling around. Blake was content that everything was fine with Kerrie and the kids, but sad that he could not be there. Blake never heard the tape click off as he drifted to another world in the confines of truck "77".

Salem Police Department, Salem, MA

The detective knocked three times on the doorway of the Special Investigations.

"Here you go Lieutenant, you need anything?" the detective said as he handed a bundle of mail to his boss.

"All set, thank you," Hayes said as he flipped through the stack of mostly junk mail.

Everyone was trying to sell them something they neither needed nor could afford. The detective was temporarily assigned to his section from Criminal Investigations Division shortly after September 11, 2001. His job was to work with the other agencies from the federal agents to the state police in locating foreign nationals who were of "interest". "Interest" covered illegal immigrants from the Middle East and other hostile nations to homegrown terrorist sympathizers and everything in between. The job was to track down leads, monitor, gather intelligence, and detain anyone who posed a threat to the nation. He was also concerned over two big targets located in Salem: A power plant and LNG tank that had little or no security.

Ever since that tragic September day, police were called numerous times from staff and neighbors to check the status of individuals taking pictures and/or watching both areas. While most officers dismissed the calls as frivolous, the residents were truly concerned that future plots were being hatched in their backyard. Police were also chasing around "suspicious package" calls, from powder in envelopes to wrong address on their packages. Everyone was paranoid.

As Hayes was sorting the good mail from the junk, he saw an unusual return address: Heavy Company, 6th MTBN, Providence R.I. He was pleasantly surprised and relieved. Blake was alive and able to write. He opened the letter and learned that Blake had no more e-mail access and received the patch. The rest of the letter described his duties and what was going on. Hayes smiled, put the letter aside and tended to the rest of the mail.

Camp Anderson, Iraq

The drivers and assistant drivers on the convoy were working hard in the morning sun. A warm 85 degrees would soon rise to 100 degrees by noon. As the ammo was loaded on the vehicles, the men ensured the load was placed properly. This responsibility was two-fold. If the load was not stacked or secured properly, the load could come apart and kill anyone near. While this was highly unlikely it was a possibility. If the ammo never made it to its destination, marines would not be able to carry out the mission and that could lead to deaths, maybe their own. This was a more likely scenario.

Blake was ultimately responsible for delivery of the cargo to the marines in the field. His marines knew that and ensured the task would be completed safely. The drivers checked the straps, chains and equipment that held the deadly arsenal in place. The convoy would be complete before noon and it would take a few hours to get back to Camp Chesty.

TERROR IN THE WITCH CITY

The marines were eager to leave Anderson and get back to where the action was. They were also disappointed to learn that the attractive female sergeant they heard had been reassigned to another section.

Combat operations eliminated a lot of the usual stringent procedures, a.k.a. bullshit that took place at an ammunition dump. Usually a range safety officer or his representative would have to complete all the necessary paperwork in advance to get the ammo that was needed to shoot. They would also have to produce the proper certification to ensure that they knew what they were doing with the ammo. In some cases, an Ammo Tech would have to accompany the load to ensure that safety procedures were being followed for equipment being used. During the normal procedure, if one safety strap was missing or fire extinguisher out of place the whole process would be terminated. Then everyone in the chain of command would be informed and the shit that rolls downhill would begin its decent. In Iraq though, those procedures were suspended, and Blake never signed a form. The checks on the vehicle were preformed, vehicles were lined up, and convoy control took the 10 vehicles back to Camp Chesty. Blake could not help but think about today his birthday. "What a fucked-up birthday," he thought as he shook his head and concentrated on his surroundings.

Chapter 7

Anger

April

Salem Police Department, Salem, MA

Officer Steven Dawson stood in the muster room of 95 Margin Street reading to see if anything new had been posted in the "atta-boy" case. He had finished all his reports and was waiting for the end of the shift, which was at midnight. He wasn't sure what he was going to do after work. Maybe a drink before heading home or shift would open, someone calling out sick.

Dawson was pleased to learn that Blake was alive and well. Hopefully the marines were killing a shit-load of those bastards. They deserved to die for what they did he thought. While his thoughts were shocking to some, he found them justified. In fact, Dawson thought about going back in the Corps and delivering his own justice. He wouldn't though. He was not only too old to go back but had been medically discharged years prior. He had injured his back on a night operation when his unit was based in Okinawa, Japan. The unit was participating in an operation in the dense jungle of NTA, (Northern Training Area). It would be the last operation that squad leader Corporal Dawson would ever participate in. His squad was on patrol when a marine to his left wandered to close to the side of the small cliff they were on. The clouds and dense jungle made seeing without NVG nearly impossible. The marine on point had never informed the others of the drop off if he himself saw it. When Dawson heard the marine yell as his foot slid, he grabbed his jacket.

Dawson would go over the edge as well. Both marines slid down about 10 to 15 feet before getting caught up in the roots and thickets. They were very fortunate not to fall on the rocks to their death 60 feet below. They both were rescued by the marines and treated by the corpsman who was assigned to the unit. They were then medevacked to the U.S. Navy Hospital at Camp Lester. Dawson suffered cuts and bruises to his head, face, and most of the front of his body as well as his extremities. He also suffered back issues that took almost a year to recover from. Dawson was sent back to the states to recover and eventually medically discharged. His only motivation to go back would be to avenge the death, no the murder, of his wife.

Even though they were only together a few years she had changed his life for good. Prior to their courtship, Dawson was a single cop who caroused the bars and hooked up with many women who sought the former marine. That all changed when he met Nicole. He met her at the scene of an accident. Dawson was the responding officer for a motor vehicle accident and Nicole was one of the drivers. He took her information and completed the report. He thought she was cute but tried not to mix business with pleasure. The department frowned upon their officers picking up their clients. Nicole liked him and since he didn't hit on her, she needed to get his attention.

She went to the police department a few days later and requested to speak to the reporting officer about the accident report. Dispatch had him report to the lobby to speak with her. Nicole danced around the subject before she handed him a piece of paper with her number and a message to call her soon. She later told him that she went there to see if he had a ring on his finger as well. Within a few years they were walking down the aisle and planning on a few children to fill their lives and their new home.

She worried about his line of work but thought he could take care of himself. Still, she could not help but feel uneasy when her husband put on his uniform and left for the midnight shift. Nicole watched the news and worried that some junkie or thief with a gun or knife would try to kill him for nothing else than to get away. She was wrong about who would be the one killed though. It would come in the most unsuspecting place too.

Nicole Dawson kissed her husband goodbye on a beautiful fall day. She drove down the street with the thought of pushing her kids in a carriage on a day like today. She arrived at work after a 30-minute ride, checked in with the supervisor, and went to her assignment for the day. She welcomed the customers and made them feel at home. She performed some required and regulated tasks before grabbing the microphone and welcoming all the passengers. She thanked them for flying American

TERROR IN THE WITCH CITY

Airlines flight 11 from Boston's Logan International Airport to Los Angles, California.

She went through the passenger safety brief as she had done many, many times before. She smiled and looked around the cabin at the very same passengers that would be responsible for her death. She buckled herself in the jump seat after the flight preparation announcement. Aboard that plane were the hijackers who had made a decision that would change the course of American history in less than an hour. The plane gained speed and catapulted itself from the runway into the clear blue sky for its final flight that departed from Boston, Massachusetts.

Patrolman Steven Dawson left the muster room and descended downstairs to a marked patrol unit. He was surprised to see the Chief headed up the stairwell.

"How is it going, chief? Surprised to see you here tonight," Dawson said.

"Me too Steve. I'm just here to pick something up. How are you doing?" His boss replied, "Things okay? Let me know if you need anything."

"I'm all set for right now, boss, but thanks for everything you've done" Dawson replied as he continued down the stairs and left the building.

"Anytime, Steve," Chief Charles Hampton replied. He was tall with a medium build. His brown hair was just starting to grey which is why he kept it short. He trudged up the stairs to his office. The reason for the late-night visit was to retrieve a file that he would need for a meeting with the mayor in the morning. They would probably have breakfast downtown and would not have time to come back to the station before the meeting. Hampton really cared for the people who worked for him. He knew Dawson had been through a lot and that was why Hampton cut the man a lot of slack.

Dawson's wife had been killed on a hijacked plane. He would never know what truly happened in those final moments but listened to the experts provide their analysis. He was given plenty of time off to grieve after the funeral. Dawson was angry, but there was no specific person to blame; so, he blamed all Arabs and he made it well known. There were several complaints made against him by Middle Easterners who had dealt with him, most were squashed in the end. As time passed so did the aggressiveness and professionalism. Dawson had fallen apart, and it was quite evident. Only recently did it appear that he was coming back.

Hampton keyed in the code on his door lock and entered the office area. The first room contained a small conference table with several chairs. The walls were adorned with police memorabilia and pictures of the Salem Police department circa 1800's, a group shot of the patrolman of that era, and some city buildings. His office was a spacious room on the second-floor corner of the building. A few chairs were in front of the desk and a couch was off to the right side. The furniture was needed to accommodate visitors who would attempt to change his mind.

The walls were a mixture of pictures of family, friends, and political figures. One wall held his military treasures to include a new piece. The 5 by 7 picture was a hand drawn picture of a wavering Marine Corps flag with battle ribbons. A letter of gratitude and camaraderie had accompanied the picture from one of his patrolmen. They had a bond even though their service was 20 years apart. Both had worn the same uniform with the eagle, globe and anchor on the collar. Hampton was fond of him. Blake wrote that by the time Hampton had read his letter, Blake would be in the theater of operation, destination unknown. He grabbed the file off his desk.

Hampton was trying to protect his men and appease the Mayor at the same time. His officers were loyal to him and respected him. The public didn't know shit about being a cop or the bullshit that went along with the job. Chief Hampton went back down the stairs and headed to the Crown Victoria that was in the space marked "40". Hopefully his budget wouldn't be obliterated during his busiest time.

Chapter 8

The road less traveled

April

Staging Area 1st TSG, Camp Chesty, Iraq

Blake looked at his watch when the other vehicles finally arrived, two hours late, no surprise there. A different Humvee (High Mobility Multipurpose Wheeled Vehicle) was escorting the vehicles, which was unusual. The vehicle stopped, and the passenger came around to Blake's side of the truck.

The passenger spoke, "Are you the senior man?"

Blake identified the man as a Master Sergeant, two ranks above his own.

"Yes, Master Sergeant. What can I do for you?" Blake as he hopped from the cab.

"Let me talk to you in private, Staff Sergeant"

Blake followed "top" as he went around to the rear of the Humvee. The nickname was given to master sergeants not only in the Marine Corps, but the Army as well. The Master Sergeant lifted the canvas back of his vehicle. The flap was not really canvas material, but a plastic material that acted as a shell.

"I have three boxes that have to get delivered to the senior enlisted or senior officer of each regiment at RRP-26. I can't tell you the contents, but if the contents are learned then morale could be affected. Do your best to ensure that the senior marine of the unit receives these boxes. I mean the Sergeant Major, CO, or XO. Do you understand Staff Sergeant?" He asked.

"Yes, Mater Sergeant, I do." He replied respectfully.

The two shook hands and then exited the Humvee. Blake grabbed the boxes and placed them in the cab of his vehicle. The familiar MRE boxes were light and ducked taped so they could not be opened easily. The writing on the boxes was specific for their respective unit. Almost immediately Blake knew what the boxes contained.

All the drivers and passengers had been waiting to go for a while. Carr returned to the vehicle and took his place behind the wheel. He saw the boxes in the back but did not ask about them. He knew that if Blake wanted him to know he would tell him. That was one of the things Blake liked about Carr, his discretion. Blake was privy to certain information and wanted someone with him that he could trust not to run their mouth to his buddies.

Shortly after convoy control had provided a quick safety brief the vehicles started to roll one by one from the dirt lot. The trip would take a few hours if all went well. The convoy went through the first village and crossed a bridge over the Tigris River. Once it crossed a bridge the convoy left the secure area that surrounded the base.

The convoy traveled north on route 8; the highway ran parallel to the river. The Tigris River provided the towns and villages the water they needed to survive. Irrigation canals were crude but effectively grew the crops that were needed to live. In Southern Iraq irrigation along the Tigris and Euphrates Rivers were necessary throughout the year to grow crops due to the lack of rainfall. The war was very visible along this stretch of road. A burnt truck loaded with howitzer rounds and RPG's had been destroyed on the side of the road by a field.

The locals stood along the roadway as the vehicles drove past a populated area. Most waved and some begged for food, which had become a familiar sight. As the vehicles moved farther along the road there were other signs of the country's past warfare. A rusted soviet tank was parked beside a house. Some buildings were partially or fully destroyed; rubble lay scattered over the sand, rusted fences surrounded buildings that appeared to have been destroyed decades ago. There were rusted vehicles in pieces alongside the buildings. Blake tried to determine if the damage was current or old; and if the old damage was from the first Gulf War or from the Iraq-Iran war in the 80's. The old regime in Iraq was also responsible for some of the destruction itself. The dictator had made examples of the Kurds in the north and the Shi'a in the south that revolted against him.

KEVIN GILLAN
TERROR IN THE WITCH CITY

The convoy took a left and traveled up another road that would take them to the southern corridor of the capital city. The area was barren except for the open fields. There were pools of oil on the ground, ponds as they were referred to on a map. On the right side of the road an expansive graveyard appeared. They were not like the graveyards in America but made up of tombs that were entangled within each other and a complex of tunnels. The graveyards were spread out over a large area and not only held a family, but the entire clan or a tribe. The convoy started to enter a more populated area. The houses were closer together and apartment buildings were mixed in. The buildings were not very tall, but stood out in the flat, level, desert villages.

The convoys took their tolls on the Marines day after day. The men were confined in their vehicles. Depending on the situation they could be alone or with strangers, if they were lucky someone from the unit was in the vehicle with them. Even though there were other Marines around it didn't mean they couldn't feel isolated. Thoughts of being away from family and friends, stuck in unfamiliar surroundings and always in danger ran through their minds.

Whoever was leading the convoy determined that a stop was in order. It was always safer to stop in the middle of nowhere than a populated area. That way you could see who was approaching and prepare an adequate defense. Blake shook his head at the poor location that convoy control had chosen to stop. His vehicle came to a halt across the street from an apartment complex of three buildings. The tan worn buildings formed a "U" shape with an open field that faced the roadway. The complex alone would have been bad enough, but the field was currently being used to play football or soccer as the marines knew it. The locals were watching their friends and neighbors play a game, which was their national pastime. It was a miracle that the game did not come to a stop. The convoy drew a lot of looks and stares. The marines exited the vehicles and took up a hasty defensive position, as they had been trained to do, along the vehicles. Infantryman and security personnel set up their weapons on both sides of the vehicles, while the drivers and passengers checked their loads, grabbed something for the ride or relieved themselves. The stop would only take a few minutes, but that could be enough time for a sniper attack as they had learned.

TERROR IN THE WITCH CITY

It did not take long for someone to realize the poor choice of stopping. Within a few minutes word came to load up the vehicles to prepare to move out. By that time the locals had started to wander over to the commotion of the convoy. Blake wondered whether the locals knew that they could get shot or maybe they didn't care. The thought of food or water might just override a bullet to the head. The marines had realized that the locals would try to do anything they could to get their hands on the supplies or equipment. They normally approached in a group which minimized the individual's risk. Blake waited by the drivers' side door to keep an eye on things. As the convoy began to pull out several trucks ahead, an Iraqi approached on his side of the truck. The young man dressed in jeans, sandals, and a multi-colored shirt walked right up with no fear.

Carr who was watching out of the window spoke, "Come on staff sergeant, the convoy is leaving, we'll be all set."

Blake read the look of concern on his Carr's face. All the marines were watching, rifles resting in the frame of the windows. Blake raised his left hand and motioned for the man to stop. The man stopped and smiled in amusement. "Is he fucking with me?" Blake thought, "or is he going to call my bluff?" He then moved closer to the vehicle, just a few feet away from him. Blake didn't know the man's intentions or that of the crowd that was slowly getting closer. He withdrew his government issued 9mm Beretta M9 service pistol from his holster. He held the gun in his right hand in the low ready position with his index finger along the trigger guard. He had been trained to do this both from the police and Marine Corps to prevent an accidental discharge when just such an occasion arose. He did this just to let the man and crowd know that he was serious. Today was not the day that the crowd was going to surround him and if they tried then a few would die.

Just as things appeared to grow tense the vehicles ahead of them started rolling. Blake walked around to the passenger side of the vehicle and hopped in. Carr had his weapon trained on the man and kept an eye through the mirrors as they moved once again. The man had stood there as the few remaining vehicles maneuvered around him, standing in defiance. The crowd had already returned to the game. Blake sat in his seat and breathed a sigh of relief, would he have shot the unarmed man in front of everyone? Unprovoked? What about the crowd or mob, as it would have been? Another day in Iraq just waiting, waiting to get the fuck out of here, waiting to go home to his wife and kids. He sat there without saying a word. Hopefully nothing else would happen on the rest of the convoy.

They moved through a more populated city. Businesses were open, people walking on the side of the road stopped and watched the convoy pass. Traffic was stopped, and a heavy-duty tow truck pulled alongside their vehicle. In its pristine state it probably had been a beautiful blue and white color combination; now however it was burnt in all, but a few spots. There were three people in the cab and every window in the truck was blown out. They all looked at the marines that were next to them and started smiling and waving. Carr and Blake waved back smiling and laughed. As traffic turned right Blake knew the supply point was ahead.

At the intersection there were a few hummers with gunners manning the weapons. Marines were instructing them to continue down the road. The convoy headed east along the southern corridor of Baghdad. There were two distinct, thick plumes of smoke rising from the heart of the city. They could only image what caused the smoke. A few minutes later, the vehicles drove through the makeshift gate and jersey barriers that would stop a truck or car bomber. The marines had set up the barriers in such a way that the supply vehicles could barely maneuver around. The camouflaged netting was all over the entrances, hiding the armed sentries.

The vehicles were guided to an abandoned warehouse that contained supplies for the Marine Expeditionary Force assigned to the area. Every unit operating in the area would re-supply themselves with food, water, ammunition and a host of other supplies through this depot. Medical personnel were available at the aid station. Smaller convoys were also run out of the area as well. The trucks were guided to the designated drop-off spots.

Forklifts drove out from the warehouses as marines with hard hats approached the vehicles. The drivers immediately began taking off the air force straps that held down the pallets. The small forklifts started to remove the pallets of food and water. Blake left his vehicle and stopped by a marine that wore the rank of major. Blake explained to the field grade officer that he needed to speak to the sergeant major or commanding officer of the respective units. The major agreed to take the two boxes himself but was soon sidetracked by another task. Blake used this opportunity to find a senior enlisted marine and explain the situation. After a lot of running around he located a Sergeant Major.

Sgt. Major White carried a canteen cup that contained a brown murky liquid that appeared to be black coffee. The standard issued cup had burn marks that seemed to be permeated to the stainless-steel cup. He was informed of the boxes and the orders that had accompanied them. White never asked him about the contents; he knew what they were. He grabbed two marines to walk with Blake back to the vehicle and take possession of the boxes. No words were spoken as Blake climbed up in the cab and reached in, then handed the boxes to the tired and filthy looking men of the 1st Marine Regiment.

It took a long time to unload some vehicles. As they were emptied, they were sent to a staging area, Blake took the opportunity to look around.

"Corporal Jackson make sure all the vehicles are unloaded and staged where they need to be. I am going to peek around to see if there is anything we need," Blake said.

"No problem Staff Sergeant. Maybe we can take a convoy into downtown Baghdad?" He asked.

"We are going back tonight. You'll get another chance later, I'm sure," Blake replied.

Jackson was eager to see what Baghdad looked like. He almost pissed his pants earlier when he learned that he was going there. Not many marines from heavy company had made it that far north just yet. Jackson did not fit Blake's image of a marine. He would have fit better on a beach in California with his wet suit half on and surfboard in hand waiting to catch the perfect wave. Jackson was a good marine, somewhat of an oddball amongst his peers, but one who knew what he was doing.

Blake headed to the rear area of the compound, checking out the rundown warehouse. Several offices were in use. One window displayed the sign of the Red Cross not the Arab version, a half crescent, but the American Red Cross. He noticed a fuel truck close by and saw the "TSG" insignia painted on the front of the vehicle. Blake stopped the first marine he saw and asked him if his buddy was around.

TERROR IN THE WITCH CITY

The marine banged on the door of the truck, "Staff Sergeant Hall, someone's here to see you."

Hall popped up from the passenger's seat and looked at Blake, "What are you doing?"

"What the fuck do you think, dropping off supplies" Blake shot back, "Nice to see you too?"

Hall came out of the truck and the two of them walked a short way to a palm tree nearby. They sat down for a smoke. Hall went on to explain a bizarre tale of a convoy that he took through Baghdad.

"We were traveling through a business district in downtown Baghdad," Hall paused to light his cigarette, "when we were stopped by military police in a hummer and two black Chevy Suburban's. They said there was money locked in the safety deposit box in the bank. They asked us to use one of our vehicles to ram through the front doors of the bank."

Hall paused for a long drag and didn't continue speaking until he forced the smoke back out. "We did. Once inside they blew the vault doors apart. They located a single safety deposit box and took it. The box contained millions in American currency. They took nothing else. I asked what to do with the bank and they said anything we wanted. The money was worthless since the government collapsed, so we took bags of money out and threw the money at the crowd as we moved along. I sat on the top of the cab and threw bundles of cash as we drove by. I felt like I was the king as we went down the road. Nobody was injured, and the supplies made it to the unit. It was the safest trip in Baghdad."

Hall then produced several brand new, crisp bills from the Bank of Iraq. They sat there and finished their cigarettes as darkness fell. A marine found Blake and informed him that the order from convoy control came was to return to Camp Chesty. Jackson would be heart-broken that he would not make it to the heart of Baghdad tonight.

Chapter 9

Tea Party

May 2003

College Hill, Providence, R.I.

"Hello," Amy greeted the caller with a smile while she talked on her black cell phone. She was walking up Brown Street that overlooked the City of Providence. She did not have time to stop at her favorite coffee shop, but the other one would have to suffice.

She was a student at Brown University, which had been admitting women since 1891 when it was the College of Rhode Island. Amy was headed to chemistry class on this beautiful sunny spring day at the prestigious school which was dedicated to diversity and intellectual freedom. She was in her junior year of studies as an engineering student. The cell phone was pressed against her right ear and she held the familiar white Styrofoam cup with the other hand. Synched on her shoulders was a grey backpack with the embroidered logo of the university that she was proud to attend. She was not happy about the weight of the bag as she walked up the tree-lined street.

"Hey, I got a letter you sent that was not intended for me," Dan said.

She felt sick in her stomach as the reality of her actions started to take form. "What?" she said.

"Listen I just got the letter. The envelope says my name, but the letter's meant for someone else," Dan said trying not to be a prick about it.

Amy was silent for a moment, then finally said, "I have to meet you to figure out what we are going to do."

"What we are going to do?" He thought.

He told her, "I can't right now I'm on lunch. Give me a call later tonight."

Then the phone went dead.

TERROR IN THE WITCH CITY

She stared at the phone, the time of the call flashed until the screen went black. Her relationship might just have come to an end. Amy resumed walking to class. She wanted to skip it now, but knew she had to attend. It was too important to miss. She had to think this out. Amy needed to remember the letter she had written to Richard. He would be furious with her. The good thing was that she had a lot of time to weigh out her options. She would apologize, kiss his ass and do whatever he wanted. After some time, things would return to normal; she knew that she would be the trophy wife that he needed for his political aspirations.

Salem, MA

Even though it was cool outside on this May afternoon, the postman wore his shorts to work. He had been on this route for a year or so and generally liked the neighborhood. There were no vicious dogs yet and some decent looking housewives. His coworkers would banter about the fantasies they would like to live out with yummy mommies or lonely ladies on their routes. He knew that it was just "boys being boys" and he did his job professionally always. Some of his previous coworkers who had worn the uniform had tarnished the reputation of the organization. He saw it as his responsibility to try to change all that.

As Postman White approached the side yard of the blue colonial, he saw the multi-colored contraption that the kids played on. It had tubes, slides and windows like a fort, but was made of plastic. There was also a green sandbox shaped like a dinosaur and a wooden swing set. The yard wasn't different than the others in the neighborhood. The only thing that separated this house from the others was the big yellow ribbon on the front door.

He was familiar with it and recalled seeing a lot of them 12 years prior. The yellow ribbon stood out on the door as he approached. He rummaged through his bag for the bundle of mail and deposited it in the black mailbox on the right side of the door at 100 Gallows Hill Road. He turned, walked down three concrete steps and headed for the next residence in the cul-de-sac. He caught a glimpse of a Red Sox sticker on a car and made a mental note to himself.

TERROR IN THE WITCH CITY

He needed to stop at the liquor store on his way home to resupply the beer that would be chilling in the fridge. The Sox were playing the New York Yankees, a team he despised. This was their first game together this season. This could be the year that they break the curse of the Bambino. While highly unlikely there was always hope from the Fenway Faithful, a group he considered himself a member of.

In hearing the mailbox lid slam shut, Erin leapt from her chair and headed for the door. She nearly knocked the small table over that held the plates, cups and silverware that were in front of her guests. Her guests didn't mind nor knew what was going on; the teddy bear and two dolls just sat there. The baby in the house was also unaware of what was going on as well. Breyden who would be one-year-old in a few days was in his wooden high chair in the dining room. Oatmeal mush was the first course followed by green peas. Kerry Blake was thinking about the people coming over in a few days while she spooned the gray matter to the baby. She had to clean the house, get all the food prepared, and take care of all the gifts all with two small children by her side. Hopefully her mother would drop by after to work, like she had been doing for the past few months, so Kerry could run some errands. Her thoughts were stopped immediately when she heard the door open.

"Erin," Kerry yelled loudly, startling the baby.

"Ya, mom," the little voice replied.

"What are you doing," Kerry asked.

"I heard the mailman and wanted to see if daddy's letter came" she replied.

Kerry let out a sigh of relief and sadness. The poor thing could not wait for her father's letters. Erin had a stack of letters in her hands as she came back from the hallway to the kitchen.

"Well honey look to see if it's in there," Kerry said as she gave Breyden a heaping spoonful.

Erin dropped the letters on the tan carpet in the living room. She slid the letters on the carpet, so she could look at them to find the right one. Even though she could not read well she knew his letter. She knew it because there was no stamp in the right corner. Instead the word "free" was written. She grabbed the letter and handed it to Kerry.

"Mommy is this it?" She asked.

"Yes honey, good job," Kerry said and gave her a smile, "Give me a few minutes to clean up your brother and we will read it together."

Erin stood there wearing her favorite pink shirt with daises plastered all over it. She wore blue jeans and Stride Rite sneakers that were pink and white. She stood 42 inches tall and had long thin auburn colored hair that always drew attention. The chain around her neck, which was a gift from her father, stood out against the milky color of her skin. Attached to the chain was a sterling silver cube that had two hands, palms facing out with the inscription "I love you this much." She wore it every day and sometimes at night if she was missing him badly. Kerry would normally tell her to take it off at night, so it wouldn't wrap around her neck or break, but not now. It was keeping her together. Her husband had given it to her the night before he left on a cold January morning.

Safwan, Iraq

Even though it was dark out, Blake knew where he was. The last time he had been through this village was when the vehicles were hauling bridging equipment for an engineering battalion. During that convoy, the vehicle had come to a stop at about 4 a.m. Blake moved his vehicle up to the snag in the convoy. A wall of cinder blocks had been erected to prevent vehicles from traveling down the road.

The driver was exhausted from the lack of sleep. He had either dozed off or failed to realize the wall existed until it was too late. The cab of the truck crashed through the blocks and the rear wheels were hung up on the ruble. Blake was still in his truck trying to figure out the most effective way to recover it. As he sat there, he heard a marine from the engineering unit yelling and pointing at him.

"Hey driver, get your ass out of the vehicle and help!" The lance corporal shouted from about 30 feet away.

Blake's passenger who was a sergeant with that unit said, "Hey Staff Sergeant he doesn't know who you are I'll go tell him." He reached for the door.

"No, you won't. This shit is going to stop here and now," Blake told him.

"Get the fuck out here and help!" Ordered the approaching marine.

Blake's fury was building as he sat in the cab. He let the kid dig himself deeper. As the shouting continued the senior staff and officers started to take notice.

"Are you listening to me driver. Get your ass out here before I drag you out," he yelled as he walked up to the truck now only a few feet away.

Blake flung the door open with so much force the door sprang back hard and whacked him in the knee. It didn't hurt but slowed him down as he jumped to the ground. The cocky marine stopped dead in his tracks and moved back quickly as Blake jumped down.

The kid stood there shocked, "I am sorry Staff Sergeant, I didn't know you were driving." He said.

Blake who under normal circumstances would never move to strike a junior marine was not in his right frame of mind. He moved closer and aggressively toward the kid when a familiar face stood in between them with his hands up by his face.

"Relax Staff Sergeant, it's not worth it, he didn't know," the Staff Sergeant said in calming voice.

Blake stood staring at the marine, extremely pissed for a few minutes until he could control himself. The Blake looked over as the 1st Sergeant who was approaching.

"There are too many witnesses anyway," the Staff Sergeant said trying to lighten the situation.

"I am tired of my drivers getting fucked by your people. Our mission is to move your equipment and help you out." Blake spoke loudly.

"We have only slept a few hours over the past few days, then get back behind the wheel, all the while your punk marines give them shit. This either stops right here and now or I will order them to stop driving!" Blake told him and the 1st Sgt.

Staff Sergeants in the Marine Corps did not make threats or tell higher ranks what was going to happen, but this was not a typical situation.

"Staff Sergeant we appreciate all your marines and what they have done. We'll stop for some rest as soon as it is safe to do so." 1st Sgt said, "And that shit will stop right now," he said.

"Let's see if we can get the truck to move," he said and walked toward the disabled vehicle.

Blake never responded to him. He walked over to the truck and looked around. Everyone had stopped and watched the drama play out. No one said a word. The driver leapt from the cab when Blake approached him.

"The rear wheels are stuck," the driver said.

Blake looked at the back of the truck, which was weighed down with gear. He went to the cab and climbed into the driver's seat. He started rolling the truck back and forth like it was stuck in the snow or mud. After a few attempts, the concrete gave way under the immense weight of the steel bridging plates that it carried. The vehicle moved forward, and Blake drove it clear of the debris.

"Just monitor it and let me know if anything is broken," Blake said to the driver.

"Yes, Staff Sergeant," the marine responded and resumed his place behind the well.

Blake looked and nodded to the Staff Sergeant whom had intervened.

"Mount Up!" the marine said.

Within 20 minutes the convoy was moving again through the deserted streets.

100 Gallows Hill Rd., Salem, MA

Kerry Blake was average height of an American woman, 5'4 and maintained a normal weight. She had long black hair, sparkling blue eyes and a large chest which drew men's attention especially her husband who was a boob guy. Kerry and Kevin had gone to high school together, but she never knew he existed. He approached her at a keg party after he had enough liquid courage to do so. They dated in school and the rest was history.

"Erin, come here please," Kerry said as the baby crawled around on the floor, "Let's read what your father has to say".

Erin took a seat on the cloth green couch by her mother's side. She leaned her head leaning against her mother's right shoulder. Kerry read the letter aloud.

"Dear Kerry, I love you and the kids and miss you all very much. The mail is coming through fine. You don't have to send any more

56

packages we have plenty. I know you have your hands full and don't want to be a burden. The guys from work sent a big box of music cd's, food and cigars. Someone sent a bottle of scoop filled with booze

She read the letter and smiled.

"What is booze mom?" she asked.

"I'll tell you when you're older," Kerry said.

Chapter 10

Last call

May

1st TSG, Camp Coyote, Kuwait

The convoy arrived late at night or early in the morning, depending on your prospective. The trip lasted five hours and was uneventful, both mechanically and enemy wise. It left from Camp Chesty, which was about 65 miles south of Baghdad.

Camp Chesty was a reference to Lieutenant General Chesty B. Puller who was the most famous and decorated Marine Officer in the History of the Corps. Puller joined the Marine Corps as an enlisted man after leaving The Virginia Military Institute just shy of his graduation, He enlisted in the Corps in 1917. He was commissioned in 1930 and served for 37 years on active duty. During that time, he earned more awards than any marine in history, including, but not limited to five navy crosses, distinguished service cross, silver star, bronze star, and purple heart. He was known as a marines' marine and cared more about the enlisted marines than his fellow officers.

The vehicles parked in a designated area outside the Camp Coyote which was 33 miles south of the Iraq border in Kuwait. 6th Motor Transport and 1st Transportation Support Battalion used the base before the ground invasion started on March 20th, 2003. Blake and his marines did not look for a tent to sleep under when they arrived. They removed their gear and slept like they had for the past few months, in or around the vehicles. Some used cots while others slept in the cabs of the vehicle. Blake woke up to the blazing sun against the glass of the front windshield and a marine calling out his name.

"Staff Sergeant Blake, your presence is requested in COC," the voice called.

"Alright I, will be there shortly," he replied.

TERROR IN THE WITCH CITY

Powers had heard the voice as he lay on the government issued green cot that he had been lugging around since they arrived in country. He was in his sleeping bag and had been awake for some time. He had been awoken by a bizarre dream. He dreamt that Amy and he had been in a church that he did not recognize. They were standing by an alter with no one else around. She wore a white dress complete with veil and flowers and he was wearing green camouflage utilities. He heard a voice from the altar area, but saw no one, then he woke up. The dreams had begun a short time after the letter arrived and had become more frequent. They were starting to take their effect on him. He could not escape her, night or day. He lay there wondering what she was doing and who was with her.

The combat operation center which he was summoned to was in a tent on the inside of the compound surrounded by Constantia wire. Blake was surprised to see a guard at the entrance who requested his identification card. A minute later he entered the tent. Normally all missions would be passed to the appropriate company or unit that could support it. However, the companies and units were now either in or headed to Iraq. A skeleton crew was left behind who would join their parent unit in a few days.

Blake's mission was to report to the 3rd Marine Air wing by 1600 hours with his vehicles to move equipment. They would load the vehicles with the unit's equipment and drive to Camp Chesty in Kuwait. There was a section of the base that had been built for fixed wing operations. The air wing would provide the security for the convoy. Blake had known all this before he left Chesty. He also knew that they would spend the night at the wing, which meant they would live a good life for the short time: good food, women to look at and possibly have phones to use.

"Thank god," Blake said to himself in relief.

"You're not enjoying your stay here, Staff Sergeant?" asked Lieutenant Colonel Bryan Keating with a hint of sarcasm.

"I will invoke my 5th amendment right at this time, counselor," Blake replied then added, "Sir."

That comment drew some chuckles and laughs from the staff and officers.

Keating smiled genuinely. Not only was he a Marine Corps reserve officer he was an attorney who worked at the attorney general's office in New Hampshire.

Blake shook the officer's hand and smiled, "Nice to see you again sir."

Keating was a tall guy and had short black hair. "How are things up north?" Keating asked.

"So far so good sir. No injuries or deaths to report." Blake responded.

The two had known each other for several years when Keating reported to the command as the executive officer and Blake was a Sergeant in one of the platoons. Blake knew him to be fair and even tempered.

"I'll let you go Staff Sergeant. Take care and be safe," Keating said.

"Thank you, sir and we'll see you in Iraq."

Blake copied the pertinent information and went to gather the marines. While at the camp the marines could take advantage of several things: hot showers, hot food, movies, FOX news, and for the motivated few, a makeshift gym. Blake would also grab any mail that was going forward to Iraq. The mail had been sorted by unit and placed in the nylon orange bags that they were shipped in from the United States. They were stenciled U.S. MAIL in large black letters. The noncommissioned officers were rounded up and given the mission and all the details. Blake instructed them to locate as many cases of MRE's (meals ready to eat) and as much bottled water as possible without stealing from other marines. Food and water were becoming scarce up north.

"Staff Sergeant, is there any way to make a call here? Power's is whining again?" One of the corporals asked.

"No cell phones, there is a satellite phone, but reserved for real emergencies. I'm sure there will be some at the wing, they have everything else. We'll be leaving at 1600," Blake replied.

"Roger that, Staff Sergeant," He said then walked away.

Blake grabbed the last bag of mail and thought about Powers. He felt no sympathy for him. Blake missed his family like hell. Powers had a girlfriend and that's it. The other guys in the unit had wives and kids they missed but didn't cry about it. All the letters and boxes were set aside while the orange bags were tied up and dragged over to the tent while everything that needed to go forward was collected. Blake found a few marines to help move everything to the staging area. The staging area was no more than a parking lot where they would prep the vehicles and organize the supplies.

Lance Corporal Robinson approached Blake with a clipboard and a smile, "Can you sign for the water Staff Sergeant?"

"I hope it's legit." Blake said as he signed his John Hancock on the form.

"Of course, it's through supply and I didn't want to forge your signature, at least not yet," Robinson said smiling and serious.

"Well I appreciate that, thank you. Take who you need and be ready by 1600," He said shaking his head and smirked.

Robinson was one of Blake's most resourceful junior marines. There were a few marines who could be counted on to perform certain tasks that went outside the norm of military requirements. They also took care of the delicate matters with certain finesse. Everyone was different, Blake thought as he walked away.

Fox Point East Providence, R.I.

Amy was waiting for her coffee maker to stop brewing the Folgers French Vanilla blend that she liked so much. She was leaning against the counter with a few things on her mind. Her relationship of six years could be over, and she had tests to study for, so she could pass her classes and graduate next year. As much as she needed to study, she could not concentrate on anything right now. She grabbed a cup and saucer from the second shelf of the cabinet and placed them on the counter. She took a spoon from the drawer and grabbed the ceramic white bowl of sugar. She heard a knock on the door. She walked to the door and unlocked the 2-inch deadbolt that her father insisted he install on the door himself.

Amy lived on the Eastside of Providence close to the Fox Point section of the city. It was far pricier than the other parts of the city, a fact her parents knew every month when they paid her rent. She opened the door. Dan stood in the doorway. He was wearing a filthy dark blue shirt with a white insignia on one side. His dark blue workpants and tan work boots resembled the condition of his shirt. In his left hand was the letter that had caused all the problems.

He read the look of surprise on her face, "Remember you said to come by after work?" He said trying to sound like he was being nice. He knew by her posture that this was going to be all business.

"Sorry, I, forgot, I have a lot going on today," Amy said and stepped to the side of the doorway.

He walked inside, "Here look at this," he said handing her the letter.

"Do you want something to drink or eat?" she asked.

"No thanks, I have to get going. What do you want me to do?" He asked her.

"He doesn't know about you, only that there is someone else," she said. "I will hold onto this and figure it out.".

"Okay. If there is anything I can do, let me know," Dan said.

"You have done enough," she said.

3rd Marine Air Wing, Kuwait

The marines woke up in the supply area of the air wing compound. It had taken until midnight, but all 10 tractor trailers were loaded. After they were woken up, they got dressed and stood in a formation.
The man in front of them was Sgt. Ward, a light skinned black male. He might have only stood 5'6, but he was strong and powerful. The troops were loyal to him because he was fair and would never have them do anything that he wouldn't do himself.

"Listen up marines" the voice boomed, "the convoy leaves at 0900 hours. Safety brief at 0830. You have two hours to clean up, pack your stuff, and eat. Chow is going on now. We are headed to Camp Viper and the war is still on. Chow is over by those tents," He pointed to the cluster of tents.

"Any questions?" He added. When no one answered, Sgt. Ward commanded, "Atten-hut, Fallout!" Sgt. Ward commanded.

TERROR IN THE WITCH CITY

Powers left the formation and made his way with the other marines to eat. As much as he was dying to call Amy it could wait; he had time before they left. The food here was too good to pass up and he had to eat. He knew without a doubt that there would be phones available, after all it was the air wing.

Third Marine Aircraft Wing (MAW) was commissioned on the Marine Corps birthday November 10th, 1942, and located at Cherry Point, North Carolina. Its combat history began in World War II with a single bomber squadron and after the war it was decommissioned. In 1952, it was reactivated for the Korean War and would remain a permanent unit.

The pilots and support staff of the 3rd MAW lived a far more comfortable existence than the ground troops who did the actual fighting and dying. While the flight lines and skies were not the safest place, they did not compare to the roads and alleys of Baghdad or Nasiriya, to name a few. It seemed that no expense was spared from the state of the art multi-million-dollar aircraft all the way down to the catered mess hall.

The marines of the air wing lived worlds apart from the other marines in front line units. They entered the air-conditioned tent, grabbed a tray and chose a line on either side. The warmed metal pans contained scrambled eggs, sausages, waffles, potatoes and a few other items. Civilians from third world nations were employed to handle all the catering duties. The next area contained other trays that were loaded with fruit, yogurts, bagels and muffins. At the end of the line there was a conveyor belt toaster where bagels and toast were loaded and came out toasted below. The table also contained condiments of every sort. The marines smiled as they placed their loaded trays on the tables that were set up in a connecting tent. The general rule at the mess facility was you could take as much food as you wanted as long as you did not waste it. The chairs were white plastic resins that were common to backyards in America.

The marines took off their gear: helmets, flak jackets and rifles were placed on the side of the chairs by their feet. There was minimal conversation as they devoured their food. The only chatter was about how good the food was. To top off the meal, the dining hall had a large flat screen television that aired round the clock coverage of U.S. national news that included sports and weather updates. Patrons, as they were called, could come in at off meal hours and watch the television and hang out.

Powers finished his meal, collected his gear and quietly slipped away from the table. He separated and placed his trash in the proper trashcans and spoke to a marine who was changing out bags, "Excuse me PFC, are there any phones available? We are leaving for Iraq in an hour."

"The phone center is over there by the water bull," he said pointing to an area of tents. "It's closed, but they might let you in," he added and turned back around to his business.

The water bull was merely a tank on a trailer used for potable water. It was painted the standard desert tan color scheme that was supposed to blend in with the landscape. The tent next to the water bull had several antennas around it and many thick cables that snaked underneath it. The cables ran to a generator that powered the communications equipment. Powers placed his tan boot on the wooden pallet that was located by the opening flap of the tent.

At that exact moment a large sized marine in digital desert camouflage utilities exited the tent. He had dark skin and a trimmed regulation black moustache. He had an M16 A2 service rifle in one hand and wore the rank of sergeant. The rank insignia of sergeant in the Marine Corps was three stripes up with cross rifles centered in the middle. The regulations on maintaining a moustache required that it must be 1/8 inch below the nose and a 1/8-inch above the lip and not allowed to exceed the corners of the mouth. Due to this strictly enforced regulation marines who wore moustaches were few and far between.

"Can I help you marine?" He said a deep Mexican accented voice.

"Yes, Sergeant. I'm here on a convoy and was wondering if I could use a phone to call home?" Powers asked.

"The phone center hours are posted on the wall over there and don't open until later," he responded.

"Our convoy leaves in an hour for Iraq. I was just hoping it would be open. Thanks anyway Sergeant," Powers said politely, and started to turn around. He was hoping the last line would sound sympathetic.

"Hold on Lance Corporal. What unit are you with?"

"Heavy Company, 1st TSG. We are moving parts of the wing to Camp Viper. There are no phones up there." He assumed he was telling the truth.

The Sergeant thought about it for a minute then grabbed the flap of the tent.

"Corporal Biddleman, let this marine use the phone to call the states," the communications chief ordered.

"Roger that, Sergeant," Powers heard from inside.

"I really appreciate this Sergeant," Powers smiled dutifully.

"Good luck, and be safe out there," he said as he placed his cover squarely on his head and slung his rifle over his right shoulder.

Fox Point East Providence, R.I.

Amy was in the kitchen pouring the coffee into a mug when her cell phone started to play her favorite ring tone, which was the sound of an old rotary phone. She never had a rotary phone in her house growing up, but she remembered the one at her grandmother's house; she loved when it rang. She picked up the phone and flipped the top open. The number was unfamiliar to her but had a 401-area code.

"Hello?" she said curiously.

"Amy, this is Ming, from your Chemistry class."

"Hey, what's going on?" she asked surprisingly.

"Sorry to bother you. I have your notebook and wanted to return it to you before class," Ming explained.

"Damn" she thought, "I forgot all about it, thanks for reminding me. Life has been really crazy," she said as she looked at Dan.

"You live in College Hill, right? I got your address from the professor, so I could return your notebook. Hope you don't mind."

"Not at all, thanks," Amy replied.

"I'm going right by there and can deliver it to you right now."

Amy could see her coming to the door and meeting Dan. Did she know about Richard? Had she ever told her? What would she think about her?

"Listen Ming, I'll meet you outside, so you don't have to come up. I really appreciate you dropping it off."

"Alright I'll be there in five minutes," she said, and the line went dead.

"I'll be right back. I have to get my notebook. Help yourself, you know where everything's at," she said, emphasizing the last words as she shut the door behind her.

"I do," he thought.

He had been over a few times, sometimes staying all night. He was as proud as he was ashamed. He had conquered what he had set out to do. He also had betrayed a friend and felt like a piece of shit for it. He sat at the large light-colored table between the kitchen and living room.

The table was littered with books, notebooks, bills, and junk mail. A clear vase with a bunch of half dead flowers was centered on the table. She must have bought them a few days ago. An admirer would have bought roses, probably a dozen, or a bouquet that was more presentable.

3rd Marine Air Wing Camp, Kuwait

There was no doubt in his mind that corporal Biddleman was from the Deep South, south of the Mason Dixon line at least. The only question was what state he from was. It took Powers a few minutes to understand what he was saying because of his accent. The phone was a TA-95 non-secure digital voice terminal.

He handed Powers a list, "Here are numbers to bases in the states. Find the one closest to your house and dial it. The base operator will answer. Ask for an ATT operator or whatever card you have. You know the rest, Okay?"

"Thanks Corporal," he said and searched for the Unites States Naval War College in Newport Rhode Island.

He dialed the number to the base and asked for an operator. She then connected him to the AT&T operator. He provided a pin number off the 250-minute calling card and was connected to the number he requested. He placed the card back in his wallet. The caller would be charged accordingly depending on what base the call originated from, where the call was going to, the time, and duration of the call.

After a while each marine had their own list of numbers based on the ease of the call. Powers was thankful that he listened to Blake before they left Rhode Island. Blake told the marines that they should bring items to ease the burden of the activation: batteries, electronics, calling cards, and plenty of cigarettes.

Fox Point, East Providence, R.I.

The loud ring of the home phone startled Dan in the silence of the apartment. He looked at the phone as it lit up. It was probably her parents or a girlfriend. She had told him to answer it if she stepped away. He voiced his concern if Powers called, but Amy would give him shit if he didn't answer when she wanted him to. So, without a thought he answered the phone.

"Hello," he said.

"Dan is that you?" The caller asked.

Dan was speechless. "Fuck," he thought to himself. He knew it was Powers.

Dan never heard another thing on the phone and after a minute of silence he realized the connection had been terminated. The window of the phone confirmed the call had ended. He hit the "off" button and brought up the number again and erased the existence of the call. She'll never know he called. He would play dumb.

Chapter 11

Natives are restless

May

3rd Marine Air Wing, Kuwait

Blake made some adjustments to the cardboard he had place in the window of his vehicle. The police patch was not just a memento, but also a marker. If anyone needed to find him all they had to do was look for the sticker in the window.

Carr chuckled as he walked by the cab of the vehicle, "looks pretty cool Staff Sergeant."

"Thanks, I'm the official representative from the Salem Police Department, Iraq division," Blake said and smiled.

"Okay," Carr replied rolling his eyes and laughing.

Most of the marines were returning to their vehicles. They finished packing their gear and bullshitted around until the safety brief. The vehicles were already staged in 3 columns.

At 0900 hours, late of course, vehicles from the 452 security forces started to roll through the area. The marines' task was to escort the supply vehicles up to the new airfield at Camp Viper. The vehicles consisted of 5 hardback Humvees. These models were the M1026 with wench. Hardback or slant back nicknames given to the vehicles due to the hard-rear shell. Most hummers in Transportation Support Group were the soft back versions or M998. The hardbacks can carry 4 marines with room for their gear in the back-storage area.

The armament could be one of several versions. There was a tow version which stood for tube-launched optically tracked wire command-link guided missile, or anti-tank missile. The guns used on these hummers were MK19, M2 or M240g depending on the unit mission and availability. Blake was most familiar with the M2 machine gun or Browning .50 caliber. He knew the weapon well since it was one of the crew served weapons on the M60 main battle tank. Known better by its nickname, "Ma deuce." The weapon was old yet durable. It was used before World War II and could make a hole in anything that it shot at. Blake watched it tear up a few Iraqi tanks and armored personnel carriers in Kuwait in 1991. Blake wanted the hardbacks dispersed amongst his vehicles in case they were attacked.

Powers, who was headed back to the staging area, started to suffer what was clinically known as the broken heart syndrome. Everyone reacted differently to one of the most stressful life events. If that wasn't bad enough, he was in the middle of a war zone. That alone could put a tremendous amount of strain on the most mentally strong and sound person. There was nothing Powers could do about it. He could not call her, see her, e-mail her, or even text her. He was trapped here.

Throughout all this time there was a non-stop flood of intrusive thoughts and images. Powers thought, "Maybe I should talk to Blake." He reconsidered. "What the fuck was he going to do about it? Tell me everything will be all right?" Blake would probably refer him to the chaplain. No, he didn't want anyone to know his problems. So, Powers did the only thing he thought he could do, kept it to himself. As he wondered back to his vehicle, he began to replay the images of her, the letter, the phone calls, and everything else his imagination could stir up.

As Powers walked back Blake said, "Sgt. Ward, I have to speak to the security force then we are going to begin the safety brief."

"No problem staff sergeant. I will have them ready".

"Thank you," He replied and walked away.

As Blake approached the lieutenant a staff sergeant was waiting with him. Blake would normally have saluted the commissioned officer, but they were in a combat zone. Saluting could get those killed, so they avoided showing signs of authority.

"I am Lieutenant Maxwell, and this is Staff Sergeant Gutierrez, the platoon sergeant for the security detachment," Maxwell said.

"Hello, I'm SSgt. Blake. I am the convoy commander for this mission," Blake shook hands with both men.

Maxwell had thick short black hair, and he was of medium height and stocky build. Gutierrez was young looking, medium height and light skinned Spanish marine. Both men were on active duty.

TERROR IN THE WITCH CITY

"Here is a map of the route. Have you traveled this road before?" Lt. Maxwell said as he unfolded a laminated map on the hood of the vehicle closest.

"Yes sir, a few times," Blake replied.

"Is there something we should be aware of?"

Blake looked at both men, "There is a border town here," he pointed at the small knot of roads. "Safwan. I've never seen anyone on the streets, but people live there. I always have a bad feeling going through there and I don't know why".

Blake looked back at them and continued, "After that town we hop on the highway all the way up to this intersection. There are a few villages off in the distance, nothing to worry about though. Pay special attention to the overpasses. They have fortified bunkers and a position on the cloverleaf. They're unmanned, but still nerve racking. The camp is about 4 or 5 miles off the hardball." Hardball was reference to the paved road.

"Okay we will disperse your vehicles within our vehicles. There will be a Hummer, then two or three of your trucks and so on. I would like you in the first group, so I can reach you if I need too. You have any radios?" Gutierrez asked.

"No, my drivers are by themselves, we have no radios, and no corpsman, not my decision. I will be the passenger in the first truck," Blake explained. "One more thing. There is an Army checkpoint here before Safwan. I have never been through it though and don't know what it entails. I'll go with you in case they need a manifest. It's 33 miles from here to the border," Blake finished.

"Staff Sergeant, if we can have your drivers over here for a safety brief, say in 15 minutes, that would be great," Gutierrez said.

30 minutes later Gutierrez had covered everything and was just finishing up.

"If you have any questions please ask them now. Later might be too late," he looked around and waited. "Okay, then we roll in 20 minutes. Line up on that first vehicle." Gutierrez pointing to the hummer with the .50 caliber in the turret.

The marines broke rank and headed to their assigned vehicles. Powers just stood there for a moment with a blank look on his face.

"Did you get that Powers?" Ward asked.

"Yes, sergeant," he replied hesitantly.

"You better get your head in the game, understand?" The sergeant said loudly.

"Yes Sgt. Ward," Powers said without making eye contact.

One by one the drivers fired up the engines of their vehicles and rolled in line to the forming convoy. The wheels kicked up dust as the trucks took their place. Weapons were checked, goggles and helmets adjusted by the security personnel that rode in their vehicles. They knew it would be an uneventful ride at least to the border. The convoy moved 10 to 15 miles per hour along the access road. The vehicles snaked around pits, jersey barriers and gun emplacements as they exited the base. These deterrents were made to stop a truck or suicide bomber from entering the base. They were hard lessons learned by the Marine Corps while on supposed peacekeeping operations in the Middle East in previous decades. The large trucks barely cleared the barriers as the wheels scarped along the concrete crawling through the maze. The vehicles drove another 10 minutes on the bumpy, winding, dirt trail that led to the highway. They took a left and proceeded north on highway 80.

The highway did have a history and was dubbed the highway of death. It attained this notoriety after the United States forces bombed the congested traffic between February 26th and 27th in 1991. Iraqi troops and vehicles were fleeing Kuwait when an allied aircraft spotted the exodus and called it in to headquarters. The bombing lasted hours and thousands of vehicles were destroyed, and thousands of Iraqi soldiers killed. Blake remembered seeing the destruction as the tanks drove past. The burned, charred vehicles lay twisted about. There were buses, trucks and cars that ranged from slightly damaged to barely recognizable. The road then consisted of large craters and angled asphalt. The marines watched in silence as they passed the vast destruction. Some media outlets claimed the bombing was illegal and inhumane, but Blake knew that Iraqi soldiers had raped, pillaged and murdered Kuwait nationals during their reign of terror. Blake felt no sympathy for their demise.

TERROR IN THE WITCH CITY

25 minutes later the vehicles slowed down for a right arrow sign reading "Checkpoint ahead prepare to stop." The lot consisted of five or six lanes to accommodate many vehicles and a concrete structure that may have been used by Kuwait customs officials for processing vehicles entering and exiting. It was apparent that the army had turned the open land into a large parking lot for the convoys passing through.

There was a sign at the end of each travel lane that read, "Convoy must check in with convoy control." The sign was a sheet of plywood with the words spray painted in black with 2x4 boards and a scrape piece of wood that supported the base. Two sandbags leaned against the bottom for more support.

When his vehicle stopped, Blake leapt from the passenger's seat and joined Maxwell and Gutierrez. They walked to the sand colored building that was now U.S. Army Convoy control. A short, balding, mustached man wearing desert camouflage utilities stood behind the wooden counter.

The man who could have passed for an accountant was wearing the rank of a Sergeant First Class asked, "What can I do for you gentlemen?"

Gutierrez assumed responsibility for the three and answered, "We have a convoy of 16 vehicles headed to a Marine base south of Baghdad. Do we need to check in with you?"

"No, only Army convoys are required to provide manifests, but we can provide maps, directions, and Intel if you need them," the Sergeant First Class said in his southern drawl.

"We will take any help you can give us."

"Okay then," he said and grabbed a detailed map of the area and laid it on the wooden counter. "The natives are a little restless today. Aside from lining the convoy route they decided to fuck with us," He looked at the three marines. He continued in detail about everything he had gathered about the climate of the town. He showed them a map of where they could expect trouble.

Safwan, Iraq

Safwan once serviced travelers that were either headed into Iraq or Kuwait. Now a vehicle graveyard from the first gulf war. The graveyard was on land where tomatoes once grew. Tarps covered the crops near the graveyard due to the possible radiation from depleted uranium munitions used on the vehicles. Troops, vehicles, and supplies were constantly traveling on this section of roadway that led directly to Highway 8 which led to Baghdad and Highway 6 to Basra.

The paved roadway went along the outskirts of the town of Safwan. The villagers had hidden during the initial invasion, but after several days they started to emerge and watch the visitors. They watched as humanitarian aid arrived several days after the initial invasion on March 20th, 2003 to deliver food, water and medical supplies. Several civilian tractor-trailers arrived from the United States and Kuwait. The drivers and reporters that accompanied them were overwhelmed and surprised by the villagers' reactions. While some in the crowd chanted praise and support for Saddam Hussein, strong young men overpowered the women and children then swarmed the trucks. Other villagers felt humiliated and insulted by the foreigners who brought the supplies. What was believed to be a chance to win the hearts and minds had turned into a riot. The military and civilian vehicles rolled through the streets day and night to deliver supplies to the troops and to prevent the turmoil from spiraling out of control.

As the days progressed, the villagers became less fearful of the coalition forces' actions. The beggars lined the convoy route and started yelled and screaming for food and water. Eventually, the American troops that drove past threw food and water out of the vehicles. The Americans spoiled the children by giving them candy and in some cases toys. Entrepreneurs had popped up along the route; the thieves in the crowd realized that they could capitalize off the Americans as well. Those in the crowd started to identify which boxes held the water and food. The soldiers who tied their packs on the outside of the vehicles to create more space inadvertently made them easy to steal.

It did not take long to realize that if a vehicle stopped long enough, something could be stolen before the troops realized that it. Some of the Americans appeared aggressive, but others did not, especially not the females. The brave villager wondered, "Would they shoot someone who tried to steal their cargo or pack? Would they stop the truck if someone were in front of them? What if the thieves were children?

Chapter 12

Chaos

May

Safwan, Iraq
    Umarah Sawaya was kicking his football in the open field on the western side of the village. Football was his nation's pastime, and he dreamt of playing on the Iraq national team. However, Umarah was unaware of the checkered history of the team. He knew that Uday Hussein was the coach at one time. He didn't know that Hussein used the secret police to detain players, as well as torture and injure them for penalties they had gotten during a game or if they played poorly. He also didn't know that Uday forced players to train on a whim and anytime he desired. Umarah and his friends had been playing for about an hour and were hot and thirsty. As they gathered in a small circle, they talked about the trucks going through town, and they decided to see the Americans for themselves. One boy told them that the day before, he grabbed a chocolate bar that was thrown by an American soldier. He told them that his parents did not know, and he would be punished if he took gifts from the infidel soldiers.

    "Let's go," Umarah said in Arabic and the group of 10 boys ran to the convoy route.

    Umarah was intrigued since he had never met anyone who was not from the village, let alone a westerner. He had learned many things about them on television and from listening to his parents and the elders in the village; however, he heard nothing good. Umarah kicked the ball to one of the other boys, dirt and dust kicking up from his sandals.

    "Maybe we'll get some candy," shouted one of the boys.

    "I saw some water bottles on one of the trucks yesterday?" reported another.

    "This is going to be fun'" Umarah thought, as they kicked the ball down the road that outside of the village.

TERROR IN THE WITCH CITY

About a half mile away, Hadid Sawaya looked out the window to the crowd that had gathered in the street. Sawaya was a tall and slim with tanned skin from working outside. He had a thin moustache with a full head of hair and intelligent eyes.

"Look at them out there, half of them are nosy and the other half are begging to the Americans. What is wrong with our people?" Sawaya said to his wife as she sipped his tea. "Things are worse now than then they were with Hussein around. At least we had electricity when we wanted it," he complained.

Sawaya, like the other Shias, didn't like or trust Hussein. He remembered night curfews in late 2001 when people and cars were searched at night. The men entered homes and businesses at will under the guise of keeping people safe. Now, there was no real government. He listened on the radio when the US government spoke, but that was sporadic. Al Jazeera radio broadcasts filled in for the lack of government and preach their hatred.

Sawaya's beautiful wife, Ghanda just smiled as she continued to sew her sons "thawb" to wear to the mosque for prayer. It was the traditional garment worm by Arabian men. Ghanda meant beautiful in Arabic, and the name suited her very well. She had long black, curly hair that complemented her dark skin and brown eyes. Ghanda was born in Iran and moved to Iraq with her family. While she missed her homeland, she didn't miss the way the women were treated there. She remembered that when she was a girl woman could wear mini-skirts. That was before the Shah took over in 1979. Now, women always had to be veiled and wore long coats even in the brutal heat of the summer. She was told it was a violation to have too much hair revealed. Apparently, it posed a serious threat to the Islamic republic's core values.

Safwan is where her family and home were now. She knew better than to comment to her husband. There was no need for her to add fuel to the fire. They had been married for over 20 years and she knew he would never change. That's what she loved about him too. He was a hard worker, great provider, wonderful husband and father.

Kuwait/Iraq Border

"We better let them know," Blake said to both marines as they left the office.

"Staff Sergeant, let's have a quick formation in about 10 minutes, is that good with you?" Gutierrez asked.

"Yes," Blake replied.

Some of the drivers had already gathered by the first vehicle.

"Formation really quick, go down the line and tell them to hurry up," Blake said to the group.

Without being told, Lance Corporal Black, who had been standing by the first vehicle grabbed his rifle and helmet and walked quickly to the trucks down the line.

The three bangs on the door startled Powers who jumped in his seat breaking him from a deep trance. He barely understood Black who yelled, "Formation up front now."

Powers stomach was in knots from the blow he had suffered by Amy. Even though it had only been a short time since the relationship ended, he now felt alone in the world. This was the most depressed he had ever felt in his life.

"Let's go Powers, formation!" He heard Black yell again.

10 minutes later all the marines stood in a large semi-circle around Blake.

"Listen up!" Gutierrez called to the Marines. "The Army just informed us that the locals in Safwan are restless. They have lined the streets and there are a lot of them. It has been reported that they have long bamboo poles with knives attached to the end. Drivers and passengers pay attention. They also have been running wires under the overpass to behead the gunners. Again, pay attention and warn someone if you see anything. We'll try to avoid anything unusual. No one is to stop for any reason or throw food out to the crowd, no one! Do not stop for any reason, unless we are on the highway. Any questions?"

"My drivers," Blake announced, "helmets and flak jackets on, rifles at the ready, gas masks attached. No fucking headphones or distractions!"

"That goes for 452" Gutierrez interjected. "We depart in 5 minutes, Fall out."

15 minutes later, all the vehicles proceeded to the border. The lead element passed an Arabic sign that probably informed the traveler that they were leaving Kuwait. The last building was on the left, a sand colored shack that had been occupied by the United Nations Security Forces just before the United States had invaded Iraq. The force established by UNIKOM, United Nations Iraq-Kuwait Observation Mission, created a demilitarize zone along the Iraq-Kuwait border which provided security. The force was removed on March 17, 2003 after its operation was suspended for their safety and to keep the peace with the United Nations. They had been replaced with elements of the Kuwaiti Army.

A quarter mile ahead was a 20-foot fence that ran as far as you could see. The fence had razor wire on top and was only broken for access to the road. There was a deep channel that ran the entire length of the fence. Blake knew it was as a tank trap. No vehicles including a tank could breech the gap. The demilitarized zone was six miles into Iraq and three miles into Kuwait. The lead hummer slowed down and stopped before the elevated section of the Iraq town ahead.

The gunners in each hardback Humvees' sat in the middle of the vehicle. A piece of canvas was attached to both sides of the cupola. The vehicle had four seats and a cargo area in the back. The back hatch had specific spots to store 5-gallon jugs of water and gas along with whatever else the crew carried. There was also a dedicated spot for the pioneer gear, which was a heavy-duty tool kit that consisted of a pick, wooden handle, shovel, sledgehammer, and an axe. The vehicle's body was tempered aluminum and the doors were composite fiberglass, neither of which would stop a round. The cupola was in the middle of the vehicle and rose a few inches above the roof. The gun mount was forward, if there was one at all. Some crews resorted to tack welding mounts or using wood and straps. The cupola spun 360 degrees by a ring of holes underneath, two handles locked in place to prevent movement. The pads in the back of the ring protected the gunners' spine. There were only three weapons that the Marines in the 452nd Regiment used in the gunner's cupola: the MK-19 40mm machine gun, M240g medium machine gun, and the Browning M2 50 caliber machine gun.

TERROR IN THE WITCH CITY

Corporal Scott's feet more than reached the platform of the Hummer, they could have passed through the platform entirely. His 6"3" 250 lb. frame consumed most of the hole that was the gunner's cupola. Scott turned the latch on the top of the cover and opened the cover of the weapon. He wanted to ensure that the belt of .50 caliber ammunition was loaded and there was plenty of it. He checked the belts that lead to the green ammo box. The gun was named after John Browning and had been in production since 1933, and it was extremely reliable. The reason it was being used 70 years later was because that the rounds could penetrate anything, including the cinderblock that the enemies hid behind.

Scott closed the ammunition cover and sat back in the large swath of canvas that was his seat. He grabbed his helmet and adjusted his tinted goggles that kept out the dust and blinding sun. He pulled up the bandana that covered his mouth and nostrils from the choking dust and dirt. The driver and the passenger checked their weapons. They also pulled on the chicken wire that had been tack welded over the windows, making sure it was secure.

Mechanics had added the wire to prevent objects from being thrown at the marines. Rocks and bottles had been thrown in the past few weeks which injured the previous occupants of the vehicle. It would only be a matter of time before a grenade made its way in the vehicle.

Scott had created a means of communicating with the driver and passenger in absence of electronic communication. If a target appeared on the drivers' side of the vehicle, he would tap his left foot; or if on the passenger's side, he'd tap his right foot. The marines learned to improvise, adapt and overcome. The gunner taped both his feet on the platform to signal he was ready. The lead vehicle started rolling into Iraq. The most dangerous part of the convoy was the next 3 miles.

*

About four miles ahead a group of a few hundred villagers were standing on the left side of the road. The people had watched as trucks had passed earlier in the day, and they knew more would follow. Among the crowd was a group of boys. Aashif looked over as Umarah and his friends came over to watch the trucks pass. Aashif was a few years older, shorter, and rounder than Umarah. He was also more street wise and savvy them the younger kids. Aashif did not really like or get along with the younger boy who had embarrassed him during a football game in front of everyone. They were the only ones around for him to play with though. The boys were excited and hoping to get some food or water, maybe even candy from the Americans that were driving their trucks.

Aashif believed that the trucks would stop if someone was standing in front of them. That was based on what he had seen in the past few weeks, especially if it was a kid standing in the road. Since he was the oldest of the group, he considered himself to be the leader. Aashif thought he was the toughest of the group, but not the bully that they considered him to be. The boys could see a lot of dust was being kicked up down the road. "We might get lucky," Aashif thought to himself.

*

"There are a lot of a people out there," Carr said with his left hand on the steering wheel and a loaded 9mm pistol in his right hand. His bottom right palm was resting on his left forearm. The barrel of the gun was a foot from the open window.

"This could get ugly" Blake said as he sat angled to the right on the passenger's seat with the barrel of the M16A2 rifle pointing out of the window at the roadway. The safety was off.

Carr monitored their speed by watching the vehicle in front of them. No faster than the slowest vehicle was the rule. The vehicles were spread out one to two vehicles lengths. They were the third vehicle in line.

*

Powers drove his vehicle but was thinking of Amy. He imagined her naked in bed with Dan on top of her kissing and making love to her. He could not drive the image from his head. He was alone in the cab of the truck, all alone in Iraq, all alone in the world. No one loved him now he thought. How she could have done this to him? Powers was almost oblivious to the huge crowd that was up ahead.

*

Aashif pointed and waved to the American who was behind the powerful gun mounted on the vehicle. He called the vehicle a "Jeep" because of the old movies of the American military that he had watched with friends and family. The men looked intimidating and scary all covered up. Aashif noticed that there was only one person in the cab of the large trucks that were spread out. If the vehicle was stopped and the driver distracted, he could probably take something off the truck and get away before anyone caught him. What would they do to him anyway? He saw the truck making the bend in the road, he saw the familiar boxes stacked high on the back. "It might even have cases of water," he thought to himself. Aashif knew what he had to do.

*

"Where is Umarah?" asked his father as he sat at the dinner table reading the local newspaper.

"Playing with his friends", Ghanda said while studying her sewing. He looked up from the paper when he heard the now familiar vehicle noise emanating from the street below. The Americans were driving through town again.

"Those Americans kept me up last night again with their loud vehicles" he complained to her. He ruffled his paper and continued reading, his eyebrows furrowed.

*

Aashif looked down the street and saw a truck that had pallets stacked atop in a certain way. He knew he could wiggle a case out of the stack if he was quick. One box would feed his family for a week. Umarah was standing in front of him. Aashif saw the truck with the boxes he wanted to steal, it was the second to last vehicle. With a quick push of his left arm, Aashif shoved Umarah in the roadway into the path of the oncoming vehicle. Only a few people saw the boy and at first, they thought that he was going to cross the street.

*

The vehicles were moving at approximately 25 miles per hour and the front grill was about 30 feet away the boy. Powers, who was lost in thought, now realized that something was in front of him, something small.

*

The boy stood frozen in the road. He saw the grill of the vehicle was getting closer. Some in the crowd started to yell at the boy and call him over. Panic was starting to flow in their bodies, their hearts started to beat faster.

81

TERROR IN THE WITCH CITY

*

Shock and terror were starting to overcome Powers when he realized the thing in the street was a little boy who was not moving at all. Powers' brain was signaling his feet to jam on the brakes.

*

Umarah's feet would not move as the silver grill grew larger and larger.

*

Aashif's heart started to pound in his chest. He did not intent to hurt Umarah, but just wanted to give him a scare and stop the vehicle. Aashif realized what he done. Umarah was going to die.

*

Powers grasped the steering wheel tightly at the 10 and 2 o'clock positions, just like he was taught at driving school in Rhode Island. With all the force he could exert from his legs, he jammed the brakes. Now with 15 feet to impact the vehicle was sliding on the gravel of the road. The air brakes were engaged; but were fighting the weight of the vehicle. The flat bed of the truck was loaded with boxes of meals ready to eat and cases of water. The pallets were fastened to the vehicles with tie down straps capable of securing 5,000 pounds of cargo.

Powers lost sight of the boy then he heard the thud. The metal grill of the vehicle struck Umarah in the nose and drove it with tremendous force into his head. There was no pain to speak of since his neck was snapped almost immediately. The front bumper threw his small body 35 feet ahead of the vehicle and a little off to the left side of the road. The vehicle slid 25 more feet to a stop after it struck the boy. Powers stared at the body as the dust of the road rose. He stared out the window hoping and praying for movement, but there was none.

The crowd who watched froze and stared in disbelief as the boy lie motionless in the gravel and dirt. Then people in the crowd rushed to the boy, women started to cry, men started to yell and shout. The tractor-trailer in front of Powers' vehicle masked what the gunner ahead would have seen. The truck behind Powers blocked the view of the last gunner in the convoy as well. After a few minutes, the driver of the last Humvee sensed something wasn't right when his vehicle came to a stop.

TERROR IN THE WITCH CITY

"Black Six Alpha this is Echo Four Golf. A vehicle has stopped ahead of me and there is a crowd forming, Over," he said into the handset.

Hearing this, the driver of the lead element looked out the side mirror and noticed the crowd was rushing to a vehicle that had stopped. Before he could say anything, he heard Lt. Maxwell say, "Echo Four Zulu this is Black Six Actual. What is going on?"

"Sir, something has happened behind us, the crowd is surrounding one of the supply trucks," his driver said quickly while still looking at the mirror of his vehicle.

"React teams, form a perimeter around the stopped vehicle," Maxwell yelled into his mic. The driver of his vehicle came to a stop as the gunner swung around in his cupola to the rear. "Get back there now!" Maxwell yelled, and then keyed the handset, "All black units form a perimeter and contain the situation," He tied not to panic, but his heartbeat was racing and knew things could get ugly real fast.

*

"Oh my god!" is all Powers could say to himself as he bent down in the cab to retrieve his rifle which had flown off the seat when he jammed the brakes. All he saw was a crowd around the boy. All he heard was crying and some Arabic that seemed to be getting louder and angrier.

*

Hadid Sawaya heard the brakes then the yelling and walked over to the window that overlooked the road. "Come here, something must have happened. The vehicles are stopped and there is a crowd," he said to his wife.

She put down her the robe she was sewing and walked over to the window. "Someone must have been hit. I hope they are all right," Ghanda said as she scanned the crowd for her son. Her maternal instincts started to take over. "Where is Umarah?" she said.

"Let's go downstairs and see what is going on," her husband said in a calm voice.

*

The react team closest to Powers left their vehicle and deployed within seconds.

"Stand back!" An American voice yelled to the crowd.

Some moved aside quickly. The man wearing desert cammies was not a Marine, but a member of the United States Navy. He was the corpsman assigned to the unit for just this purpose; he was to render first aid and medical assistance until treatment could be sought.

"Let them know we have a down civilian boy, between 10-12 years of age, massive head trauma, medevac immediately" the corpsman said to a marine standing by, who left immediately after he spoke.

He started performing CPR on the boy with the assistance of a squad member. "Get the crowd back," he yelled and could barely be heard over the hysterical group.

Powers did not understand what the crowd was yelling or saying, but knew they were angry. They were pointing and screaming at him. The squads of marines were trying to push the crowd back. CPR was being performed on the ground by Powers' feet.

"No pulse," The corpsman said.

Powers was having problems comprehending all of this; he was in shock. A hummer came flying up to them with the machine gun pointing in the direction of the mob. The crowd cleared quickly as the vehicle appeared on that side.

"Request immediate medevac to this grid," Maxwell said to his radioman.

The radioman was well trained and familiar with procedures; he pulled out a map and obtained the grid where they were at. He switched to the "guard" frequency that was used for this type of emergency. He began with the unit call sign and then the medevac request. He finished by telling them that he would mark the area with green smoke.

Gutierrez was barking orders to his platoon to ensure the perimeter was secure and to control the madness. Blake saw Maxwell's vehicle fly past him and yelled at Carr to stop. He knew the supply vehicles couldn't turn around, but it was a short run back.

"Grab your shit and let's go back there. Just leave the truck here," Blake yelled and leapt from the vehicle.

Blake appeared at Blacks' window and yelled, "Come with us, leave the truck, now!"

Blake and Carr worked their way down the line of vehicles. Orders were given to move and secure the vehicles as others were taken to assist the scene. The security vehicles were moving into place, forming a secure area. Blake saw one of his vehicles was at the center of the riot. The locals that were in the area were being pushed back.

Gutierrez's Marines were dealing with the angry crowd. Blake was close enough to see the boy with his mangled head and lifeless body, the corpsman and some marines working on him. Blake had dealt with plenty of death in his law enforcement career to gauge that the boy was probably dead. Powers was standing there in a daze.

"What the fuck happened?" Blake yelled at him as he approached.

"I don't know. He was just standing there in front of the truck. I tried to stop!" Powers said in a cracking voice.

Blake heard a woman screaming in Arabic as she plowed through the marines trying to hold back the crowd. A middle-aged man followed yelling what might have been the boy's name. Blake had seen this before, at crime scenes and the hospital when the victim was transported. The woman yelled something at the corpsman in Arabic which was probably to leave her son alone, then pushed him away. She knelt in the gravel road holding Umarah's bloodied head, crying and yelling in Arabic. The father was consoling his wife and yelling for answers to what had happened to anyone who would listen. The corpsman stood there and watched helplessly.

"Medevac on its way, but he's dead," Gutierrez said quietly to Blake.

"My guys are coming to help," Blake said, "Any of your guys speak Arabic?"

"No, I'll tell the Lieutenant what is going on" he said and walked away.

"Does anyone speak English?" Blake yelled to the crowd gathered 20 feet away. He could see the angry faces looking and shouting at him with hatred. "Please we are trying to help the little boy?"

"I do," said a short balding dark man in broken English.

"Let him through," Blake ordered to the marine in front.

TERROR IN THE WITCH CITY

The man was wearing a white buttoned-down shirt, black pants, and sandals. He was too dark to be Iraqi and from his accent, he was probably Indian.

"Can you translate for us to the boy's parents?" Blake asked as he ushered him to the boy. The man nodded his head as he walked slowly and carefully through the marines with their weapons.

"My name is Blake. I don't know what happened to your son yet, but I am sorry. He must have run in front of the vehicle and it could not stop in time," Blake was talking and looking at the woman who had her head down crying.

After some thinking the man started speaking in Arabic to her. Blake did not know if she was listening to him.

"Our medical personnel are trying to help him. We have a helicopter coming that will bring him to the hospital if you want," Blake said sympathetically.

It took a few seconds for the translation before the enraged woman started screaming and yelling at him as she held her dead son. Her husband was by her side holding him and crying. Blake and the translator watched her in silence.

"You killed him and now you want to take him with you. Don't touch him" the man said as he translated for the woman.

Blake could see the hatred in her eyes and hear rage in her voice. Then a few rocks bounced off the cab of one of the trucks. A few more were thrown at the marines on the perimeter. Blake turned to see the lieutenant quickly approach.

"The boy is dead, and I found an interpreter. The mother and father are here, and I tried to explain the situation to them. The mother went off on me," Blake reported.

Lt. Maxwell appeared to be a little overwhelmed by the incident. They never prepared him for this while he was at the basic school in Quantico, VA. He walked over to the chaos and watched as the woman held her dead son tightly.

"Sir, the boy is dead. There's nothing else we can do for him" said the Navy corpsman.

At that moment, the mother placed her sons' body on the ground, stood, faced him and started yelling and screaming wildly. Her husband got up and held her back by her waist. Like pouring gas on a campfire the crowd acted accordingly. A few more rocks were thrown, one bouncing off the Kevlar helmet of a marine who was ducking for cover.

"Have them hold the fucking line, Staff Sergeant!" Maxwell yelled to Gutierrez.

A shot wrung out from somewhere and the windshield of Powers' truck exploded. The crowd screamed and started running from cover. Gutierrez yelled to a sergeant in the area, "Find the shooter and clear the crowd now!"

The sergeant barked some names and orders and two squads headed to a nearby building as the other marines widened the perimeter, shoving anyone in their path out of the way.

Chapter 13

Last Straw

May

Safwan, Iraq

Powers was in shock as he watched everything around him collapse. He killed a boy and the crowd was rioting. He could not grasp the intensity of what had occurred. Powers could hardly think as he looked around in slow motion. He could barely hear anything outside of his brain. It then occurred to him what he needed to do. With his left hand he reached over to grab the rifle that was slung over his right shoulder. He grabbed the barrel and brought the weapon down in front of him. He grabbed the stock with his left hand and placed his right thumb in the trigger guard. The magazine in the well of the rifle was full and there was a round in the chamber of his service rifle. The rifle that was manufactured in Springfield, Massachusetts not too far from his home. He thought of Amy, the dead boy, and all the problems he had caused in the last 10 minutes.

"Powers what the fuck are you doing?" Blake said after he saw him move his rifle.

Blake tried to move toward him, but it was like he was frozen for a few seconds and could not react. The feeling when you're dreaming, and your legs will not move even though you want to. Blake could only look into Powers' eyes and see the despair. He stared at the bright blue eyes that were about to go out forever. He knew through those eyes what decision had been made, a look that he would remember for as long as he lived.

Everything came to a complete stop. Blake went to raise his left arm in a motion for Powers to stop. Within that second, Powers depressed enough pressure with his thumb to engage the trigger mechanism. The 5.56-millimeter round exited the barrel of the rifle at 2,800 feet per second and entered Powers mouth. Blood, hair, and brain matter exploded from the remnants of Powers' head against the cab of the truck.

Everything in the immediate area stopped and everyone stared. Several seconds went by in absolute silence as the witnesses mentally digested what just occurred.

"Oh my god!" Blake said, still frozen in place.

Powers' body simply collapsed to the right side of where he stood moments earlier. The noise of the rifle falling to the ground was all that could be heard. The corpsman ran over with his medical kit.

Lt. Maxwell had also heard the shot and turned around to watch Powers slump over and fall. He hurried over to Blake.

"What the fuck just happened?" Blake heard Maxwell ask.

"He just killed himself" Blake said staring straight ahead in shock.

Maxwell looked at Blake. He waited for a while before he asked, "Are you alright?"

Blake didn't reply he just stood there. He heard the Lieutenant saying something but didn't understand.

Maxwell turned to Gutierrez, "Give me a hand with Blake. He might be in shock." Then he grabbed Blake by the arm.

"I'm okay. Just give me a minute" Blake said and stood there.

Maxwell let him go and watched him. Maxwell turned to his communications guy, "Get HQ on the line now, and let them know what happened. Tell them that only one medevac will be needed, the one on the way. The parents refused assistance," he said.

Gutierrez came over to Maxwell, "The perimeter is secure and the LZ is ready, sir."

Black and Carr then both appeared and stared at Powers body.

"Carr, get Sgt. Ward over here now!" Blake said, "Black, move the rest of the vehicles to a secure area. Also, assist SSgt. Gutierrez with anything that he needs".

"Yes, Staff Sergeant," Black said and left.

"My unit is 6th Motor Transport Battalion. We are assigned to 1st TSG, Colonel Dalton is the battalion commander," Blake said to Maxwell.

"You got that?" Lt. Maxwell said to his radio operator.

"Yes sir," he replied.

Blake stood silently for a few minutes. The boy's mother was crying again. The quiet crowd started yelling and screaming again, some even clapped and cheered about the suicide. The corpsman took a camouflaged poncho that was rolled up in his medical kit and draped it over the body of Richard Powers.

Ward came running over to Blake.

"What the fuck?" Blake said to Ward as he watched the now covered body.

"I heard the shot and looked over," Ward said looking at the camouflaged poncho.

"Besides him running over a kid by accident, do you know if anything else was bothering him?" Blake asked still staring at the covered body.

"He's been out of it lately, not paying attention. He snuck out of chow before we were finished and returned 15 minutes later, could have made a call," Ward said.

"Did he know anyone there?" Blake asked referring to the air wing unit.

"If he did, he would have said something that I am sure of'', He replied.

"Get a corporal to stay with the body when the medevac gets here. He will stay with him until relieved by someone in the command. I want them to keep his personal effects and write down who takes him and where." Blake added, "Make sure they have their day pack ready for a few days. food, water…you know what to do."

"I know Staff Sergeant. We'll be down two drivers by the way."

"We'll figure it out," Blake said as he looked over the scene again.

Sergeant Ward looked at him for a moment then left.

"Sir, incoming from HQ. Report directly to the wing HQ as soon as we arrive," The radio operator said to Lt. Maxwell. "Do not speak to anyone about the incident until cleared by the command."

"No shit," Lt. Maxwell said more to himself than anyone.

"Understood" he told the radio operator and walked to the front of the vehicle.

"Is there anything that I can do?" Gutierrez asked Blake, "The chopper will be here in 10, and we have a body bag to take him away."

"One of my guys will be accompanying the body. I will need one of your guys to drive a truck. It's a standard transmission," Blake said.

"No problem," he replied. "We'll all in this together," He said and walked away.

Blake felt like someone punched him in the stomach. "Why did he kill himself? What the fuck did he I miss? He thought. Blake was prepared for a lot of things happening on a convoy or with the marines in general, but not this. He felt partially responsible, like he could or should have done something to stop this. After all he was entrusted with the lives of the marines, but what could have he done. The woulda, coulda, shoulda was not going to help now.

Blake turned to boy's dead body lying in his mother's lap again. He pointed to the man who had been translating.

"Tell her a helicopter will transport her son to a hospital if she wants. She and her husband can both go with him. It's their choice. If not, we will leave her alone," he said with less sympathy now.

The man then translated this to her, but the parents did not look up or acknowledge him.

A few minutes later, Sgt. Ward and Corporal Christos came over to Blake. Christos had a day pack synched on his back. Blake had insisted that all the marines use their day pack, which was part of their issued gear, in case they had to take off quickly and would be gone for a few days. This had happened from time to time while they had been deployed.

Ward said, "Staff Sergeant Gutierrez wanted you to know that they don't have any body bags, but the medevac will have some. I'll wait for it to arrive, okay Staff Sergeant?"

"Sounds good," Blake said.

Ward headed for the landing zone.

"Cpl. Christos stay with him until someone from the unit arrives and make sure you get all of his belongings. I'll take care of your gear in the truck," Blake said.

"Yes, Staff Sergeant," Christos replied as Blake turned and walked away.

TERROR IN THE WITCH CITY

100 Gallows Hill Rd., Salem, Ma

Kerry was standing at the island in the kitchen. She just finished slicing tomatoes and cucumbers for their salad at dinner. From where she was standing, she could see the television that was on in the "playroom". The couple had changed the room that was a formal dining room to a playroom for the kids. Blake had hooked up cable to the other TV a few months ago. Now Kerry could watch television while she was in the kitchen. She was watching some daytime talk show, but really hadn't known what they were talking about only that some female was arguing with the host. She did pay attention when the breaking news logo flashed on the screen.

Channel 7 news was live from their studio with breaking news from Salem. Kerry placed the knife on the white plastic cutting board and moved closer to the TV. The female anchor was reporting that an American Service member from Salem had been killed in Iraq. Future details would be reported when made available. Then the television show was back on the screen. The audience who was mostly made up of white middle-aged women were standing up and clapping at the host who was smiling and waving her thanks.

"Was it a marine? What service? My god," she thought. A lot of thoughts passed through her mind. Kerry remembered something Blake had told her a long time ago; the Marine Corps will never call, send a letter or telegram if something happens to him. They will send two marines, an officer and a senior enlisted and they will tell her.

The phone rang. Kerry held it to her ear, "Hello?" She said mechanically.

"Hi, honey." Her mother said. "Everything all right?"

"I don't know?" she said.

Safwan, Iraq

Blake looked around and noticed an older man dressed in a traditional Arab garb. He was looking at Blake, studying him. There was something about this man, his presence and statue, that was different from the others he had seen. Blake had read some things about life in the Middle East while he was in the region during the first Gulf War. When he was a corporal in 1st Tank battalion. He bought a book about life in Saudi

Arabia when he was in a market place at one of the camps that the marines could visit. He was intrigued by how different life was in this part of the world. Blake knew this man held power in the village, maybe through the mosque or a town elder. Blake looked up when he heard the noise of the chopper blades from the black hawk helicopter that was circling above.

*

"Come here boy," the elder man said.

The boy who wasn't wearing shoes came over cautiously to the man.

"Go over to the convoy and watch them. If they look like they are going to leave, let me know," he said. "I will be in the electronics shop by the market" and pointed in the general direction.

The boy bowed his head in acknowledgement and headed for the trucks. He knew that he did not want to offend this man.

*

After about 20 minutes, Blake stood and watched in disbelief as the Helicopter rose above the swirling dust in the sweltering heat of the early afternoon. Powers body had been loaded in a body bag and was now headed to an aid station. Blake kept replaying the scene in his mind. How could he explain this to Powers' parents or his girlfriend, those who trusted him to Powers safe? He felt responsible for what happened even though he could not have prevented it. Whatever had happened must have hit Powers hard.

Blake turned back to the area where it happened. The crowd had left. The boy's parents didn't want their child brought to a hospital. They had wrapped his body in a blanket and hoisted him above the crowd and moved down the street. Blake walked to Lt. Maxwell and SSgt. Gutierrez who were leaning against a hummer.

"We're all set Staff Sergeant. One of our marines took over the truck" Gutierrez said.

"They told me, Thanks" Blake replied.

"Are you okay?" Gutierrez asked.

"Yeah, I guess," Blake turned to the Lt., "I will be ready in 15 minutes. I will be driving the last vehicle".

All the vehicles had been lined up and the security vehicles had fallen back in place. Vehicle traffic had resumed along the main supply route. A small crowd lined the route to watch the other vehicles proceed.

Only a few adults and kids were around the marines of heavy company. Blake went back to the cab of the truck where he was the passenger.

"Let me grab a few things and you are on your own. See you at camp Viper," Blake said as he grabbed his gear.

As he looked out the window Blake stopped what he was doing. The man from earlier was standing closer still watching him.

"What's up," Carr said as he looked where Blake was looking.

"That old man there keeps staring at us. He was there when the kid was hit then followed us over here."

"I wouldn't worry about some nosey old guy," Carr replied.

Blake grabbed his stuff, shut the door then headed down the row of vehicles. He turned around to check if he was still watching him which he was.

*

The man with the gold-rimmed spectacles had a neatly trimmed moustache and short beard. He was average height and slim. His skin was weathered and tanned from the harsh sun. He studied the man who wore the tan camouflage uniform. He knew the American oversaw the men, at least the ones driving the big trucks; they responded to him when he gave them orders, and he wore a pistol on his belt, while they only had rifles. The elder had no doubt these were signs of leadership. He would need to know more about the leader though.

The elder took out a small digital camera. He looked through the frames that he had already taken of the marine who was responsible for the boy's death. The pictures were taken before the man even knew he was being watched. The elder had taken a few shots of the sign that was in the window of the truck, a patch of sorts. He would have to research the patch, maybe find out where the Marine was from in America. The elder looked up to see the boy returning from the truck area.

"Bring this to the place I told you about earlier. You know where I am talking about? he asked and handed the boy the camera.

The small boy looked at the powerful man and said, "Yes sir."

"Then have your family pay respect to the dead boy's parents," he told him.

"Yes sir," the boy replied again, took a step back then ran off.
*

Blake moved around the driver's side of the vehicle and opened the door. Someone had poured water on the vehicle to wash off the blood and brain matter. He hopped up in the seat of the cab and looked around before he settled in. He saw that someone had piled Powers gear on the passenger's seat and floor as neatly as possible. Would Blake have killed himself for the same reason? Did the child run in front of the vehicle? Was he pushed?

Blake wouldn't be investigating this and would probably never really know the answer. The locals hated them too much to answer any questions. The best thing they could do was leave now. He would question all the Marines in the unit to see if they knew anything further.

Blake started the vehicle and let it run to build up air pressure in the brakes. He reached down to his right ankle and removed a pack of cigarettes that was tucked up in the blouse of his boots. Marine Corps regulations stated that a marine's boots would be bloused. That meant that the individual would put a band around the top of the boot between the first and second hole and fold the excess trouser material under the band. This was done for a few reasons, uniformity and neatness were the main reasons. It also prevented insects and debris from moving up their legs while they were in the field. A drill instructor in boot camp told Blake and the rest of the platoon that it kept cigarettes' and chewing tobacco from getting crushed in the pockets and looked neater.

Sixteen years later Blake took the unopened pack from his pant leg, flipped it upside down and whacked it in the palm of his hand. He flipped it right side up and opened the packed box. He removed the cellophane and foil before extracting a cigarette. He used a book of matches that came in the M.R.E. (meals ready to eat) package to light it. Smoking was prohibited in military vehicles. However, this was not a military vehicle and he did not care.

That was the least of his worries right now. He thought about what had happened. If they had marines as passengers, this probably would not have happened. They had no radios to communicate, no corpsman for medical emergencies, and only enough marines to drive. This went against all Marine Corps orders published and common sense. He would have been disciplined and punished if he ever did any of this in the states. The vehicles started forward and took a left out of the lot. They were on the main supply road again. Blake saw the ramp to the highway ahead. He also saw the old man on the right side of the street watching them again. Blake thought about giving him the finger but thought the better about it. He watched the elder through the passenger's side mirror. The man faded in the dust kicked up by the vehicles.

One by one the vehicles turned right until they were all on the ramp to Highway, Route 6. The city was behind them as they drove in a single file. The convoy looked quite impressive, 15 vehicles were spread out by three truck lengths apart in a perfect line, driving at about 45 mph down the abandoned three-lane roadway.

Blake enjoyed the breeze coming in through the open windshield. He had about two hours to enjoy the quiet before the shit storm started. It would begin with compassion about the loss of a marine, then the accusation that he failed to take the necessary precautions. All the Monday morning quarterbacks and desk jockeys would line up to scrutinize, analyze and dissect all the information. He had never been in trouble in all his 16 years in the Marine Corps. He was threatened once with the court-martial when he was on guard duty, back when he was a Lance Corporal. In that case he had followed the orders of the corporal of the guard. After a few days he was cleared of all blame and released back to his unit with an apology from the battalion commander for all the confusion. However, this time one of his marines had died.

100 Gallows Hill Rd., Salem, MA

Kerry was bent over the bathtub. Her hands were full of the baby's arms and legs that were flailing as his mother attempted to wash his hair. The baby was yelling, crying and trying to inform her that he did not want to be washed. The baby was seated in a small plastic tub specially designed for an infant bath. The tub was placed in the empty bathtub. Kerry wanted to clean him up before his afternoon nap then maybe she could get something done. She had been so busy the past few weeks. She barely heard the front doorbell ring.

"Erin can you find out who it is?" She yelled, startling Breyden.

TERROR IN THE WITCH CITY

Oh, it's okay," she said in her calming voice to the naked boy until he was smiling.

The little girl walked up the stairs and said, "Mom it's two men in uniform."

Oh my God! Kerry thought. Her heart started to race as she started to get scared. The Salem serviceman who was killed last night, the two men in uniform at the door. My God, she said to herself as she fearfully descended the stairs. She could not leave the baby there. She went back to the tub and grabbed him and headed downstairs. The baby was crying, dripping wet, Kerry was frantic and didn't even hear him. She reached the door and flung it open.

She blew a breath out in relief after a minute when she realized who was at the door. The two men in uniform looked in shock. One man carried a box while the other carried a large clipboard. They were both dressed in brown. The UPS truck was parked in front of the house in the cul-de-sac.

"Sorry to bother you, Ma'am. If it's not too much of a problem, could you sign for it?" He said with a disappearing smile. "We can come back later if you want?"

She half smiled, tears streamed from her eyes as she signed with one hand and held the naked baby with the other. She didn't want to burst out in tears.

"Erin grab the box." Kerry said to her daughter, the turned back to the UPS deliveryman, "I'm so sorry."

"We're sorry to bother you," he said. The two, men turned around and walked back to the truck.

Erin shut the door and Kerry embraced Breyden as she sat on the carpeted stairs behind her. "Where was he?" She wondered. She did the best she could to compose herself so as not too upset the kids. Her eyes watered up as she held the baby tight against her chest. It was only a matter of time before she would lose it.

Chapter 14

The Heavens

May

3rd MAW, Camp Viper, Iraq

The vehicles entered the compound, snaking through a series of Jersey barriers. The vehicles continued about a mile further to a supply depot. There were stacks of crates, boxes and drums of oil and lubricants. There were already a few forklifts in place when Blake's vehicle came to a stop. The drivers stopped the trucks in a straight line. Blake watched as the drivers unfastened the straps and chains. He knew it would take hours to complete the off-load. He also knew he would be debriefed as soon as the command realized the convoy had arrived, so he tried to milk the time until then.

He found Ward stretching and approached him. "Sergeant Ward take care of the off-load and vehicles. I don't know when I'll return?" Blake saw Maxwell's vehicle approaching.

"Yes, Staff Sargent, good luck," Ward told him.

"Thanks," Blake replied.

"I'll try to find out if anyone knew what was going on in his head. I knew something was going on before the convoy left. Powers was in a daze after the safety brief." Ward said.

Blake nodded and started walking back to his vehicle when Lieutenant Maxwell's hummer stopped. Gutierrez was in the back.

"They want to see us in the coca." Gutierrez said. "Staff Sergeant. your unit's commanders are there already."

"Then let's get this over with," Blake said as he opened the door and hopped in the rear seat.

The four occupants rode in silence. The combat operation center was hidden within a few tents and surrounded by concertina wire. The guard had a clipboard and requested military IDs from all three passengers. Security had to be tight due to the air requests that were received and conducted. Maxwell's driver and communications man was not needed so he sat in the vehicle. As Blake was putting his identification back in his wallet, he saw his Commanding Officer, the First Sergeant, The Battalion Commander, and Battalion Sergeant Major were all waiting in the breezeway of the tent. Major Morgan and 1st Sergeant Warwick looked at Blake in acknowledgment but did not move. Neither did the Battalion Commander and the Sergeant Major who had spoken with Blake on several previous occasions. Blake knew that they were told not to talk to him until the CO of the air wing had spoken first. The seven Marines now waited in the tent for the "old man" to arrive. The term, "old man" was given out of respect to the unit's commander, but never to be used in his presence.

A tall man in his mid-fifties with salt-and-pepper colored hair, with very tanned arms and head, wearing a pair of silver birds on his collar approached the tent, "Gentlemen, there's an empty spot ahead."

The enlisted men fell in line behind the officers as they made their way to the empty section of the tent used as an office. The Colonel introduced himself to the group and waited for the rest to do so as well. The nametape affixed to his digital desert cammies stated that his name was Baxter. He told the men that this was an informal inquiry to give the general in charge of the wing a report of the incident. Lieutenant Maxwell was instructed to tell the facts as he saw them. Staff Sergeant Gutierrez spoke next, but only for a short time.

Baxter, who took charge of the questioning, was sympathetic when it was Blake's turn, "Staff Sergeant Blake, my condolences for the loss of one of your marines. For those of us unfamiliar with you, could you please explain your position within your unit and a summary of your military experience."

"Yes, sir and thank you," Blake said. He kept eye contact with Baxter and the air wing sergeant major as he provided a brief snapshot of his military career.

"Thank you, would you proceed with the events of this morning," Baxter asked.

Blake gave them every detail he could remember; he had nothing to hide. He made it a point to make eye contact with each of the six marines who listened to him, judging him. Blake had learned a lot about reading a person's face, eyes and body language while being a police officer. He finished speaking and the room fell silent as the men let everything sink in. Baxter asked Maxwell and Blake a few questions.

"Gentlemen, if there are any questions for these marines, please ask them now," Baxter said.

Several questions were aimed at the procedures that Maxwell had taken on the convoy. Blake was asked about Powers state of mind, past dealings and what had occurred prior to the convoy leaving.

Blake answered, "I have Sergeant Ward asking the marines if they knew anything. He did inform me that Powers was in a daze prior to leaving Kuwait. I wasn't informed of that prior to leaving and that probably would not have made a difference. He was known to be preoccupied with things while we have been on deployment."

Blake continued without being asked, "Corporal Christos accompanied his body on the medevac. He was instructed to ensure we have his entire belongings that may shed some light on the incident. I have his pack in my vehicle and will go through it later," Blake felt like he was talking to the street sergeant or shift commander about a case he was investigating.

"Will you excuse us for a few minutes?" Baxter said to the three that were on the convoy. "If you could just wait in the lobby where you came in"

"Yes, sir." All three chimed in unison and then proceeded out of the tent.

The trio waited patiently as instructed. Maxwell and Gutierrez spoke about what they needed to do that day. Blake silently looked around. 1st Sergeant Warwick came out and called them back into the tent. Colonel Baxter determined that the three marines had followed policy and procedure and could not foresee the events that took place. Both deaths had been tragic, and neither could have been prevented. Lt. Maxwell and SSgt. Gutierrez were instructed to complete reports and to include the marines who were in the immediate area. Blake was told that he would file his own report at the battalion that would be sent to the air wing. The reports were to be forwarded up the chain of command. The unofficial meeting had ended.

All the men shook each other's hands and parted ways.

Before leaving, Blake turned to Maxwell and Gutierrez, "Thank you for all your help," he said.

"Good luck, Staff Sergeant," Maxwell said, shaking Blake's hand.

"Thank you, sir," he replied.

"Any time, Staff Sergeant," Gutierrez said with a smile.

"I'll be riding back with my boss. Take care and be safe." Blake said and watched them walk away.

He would never see them again but would not forget them for the rest of his life.

      *

"If we had some booze, I'd get you shit faced." Warwick said as he came around the corner and grabbed Blake by the shoulder.

"I wish you did," he replied as they walked toward the hummer with TSG stenciled on the side.

Blake turned around when he heard his name being called. The Battalion Commander approached him with the Sergeant Major in tow. Lt Colonel Dalton, Blake knew, had spent over 25 years in the Marine Corps and had started out a private in the Marine Corps. He was commissioned as a lieutenant on the battlefields of Vietnam and never forgot his enlisted roots. He was a true to life mustang officer. Dalton spoke to Blake with all the kindness and sympathy that a father would give his son. He spoke quietly, and his eyes never left Blake's. He was truly concerned about the welfare of his marines, unlike other officers, which said and acted concerned.

They shook hands after the conversation and Dalton walked over to Major Richard Morgan. Dalton said, "We're going back, Richard. Come by later and we will go over some things. Tell your marines, what happened. Then I will have a battalion formation first light."

"Yes, sir," Richard Morgan replied.

"I have to call New Jersey now," he said and walked away to a waiting vehicle.

"Come on, Staff Sergeant, let's go see the marines," Morgan said to Blake as they headed to the Hummer.

TERROR IN THE WITCH CITY

The commanding officer, Richard Morgan, was medium height and average weight for a man of his size. He was an accountant by trade and above average intelligence. He had attended The U.S. Navy War College in Newport Rhode Island, which no doubt gave him the upper hand in promotions and becoming the commanding officer of the unit. He explained to Blake that he had to call back to Rhode Island to start the death notification process. He also told Blake that he would speak to the company tonight. He wanted Blake and the others to stay at the wing until morning.

"Sergeant Ward get everyone together." Blake said as he opened the rear door of the Hummer.

"Right away," he replied.

A short time later the marines had gathered on the side of one of the trucks. Blake reminded his boss that Christos accompanied Powers' body.

"We will find him," Warwick responded.

Morgan tried to give a comforting speech to the mentally exhausted Marines.

"I was saddened to learn about Lance Corporal Powers. I know some of you were very good friends and you have my deepest sympathy. Please include him and his family in your prayers. If any of you would like to speak to the Chaplain, let Staff Sergeant Blake know. If you or any other marine can help us find out what was troubling Lance Corporal Powers, please let us know. We owe it to his parents."

Morgan continued, "I spoke with Staff Sergeant Blake, who agrees that it is in the best interest of the company to have you stay here tonight and return tomorrow morning. I will inform the company tonight. I have ordered all conveys to return to camp. It is not fair that they learn of what had occurred through the rumor mill and they also might know something we don't. I also ask that no one call home. I don't want this information to get out before his parents are officially notified. We are not here to restrict you but act out of respect for his family and friends. Please no calls until tomorrow."

Morgan added, "I will be calling Major Alvarez in Rhode Island later tonight. Get some rest tonight, you been through a lot. We are all devastated from what occurred. Reflect on what happened and include Powers and his family in your prayers," he concluded.

Morgan turned to Blake as they walked away from the group, "Staff Sergeant, if you need anything and can't get it, notify the Sergeant Major. He will probably be out to see you later."

"Yes, Sir," Blake replied.

Warwick, who was following Morgan, said "Hang in there. Someone will come get you tomorrow with two drivers."

Blake watched Warwick hop in the driver's seat and Morgan in the passenger's seat. Blake, who was the motor transport chief, dismissed the fact that Warwick was not licensed to drive the vehicle.

It wasn't until early evening that all the vehicles in Blake's convoy were unloaded. At the air wing base the Sergeant Major had visited the men and gave some inspirational words. The vehicles were relocated to a better area of the compound and everyone headed to the chow hall. Blake learned nothing further about Powers.

Heavy Company 1st TSG, Camp Viper, Iraq

When Morgan returned to the heavy equipment company area, he located Captain Foster. Foster was a platoon commander and the executive officer of the unit. He was also very intelligent and competent which was probably the reason he did so well working at a financial institute in Boston. They both went for a walk where they were out of earshot of anyone. Morgan informed Foster that his mission was to find the aid station, locate Christos and attain Powers belongings. Foster was to learn everything he could about the death and return immediately. If the aid station was far, a helicopter would be made available to him from 3rd Air Wing.

Foster was instructed to grab one of the warrant officers in the unit and tell him what happened after they left. According to policy, no one could leave the base alone. Foster was told that the battalion sergeant major would give him all the information he needed.

"Time is of the essence, Captain, you need to leave now," Morgan said.

"Aye, Aye sir," was the response which Foster was taught at the basic school in Quantico, Virginia. It was not that Morgan did not believe Blake but had to confirm the facts and cover his own ass.

3rd MAW Camp Viper, Iraq

Blake sat on the bed of the truck in the cool night. The starry night was the most beautiful view he had ever seen even though he would not admit it at the time. Blake was having his last cigarette for the night along with Black and Carr. Ward did not smoke but hung out with them anyway. They were still trying to figure of why Powers had shot himself. They were going back and forth with their suspicions.

Now, they were looking up and admiring the heavens. Blake remembered seeing such beauty in the night sky when he was a teenager, on a mountaintop in Maine, around Sebago Lake. That night in Maine he thought he could reach out and touch the stars because they seemed so close. No skyline or lights to ruin the view.

A light off in the distance caught the marines' attention, and then there was an explosion. It was too far to really make out what had blown up. Afterward, there was no noise, and no one spoke a word only watching silence.

Finally, someone said, "What the fuck was that?"

"Missile or rocket?" someone guessed.

"We're in a war zone, you know," Ward said.

A few minutes later Ward turned to the three of them. "Goodnight see you tomorrow." He walked back to his vehicle in the darkness.

"Goodnight gentlemen," Blake said as he jumped to the sand.

"Night Staff Sergeant," Black and Carr said in unison and they hopped off the vehicle and walked away.

Blake opened the door and climbed into the cab of the truck, which was his bedroom that night. "This had been the longest day of my life," Blake thought to himself in the silence of the dark cab of truck number 77. He dugout his sleeping bag, set up his stuff, and undressed. He slept in a t-shirt and shorts.

He laid there and reflected about the importance of the day. Not the suicide or child's death, but his son's birth. The next day his son would turn one year old. This was not how he envisioned the baby's birthday to be. In a few hours the family would wake up. Guests would come over and there would be cake, ice cream, and plenty of family around, especially because of his absence. By the time Blake woke up, his wife would be cleaning up the mess (putting the chairs away, doing the dishes, and putting the leftovers away in the fridge) and being the good mother she was.

Blake had his head propped up on a rolled-up poncho. He was contemplating what he would do when he finally left here, when the nightmare would be over, and he would be home. He would have cried from missing his son's birthday, but he was mentally exhausted from the day. His last thought was Breyden sitting in his high chair with a piece of cake in front of him, wearing a cone shaped hat, showing his toothless smile.

Interstate 95, Providence, R. I.

"Hello," Jose Alvarez said into his phone as he drove his black 2001 Ford F-150, down Route 95 southbound, before the morning rush hour began.

"Jose, Morgan here. Sorry this is early, but it couldn't wait." Richard Morgan said.

"I was just on my way to the gym. What's wrong?" Alvarez said, "Richard, let me pull over first, give me a second."

He was taking exit 18 Thurber's Avenue, off the highway when the call came in. He pulled to the right under the overpass. "Alright, go ahead."

"One of our marines shot himself yesterday," Morgan said somberly. "He was on a convoy, a kid ran in front of his truck, and he could not stop in time. It was Lance Corporal Powers." Morgan paused for a moment, then finished the report. "He shot himself when the crowd started rioting over the incident. Staff Sergeant Blake watched him take his rifle and put it to his mouth."

Alvarez sat in the cab of his truck, staring out the windshield. "Oh my god!" was all he could say at first. "When did it happen? Where?"

Morgan went on to explain everything he could. He told Alvarez that he was waiting for some other details before he finished his report, and when it was complete would fax it over.

"Okay I will take care of things on this end and tell his parents," Alvarez said.

"I was afraid someone would get killed, but never expected that," Morgan added.

"Me neither," he replied, and the conversation finished a few minutes later.

Alvarez continued his original course for the reserve center. He was going to work out in the gym, but that was going to have to wait. He decided to stop at the Dunkin Donuts instead. He grabbed the cell phone again and pressed the numbers on the pad.

"1st Sergeant, sorry to bother you." Alvarez waited for Charles Wood to respond. "You better come right in. One of the reservists has died. I'll explain everything when you get here."

He did not have to tell Wood to bring his uniform because all the Inspector & Instructor staff had their dress blue uniform ready at the drill center. He drove up to the box to place his order. He needed the coffee already. He pulled up to the window and paid the smiling Latino girl. She was cute he thought and young enough to be his daughter if he had one. Alvarez and his wife had been too busy for children. His duty assignments took him to new duty stations every three years or so. His wife followed him all the while selling real estate when she could find a position and get licensed. They loved to travel and hated to be tied down. They owned their share of property and the rental income helped pay for their trips. The Marine Corps assisted with their travel in Asia and the military paid for all the moves. He took the left onto Allens Avenue, about 1 mile from the reserve center.

Chapter 15

Breaking Point

May

3rd MAW, Camp Viper, Iraq

Blake woke up to banging on the metal door of the vehicle he looked at his watch, 0700 hours.

"What is it?" Blake yelled.

"I'm Warrant Officer Johnson. Are you in charge of these vehicles?" The voice responded.

"Staff Sergeant. Blake here, sir." Blake sat up and opened his door.

"Sorry, I didn't know who you were. Give me a minute to dress and I'll be out to speak with you".

"Take your time," he said.

Five minutes later, Blake left the cab.

Johnson continued. "Did you or any of your men see an explosion last night?"

"Yes, over there," Blake said pointing to his right "There were four of us who saw it."

"Did you see anything else?"

"We saw a light off in the distance, not a shooting star or nothing like that. It was a bright light, then an explosion. We thought it was a missile or rocket."

The man who wore the rank of Chief Warrant Officer 3 wore a silver stripe on a maroon field. He paused a minute before continuing. "What you saw was one of our helicopters, and it wasn't shot down." He briefly explained what had occurred. He used a lot of technical terms, but Blake understood that a flare ignited the gas tanks and caused the explosion.

"Four marines were aboard that helicopter, and they all died." Johnson was finished and about to leave.

"Thanks anyway Staff Sergeant"

"Sorry I couldn't help, sir, I'm sorry to hear the news." Blake said.

"Thanks, me too," he said and walked back to the camp.

Blake stood there and watched him walk away and thought it was just another horrible day in Iraq already, and he hadn't been awake for five minutes. He would tell the others later. He had to wait for the company to come get the men anyway. Blake walked back to the cab to pack up his sleeping bag and gear in preparation of their departure.

Heavy Company 1st TSG Camp Viper, Iraq

Approximately four hours later the vehicles pulled into the motor pool. The wind was blowing the sand that was kicked up by all the vehicles. Everything had dust on it. It was impossible to stay clean for longer than one day in the desert. Morgan heard the roar of the engines getting louder as he sat in the company office tent.

He stopped typing on his laptop and addressed the company clerk.

"Could you please have Staff Sergeant Blake come see me?" It was an order more than a question.

"Yes sir," he replied and grabbed his helmet and rifle before leaving the tent.

Blake had just shut off the vehicle when the clerk appeared at the door. Blake knew what he wanted.

He opened the door and heard the clerk say, "Sorry to hear about Lance Corporal Powers, Staff Sergeant. He was a friend."

"I know, and I am sorry for your loss." Blake responded, "I'll go to the office to see Morgan."

Blake tried to avoid everyone along the way, so he didn't have to answer any questions. Blake entered the tent and went through the right partition, the commanding officers' office.

"Staff Sergeant. Blake reporting as ordered," he said in a loud voice. He kept his eyes straight ahead, stood at attention with his feet at a 45-degree angle, and his hands were along the side of his trousers. While this was the proper way to report in to a commander, he knew he should not be pissing Morgan off right now. He felt Morgan staring at him.

"Cut the shit!" Morgan said in a quick loud burst that caught Blake off guard.

"Sorry sir, it wasn't a pleasant night," Blake said feeling bad. "Why?"

Well we didn't know it at the time, but last night we watched a helicopter explode killing four marines aboard. I was told this morning by a warrant officer investigating the accident. Something happened, and the flares ignited the gas tanks. To top it off it was my sons first birthday yesterday or this morning," Blake said.

"I'm sorry," Morgan said and moved his chair away from the desk.

Blake saw a picture as the background to Morgan's computer. The picture was of he and his wife, two small children and a baby. "Fuck, his kid is not even a year-old," Blake thought to himself.

"Sorry, I know you're going through the same thing," Blake said.

"Here," Morgan said and handed Blake a plastic bag that contained a few papers. "This was in Powers' pocket," Morgan said wanting to avoid the topic any further.

Blake removed the papers from the from the bag.

"Go ahead read it," Morgan said.

He read the return name and address, "his girlfriend?" Blake asked.

Morgan nodded in response as the 1st Sergeant Warwick walked in and took a seat in a white plastic chair. The yard chair could not have been more out of place.

Blake took out the letter and started to read, "Wow, romantic?"

"Well detective," 1st Sgt. Warwick said with a grin, "what is your analysis?"

"She was fucking someone on Valentine's Day while we were here. He found out because she was stupid," he said and looked at them both. "It must have eaten away at him and running over the kid was the breaking point. Wow!" Blake said.

"She supposedly goes to Brown University for some engineering degree," Morgan said.

"Well, her parents are wasting their hard-earned dollars. Another tragedy at the hands of a woman," Warwick said.

"Can I keep this?" Blake asked holding the letter in his hands.

"Not yet, after we learn more," Morgan said. "Go see Captain Foster and fill out an after-action report. He is at the battalions' executive officers' office. Do it there in peace. After, you need to see medical, battalion commander's orders," he finished.

"They might want to give you a tune up while you're there" Warwick said pointing to his head.

Blake hadn't known Warwick as long he had Morgan. Warwick was tall and lean. He was black, officially referred to as dark green marine, in the Marine Corps. He was born in the south and loud as well as quick witted. He made Blake smile when he acted like a clown, which was only in front of the enlisted staff and occasionally in front of Morgan. Blake didn't like that he was extremely loyal to the commanding officer and not so much on the enlisted side.

Blake smiled at Warwick, then addressed his commanding officer. "Yes, sir."

Morgan continued, "There will be a memorial service at 1500. Neither of you will miss it, unless you're in a padded room."

"Aye, Aye, sir," Blake said as he stood up then about faced and the left the tent.

He headed for the berm that separated battalion headquarters from 1st Transportation Support Group. The berm was a pile of sand that was bulldozed to form a wall. The report was tedious, but necessary. Captain Foster told Blake what he had learned at the aid station. Blake completed his after-action report and handed it to the captain for his approval. After that, Blake, went to the battalion aid station.

"Son, I'm going to have the corpsman give you a quick checkup, and then I'll see you after," the Navy doctor said. He wore the rank of Captain.

Blake thought the Captain was young enough to be his son.

"Yes, sir." Blake replied and followed the corpsman to a secluded area.

Several checks were made on his body. They had his medical records and many annotations were made to it by the time the corpsman was done. The corpsman disappeared and soon later the doctor summoned Blake to a different area. The doctor spoke to him with a copy of the battalion commander's report in his hand. While the doctor spoke, Blake could only think of Warwick's comments about a tune up.

TERROR IN THE WITCH CITY

"Well, if you change your mind, Staff Sergeant," The doctor said, "I'm available, anytime."

"Thank you, sir, I really appreciate that," Blake stood up and shook the doctor's hand.

Blake crossed back to his small "two-man" tent that was his home. The zipped, nylon tent was a vast improvement from the shelter half that was part of his issued gear from several years prior. The shelter half was just that, half of a canvas tent. Each marine carried a shelter half with three poles and several stakes. The idea was to find someone to share their half with. The tent leaked and did not prevent any insects from coming in. However, the new tents had an exterior cover as well as zipped netting. Blake was very thankful that he did not have to share it with anyone, thanks to his rank. One of the few perks of his position.

He unzipped and entered the tent that heated up well above 100 degrees, the temperature of the day. He removed a clean set of cammies, t-shirt, underwear and socks that he had stashed away in his pack. He would have to do laundry soon which was a pain in the ass. He grabbed his toiletries and headed to the shower.

First, he made sure that the 5-gallon water jug in the shower stall was full. He put his clean clothes aside. The stall was plywood boards with a door situated on top of a pallet. A shelf had been built to hold the water jug on its side. Blake took off his filthy clothes and hung them on the nails that were on the side wall.

Out of the reach of the water was his towel and clean clothes. He made sure the shampoo and soap were ready before he opened the cap slightly. This allowed water to trickle out, enough to rinse off the grim. The tan foam that came off his body mortified him. The trick was controlling the flow of water from the jug. Too much water poured out and you were screwed, there'd be none left, and you'd be stuck with shampoo in your eyes. Convicted felons could take showers, why the fuck couldn't the marines? They were fighting a war for their country subject to injury and death at any minute. This was what was wrong with the country he thought to himself.

15 minutes later Blake felt like a new man. He finished his transformation by brushing and scrubbing his teeth. He put the laundry on hold until he found some detergent. While at the airport the marines had

used the laundry service that was provided by the Army, which was unthinkable in the Marine Corps. He went to check on the men before the service making himself available in case, they needed him.

One of the tents in the company area was used for recreation and meetings. There were a few small tables made from stacked cardboard boxes with plywood on top. The "tables" were used for dominoes and card games, especially spades. Spades was a huge card game for military personnel and was played repeatedly in the tent. Most of the seasoned spades players had found partners in the unit early in the activation. Blake's partner was a sergeant from the Texarkana unit. The spade games usually got out of hand when people got pissed because they were losing, or their partner had screwed up.

The cots that lined the wall were used as chairs during the day and as beds at night. There was a section with boxes that contained toothbrushes, soap, gum and candy, books, and everything else that was donated. As the packages and mail started flowing in, so did the generosity of family, friends, neighbors and appreciative citizens. The boxes took up a quarter of the tent and had to be organized. One day when he was bored, Blake countered 167 toothbrushes. Bags of coffee from Dunkin' Donuts and Starbucks had made their way in some of the packages. The coffee drinkers got lucky when someone provided a coffeemaker for the tent. Since the generator ran all day, and most of the night, electricity was never an issue. When paper filters ran out for the coffeemaker clean T-shirts were used instead. There were even nylon folding chairs that somehow found their way to Iraq.

When Blake entered the tent, he found marines from another platoon playing cards and dominoes while jamming to some music. Blake went out the rear door of the tent and checked the volleyball court to see if anyone was around. The volleyball court that had been created was a huge morale booster. They played hard-core games of "beach" volleyball, minus the water. According to some of the guys, the court was regulation. It was complete with staked ropes that marked the boundaries. The net was an unused section of camouflage netting that was used to cover tactical vehicles from being located by enemy air assets and radar. There were two volleyballs that also made their way to the unit. Blake was always amazed at the creativity and imagination of some of the marines.

Chapter 16

Death comes A Knocking

May

Warwick, R. I.

The white Chevy 15 Passenger Van snaked through the remaining two miles of their trip. The license plate identified the Chevy as being registered to the U.S. Government. The sign had told them that Warwick Neck in Rhode Island had been established in 1642. The GPS instructed the operator to take a left. They drove past the John C. Delguidice Memorial Field.

"He probably played ball there," the passenger said to the driver.

"Less than 10 years ago, I bet," the driver replied. "I wonder if they'll rename it after him."

From the end of the street, there was a great view of Narragansett Bay. The house would have cost a pretty penny if it was for sale in 2003. Alvarez assumed the owners had probably paid a small fortune at the time they bought it. The van took a left, then a right and stopped at 18 Alden Avenue. The weather was beautiful, and the sun was shining off the water. It was all business today, and it was going to be one of the worst days of the residents' lives.

"I hate this shit," the driver said as he used the rearview mirror to adjust his collar.

"I know. We all do," Álvarez said and opened the door.

Both men had received training in this exact type of situation. The official title was CACO or "Casualty Assistance Call Officer." The senior man would have brought along a naval chaplain of the deceased marines' religious denomination according to military records, but he was not available at the time.

*

Mr. Leonard Powers sat in his office that overlooked Narragansett Bay and East Providence. It had been his son's bedroom before the boy moved into an apartment in Providence. A cup of coffee was on Leonard's desk next to a laptop. He was putting the final touches on a proposal to the Town of Warwick as well as checking on some stocks on Morningstar. The proposal was to rebuild the abandoned property where Rocky Point Amusement Park stood.

Leonard was first taken there as a kid. Years later, he got a job there running the rides, and fixing them. He eventually moved on and worked his way through college; then entered the real world as an engineer. He had started as a worker at Rocky Point, and now he was trying to become the owner.

He sat back in his leather chair, sipping his coffee, and glancing at the picture of his son. His son wore a crisp white hat, or "cover" as he had been corrected, and the famous dark blue jacket with red piping. Leonard then went back to the stack of papers on his desk.

"Okay, 60 luxury condominiums, some storefronts and the boardwalk," he said.

Rocky Point was closed due to unpaid taxes, and then the owners declared bankruptcy. People couldn't even the access the beaches there since the property was held up by the state of Rhode Island and the federal government. He would have to jump through some hoops, thanks to those bureaucrats.

He heard a car door shut but resumed his thoughts. Then he heard the single chime of the front door. He waited a minute or two, to see if his wife was going to answer. The bell rang again, so he went down the stairs, to see his wife in her gardening clothes on, approaching the door as well. "Feel free," Elizabeth said sarcastically, and her husband opened the door to see two Marines in their dress uniforms.

He noticed the gold oak leaves on one uniform and numerous gold stripes on the other. Powers recognized the man on the right as the officer in charge of the unit, not his son's CO, but the active-duty officer. He did not recall the other man.

"How can I help you gentlemen?" He asked cautiously.

"Is everything all right?" Elizabeth asked.

"Good morning. I am Major Jose Alvarez, the CO of the active duty component of the reserve site, from your son's unit. Could we come in for a minute, please?" He said respectfully.

"Of course, please come in. Sorry," Leonard said and made way for the marines.

His wife led them toward the kitchen table. She looked back at Leonard as the marines entered the kitchen. The husband and wife, of 28 years, exchanged looks. They didn't need words to know what the other was thinking.

"This is 1st Sgt. Charles Wood. He is also part of our staff." Alvarez realized he had forgotten to introduce his colleague.

"Hi, nice to meet you," she said as she shook his hand.

He smiled. "Nice to meet you ma'am."

"Is my son alright?" Elizabeth asked Alvarez, her eyes were starting to water.

He looked straight into her eyes and repeated what he had said more times than he cared to remember. "No ma'am. There has been an accident. I am afraid your son, Richard, died," he said with all the caring and compassion that he could muster.

The marines braced themselves for the yelling, screaming, and crying of two parents who had just learned that their only son had shot himself. They would never know the real reason why. They would never learn about the letter in his pocket. The senior marines spent the next few hours explaining what had happened, then trying to console and assist the family in any way they could.

1st TSG Camp Viper, Iraq

Gunnery Sergeant Evan Jones halted the company squarely in the middle of the rectangle u-shaped formation. The marine was on active duty and a member of the Inspector and Instructor staff of Texarkana, Texas. He gave the proper commands in a deep booming voice that could only have been from a former drill instructor. It had been several years, but he never lost the art of marching from his days at Marine Recruit Training Depot Parris Island, South Carolina. He moved the unit impressively through the other companies and parked the men, like a car being parallel parked on the driver's first attempt. He gave Blake a break, who should've been marching the unit, but he had been through a lot.

Blake was the junior platoon sergeant, and reservist, a double negative as they had joked around with him at one time. Jones made sure the marines were lined up properly then turned them over properly to the 1st Sergeant, who in turn turned them over to the CO. The major took his place in front of the unit along with the company guide. The guides' purpose was to present the company guidon which was a military flag that each company carried to signify their unit. His title in the unit was the Company Guide. The guidon itself was covered under the Flag Manuel or Marine Corp Order 1051.3. The flag was scarlet red with gold lettering and numbers that indicated their unit as well as the letters USMCR. The ceremony started with a service by the Chaplain. The battalion commander spoke for the reserve side of TSG. Major Morgan spoke about Powers dedication to the company and his country. Three marines from Providence spoke personally about their friend. One marine, who was attached to Light Company, had been a classmate with him in high school and joined the unit a few years after Powers. The other two were from Heavy Company were not only knew him from the unit but attended the same college.

The marines lined up individually to pay their respect to the fallen marine in front of a memorial that had been erected. A wooden cross was atop a table that was covered in camouflage netting. Powers' helmet was on one side of the cross with a picture of him in a frame placed on the other side. His dog tags were placed in front of his picture. Two sandbags were placed in front of the table, so the men could kneel and pray.

The Chaplain led the way followed by the Battalion CO and Battalion Sgt Maj. Heavy Company were the first company to pay their respects. Blake knelt and looked at the photo. It looked like it had been from Powers' identification card. He prayed for several minutes, got up and headed back to the formation.

Once the companies were back in their formations, seven marines were called to attention a short distance away. Their commands were to shoot three seven round volleys into the desolate desert. As the last loud crack of gunfire faded, instruments began to play. The song was "Taps" being played by two marines. They played seconds apart, which gave the music an echoing effect. The buglers played flawlessly, and goose bumps formed on the marines who stood at attention. The song ended, and every man stood silently for a few moments. The units were dismissed by their commanders and they headed back to their company areas.

Blake had trouble digesting everything that had taken place. "Killing himself" over a girl" he thought. What he would have given for some alcohol right now. Instead he went back to his tent and dug up the cigars that his friends from the police department had sent him. He cut the tip, as one of the police officers had instructed him to do and found a book of matches to light the stogie. It was a Dominican brand that had a nice smell about it.

He grabbed some water, headphones, and a CD player with along with an Aerosmith cd then found a quiet part of the berm. He sat overlooking a vast desert, devoid of building, vegetation, and any form of life. The sun was setting, and it looked spectacular, with nothing in the way to spoil it. Blake, once again, thought of home. He thought of his job and whether to seek a less violent career. It was here that he realized that he had violent jobs for almost 20 years. He thought about his kids getting older, his wife, and new home. He leaned back in the huge pile of sand and watched as day turned to night. "One more day…." he thought, as the end of the cigar now gleamed a little brighter in the fading light.

Safwan, Iraq

Four hours south of Blake's position, Hamden Khalifa had almost forgotten about the folder on his desk. He finished his tea and entered his office. This was his favorite room to be at peace in. The only three things which brought him peace were the room, the Koran and Allah of course. He sat in the comfort of his leather chair that complimented his beautiful oak desk, the showpiece of his office. The desk was a gift left by one of his friends who was now in paradise along with the boy who was run over. They were both with Allah, he thought. He thought about the infidel who did his biding for the great Satan, the one responsible for the death of the boy.

He pushed his wire rim glasses up off his nose and opened the lower right draw of his desk. He grabbed the ivory folder. He opened the folder on his desk and removed the six 8 x 10 digital photos and arranged them across the desk. He studied the photos of the American and read the tag on his chest US Marine.

TERROR IN THE WITCH CITY

He had heard rumors about United States Marines from Russian soldiers whom he had known when they were advisors to the Iraqi Army. The soldiers told him that the ranks of the Marine Corps were filled with criminals released from jails, prisons, and from mental asylums. They were trained and released by the Infidels to rape and pillage. At the time he really did not believe them, but now it made sense. They looked different with short hair and bald heads. They acted different and fought like savages. He took out a magnifying glass and studied the picture of the man in the vehicle. There was a picture in the window of a witch on a broomstick, how bizarre, he thought. He would have to find out about that picture. He put down the magnifying glass and thought about the boy's father hoping the man might agree to his plans. Khalifa collected the photos, put them back in the folder and got up from his chair.

Chapter 17

Coyote Ugly

July 2003

Heavy Company 1st TSG, Camp Viper, Iraq

Things had returned to normal over the past few months, or what could be normal in a war zone at least. The average temperature of the day was between 105 and 110 degrees, and maybe it would get hotter. Much to everyone's relief, there had been no further injuries or deaths among the unit. Missions came and went, and battles were fought along the way, same shit, different day.

The war appeared to be going well or at least that's what they were told at the nightly staff meetings. Blake attended the 7 p.m. staff meeting then gathered the platoon. Blake was in the process of talking to the remnants of his platoon in the recreation tent, as the rest of the men were on a convoy. The Domino game and "combat uno" was temporarily placed on hold. Blake took out his notebook and was about to speak but was interrupted when Major Morgan entered the tent.

"Attention on deck," Blake heard and sprung out of his seat and stood at attention along with everyone else in the tent.

This was the protocol and respect given to field grade officers, Majors and above, in the United States Marine Corps when they entered a room.

"At ease," Major Morgan said and walked over to Blake.

"What's going on sir?" Blake asked cautiously. He had just left Morgan less than thirty minutes ago. He wondered what could have gone wrong

"Ye of little faith, Staff Sergeant," Morgan said with a grin.

Everyone looked at each other puzzled. "He lost it," Blake thought to himself.

"Let me have your attention and feel free to pass this along to anyone," Morgan said looking around to make eye contact with everyone.

"We have a flight date."

The tent erupted in cheers and celebration as handshakes and high fives were exchanged. It was the first time in a long time that anyone was happy and smiling. Morgan let them enjoy the moment before Blake settled them down so the Major could finish.

"I'll learn more tomorrow, but we will be leaving here in a few days and going back to Coyote, then on to conus," Morgan said and left immediately.

Conus referred to the continental United States.

*

Three days later, a large convoy was lined up where the motor pool used to be, and the tents had stood hours earlier. The convoy was broken up into three sticks. Blake, who was in the first stick, was behind the wheel of a Humvee. His front seat passenger was the Major Morgan and in the back seat was 1st Sgt. Warwick. The vehicle was packed with as much gear as it could hold, and they were waiting for convoy control to escort them back.

Blake sat staring straight ahead. He was pissed off but tried to hide it. He adjusted his helmet and gas mask. He removed his 9 mm Beretta from the holster, ensured a round was in the chamber and the safety was off, then he returned to the holster.

"Is that how you carry your pistol at work?" asked Morgan who was watching him.

"Yes sir, departmental policy," Blake replied without looking at him.

"Aren't you afraid it will go off?" He asked with genuine curiosity.

"It will not go off by itself." Blake said. "Guns don't kill people, people kill people." A moment later, he added, "Sir."

He knew that not making eye contact would piss his boss off. The brake lights of the vehicle ahead came on. He put the gear selector in drive and began the long Journey.

"I know you're pissed that I am not sending you on advanced party back to the states," Morgan said, "but the Warrant Officers can get it done as well."

Blake looked at him and thought about it for a minute. "Okay sir," he said in a neutral voice looking at him, acknowledging him. Blake continued, "Have your pistols ready in case something happens along the way, sir, 1ˢᵗ Sergeant" he said looking at him then looked in the rearview mirror at Warwick.

At 7 a.m. that morning, Blake was told in a staff meeting that he would not be on the advance party going back to California like he was supposed to. Instead, two warrant officers also from the Providence unit, would be obtaining transportation, billeting, vehicles and everything else needed for the unit when it arrived in the states. The rest of the company was supposed to leave for the states 10 days later, but Blake knew that wouldn't happen that quickly. Blake drove the vehicle trying to avoid the dust from the vehicles ahead and kept his proper interval. It would take four or five hours to leave this God-forsaken place and be back at Camp Coyote, but at least they were that much closer to going home. Blake remembered the $10 pair of sunglasses that he bought at the Post Exchange and put them on, then continued to concentrate on his surroundings.

Safwan, Iraq

At that very moment, Sawaya, found the person he was interested in talking to outside of the Mosque. Sawaya knew he volunteered and spent a lot of time there. The man owned an electronics shop in the village. Sawaya waited until the older man were done talking before, he approached.

"Excuse me, sir. May I have a moment of your time?" Sawaya said in his native Arabic.

"Yes. Let's go for a walk," Khalifa said softly.

Sawaya walked a pace behind the man to show respect. "I thought of what you suggested and would like to proceed. My wife cannot learn of this right now though," he said.

"She will not know unless you tell her," Khalifa said as he stopped and turned around to face Sawaya. "She will ask you though, when you leave to perform your task." He said putting emphasis on the last two words.

"I will worry about it then." Sawaya said.

"Good, I will make the call. Plans will have to be made which will take time. I will contact you when a meeting with the handler is scheduled." Khalifa said. "Now, let's go pray to Allah for your son and that he will watch over you and bless us with success." He turned around and the two walked back in silence.

Sawaya had been approached by Khalifa several weeks after the death of his son, inquiring of seeking revenge on the American who was responsible. Sawaya was more than happy to listen to the man tell his plan since the boy's death had consumed him and his wife. Sawaya had heard rumors that this man had connections to Hezbollah, but Sawaya didn't put stock in rumors until he entered Khaifa's store and heard the radio that played news from Al-Nour, a pro Hezbollah radio station.

6th Motor Transport Battalion, Camp Coyote, Kuwait

It had been 21 days since Blake parked the Hummer when the unit returned from Camp Viper in Iraq. Eleven days longer than they were told. Since then, the reservists assigned to 1st TSG (Transportation Support Group) had been returned to their parent unit which was 6th Motor Transport Battalion. All the reserve sites were reconfigured.

Blake sat in a white resin chair and waited for his turn to call home. He wanted to reach Kerry before she went to bed, and the kids were asleep. Blake looked at his watch, 1400 hrs. He sat in the remaining shade provided by the camouflage netting that hung over the roof of the trailer. The trailer was a desert tan color and was used as a store and phone center. He had put his name on a list that was maintained by a marine who had several cell phones on a desk.

The customer purchased several minutes which were loaded on a small chip that was inserted into a cell phone. The price of a minute was one dollar which might have seemed outrageous, but to marine stranded thousands of miles from home, it was well worth it. There were no other means of communication that had been set up for the marines at Coyote. Blake thought this arrangement was odd compared to other times he was in other remote places. Phone centers typically consisted of a bank of phones that were sponsored by a major phone carrier. Phone cards and credit cards were used, but money was never exchanged. Blake had overheard a conversation about an investigation being conducted on the officer who was running this call center.

TERROR IN THE WITCH CITY

Blake had his $20-dollar bill ready to talk to his wife and let her know he was still there. He would have to reassure her that he would be leaving soon, even though he didn't know when they were leaving. Once the unit returned from Iraq, the command told the marines to call home and have their family and friends stop sending mail since they were leaving soon. They did so, and now three weeks later, their family and loved ones wanted to know why they were still not home.

Once they were back in Kuwait they inventoried, inspected, and prepared their gear for departure, which included tools, supplies, and vehicles. Their equipment was moved to the port for shipping. There were still missions going to Iraq, so the marines volunteered to drive. Mostly they were trying to escape the boredom and busy work of camp life. After a while though, another unit took that responsibility over.

While the men and woman enjoyed the down time and a chance to play sports and exercise, it started to grow old. They were becoming bored. The Battalion staff thought they had a way to fill the void by giving classes to the marines to occupy their time. The classes varied in military subject. Since they just survived months in a combat environment, they felt insulted. It was like teaching an NFL player how to play a game of football. The marines were getting angry, and Blake had enough of the bullshit himself. However, he did know that things could be a lot worse. Improvised explosive devices (IEDs) were being deployed by the enemy along the same convoy routes that the American troops had driven. IEDs would create a horrific way of life for his fellow marines and soldiers. Arms, legs, and lives would be lost daily and with no warning whatsoever. In fact, they didn't know it at the time, but if 1st TSG had delayed by two more weeks then they would have never left. The command would have been ordered back to Iraq to serve at least one year of active duty. Had the troops known this at the time, maybe some of the youngsters (who were full of piss and vinegar and complained about the boredom) would have been reminded of the reality outside of Camp Coyote and kept their mouths shut.

Blake got up to see where he was on the waiting list.

Chapter 18

California Dreaming

August 2003

Central Iraq

"I have some business for you if you're interested," the caller said into the cell phone. 'It's against one of your friends. It will require some travel, but it would be worth it."

"Okay, you have my interest," Abdallah said. "I will see you in a few days then at the usual time and place." Abdallah was a large man in his late 30's. He had thick black hair, medium complexion and a neatly trimmed beard.

"Yes, in two days. I will see you then," the man on the other end said then hung up.

Abdallah knew to keep the conversation short and not specific. The American spy satellites were great at monitoring phone calls. Programs installed on them recorded conversation based on key words and phrases, known phone numbers, and speech recognition. He believed he was not known to them and hopefully would keep it that way.

Many of his associates had gotten sloppy and careless, then were tracked down and killed. Abdallah's "friends" were his enemies and he had many, but based on the current situation, it was the Americans. He would travel to the house in a few days to see his ally in the Jihad against the west. Abdallah knew he had to be careful with this man. The man had spent time in the Bekaa valley in Syria and had ties to Hezbollah.

6th Motor Transport Battalion, Camp Coyote, Kuwait

105 Marines stood at attention in the morning sun of the Kuwaiti desert. The four platoons were evenly spaced and covered in three neat rows.

"At ease," the man in his clean desert utilities bellowed.

The verbal command allowed the marines to relax slightly and move only their left foot. but not their right. The noise of the moving rocks under the soles of their boots could be heard when they adjusted themselves. The rocks were spread all over the compound to keep down the dust that would be kicked up by winds and the 700+ marines that lived there and moved about. The soles of their boots indicated the scars and tears left by the rocks.

The man's gold oak leaves were centered and one-half inch above the end points of each collar. "Let me get right to the point." Major Morgan began. "Our plane is scheduled to leave from Kuwait Airport tomorrow night. Inspectors will be here tomorrow going through our gear. Once it has been cleared, it will be loaded in trucks and taken away. Then buses will be picking us up in the afternoon."

Morgan continued. "I was told this was pretty solid information but cannot make any promises. Details will be worked out today, but everyone will be ready tomorrow. Your platoon commanders will keep you informed." He turned and called, "1st Sergeant!"

1st Sgt. Warwick appeared from the rear of the last platoon. He centered himself at the position of attention in front of the commanding officer and presented a crisp salute.

"Take charge of the company and carry out the plan of the day," Morgan said returning his salute.

"Aye, Aye Sir." Warwick said and cut his salute.

Morgan then walked left and headed back to the tents. At that same time, Captain Foster, who was in the rear of the formation turned to the right and followed Morgan.

1st Sgt. Warwick took one step forward and made an about face, "Company Gunny," he said.

Staff Sergeant Blake then took the same path as Warwick and repeated the same moves. After, he cut his salute and waited for Warwick to leave.

Blake took one step forward and about faced, "At ease."
This time, those enlisted Marines who were senior to Blake left the formation.

Blake spoke to the remaining men. "Alright, all our gear is gone except your sea bags and some miscellaneous items. No one leaves the camp without my permission for any reason unless an officer orders you, and I still want to know. I want everyone to make sure you have no contraband, weapons, knives, or empty casings, nothing that would cause customs to delay this unit from going home."

Blake continued. "Remember, if anyone gets snagged at customs the whole unit is delayed for an unspecified time. I don't know if that's true or not, but we are not going to find out. Platoon sergeants will make sure that happens." He waited for some recognition from them.
Once they nodded. he continued, "There is nothing further at this time. You might want to wait to call home until we have something more substantial. That's your call though. Company Atten-hut!"

Blake added, "Platoon sergeants take charge of your platoon and carry out the plan of the day." He waited for the salutes and acknowledgements from each of the platoon sergeants. Then, he turned to the left and walked toward the staff tent that he had been residing in.

Chapter 19

Home Sweet Home

August

Oceanside, CA

Blake was completely wasted and barely could comprehend where he was at.

"It's two in the morning, time to go," his tablemate said.

"No way!" Blake shot back.

"Shut up and let's go." Burton was aggravated. "You're drunk."

"How do you know?" Blake was being a smartass.

"I run one of the biggest night clubs in Boston." Burton replied.

"And I started out a bartender asshole."

"That's right, sorry," Blake said.

Blake knew that his crazy job and hours probably led to Burtons' divorcee after four years of marriage.

"Are you leaving?" The attractive blonde asked him from across the table.

"Sorry," Burton told her. "We're taking him home." He grabbed Blake's arm and pulling him up.

Sergeant Xavier Reyes just stood there with his arms folded across his chest watching. Reyes was newly promoted sergeant from the Rhode Island Unit. He liked and respected Blake.

"I wish I could join you," Blake said to the blonde woman, "but I have to go home tomorrow." He steadied himself while he got up.

She rose to her feet and moved over to hug him, "You're cute, too bad you can't come with me." She kissed him on the cheek.

"Come on lover boy, let's go," Burton said and moved Blake along.

They were at the Platinum Club, a gentleman's club. It was there, hours earlier, when they had met the blonde woman when she performed on stage. She later came over to Blake and struck up a conversation. She wanted him to fly to Vegas with her in the morning. Apparently, she found employment with one of the big casinos and would be performing there.

Reyes had gone ahead outside and unlocked the van. He was the designated driver for the two Staff Sergeant who wanted to continue drinking. Blake and Burton wanted to take all the sergeants in their unit out for dinner as a celebration for their hard work during the deployment. All the other sergeants had left during the evening. Now, Reyes watched as Blake climbed in the side door and fell into the second-row seat of the white passenger van.

Interstate 5, Southern California

The van with the Marines had just exited the highway and headed for the San Mateo gate to enter Camp Pendleton. It was their last night in California before they flew home tomorrow night. Formation was not until noon so there was no reason to rush back to the base. It was around 2:30 a.m. when the bright lights of the gate appeared before them. The warning signs appeared along the road, informing them that they were about to enter government property. As they crested the hill, the massive floodlight illuminated the guard shack that was manned by a young Lance Corporal who was standing tall at modified parade rest.

The Marine was highly visible with his orange reflective vest, crisp starched cammies, and spit-shined boots. Inside the guard house stood another young marine, they both kept their eyes fixed on the approaching vehicle. Sgt. Reyes killed the headlights, which was a standard practice when approaching the guard shack during the night. The young MP then motioned the van to the right where a serious looking Corporal was waiting. The van came to a stop and the Corporal approached the driver's side of the vehicle. Reyes put down the window and immediately handed the MP his military identification and driver's license.

Burton and Blake already had their military identification cards out and passed them to the front. The Corporal Informed Sergeant Reyes that they were conducting a sobriety check point and began a series of routine questions. Once convinced the three Marines were in fact Marines and the driver was not drunk, the MP handed back the three I.D. cards.

The bill of the Corporals cover was down so low his eyes were barely visible, "You're all set. Have a good night gentleman," he said firmly. He gave a slight wave of his hand to indicate they were free to proceed on base.

"Thank you," Reyes said and accelerated the van slightly and headed into the darkness.

100 Gallows Hill., Rd Salem, MA

"Hi Mom, Good news Kevin is coming back home Sunday!" Kerry said excitedly. "That's great, when did you find out?" Her mother responded.

"He called at dinner after he made sure the flight was confirmed."

"The kids must be excited!"

"Erin can't wait. She is going to make him a card tomorrow. I was wondering if you and dad can come up early on Sunday to watch the kids while I go down to Rhode Island." Kerry waited a moment before continuing. "His flight arrives at eight in the morning, and they will be at the unit by nine. They want everyone to meet at the unit instead of the airport."

"Is six early enough?"

"Yes, six is perfect! Thanks, mom"

"You're welcome, dear. I've gotta run."

"Ok, talk to you later."

"Buh-bye." Her mother made a kissy noise and hung up.

Kerry put the cell phone on the counter, then turned to grab a glass from the cabinet. She went to another cabinet and pulled a bottle of Captain Morgan from the top shelf. She added some Pepsi, and a few ice cubes and the drink was complete. She wanted to relax her nerves, hoping to save her excitement for Sunday. She went to the living room and sat down in the big comfy chair for a little quiet time.

TERROR IN THE WITCH CITY

Somewhere over New England

"Ladies and gentlemen," the pilot announced, "please fasten your seatbelts as we will begin our descent within the next few minutes. Thank you."

Blake was awakened by the announcement. They had left San Diego at 10 p.m. the night before. He wondered how long he had been asleep since he usually never slept on a plane, not even during a redeye flight. The fact that he had not sleep well the night before, due to the bed spins had probably helped.

Blake wiped the sleep from his eyes and brought his seat into the upright position. He opened the window shade and saw the sun in a cloudless sky. The journey was almost over, and he would be home in a few hours and finally see his wife and kids. He adjusted his seat belt and gathered a magazine he was reading and a CD player that had fallen after he fell asleep. The CD player had been through hell and survived with all the sand. He stuffed his items into an olive drab green helmet bag that had also been through hell throughout the deployment.

About one hour later, the plane vibrated, and motors reversed as it contacted the runway. The Captain of the plane, a retired Air Force pilot, gave a nice heartfelt speech to the war veterans aboard the plane as he welcomed everyone to TF Green Airport in Rhode Island. Since they were the only passengers aboard the chartered plane, it did not taxi to a gate at the terminal. Instead, it taxied to the far side of the runway where the hangars and warehouses used for cargo were located. There were three chartered buses, two passenger vans, and several unknown marines standing by the vehicles waiting for the plane to arrive. After a while, the door to the plane opened and a cool morning breeze whipped along the aisle of the plane.

A truck with passenger stairs was being moved into place. Blake heard the noise as the door to the cargo hold was being opened. On the night they had departed, Blake had personally supervised several marines in loading the units' sea bags, packs, and boxes into the cargo hold of the plane at the Kuwait international Airport. The marines loading the plane were amazed at how much cargo it could hold.

Blake shook hands with the pilot and thanked the stewardesses for their help as he exited the plane. The marines who were waiting for them to arrive were running around unloading the plane and assisting in whatever needed to be done. The passengers stretched their legs and greeted the active duty inspector and instructor staff. A few of the guys snuck off to have a cigarette before they had to board the buses. Major Alvarez gave a quick speech and informed them that several hundred family and friends waiting patiently for them at the reserve center.

Armed Forces Reserve Center, Providence, R. I.

About 20 miles due north of the airport, Kerry was surprised to see a police officer directing traffic on Narragansett Boulevard at such an early hour. The officer stopped traffic, so she could take a left, which led to the unit. She proceeded down the hill and was shocked to see what seemed to be hundreds of people in the open fields next to the building. The parking lot was packed, and she was directed to park in a grassy area.

After she left her car a young marine directed her to check in at a table at the end of the lot. Kerry wandered through the banners, signs, balloons, and a small stage to woman sitting behind a table.

"Name, please?"

"Kerry Blake, husband's SSgt. Kevin Blake."

"We have shirts for all the dependents. Just give me the sizes and you can wear them before the marines arrive," she said politely.

The woman dug into a box and pulled out four white shirts that had the unit's name, logo and dates deployed. Kerry put her shirt on over what she was wearing and made her way through the crowd. She really did not know anyone there; she only communicated with a few of them on the phone and exchanged e-mails.

"Let me have your attention please," the tall Marine said into the microphone, "The buses have left the airport and the Marines will be arriving in 15 to 20 minutes." His words were drowned out by the cheers.

"Please keep the road clear and let the buses come to a stop," he said. "Thank you," was barely audible to the crowd.

"Let's move closer," Kerry heard a woman say to her while smiling and dragging a small child.

TERROR IN THE WITCH CITY

*

Blake's bus was surprisingly quiet. Everyone was taking in the scenery. Since it was early on a Sunday morning, the sidewalks and roads were barren. Blake knew that everyone was a little apprehensive about returning home to their family. Their lives, attitudes and viewpoints of the world had changed, some more than others. They had spent the past nine months, day in and day out with each other through the most challenging of circumstances of their lives. They ate, slept, laughed, fought, cried, killed, and shared everything with each other. Now they would be apart. They would be alone from the only people who knew what they were going through. It would take time, but everyone would get accustomed to their lives again.

As the bus moved closer, the marines grew silent. The bus passed by a "Welcome Home Troops" sign on the lawn of a Municipal Building in Cranston, that was along the way. On the road in front of them, they saw a police officer directing traffic by the reserve center.

"What's that all about?" Someone asked.

"Us," another replied.

The bus slowed down and took a right on Narragansett Boulevard. There were about six houses on the road that led to the reserve center. The residents of those houses would constantly complain about all vehicles that would come and go all weekend long during drill. They had called the police, and the drill center a few times to complain about the military vehicles moving late at night and very early on weekend mornings.

When the buses came down the hill, the marines were speechless as they saw hundreds of people waiting for them on the field. Cars were parked all over the lot, on the grass and on the sidewalks. There were two news trucks with their antennas up toward the sky. The crowd was cheering and waving signs and banners with the names of their sons, husbands, boyfriends, wives, and daughters. Blake scanned the crowd and tried to find his wife, but there were too many people.

Blake was the third one off his bus, which was met by a chaotic crowd of women and kids. He was trying to find his wife in the bedlam when someone grabbed his arm and yanked him. Before he knew it, Kerry gave him an intense hug. She buried her head in his neck and began to sob. He kissed her head as he felt the tears run down the front of his shirt.

TERROR IN THE WITCH CITY

"It's all over honey, it's all over" he whispered in her ear.

The marines had to locate their gear, which was dumped into a huge pile. It was about three hours before Kevin Blake had his sea bag and pack in the sport utility vehicle. While the marines were processing out, the family and friends gathered had to endure a few speeches. A formation was given, and the men and women of 6th Motor Transport Battalion, Providence were given a "96" off, which meant they had 96 hours (or 4 days off) to get reacquainted with their lives. They were reminded that they were still on active duty and were expected to act accordingly, and more importantly, still fell under the Uniform Code of Military Justice.

They had another week of active duty to complete many tasks before they were reservists again. Blake knew they had to complete medical physicals, dental exams, update personnel records, new identification cards and a slew of forms. The Marine Corps truly floated on a sea of paperwork.

Kerry called home to let her mother know that they were on their way. Once they were headed home, Kevin tried unsuccessfully to convince his wife to stop at a semi-secluded rest stop that was just over the Massachusetts border along Interstate route 95 for a quickie. It would have to wait, though, the kids were waiting and there was a backup in traffic.

About an hour and half later, Kerry said into the phone, "We'll be there in about 10 minutes." She spoke to Kevin, "The kids are excited."

They left the highway in Peabody and headed to Marlborough Road which ran into Salem. They turned left to the Witchcraft Heights area of Salem, a typical suburban middle-class neighborhood. They rounded the corner on Valley Street and Blake saw the familiar sight that marked their house, a light blue water tank. The tank had a witch on broomstick painted in black under the word Salem.

He realized he was home and could not wait to see his children. The silver Toyota Highlander drove into the cul-de-sac where the house was centered in the middle. Blake saw the kids playing with his mother-in-law in the front yard.

He saw his daughter jumping up and down and yelling, "Daddy, Daddy, Daddy!"

TERROR IN THE WITCH CITY

The vehicle barely came to a stop when Blake flung the door open and ran to scoop up his daughter. He grabbed her up and held her tight, "I missed you so much!" He tried holding back his emotions.

"I love you," she said as he continued to squeeze her tight.

He looked at Breyden who was in Anne's arms, "Wow, he grew up," Blake said, holding Erin with his left arm against his hip and then took the 16th month old in his right arm. He received a smile from his son who now had curly red hair.

"That's what they do, grow," Anne said with a smile.

How many times in Iraq had he dreamed and wished for this very moment? He now knew that the nightmare was over. Blake stood on the lawn hugging both children and cherishing them for what seemed like a long time.

"Daddy come see what we made you," Erin said. "Breyden helped."

He put her down and grabbed her hand. Erin was about to lead Blake toward the house, but Anne stood in his path.

"My turn," Anne Curran said, and she gave him a hug. "Let me take him," she said referring to Breyden.

Erin ran toward the house. Anne followed her, not waiting for the rest of the group. Blake's father-in-law, who was next to Kerry, shook Blake's hand and gave him a hug.

"Welcome Home," Robert Curran said.

"Thanks," Blake said.

"I like the ribbon," Blake said to his wife as they entered the house.

There were some changes that Blake hardly noticed, but mostly everything was the same. He could not shake the feeling that he did not belong there in some way. There was a banner hanging on the wall with words written in crayon and marker. There were different colored streamers hanging from the ceiling and around the kitchen table. A few balloons were scattered about.

"Are you hungry?" Anne asked. "We baked you a cake. Erin helped decorate it, if you couldn't tell," She laughed.

"Not yet, but when I am hungry I will," Blake said. "We stopped for iced coffee,"

"Nothing like that in Iraq I bet," she said.

"They don't know what ice is," he replied.

Kerry was holding Breyden now and handed him to Blake as he sat at the kitchen table. His son started exploring his face, smiling at him. Blake kissed him on the forehead.

"Look what we made for you," Erin said and handed him the folded paper.

"Its beautiful honey, thank you," Blake spoke enthusiastically.

"Thank you," he said and started to the card.

Chapter 20

Reality Check

September 2003

Main St Peabody, MA

Khalid Yassin was tall and had a medium build. He had thick black hair with dark skin and well-groomed moustache. He was at the counter of the store when the familiar man came in. He carried a single envelope.

"Good morning, Jake," Yassin said in English which had improved over the years.

"Good morning. This is all I have for you today," The man replied.

"That means no bills" Yassin said. "Too bad." He grabbed the envelope as they both laughed, "Have a good day."

"You too," He walked out of the store and back to the running UPS truck.

Yassin looked at the Worldwide Express envelope that was from his sister and went to the office that was next to the counter. His sister still lived in Iraq not too far from the village where they had grown up so many years ago. He was surprised she didn't mail it to his home address. He opened it and found two sealed white envelopes inside. One was clearly from his sister, he could tell by the hand writing. The other letter had Yassin's name written on the front and a seal over the flap in the back. He opened the letter from his sister which was written in Arabic and explained that a man had dropped off the letter at her house. She told Yassin that the stranger had told her that he was friends with him at one time, but lost touch. She further explained that he had insisted that she send the letter through a secure means. Also, the stranger gave her more than enough money to send it through a private business. She decided to give him the business address since it seemed odd.

TERROR IN THE WITCH CITY

"What's this…." he said to himself. He opened the letter and began to read.

As he read, he felt his heart rate quicken. He inhaled deeply as the instructions sunk in. "Oh shit! This cannot be happening," he told himself as he read the letter again.

"John, can you come here please?" Yassin said.

"What's up, boss?" The young man said.

"I have some business to attend to. Can you take care of the store?" Yassin said.

"No problem," John replied.

John had been a loyal and trustworthy employee for a year now. He had worked there when he was not going to classes at Salem State College. Yassin liked the kid.

"I won't be back until later so you're in charge," Yassin said as he walked toward the front door.

"Okay boss take care."

Yassin left the store and got into his 2002 Mercedes C class Kompressor. The car was a gift to himself for years of hard work in starting the business. He pulled out of the lot onto Main Street in Peabody. He needed to go for a ride to think about things right now.

Salem, MA

It felt great to be home. Blake decided to take Erin out to the park for a while and then get some ice cream. There were only a few places to get good ice cream in the area. It was a sunny day, neither too hot nor humid. They went to Forest River Park, his favorite park while he grew up.

The park was big, had a decent playground, huge picnic area, public pool, and two rocky beaches. The only people they encountered at this time were either elderly or people walking their dogs. Some let their animals run free even though the signs planted all over the park deemed the behavior illegal. At least, most people had bags in their hands to pick up the poop.

TERROR IN THE WITCH CITY

Blake was pushing Erin on the swing when the cell phone in his pocket rang. It was his wife's phone, but they shared it. The person who was not home usually took possession of the phone. The incoming call had a 401-area code, which was from Rhode Island, he assumed it was probably someone from the unit.

"Hello." Blake said.

"Could I speak to Staff Sergeant Blake, please?" The unfamiliar voice said.

"This is he," Blake said while he pushed Erin slowly on the swing.

"Staff Sergeant, this is Lance Corporal Macdonald from the reserve center. 1st Sgt. Warwick wants all marines to bring their dress blues, or alphas if they don't have blues. It's for a memorial service for Lance Corporal Powers on Friday."

"Okay, thanks," Blake replied then the call was ended.

Under normal circumstances, Blake would have been responsible for making sure that everyone underneath him received the message, better known as a frost call. It was a tedious and stressful process that was ineffective. It was a frustrating process made a little easier by e-mail, but that had its limitations as well.

"Go higher, go higher!" His daughter yelled from the swing.

"Okay honey," he said.

His mind was back on that day, like it was every day. He had not spoken to anyone about it back home. They could not possibly understand or relate to him. He pushed his daughter a little higher each time to keep her happy. She cried out loud with joy and had a big smile on her face. Powers would never get to push his kid on a swing or play with them at the park. He wouldn't watch them, worry about them, spend time with them, or watch them grow up. Blake knew that he would have to meet Powers' parents. He would have to look them in the eye and explain what happened to their son. What would they think of him? He was the person who was supposed to keep their son safe and alive but failed. Now they would have to relive his death. "Was he their only son?" Blake wondered. Blake grabbed the chair of the swing, slowing Erin down to a stop.

He bent down and whispered to her, "How would you like to take a ride to find some ice cream?"

"Yeah, ice cream!" She said, and he helped her down.

They walked back to the car. He opened the back door of his green Saturn sedan. She hopped onto her safety seat, he adjusted her straps and buckled her in. He closed the car door and stood for a moment to breathe and settle his thoughts. Eventually, he took his place behind the wheel. The car had 105,000 miles on it, but it looked and ran like new. He opened the sunroof to view the blue sky. He liked driving a standard. He never worried about it being stolen because thieves didn't know how to drive a standard transmission. He would have rather been driving something sporty and expensive, like he always wanted, but needed something practical and cheap. He left the park and drove straight until he reached Lafayette Street. He took a right and followed Route 114 to Treadwell's Ice Cream.

Armed Forces Reserve Center Providence, R. I.
Blake had just given the final instructions to the marines for the memorial service. They filed off the drill deck and headed to the locker room, and after they changed clothes, they went outside to their vehicles. Technically, they did not have to go to the service, and no one would force them. They had received their DD214 form.

The DD214 was a certificate of release or condition of discharge with a complete verified record of service with all pertinent information. The unit had just completed five days on active duty. Since they were reservists again, new ID cards were issued, and ranks were adjusted for those who were promoted.

Forms, forms, and more forms were completed. Pay problems were rectified, and their issued gear was checked for serviceability and replaced if necessary. Most of the marines had rushed to have their dress blue uniform tailored in time for the memorial service. Some needed to change their ranks; others needed their waistline altered both in and out. Those who did not have dress blues had to wear their alpha uniform.

The alpha uniform was comprised of green pants, green jacket and a green cap (better known as a piss cover) that was issued to every marine in boot camp. The uniform was tailored to the individual and was worn at graduation. It was required when checking into a new command or attending a school. The alpha uniform was also worn at ceremonies and functions in lieu of dress blues. The alpha uniform was worn and inspected at least once a year by the unit's command.

The dress blue uniform was by far more popular and desirable by the marines, but it was not issued and cost over $700 dollars when all was said and done. There were no formal uniform inspections of the dress blue uniform unless a marine was assigned to a special unit such as embassy duty or presidential duty at the White House.

"Sir," Blake said as he appeared in the doorway of their COs office.

"Come in," Major Morgan said from inside his office. "Everyone all set?"

"Yes, sir," Blake replied, standing at parade rest.

"The I & I staff will handle all the details. It will be informal at the church and the gravesite. We will be speaking to the parents, though. We'll let them lead the conversation, all right?"

"Yes sir," Blake said.

"One more thing. Here is the letter that Powers had. His parents don't need to know about it," Morgan said as he handed him the envelope,

"Be careful with that."

"I will sir," Blake said as he turned around and walked back stuffing the envelope in the cargo pocket of his pants.

Warwick, R. I.

Blake decided to ride down to Warwick where the service was being held, with Staff Sergeant Burton. Burton entered the address in the Garmin GPS and 35 minutes later they were in the parking lot of the church. Blake was happy to see that everyone had made it on time, and most were in their proper uniform. About 20 or so family and friends had turned out for the service, including Powers girlfriend. He wondered if anyone else knew about the affair. Morgan had made sure that only a handful of people knew about the letter. Blake spotted an older couple who must have been Powers' parents. If they found out about the letter, they would be devastated.

The mass lasted an hour. The church was very old and gothic. Powers had probably gone to this church his entire life. Blake attended a similar church in his neighborhood when he was younger. He loved the look of the stain glass on a sunny day. The priest spoke about Richard and remembered when he was an altar boy at the parish. Two women did the readings during the Mass. The priest gave directions to the cemetery and reported that there would be no formal ceremony there. Blake watched the parents and family file out of the church behind the priest and wait outside to thank the marines. Majors Alvarez and 1st Sergeant Wood who had been with the Powers since they informed them of Richards death had a bond with the family. They introduced Major Morgan and 1st Sergeant Dineen. Now Staff Sergeants Blake and Burton waited behind them.

"Staff Sergeant Blake," Major Morgan called over politely.

"Yes sir," Blake responded and walked to Morgan with Burton following behind him.

"Mr. and Mrs. Powers, this is Staff Sergeant Blake, Richard's platoon sergeant."

"I am so sorry for your loss," Blake said as he shook their hands.

"Richard spoke highly of you," his father said as he looked into Blake's eyes. Leonard Powers was a big man with white hair, blue eyes and a strong grip.

Blake felt ashamed of the statement because he couldn't protect their son, so he did not know what to say at first. "He was a good marine and will be missed by all of us, I can assure you," Blake managed to say.

"Were you with Richard when he killed himself?" His mother asked.

The direct question shocked Blake. She was average height, long blonde hair and attractive woman. He looked at her for a moment admiring her strength. "Yes, Ma'am I was." He replied without breaking eye contact.

She stared at him, trying to read him. She nodded her head in understanding, which Blake took as forgiveness, because she could empathize with him. Mrs. Powers then grabbed his hand and introduced him to some other family members. Blake learned that Powers was an only child. There was nothing worse than parents outliving their children.

Blake saw an attractive woman in a simple black dress. Her dirty blonde hair was pulled back in a ponytail, and she wore minimal makeup. She was surrounded by a few people who he did not recognize. Blake stepped in front of her and knew what he wanted to say but thought better.

'You're Staff Sergeant Blake, right?" She put out her hand.

"Yes, I'm sorry, I forgot your name." He shook her hand.

"Amy," she said.

"Right," he smiled. The one who drove Powers to his death, he thought to himself. "I'm sorry for your loss. I knew you were dating for a while," Blake said with the utmost sympathy.

"Yes, we were together for seven years," she said while looking down.

"Richard will be deeply missed by us all," he said.

"He already is," she replied.

I am sure he is, you cheating bitch, he thought.

Blake proceeded through the crowd and waited by the stairs until Burton found him.

"Someone here will try to get in her pants," Burton said as they headed to the vehicle.

"You're nice," Blake said and looked at him, "but, no doubt, you're right. They won't if they're smart."

Burton looked at him, "What's that supposed to mean?"

Burton was never told about the letter, but not because he couldn't be trusted. It was simply that the fewer the better. Blake wanted to avoid further explanation.

"Too much baggage," Blake said.

"Dead boyfriend and all, I guess," Burton said in agreement.

The cemetery was a 15-minute ride away, and it overlooked the water of Narragansett Bay. Blake walked to the group of marines who are gathered along the small road by the marble headstone. The grass had taken and was growing in nicely. The priest arrived with the family and a few prayers were given. One by one the marines stood by the headstone and gave their prayers. Some would never come back again, others would visit occasionally, and his parents would come every day for as long as they could.

Sergeant Reyes waited for Blake by the road. "Staff Sergeant we are headed to the Foxy Lady for a toast. I hope you and Staff Sergeant Burton can join us," he said.

"Of course, we'll be there. Thanks," Blake said.

Chalkstone Ave., Providence, R. I.

The Foxy Lady was in Providence right off Interstate 95 and had been in business for over 20 years. It was considered a jewel by some. The club was on the classy side as far as strip joints were concerned. The women were impressive, Blake thought and expensive. The business was well known, and patrons drove quite a distance to visit the lovely ladies. Everyone in the club had looked at them as the 30 or so Marines walked inside that dark room. Some stood by the tables, as others sat down most in their dress blues. Not a typical site on a Friday afternoon. Blake looked around and noticed the beautiful redhead onstage performing, a natural redhead, he thought.

"Good afternoon gentlemen. What can I get you handsomely dressed marines?" she spoke with a smile.

She was in her late 30s or early 40s and wore a tight white blouse that held back a large set of breasts. She was not a stripper, Blake thought. As the marines gave her their orders, Blake wondered why she approached him. Was it the fact that he wore more stripes or because of his age, probably the latter? His wife would be pissed if she found out that he was at a strip joint no matter what the reason. The waitress took everyone's order and asked Blake last.

"Corona please," he said to her.

"I'll be right back," she said with a smile.

After the first round of drinks arrived, the men were engrossed with the women and conversation. Blake switched to his favorite drink for round two, Jim Beam and Coke.

"All right listen up Marines," he said to the guys. He waited for everyone to gather around with their drinks. "Before we forget why we're all here, would everyone please grab a drink and join me in a toast."

He waited for all the chatter to cease and the seriousness set in before he continued. "To Lance Corporal Richard Powers! You will be missed by family, friends, and the United States Marine Corps." He raised his glass. "Richard may you guard the streets of heaven well."

The clangs of glasses could be heard over the music. They all took a swallow of their poisons. The drinking continued for a while longer.

Blake had the sense to stop before he was too drunk and couldn't drive home.

"Let me know when you're ready to go," Burton said to him at the end of his third drink.

"How about now?" Blake replied.

They got up and told the guys that they would have to leave. They both put down some money, only to hear the arguments of why they shouldn't have to pay. The money stayed on the table as they shook hands and said goodbye.

"It's time," Blake thought as they left the darkness of the club and staggered into the bright sunlit parking lot. They found Burton's car and Blake got in the passenger's side. He removed the envelope that he had previously stuffed in his pocket.

"Would you mind going for a ride to East Providence before you drop me off?" Blake said.

"What are you up to?" Burton asked. "Especially dressed like that."

"Nothing you really want to know about." Blake said. "It's not illegal. I just want to pass a message along to someone who needs a dose of reality. I'll tell you if you really want to know."

Burton looked at him intently for a minute. "Does it have something to do with that letter?"

"Yes," he said.

"I'll take you. Will things go bad where we are going?"

"No," Blake replied.

Blake looked at the return address on the envelope and punched it in the GPS unit that was suctioned to the windshield. Burton backed from the parking spot,

"Calculating," the machine announced.

"You better not get me in trouble with Morgan either," Burton said with a smile, "Officer Blake."

"How do you know it's anything to do with the military?"

"Look at the way you're dressed, where we just came from, it's probably about Powers, but I don't want to know," Burton said not looking at him, but focusing on the roadway.

"Good job detective," Blake said.

"Fuck off," he laughed.

Fox Point East Providence, R.I.

15 minutes later, the car stopped in front of an apartment building. Blake saw the black Capri that he thought she drove.

"Wish me luck," he said as he reached for the car door.

"How long you going to be?" Burton asked.

"Five minutes."

"You're that quick?"

"Quicker," Blake said as he hopped out of the vehicle, "Just ask my wife."

He crossed the street, walked up the stairs, and entered the lobby of the apartment. Amy's name was on the panel by the buzzer. The inner door was locked, so he pressed the buttons for the first and third floor residents. As predicted, someone buzzed him in without checking who was at the door. He had done this many times at work to gain access to an apartment building without tipping off the bad guy.

Surprise was the key after all. He wanted to catch her off guard. He felt obligated to confront her once the letter was revealed, and after the bullshit-grieving girlfriend show of today, he decided that it had to be done. The booze had nothing to do with his decision it was made when he watched Powers blow his brains out of his head. He had to live with that vision she did not.

He stood outside of apartment #2 and listened for a few minutes to speculate who was inside. He did not want her or Powers parents over while he berated her, so he came up with an excuse in case they were present. He knocked on the door and heard movement inside.

She was clearly surprised to see him. "Hello, Staff Sergeant Blake, right?"

"Please, call me Kevin," he said sarcastically.

She opened the door wider, wondering if she should invite him inside. Blake looked right at him sitting at the kitchen table, former Lance Corporal Daniel Allen. Blake knew Powers and Dan were good friends at one time.

She saw Blake staring at Dan. "You guys know each other?"

"Hello, Staff Sergeant," Dan said.

TERROR IN THE WITCH CITY

"Of course, we do." Blake answered Amy and handed her the letter. "I came here to give you this."

She took the letter and Blake continued, "I figured you might want it back. We found it in Richards' pocket." Blake noticed the tears watering in her eyes. "After he blew himself away," Blake said.

"I suppose you have the other letter?" Blake asked Dan.

"Yes, I do," he replied looking down.

"Weren't you guys good friends at the unit?" Blake asked Dan the question but looked at Amy for a reaction.

She folded her arms across her chest and looked at Dan. Neither of the two said a word.

"You're a real buddy-fucker, aren't you?" Blake said to him.

Amy turned back to Blake. "What do you want?" She said angrily.

"Nothing. I just wanted you to know that the command found the letter and figured out what probably happened. The marines don't know, and his parents don't either unless you tell them. We don't care what you do, but I do have one question?"

Blake didn't wait for an answer. "Did he call you before he killed himself? Did you tell him you were fucking around? If you did talk to him, it would have been one day before his parents were notified."

"What are you talking about?" She said defiantly, "It had been weeks before he died since I had talked to him," she sounded confused and tears started rolling down her cheeks.

Blake looked at Dan who was looking down at the floor with no expression on his face.

"He made a call before we left on the convoy that morning," Blake continued, "which was at night here. He was out of it after the call. I thought he might have called here and spoke to you or him?" Blake said and glanced over at Dan.

Amy turned to Dan. "Did you talk to him?"

"No," Dan said quietly, he looked up at her, his guilt was unmistakable.

"Anyway," Blake interjected, "You have your letter back and are aware of what we learned." He turned to exit, but before walking down the hallway, he added, "You drove a man to his death."

"He killed himself!" She was crying and angrily followed him.

TERROR IN THE WITCH CITY

"I know what happened." Blake spun around to face her. "I watched him do it, you fucking bitch!"

He was furious, but calmly said, "I will never forget it." Blake turned back around to leave, and said over his shoulder, "Have a nice life though."

He heard the wailing and then the yelling. It started to fade as he started walking down the stairs. He thought he would have felt better about the confrontation but didn't. Powers was dead, and the lives of his family and friends would be touched forever.

He went out the front door and stopped at the curb, then looked both ways before crossing the street to the waiting vehicle. He opened the passenger's door, sat in the seat and looked straight ahead.

"Do you mind if I smoke?" Blake said while looking straight ahead.

"Normally yes, but in this case no." Burton watched as Blake took a pack of Marlboro cigarettes from his right sock. "Are you done?"

"Yep," he replied and fished for the lighter in his pocket.

"Feel better?"

"Not at all," he replied as he lit the cigarette.

Burton shifted the vehicle into drive, looked in his mirror and pulled onto the roadway.

Chapter 21

Street of Dreams

September

Derby St., Salem, MA

They sat at the weathered bar, where many drinks had come across during its lifetime. The stools had high backs, armrests, and were as worn as the bar. The bottles on the wood were ice cold. The meeting had just finished so there was a good crowd on hand. The members and guests were mingling with drinks in their hands. Some walked with canes, one had a walker. They ranged in age from mid-30s to late 80s, maybe even 90s. Most were male, some with their wives or girlfriends.

Their experiences were historic and incredible. Their contributions to the world were immeasurable. They had helped form new countries, overthrown mad man, and liberated nations. They fought on the beaches of Normandy in France, in the rice paddies of Vietnam and Korea, and in the streets of Baghdad, Iraq. They were members and guests of the Veterans of Foreign War Post #1524 which was in Salem, Massachusetts. Their monthly Thursday night monthly meeting had ended 20 minutes ago. Blake and another member had stopped mingling in the crowd and found a place to settle in. Blake looked over at the man across from him more in a friend/fatherly way than his boss.

"You're a double member here," Chief Hampton said.

"I'll be a triple member if they have their way. If I stay there, I will be back over within two years," Blake replied, referring to the Marine Corps.

"You really should get out."

"I'm four years shy of retirement. I have too much time invested" he replied.

As if on cue, they both took a pull from the long neck bottles of beer that were in front of them.

Blake said, "I think I will try another unit, something new. I am an official reservist again, I checked out last Friday. We start drilling again in October."

"When are you coming back?" Hampton asked.

"Three more days." Blake replied.

"Take another week off, to decompress. I'll let Ross know it's okay."

"Thanks Chief, but you don't have to do that. You've done enough."

"Don't worry about it, spend time with the kids. You deserve it, give him a call on Monday and work out a date to come back."

"Thank you."

"Now back to drinking, what do you want? I'm buying and don't argue with me," Hampton said smiling.

"Another Corona then," Blake said.

His boss stood up and went over to the bar. Blake liked his boss he considered him a good friend. The chief had called and checked on Blake's family when he was away on deployment. There weren't many bosses who would do that. He also ensured that his pay and benefits still flowed to the family. Hampton was a local guy who rose to serve his community. He joined the military serving his country, then later graduated from Boston College. He started out as a patrolman and worked his way through the ranks to chief.

When he came back the two continued through a few more rounds while swapping stories, Blake in the first Gulf War and Iraq and Hampton in Vietnam. They talked about the city, coworkers, politics, kids and life in general. A few of the old timers stopped by their table mostly to say hello to the Chief.

Hampton and Blake both stood up a few hours later, Blake put a $10 bill on the bar as the Chief looked at him.

"Tip, that's all, you bought the rounds," he said and smiled.

They were out the door then stopped in a small parking lot.

The chief turned to Blake and said, "I'm glad you're home safe and sound."

The two shook hands.

"Goodnight boss," Blake said.

"Goodnight."

Blake had parked on the street, a small one way that led to the ocean. He walked to his car, noticing how cold it turned at night now. Blake took his seat behind the wheel and started the ignition. Rock music played as the car came to life. Another week off was great and normally he would be happy, but it just made it harder to return. He turned his head and looked to the rear to make sure no one was coming and entered the roadway.

Safwan, Iraq

It was dark out when Abdallah pulled though the open gate in his Toyota Land Cruiser and into the gravel driveway. He had been here before, always at night, and at a specific time. He knew the owner of the residence was no one to screw with since he had strong ties to the "Party of God". The Shiite militia had formed the organization with the help of the Iranian Revolutionary Guard. While Abdallah despised the Shiites, he knew his place with this man. He grabbed his briefcase from the passenger's seat on his way out of the vehicle. He passed through the gate and pushed both sides shut and engaged the locking mechanism. The less he was seen here the better. He knocked on the side door and waited. The owner of the home heard the crunching of the gravel under the weight of the tires and was not surprised. This was their second meeting involving Sawaya. During the first meeting his host had laid out the plan and what he wanted Abdallah to do. He expected his visitor, which was the only reason why the gate was still open. He didn't trust many people.

Khailfa headed to the door to greet his guest. "Hello, my friend" he said as he opened the door for Abdallah, "Any problems getting here?"

"Hello" he said and lowered his head to the host, a sign of respect, "No, the streets are quiet" Abdallah replied.

He looked around the house as he walked in. He was amazed by all the luxuries and high-tech gadgets that the man had; the same man who he once heard denounce "the lavishes of life." As he entered the room, Abdallah noticed a man in the corner: he was the reason Abdallah was here. The host had told him all about his other guest.

Abdallah walked over to Sawaya, introduced himself and passed on his condolences for the loss of Sawaya's son at the hands of the

Americans. Abdallah then turned around and sat in a leather chair in the opposite corner facing Sawaya and Khalifa behind his desk.

"I have been told you would like to seek vengeance for the death of your son," Abdallah said looking at Sawaya.

"I would," Sawaya responded, "but I do not know how to accomplish it."

"I understand that the infidel responsible took his own life before he could be held accountable?"

"Yes, I watched him do it," he replied, "It was the other US Marine calling the shots though. He is the one who destroyed my family and is responsible now," he said.

Khalifa sat behind his desk watching while the men spoke. He opened the top drawer and removed a manila envelope and placed it on top of the nearly empty desk. He withdrew the photographs and spread them out.

Abdallah had seen the photos before and had conducted some research on the man. He grabbed a photo and held it up. "Was this the American who watched your son die, standing over his body?" he asked.

He knew how it would play on the distraught father's emotions.

"Yes, it is," Sawaya replied, his voice revealing that he was trying to keep his emotions under control.

"He told me he would take my son to the American hospital after he died. They were going to take him on a helicopter," Sawaya recalled.

"To take your son away from you forever and do what with him?" Abdallah said angrily. He waited moment to calm down before continuing. "Has Khailfa told you of our intentions for this demon?" he asked Sawaya.

"Just that we should show him what it feels like to lose a child he loves, and to teach the Americans a lesson in their own country," Sawaya said.

"Are you willing to seek revenge on him and his family in America?" Abdallah asked leaning closer.

"I am!" he said angrily locking eyes with him.

"Do you want to be a martyr with our people and teach the infidels a lesson that they will not forget for a long time?" Abdallah said with a smile on his face.

"I do," Sawaya replied enthusiastically.

"Then we will begin right now, and you will be ready when we call upon you to assist us in our mission, on behalf of your murdered son," Abdallah said emphasizing the last few words. "We will travel to America and inflict the same hurt and pain that he did to you and your wife," he said calmly, "Would you like that?"

"Yes, I would!" Sawaya responded.

"Good. There is one thing though" he said, "you can tell no one what we are planning. They will know in time. The world will know in time."

"I understand," Sawaya said.

"Also, do not cross us. We are doing this to avenge your son's death. If you do cross us you will pay with your life, understand?" Abdallah said. He failed to tell him that his wife would die if he did. Killing her would prove to the other villagers that they were serious. Once Sawaya agreed Abdallah knew that he had recruited another man that he would use to achieve his goals.

He would later use Sawaya's bomber martyrdom as propaganda to recruit more people for his cause after this was done. If he backed out in America, then Abdallah would use his connections to take Sawaya's wife and family members as hostages until he completed his part of the mission. They were expendable, Abdallah was not.

"Okay, some research has been done on the subjects so far," Abdallah said as he opened his laptop that was in his briefcase and turned it on. He brought up a file that contained some information. "His name is Kevin Blake, and he is a Staff Sergeant in the United States Marine Corps. He is a reservist and on leave from his work. He is a police officer in Salem, Massachusetts," he said to the two watching him.

All three men knew the name Salem was a name meaning peace.

"Someone called his work to verify he was on deployment in Iraq," Abdallah said, "Thanks to the chatty woman who answered the phone." He pulled up a web site and entered Blake's name and state in the locate box. His address, date of birth, places where he lived and even family names associated with him appeared. Abdallah typed a little more and an aerial map of Blake's home appeared. He looked up and smiled at the two men.

TERROR IN THE WITCH CITY

"What if someone gets a hold of that laptop?" Khalifa asked.

Abdallah pointed to a USB drive that was sticking out of the machine, "The files are encrypted, and password protected, no way to access the data. The IP address is masked, and a trace would send it to another country. It does not keep a history on the machine it's plugged into."

"Impressive," Khalifa said.

"American technology. They are their own worst enemy."

Abdallah said smiling. He saved the data and removed the drive after it was complete. "I am in contact with a person who will assist us once we arrive and possibly a second as well," he said and closed the laptop.

Abdallah continued, "All you need to do is be ready to leave for a week. I will make all the arrangements. I'll let you know a few days in advance. In the meantime, think of what you will tell your wife or anyone else who will ask where you're going."

"What about a passport, should I get one?" Sawaya asked.

"I will take care of that as well, just be ready when I tell you," Abdallah said speaking to the man like he was a child.

Khalifa watched Abdallah do his thing; he was contacted for this assignment because he was educated and spoke with a slight British accent after living in London. He was intelligent, careful, and resourceful. He could also think "outside the box" as the westerners said. Abdallah put his religious and tribal beliefs aside when it came to the mission. He had been to America several times and knew what to expect from the authorities. Khalifa knew Abdallah used fear and intimidation to get the job done as well.

Khalifa looked at both men from behind his desk, "Now let's pray to Allah for his blessing, shall we?" he said to both men.

The two men stood up and followed their elder out of the office.

Salem Police Department, Salem, MA

Blake had just spoken with the Patrol Commander. The schedule was set, and he would start at midnight in two rotations. He needed to pick up his gun and other gear that he would need before he returned to work. One rotation consisted of four days followed by two days off. It was referred to as the swing shift because they worked two midnight to 8 a.m. shifts, followed by two 4pm to midnight shifts. The killer was the second day, when you left work at 8 a.m. and returned for the second shift at 4p.m.

He enjoyed the time off and had not worked there since early January which was nine months ago. He hated working the midnight shift, especially on his first night back. He would seriously consider working the day shift on the next shift bid in December.

Blake took the elevator to the third floor. There was only one door on the third floor; he walked to the room that he knew held all the weapons and ammunition. He knocked on the thick glass door of the armory/range room until he saw a chair roll across the room. The older man stood up and walked to the main door. He smiled when he recognized Blake.

"Kevin, nice to see you back. How are you doing?" The Armorer said with a genuine smile and a powerful hand shake.

The armor's job was to inspect, diagnose, maintain, repair, and service weapons for sworn police staff. There were two other armors, but he was the only one full time. They spoke awhile about family, Iraq and the Salem Police department.

The armorer didn't wait for Blake to say what the visit was for, "Let me get you what you need," he said and disappeared.

"Here you go, just the way you left it," The Armorer said, handing Blake the gun belt. "I took the liberty of cleaning your gun. The least I could do for a war vet."

"Thank you, I really appreciate it," Blake said slightly embarrassed, "Well I have to go, but I will see you next week. I am sure they will want me to qualify you soon," he said.

Blake entered the male locker room used by the patrolman. Since it was between shifts, the locker room was deserted. Blake went to locker #62 and grabbed what he needed. He didn't want to stay to long because no one was home and he had to catch up on work around the house. He would see everyone soon enough.

He left through the door that led to the gym. The gym was small but contained a lot of machines and equipment. He went down the stairs to the side door, the detective side as it was known. Patrol had the other side where the vehicles were parked.

It was so quiet in the house that Blake didn't know what to do first. The yard work took precedence. Kerry was gone with the kids and he had a few more hours of peace and serenity. He enjoyed the chance to get something done without constant interruptions. After a few hours of laboring in the sun he called it quits. He took a shower to clean off the dirt and grime.

He laid on the bed with the ceiling fan producing a cool breeze that circulated about the room. His breathing slowed, and his body began to relax. It did not take long for him to fall asleep. As the fan cooled his body the rotation of the blades set off a series of signals somewhere deep in his mind.

Blake's dream began with him driving a Hummer down a street in Iraq. He could see and hear the crowd yelling and screaming at him. There were no other vehicles around. The angry crowd was on both sides of the street. The road seemed to go on forever. His foot seemed to be stuck to the gas pedal. He saw someone in the middle of the roadway in the distance. The person was waving their arms. Blake's vehicle was going faster now. He looked down for a brake pedal, but there was none. He went to turn the wheel, but it just spun around in his hands as the vehicle continued straight. The crowd was yelling in Arabic, which he thought the words meant for him to stop.

He watched the crowd motioning with their hands, but he shot right past them. Blake could not see a face on the person in the street, only a black circle in the middle of a head. He braced himself as the vehicle careened into the figure, knocking him into the air. The Humvee stopped immediately, and he looked around at the crowd that was staring at him. It was silent as they looked and studied him. Then they began to yell and scream and started picking up anything they could get their hands on to throw at him.

Rocks began to bounce off the glass that surrounded him, a few at first and then they rained down. The crowd surrounded the vehicle and started rocking it back and forth. The glass finally gave way in a few spots and arms reached through to grab him. More rocks smashed gaping holes through the class. Hands were all over him now.

TERROR IN THE WITCH CITY

He felt himself being dragged out through a hole and thought it would hurt, but he had no feeling as he passed through the broken glass. He was dragged on the ground and surrounded by angry faces. They started kicking him and bending over to punch him, but he still felt nothing. It was so loud and confusing. He saw the crowd move for someone or something; they were all looking at whatever was approaching him. They were smiling, laughing, and pointing. Then he saw a Herculean man with a giant boulder grasped in his hands. The bearded man was smiling. The crowd was chanting loudly as if it was sporting event. The man was standing over him now. Blake wanted to yell and scream, but nothing was coming out. He could hear himself, "No! No! No!" He was screaming, but nothing came past his lips. "What is happening, please make this stop," he thought. He was yelling, the man used all his strength to hoist the rock, the crowd was yelling, and chanting. He moved his body forward. In slow motion, the rock was in the air.

The next thing he knew; he was on a stretcher looking up at the rotating blades of a helicopter. It was loud with the whine of the engine growing louder and louder. He tried to move his head, but it was frozen. No room to wiggle. He could not feel his legs or arms. He must have been strapped down he thought. He could see men in desert Cammies bending down telling him it would be all right. He did not know who they were, but they looked scared. They were yelling at each other, but he could not make out what they were saying.

"Hold on, hold on, you'll be all right," someone got close and said to him as the motor whined above his head.

"NO, NO!" He heard himself yelling to anyone who would listen, but everyone was avoiding his pleads.

The blades spun faster and faster, the whining motor grew louder and louder. He began to rock from side to side as the helicopter shifted. It started to rise, and he could see nothing, but blowing dust and dirt. In that instance, a blood curdling scream arose from the darkened bedroom where Blake had just awoken from the nightmare of Iraq.

TERROR IN THE WITCH CITY

*

It was at the end of September and Blake sat watching a recap of football scores for week four of the NFL on ESPN. The only team that interested him was The New England Patriots with a record of two and two. He was dressed in his uniform pants, boots and a t-shirt. It was 11:25 p.m. on a Sunday night, but he had a smile on his face with good reason. He was awakened by the weight of her body on top of him. He opened his eyes to find her large breasts against his skin. She kissed his neck and head. He kissed her lips then felt her warm body on top of him. He slid his shorts and underwear off and plunged himself inside her. Blake moved her up, so he could devour her boobs as he went in and out of her. She grinded and rocked on top of him as she felt the rush of pleasure. Blake flipped her over and pinned her to the bed never losing his position. He continued this until he couldn't take it anymore. They lay in a heap after he exploded inside her. He lay there not wanting to move at all. He kissed her passionately and wished her a wonderful night's sleep.

Two hours later he was hoping it would be a quiet night, call wise, but he had no idea what was in store for him. He grabbed his Kevlar vest, shirt, and a bag that was loaded with the tools he needed for the street and headed out the door. He felt like he was starting over, first night on the job. He locked the front door of the house and went to his car. It was so quiet in the neighborhood. A few lights were on and the flickering of a few televisions. He started the car and left unhappily. The ride took all of four minutes, five if the lights were against him. He pulled in the lot of 95 Margin Street to resume his career as a police officer.

The Salem Police Department was situated across from an old meat packing company that had closed many years ago. Both buildings were at the end of the train tracks where a small freight yard was once busy. A marina now used the lot of the meat packing building to store boats in the off-season. After the boats were towed in the yard, they were shrink-wrapped to keep animals and weather out during the winter months.

Blake remembered a ramp and loading dock at one time that was used to load and off-load freight trains. When he was a kid, he thought he could ride his bicycle up the ramp, jump off, and land with ease just like his childhood idol at the time Evel Knievel. Blake learned seconds later after he was airborne that he couldn't. He was lucky that he did not break any bones or shatter his teeth when his ass went over the handlebars into the dirt. He went home crying and learned a valuable lesson about reality and physics.

Blake grabbed his bag from the passenger seat and headed to the door. He removed his wallet and swiped the card reader. The light turned green. He opened the door and headed upstairs to the locker room. Tucked away in his wallet was a card that not only identified him as a Salem Police officer but allowed access to certain areas of the building based on rank, position, and the need to know.

He entered the locker room through the gym. Blake unlocked his locker, emptied the contents of the bag, and put the final touches on his uniform. He took out his gun belt and clipped it around his waist; there was a little more room since the last time he wore it. The belt was a pain in the ass to adjust because of everything that was attached to it. He put all the items in their allotted pouches: handcuffs, flashlight, radio, and ammunition. He took out his departmental issued 9mm Smith and Wesson model 5906. The gun was ancient by today's standards. He locked the slide to the rear and inserted a magazine, which had 15 rounds and released the slide, chambering a round. He released the magazine by pushing a button on the side and inserted a single cartridge into the magazine, bringing it back to full capacity. He reinserted the magazine back into the weapon and holstered it. It was now street ready, 16 rounds at the ready and 30 more in reserve.

Blake heard some voices and lockers being opened out of his sight of vision. He grabbed the hard-plastic briefcase that contained tickets books, forms, law books, and a host of other things he needed to be effective at his job. He grabbed his jacket and eight-point hat and made his way to the muster room, passing the other lockers. He was stopped twice along the way to say hello and shake some hands. He exited the locker room, took a right, and walked to the glass door.

The shift technically did not start until 0000 hours. or midnight. In most cases the oncoming shift arrived 10-15 minutes before the shift began to relieve their fellow officers. During roll call; officers were briefed on the past shift's activities, bolo's (be on the lookout), extra checks that were requested, breaks in the area, and other police and city related business. The items were read to every shift for a week or were supposed to be depending on the matter. Vehicles and personnel assignments were also given.

Blake opened the door and saw the patrol sergeant behind the podium in front of the large room. Patrolmen were sitting at the six long tables toward the back of the room and typing last minute reports on the computer before they were relieved by the Street Sergeant.

"First night back and you're almost late," the salt and peppered haired Sergeant said with a smile. He came around the podium and walked toward him with his hand out.

Blake was putting his stuff down on a table.

"Welcome home Kevin, glad you made it home safe."

"Thank you" he replied, "It's good to be home, even here," He heard a few chuckles.

"How's the family, life returning to normal?" the sergeant asked.

"Family is good, thanks. And life little by little," Blake replied honestly.

"Good, after roll call we will go see the Lieutenant and figure out what to do with you."

Chapter 22

Cops and Robbers

October 2003

Salem, MA

It was October, and life was finally falling back into place. Blake was comfortable at home, not the stranger he had once felt. At work; he demonstrated that he still knew his job. During his first week back, he was on the desk and assisting the dispatcher; throughout the next rotation he was back in a patrol vehicle as a passenger. Now, he was a one-man patrol unit back to his assigned area, 22 Car. The City of Salem was divided into seven patrol sectors. There were only six during the midnight shift. The other beat was divided between the surrounding areas. The beats were numbered 21-26, and one other called Essex Street. If there were spare officers, they would be assigned to unit 27 through 29.

During other times, such as on a midnight shift there may be only four officers, which was the department minimal manning policy. If the public only knew there were four officers to cover a city of 40 thousand residents and handle all the restaurants, and the bars when they closed and college students they would be outraged. It was all about the money though at least as far as city hall was concerned. The Mayor couldn't have given a shit about the officers' safety. If the overtime budget was kept under control, that's all that mattered. Unit 22 was responsible for one of the smallest beats which was called the point area. It was only 1 mile by ½ mile, but it was heavily concentrated and the busiest call wise. The area consisted of a large Dominican neighborhood with a lot of college students from Salem State College.

Growing up in Salem, Blake remembered that neighborhood as predominately French-Canadian working. Then a few Puerto Rican families moved into the neighborhood, then some white families moved out to other areas of the city. When the Dominicans moved in, the Puerto Ricans moved out. The area was extremely busy during the summer months and dead quiet during the winter months. Some families in the neighborhood would leave their residence for the winter and live in the Dominican Republic, then they came back when it was warm again. Blake had learned a lot about being a cop while assigned to the point. If you wanted to be proactive and make arrests that was the place for it. From drunks to drug dealers, you earned your money and experience. Blake was surprised when a few of the people who lived in the area had stopped him and thanked him for his service in Iraq. Either the other officers told them where he was, or they read the newspaper. In either case he was surprised.

Blake made his way through the tight streets and one-ways. Parking was premium there. It was a nightmare during a snow emergency where the residents had to find off street parking or their vehicles would be towed. A group of kids were hanging out on the corner. They were not causing any problems, mostly being loud. He passed by the same people doing the same thing day after day. He saw a familiar group of guys in the corner of a parking lot on Congress Street by Palmer Street. They were older and barely spoke English, at least in front of Blake. They had a small card table with chairs and were playing dominoes like they always did on a nice day. They had blue and red plastic solo cups on the table, and Blake knew what was in them. Corona was the beer of choice in this neighborhood. He didn't bother with him them since they were discreet and quiet. He knew that if he told them to leave because the owner complained, they would leave without issue because they were respectful. Anyway, he knew they would be packing up the game soon to go eat dinner.

The area was comprised mainly of three- and four-story large brick buildings and two and three decker multi-family houses. The neighborhood had changed dramatically from when his friends had lived there. Now there was trash strewn about, graffiti on the buildings, and a general lack of care for the property. The playground in the middle of the area, named Mary Jane Park, was a mess. Trash was everywhere, graffiti all over, broken playground equipment, and punk kids that liked to hang out there.

Blake circled the area constantly to let them know he was around. He remembered when he was a kid that residents used to sweep the sidewalks in front of their houses, whether they owned the property or not.

TERROR IN THE WITCH CITY

There was still an elderly woman who continued to sweep in front of her house on Palmer Street, she had lived there for over 40 years. The kids who lived around her thought she was crazy because she did this, but Blake knew she never forgot her roots and had pride in where she lived.

There were alleys and gaps between buildings within the area that created a maze for police and an elaborate escape system for the criminals. As he was driving on Lafayette Street, he saw one of his favorite drunks on a bench at Lafayette Park as it was formally known. The police called it Dog Shit Park. It wasn't a real park at all though. Just a gathering point for drunks, junkies, and the low lives that congregated there. It was a large triangle of brown, spotty grass with several benches and trees.

Blake only knew the drunk as Norberto. It was rumored that he was once a successful businessman who fell apart after his wife left him. He apparently had replaced her with a bottle of booze and lived off the streets. He barely spoke English but managed to survive in the Spanish neighborhood. The locals gave him money for food that was usually diverted for alcohol. They let him stay in their basements when the weather turned cold.

Norberto yelled something in Spanish at Blake, who assumed it was a greeting of sorts. Blake waved back like he always did and felt bad for the man. Norberto was old and had nothing but chose to live his life this way. He seemed like a decent guy and never gave any officer the slightest hassle. Norberto had been placed in protective custody so many times he probably held the record at the police department. It was done for his safety though. If not, he would have been killed, robbed or beaten by some thugs, maybe even freeze to death because he was so hammered. Blake continued driving and took a right on Peabody Street.

He saw a known street dealer on the sidewalk that was watching him cautiously. There was no doubt that he was carrying something, coke or heroin. He had been recently arrested by detectives for selling cocaine and was out on bail. Blake knew that if he stopped the car quickly the man would run. He had no legal justification to shake him down at least for the court's sake.

TERROR IN THE WITCH CITY

The Massachusetts Supreme Judicial Court made the police jump through a lot of hoops to stop the flow of narcotics. It was not like the guy would stop selling either. He would be careful about dealing for a while, but eventually he would get sloppy again and caught.

The patrol vehicle, a 2002 Ford Crown Victoria preceded straight and took another right onto Congress Street. As he continued up the street, he heard loud music coming from the Honda ahead of him. It appeared that the registration was expired. While they waited in traffic, Blake ran the license plate number through the computer that was inches from him.

The computer was synced with the Massachusetts Registry of Motor Vehicles. He waited patiently for the response. He knew that a lot of people failed to put the current registration sticker on the rear license plate or not on at all. After a minute or so a code came back on the screen that meant the registration was revoked due to insurance.

The Honda took a right and Blake immediately followed. With his right-hand Blake activated the master control switch on the center console that turned on the emergency lights then pushed the siren button. The brake lights of the Honda came on and the vehicle pulled over to the right.

"22 to Salem Control," Blake said into the Motorola microphone in the cruiser.

"Control is on," the dispatcher returned.

"Motor vehicles stop 117 Lafayette Street with Mass registration # TYSLPD, black Honda," he said before leaving the vehicle.

Every traffic stop was supposed to be called in so in case something happened to the officer, backup units could be sent, and an investigation could be conducted. He had positioned the vehicle strategically, as he had been taught at the police academy, so a passing car would not clip him. Drivers were known to stare at the flashing lights' wondering what was going on. While doing so, they would unintentionally veer off to the right and hit the officer on the side of the road. Many officers were injured or killed by their drivers' careless hands.

Blake would normally have told dispatch how many passengers were in the vehicle, but the windows were so tinted he could not tell, a huge safety disadvantage for anyone who stopped the car. For all he knew, the occupants had a shotgun aimed right at him as he came up to the driver's side of the vehicle. Massachusetts's law defined the percentage of tint allowed on a motor vehicle with the use of a tint meter, which was not needed in this case.

Blake unclipped the safety of his holster and rocked it out a little. The gun was still in the holster, but his hand was on the grip and easily accessible. Blake stopped just before the line of the front door where the B pillar is located. Getting in the path of the door could get an officer killed.

Traffic stops were one of the most dangerous things a police officer could do. You never knew who you were pulling over or what they had just done. Cases of officers killed on traffic stops revealed that the offender had thought they were being pulled over for one reason when, in fact, it was usually for a minor violation. Many police officers had died on the side of the road through these chance encounters.

The window came down a moment after Blake had stopped. The white male driving looked at Blake with a baseball hat lopsided on his head and look of disgust on his face.

"What did I do?" he said like a smart ass.

"One, your windows are so tinted I could not see through them. Two, your registration is revoked for insurance," Blake said firmly, "Can I see your license and registration?"

The kid looked at him for second then went for his wallet and removed his license. As he did this Blake scanned the vehicle and looked over the male in the passenger's seat and Hispanic female in the back. He lowered the visor to get the registration. Blake would search this vehicle before it was towed.

"I'll be right back," he said and with the documents in hand headed back to the patrol car. Blake noticed the other police car arrive as he started back to his car.

"What do you got?" Officer Christina Spencer asked Blake as he approached Unit 25.

"Revoked insurance, tinted window, smart ass driver. Do you know him?" Blake asked as he handed her the license.

She looked at it for a minute, "No. Want to go through the car?"

"Yeah, if you don't mind?"

"Not at all," she said as she unbuckled her seat belt and got out.

TERROR IN THE WITCH CITY

*

Michael Mitchell had just crossed Lafayette Street by the fast food restaurant. He saw the blue and white flashing strobe lights and thought, fucking cops. While he didn't hate them, he didn't exactly like them either. He had been arrested a few times and had his car towed. They had treated him decently, though, and he spoke to a few of the officers who worked the detail at the building where he lived. He respected them for the thankless job they did.

Mitchell recognized the Honda and knew that the kid driving was an asshole and deserved whatever he was getting. The asshole had nearly run him over while showing off for his friends.

He crossed Ward Street and fished for the key to the lobby door. Mitchell was in good mood since he had been working for a few weeks now. He just picked up the vendors' license for Halloween and would make some good money that weekend. His plan was to get a vendors' cart from a friend and sell soda, water and candy on Friday and Saturday. There would be plenty of business and he wouldn't mark up the price too much. He could move around and away from the stationary vendors and capitalize off the crowd.

The vendor's license wasn't cheap or easy to get. He started the process in July and finally received the license after winning the lottery for licenses that the city held. He picked up the license after he paid a $200 a day fee per day for it.

His brother-in-law had felt bad for him and hooked him up with a job assisting an accountant in town. The accountant was impressed with his skills and agreed to keep Mitchell on as long as he could. He also fronted Mitchell money for the license and goods to sell.

Mitchell had not just fell on hard times, he hit rock bottom. He realized now since he was sober and off drugs that he had created this mess. It started with him drinking after work, then eventually during lunch too. He was hauled in by his boss, the head of the firm, for his behavior. They had built a nice case against him with their legal team. They told him he had one more chance before he would be terminated.

After two months and broken promises to himself, Mitchell was let go from his six-figure job. His wife was furious with him. He needed to escape and experimented with some recreational drugs. His wife left him,

165

and she took their two kids shortly after he started using cocaine. Without employment and pissing through a sizable amount of money in their joint account, the house was seized by the bank.

One night, he went to see a new friend about buying some coke. The friend told him that he was out of that but had some heroin instead which was a lot cheaper and a way better high. Mitchell went from living in a beautiful house in Lynnfield with his wife and two kids, to living in his car until the police had taken it. The insurance was revoked after he stopped paying the bill, and the police had towed it as he partied with a whore and another junkie in a rooming house in Salem. He eventually wound up living at the Salem Shelter on Crombie Street. He still had room to fall though.

Mitchell thought he had a good plan to get some money for his habit. He dressed up in the only suit he had, left the shelter, and went to a local jewelry store that he knew carried quality and expensive items. He started to sweet talk the older woman behind the counter and requested to see a specific ring. Once in his hands and with the distraction of another customer, he bolted from the store and attempted to get lost in the lunchtime crowd on the walking mall. He failed to research his escape route, because there was a police officer working for a contractor around the corner from the business.

The officer heard the call being given out on his portable radio and subsequent description. The officer then watched the suspect try to walk by casually. Once Mitchell realized that he was identified, he attempted to out run the cop who was half his age. The foot chase lasted no more than a block before Mitchell was grabbed and dragged to the ground after he refused to obey the commands to stop. He was arrested, brought to court, and then to the Essex County Sheriff's Department jail in Middleton until his trial date.

While he was incarcerated, he spoke to a treatment councilor and requested a drug treatment program. He eventually served 30 days at a drug treatment program, compliments of the Massachusetts Department of Corrections and the taxpayers of Massachusetts. He pleaded guilty, and served several more months, with the remainder of the sentence on probation. The judge was lenient since he had never been arrested before. He was on drugs at the time, and it was not a violent crime. Besides the job, his sister had given him some money to "start fresh" after his jail sentence.

Michael Mitchell was now living in a single room with his own private bathroom. It could be called a studio, but it was literally the size of a bedroom. The Lincoln Hotel was not a hotel at all. The management company that ran it was certainly not going to call it a rooming house though. You could call shit a rose, but in the end, it still stunk. The hotel was at 117 Lafayette Street in Salem and he paid $120 dollars a week that included all the utilities. His apartment was a little bigger than the walk-in closet of the master bedroom he formerly owned. He was clean now and getting on his feet - baby steps, he told himself.

He produced the key, unlocked the hall door and entered the lobby. All the mailboxes, which were built into the wall, were on the left side of the lobby. He would get his mail later when he went out tonight. His nightly walks cleared his head and made him think about what he needed to do next to get his life back. He really wanted to see his kids, but that would take some effort. It had been a long time and he was ready to see them now. Just a short visit was all he wanted. He would petition the court for visitation rights if he had to, but that would take time and the money he didn't have. His wife had never visited him in jail, only his sister and brother-in-law a few times. He had not spoken to his wife since the day she left with the kids two years ago.

Mitchell took the elevator to the 7th floor, took a left, and went to the end of the brightly lit hall. He was the last door on the left room #705. He took out another key and unlocked the one-inch deadbolt that kept the other junkies and thieves out. Mitchell knew he lived in a flophouse and was embarrassed to be there, but he had nothing else. He took out the vendors badge and threw it on the dresser next to the picture frame. He turned on the television with a click of the remote to watch the local news.
*

At the same time, the man interested in Mitchell was no more than three blocks away. Yassin was sitting at a small table at Starbucks on Washington Street on his Sony laptop; he was looking at a map and realized that he was only blocks away from the target. Yassin wondered if he should go for a walk or drive by the address. He put the man's name on the website to see if he could learn more. While he waited, he thought of how easy it was to find all the information at the stroke of a few keys.

Yassin took a sip of the overpriced, but good dark roast coffee. A few more names appeared with the towns affiliated with them. He would not dig too deep just yet. A cursory search, until they arrived. He really didn't like this and didn't want to go any further, but he had no choice in the matter. He wasn't worried about being caught since he was using a wireless access point. The only thing that could be traced back was the DNS server in the area. Yassin thought of the police stumbling upon him, and what he would do. He did not want anyone's blood on his hands. It wasn't his fight, at least not anymore. He had a job to do now, though, and would complete it.

Yassin had gotten lucky earlier when he went to the Salem City Hall annex to obtain a vendor's license for Halloween. He went to 120 Washington Street where the license/builder counter was located. A middle-aged woman in glasses told Yassin, nicely, that all the vendors' licenses were taken, and he was out of luck. As he pondered this, a middle-aged man stepped to the counter and told her that he was there to pick up his license. Yassin looked at the man who looked rough. Not in a tough sense, but in a way that life had not been too kind to him. Besides that, his clothes were mismatched, and he was unshaven. His hair was also a mess.

The woman went to a cabinet and took out some papers with a badge clipped to it. She had him sign a paper, and he thanked her and headed for the elevator lobby.

"Helen," another woman came around the wall from a large office, "your sons on the line, sounds urgent."

"Sorry, I have to go," she said and followed the other woman.

Yassin moved over to the other side of the counter and looked at the discarded form. On the form was the man's name, address, phone number, and amount paid. Yassin looked at it for a moment, removed his cell phone, and took a close-up photo of the information. He placed the phone back in his pocket and headed out of the office to the elevator. The elevator was so slow to arrive and by the time he reached the lobby floor, the man was long gone. He looked around for a bit, then went to his car that was parked in front of the building. Yassin drove down the one-way lane until he spotted the Starbucks sign. He would get a coffee and do some research as well as think about his next move. His contact would be pleased with him for the information that he obtained.

Yassin powered down the laptop and stored it in his briefcase. He thought about his wife and kids and what they would think of him after this. He reminded himself that he had to do this and knew this day would happen. That's why he was sent here in the first place. He thought he was forgotten, but that was only wishful thinking. Now it was going to happen, but he had such a good life thus far. He took out his cell phone and hit number two and waited.

"It's me, do you need anything from the store?" he asked.

Chapter 23

Checks

October

Washington St., Salem City Hall, Salem, MA

The meeting started right at 7 P.M. which was a miracle. The meetings were open to the public and held on the second and fourth Wednesday of every month. There was a lot of chattering, some of the conversations were genuine, and others were just trying to be polite. The mayor, clerk, and council members sat at their designated chairs, which were in the City Council Chamber on the second floor. With a few exceptions, the chamber had remained unchanged since 1838, and some of the original furniture was still used.

The members sat at two long tables that faced each other, separated by a small aisle and below the perch of the President of the Council. The others, such as department heads, officials and guests, sat at the tables that were shaped like semicircles on each side of the room. There were also chairs that lined the walls, as well as a room off to the side. The décor of the chamber seemed almost too powerful and formal for the city of over 40 thousand residents. It seemed like it would be better suited in the statehouse or some federal building.

The meeting was about appropriations. The budgets of at least three departments would be short due to the Halloween festivities and needed manpower to perform their duties. All the police officers were ordered to work that night as well as the need to hire additional officers from the surrounding cities and towns. The Salem Fire Department needed extra firemen for medical calls downtown, where an expected crowd of 60,000 visitors would be walking around. The Department of Public Works had to clean up the mess after everyone went home. Since the Council was not allowed to add to the existing budget, additional appropriations were being sought to fund the "festivities" as the mayor called it.

TERROR IN THE WITCH CITY

The president of the city council brought the meeting to order as his gavel crashed down. He read through the agenda that would be covered. Each matter would be discussed then put to a vote. Each matter involving finances had been discussed and endorsed for approval or declined prior to the meeting. The Chief of Police had discussed his concerns over his portion of the budget and the short fall that would ensue. The matter had even been put before the financing committee to see if it met their approval, which it had. This meeting was more of a formality.

Basra, Iraq

Basra was Iraq's former main port for shipping and the southern oil field region. The city was damaged in the Iraq-Iran war, then again in the gulf war. Some of the residents left the city and never returned due to the disrepair and lack of infrastructure. Abdallah had made the trek to Basra in a relatively short period of time. He passed by the marshes and clay houses on the outskirts of the city.

He was only stopped once along the way by British Soldiers manning a checkpoint. Abdallah knew he would have to go through it again on the way back, so he was cautious and did what he was told. He would have loved to kill the soldiers, but that would result in his death as well. Instead he provided the Infidels with the paperwork from the government of Iraq. Their interpreter looked at the papers, he did not appear to be a local, but probably understood some things.

The interpreters used by the Americans and the British were usually driven to use their language skills by money or some form of revenge against their enemies. They used their new positions for their own agenda and not the intended use. This man did not know the local dialect, only a general knowledge of the language. Abdallah gave them enough of an explanation in Arabic, then broken English. He knew this would frustrate them more than anything which was his intention.

He was forced out of his truck, so they could search it. The soldiers threw everything around the cab and the bed of the vehicle as the interpreter looked at him. They looked at his papers and asked him where he was going. After he told them he was going to a mosque, Abdallah was eventually allowed to enter his vehicle and proceed through the checkpoint.

TERROR IN THE WITCH CITY

Abdallah spoke excellent English and was complimented many times on his use of the language. He heard the soldiers insulting and laughing at him. He half smiled, half glared at them as drove away. They would pay for the humiliation of he and his countrymen. The Americans and British thought they were better than the rest of the world with their monarchy and pompous traditions. They had no shame in the way the treated the Muslims living in their capital, Londonistan as their enemies like to say. Abdallah had plenty of contacts in London that he had met at the local Mosques.

There were hundreds of Mosques in London and more being built every day. It was a base of operations on that side of Europe specially to recruit members, raise money and network. He had lived there for a few years not so long ago. The British were always trying to please the liberals and give everyone their so-called rights. In doing so, they created a base of operations for his organization right in their own backyard. It was only a matter of time before the Muslim Community controlled that government and pushed out the non-believers.

Abdallah had studied a map of the area in Basra he was headed to. He did not want to have directions on him for exactly this reason. They would have been found and scrutinized by the Americans or British. He did not want to give them any more information than they he had to. He located the place where he was to meet his contact and parked in the dirt lot on the side of the building. He entered the coffee house and gave a name that he was instructed to ask for. There was no doubt that it was not a real name. An old man nodded in acknowledgement and signaled Abdallah to follow him with the movement of his head. He led him through a curtain into a backroom.

The room was dark and lit with oil lamps that were on every table. The tables were spaced apart for privacy each had a few upholstered chairs. The room was probably used for weddings and other celebrations. Now the room was empty except for him. The elder man waited for him to sit before he left him alone at a table on the far side of the room. Abdallah waited several minutes before a young man, approached with a silver tray that held a steaming teapot, cups, plates, silverware and pastries.

KEVIN GILLAN
TERROR IN THE WITCH CITY

"Your party will be here shortly, sir. Do you need anything?" The dark-skinned man said in his native tongue.

"No, thank you," Abdallah responded looking at him and then around the empty room.

He did not help himself to the food and drink but waited for his host to arrive. It would have been rude not to do so. Five minutes later, a short man wearing a white traditional robe entered along with two large men. The short man walked over to the table as the other men took strategic positions in the room. The man had a graying beard as he approached the table. Abdallah was surprised by the size of the man, small and insignificant. What he expected was a tall, rugged fighter from one of the most feared terrorist cells in the worlds. Instead this man looked like he should be teaching science or history at a university. The man took out a pair of gold rimmed glasses from his robe which highlighted his intelligent eyes.

He studied Abdallah intently before he asked with a slight British accent, "Who sent you?"

"Hamden Khalifa. We need your services," Abdallah responded.

The man looked at him then stated, "Don't be alarmed at the men. I have many enemies that would love to capture me."

Not only was the man wanted by the United States government and British authorities, but he was hated by Hussein and his loyalist; due to his ties with Iran and Al-Qaida.

"I understand," Abdallah replied. He knew that besides the security detail, the locals were on the payroll to watch for the military and local spies.

"What services do you seek?" He asked knowing the answer and taking a seat facing Abdallah.

Abdallah spent the next several minutes explaining what he needed and when. He avoided giving too much information initially but realized that he may need the organization's help later.

"My name is Nazar and I can assist you then," the man said as he poured tea and slid a plate of food toward his new business associate.

Abdallah knew better than to refuse the tea which was their way of sealing the deal. Nazar asked several questions about the operation and gave his advice on how to elude the authorities.

TERROR IN THE WITCH CITY

"All you will need is a picture of him," Nazar said. "Khalifa has taken care of my fees. We will go soon to where your documents are waiting for you. These documents will get you through any customs official including the Americans. However, you must study them well in case you are questioned, do you understand?"

After a few seconds, Abdallah responded, "I do."

He did not like the way this slight man spoke to him but knew the man's connections were to the most ruthless organizations in the world. Abdallah was told earlier that Nazar had the ear of Osama Bin Laden himself. His work was so impressive that customs and government agents from every country had been fooled. In fact, certain governments had put a high price on locating the man and bringing him to justice. He was also told that insulting this man would result in a certain death.

"Please join me with a cup of tea," Nazar said with a slight smile, "then we will retrieve what you have traveled for. We will then ask Allah for his blessing of your work."

Both men then grabbed the cups, lifted them and nodded to each other. Nazar worked out of the local mosques. He knew the military would never enter to search and arrest him.

Chapter 24

No Turning Back

October

Salem, MA

"Salem 40 to 22?" Blake heard through the speaker of the vehicle. "22 on," he replied quickly.

"Report to my office when you have a chance?" his boss said.

"Yes sir," he replied and let go of the mic button.

Blake headed back to the station. "When you have a chance?" really didn't mean just that when the chief of police said it. Four minutes later he pulled into a parking spot. Every vehicle had its own spot and some supervisors got all bent out of shape when a patrol vehicle was not in its intended parking spot. Blake wished he had that much spare time in his working day to be concerned about such trivial matters. He went up the flight of stairs, down the hall and knocked on the door that led to the office.

"Come on in, Kevin," he heard from the other room.

Blake entered the small conference room that led to his office, then said, "Yes, chief?" Blake stood before his desk at attention, which he thought, was proper protocol for the Chief of Police.

"Relax Kevin, take a seat," The Chief said pointing to two leather chairs that faced his desk. "How are you doing?" He asked generally concerned.

"Good, everything is flowing back into place," Blake replied.

"How are Kerry and the kids? They must like having you home?"

"They missed me, and Kerry is probably getting tired of me being home already," Blake said which generated a chuckle from both.

"Seriously, everything is going well. I appreciate you asking boss," he said, feeling the need to reassure him. He really liked his boss who cared about his officers, a rarity in the police world it seemed.

"You're taking off Halloween, so you can take your kids trick-or-treating. It will be an excused absence the least we could do for your family's sacrifice," he said as an order more than anything.

"I appreciate that offer," Blake replied, "but if you need me here, I understand."

"Nonsense. We made it 10 months without you. That's an order anyway," Chief Hampton said smiling, "I will tell you this if the city goes to shit and we need a combat veteran, we will call you back, fair enough?"

"Fair enough," Blake replied standing up to shake his hand. Blake turned around and headed out the door with a smile. It was the first Halloween he would have off since he started there. Some of the officers would be pissed.

Safwan, Iraq

Sawaya was working on a Toyota truck, which was fairly new. Fairly new for Iraq was old for the rest of the world. He had been a mechanic for some time and rented the garage space from the owner of the building. Sawaya repaired small and big engines. He worked on agricultural machinery as well as motor vehicles. He remembered his business almost collapsed after the gulf war in 1991. Thanks to the government, no money was coming in to the people and no spare parts could be obtained. Luckily, once the "oil for food" program began, spare parts and money were available for repairs.

He felt like he was being watched and looked up from his work on the motor. Khalifa was staring at him.

"Are you alone here?" Khalifa asked.

"Yes sir," he replied.

Sawaya was careful around this man and knew that he was a former and possibly, still a member of Hezbollah. He had heard that Khalifa had spent time in the Bekka Valley in Syria. Sawaya had seen a tattoo of the Hezbollah flag on the man's right forearm before.

"Good," he said, moving closer with a smile, "You need to go over to my shop," He pointed across the street. "They will take your picture for a passport. You will need to be ready to go on October 22nd," Khalifa said. Sawaya smiled then said, "excellent".

"Now you can make them pay" he said.

TERROR IN THE WITCH CITY

"And I will," Sawaya replied with a smile.

"On October 22nd come to the mosque after the noon prayer. Bring your bag with you because you'll be leaving from there. Tell no one where you are going. Do you understand?"

"Yes" Sawaya replied looking at him.

Khalifa smiled then turned around and walked down the street. He knew the look on Sawayas' face. He has seen the look of doubt many times. He appeared eager but didn't have the look in his eyes. This man was not ready to carry out the mission of Allah. That was not Khalifa's problem though. He had only made arrangements after the information had been brought to him. Abdallah would certainly never implicate or mention him at all if he was caught. He was sure of that.

*

Sawaya watched him leave the garage and head down the dirt street. While Sawaya and his family held true to the Prophet Mohamad and rejected a life of possession and opulence, like all Shia's were supposed to do, Khalifa did not. The inside of his home was filed with luxuries that he preached against. He was just like the Clerics and others who publicly abhorred modernity but were surrounded by comforts in their lives. The Quran forbids marking of the skin, but Khalifa bore the sign of a terrorist organization.

This man, however, gave Sawaya the chance to seek revenge for the death of his child. He had thought of Umarah every day since then. His poor wife had cried every day after his death. Their whole world had been turned upside down by the infidel monsters who killed the gift from god that he and his wife were given.

He had thought about this for quite some time. He thought about what he would have to tell his wife; telling her the truth was impossible, but he didn't want to lie to her either. *"My dear Ghanda how will she take the news when she finds out what I am doing?"* he thought. She will learn the truth sooner or later.

Sawaya took out the rag from his pocket and wiped his hands clean of the dirt and grime. He had a few days left before he would tell her on that morning, that he was leaving for a week and nothing further. He decided to close the shop and go home during the heat of the day. He was hungry and would have a sandwich and tea while he thought about what he would do.

Iraq/Iran boarder

The dark colored Mercedes sedan cruised along the barren desert road toward the Iranian border. The three occupants hardly said a word to each other. The driver was young, tanned, with short black hair, dark eyes, and a neatly trimmed beard. He had told the two men that he was instructed to take them to the town of Ahvar in Iran. After that, they would be picked up by another contact. He apologized for not knowing any other information. Abdallah who was riding in the front seat looked over at him when he spoke. He periodically checked his phone to see if there was service and went over a mental checklist.

Sawaya sat in the back seat watching the desert go by while the air conditioning kept the car at a cool 65 degrees. He was lost in thought but managed to look up front at the driver. He caught the driver looking at him through the rear-view mirror. The driver met his eyes then resumed watching the road. Sawaya knew that the driver was too scared to look at Abdallah, though. That would probably get him killed. He had made Ghanda cry again right before he left, and he was not sure if she would ever forgive him for leaving her. He had a job to do now and right the wrong that was brought by the American Marine.

"Gentlemen, we will be at the drop-off point in a few hours if you want to rest" he said, glancing at Abdallah then looked in the rearview mirror until his eyes met Sawaya again.

Those dark eyes, Sawaya thought, were full of evil. He exhaled and slumped back in the worn discolored leather seat. He shut his eyes and tried to clear his head.

Main St., Peabody, MA

Khalid Yassin was in his office going over invoices, when a voice caught his attention.

"Boss, UPS guy just delivered this," the woman said and handed him the envelope.

"Thank you," he replied and grabbed it.

TERROR IN THE WITCH CITY

"No problem," she said and went back to the front counter of the rental store. She had been working there for a few weeks now doing "mothers' hours."

Khalid's wife and daughters were pleased to have a woman work there. His wife had adapted well to the Western women's lifestyle since arriving in America in 1995. Now she was a strong proponent of the working woman, once the children were grown.

Khalid got up and shut the door to the office. He sat down and pulled the tab to open the envelope. Inside was a sealed manila envelope with a no return address. He used a letter opener to free the contents, which were 8 x 10 glossy photos and a single sheet of paper. The photos were of a white male in camouflage utilities. A tag on his uniform stated, "U.S. Marine," and the other tag had his name, "Blake."

He looked closely at one picture that caught his interest, "*Salem Police*," he said to himself. The photo was of the decal that he had seen on the doors of the police cars in Salem. It was an unusual decal he thought to himself, a witch on a broomstick. Blake, the US Marine was a police officer in the City of Salem. This was why they had contacted him. He picked up the letter that gave a summary of the incident with the boy and the information about their target. There was nothing about the actions they would be taking. His job was to obtain all the information he could about the subject, including: his work schedule, address, family members, and habits. Family, he did not like that. The paper gave the flight information of his contacts and requests for a hotel. The hotel was not to be too close or too far away, and he was not to make reservation. They would arrive at Logan International Airport in Boston on Oct 26th. Three days was not lot of time.

This was really going to happen, he realized. He knew he would have to do something like this when he first arrived, but always thought it would then. The years had passed, and no one had contacted him. He presumed that his services were not needed. He went to college in Boston and earned an engineering degree. He met, dated, and married a beautiful, intelligent woman, built a nice business renting movies and video games, and had two wonderful, lovely daughters. His wife and he had become active members of the community. He had even helped coach his daughters when they wanted to play his favorite sport, soccer as it was called here. What would this mission entail?

He knew one thing, though, there was no turning back with these people. He knew they were ruthless, and they would kill his wife and kids if he refused to complete his mission. He read the sheet again and looked at the photos. He would put everything to memory before he placed them in the shredder. He would then burn the contents of the shredder somewhere where it would not come back to haunt him. He opened his laptop and powered it up.

Chapter 25

Settling In

Monday October 26ᵗʰ

Logan International Airport, Boston, MA

"On behalf of Lufthansa, I would like to thank you for flying with us today and welcome you to Logan International Airport in Boston, Massachusetts," the voice said and continued with the time, weather conditions, and connecting gate information.

Abdallah looked out the window as the plane taxied down the runway. He looked at his co-conspirator and said in Arabic "They're welcoming you my friend" with a grin.

"Do you know all the answers?" He asked Sawaya quietly not wanting to draw any attention. Even though there were other Arabs on this flight he had to be careful, you never know who was loyal to the infidels.

"Yes, don't worry," Sawaya replied.

The plane stopped, and the passengers were getting up and gathering their belongings from the overhead compartment. When the aisles ahead began to clear out Abdallah bent down and grabbed his briefcase from under his seat. The briefcase was more of a prop than anything else. Sawaya only carried the Quran. Abdallah was impressed with him for taking it along and convincing customs officials. Sawaya didn't bother to tell him that he read the holy book even though it had been a while. Telling him this would have been a waste of time.

During the flight, and while reading the *Suras*, he had time to think and consider what had taken place. He stood up and headed to the front of the cabin, where the smiling stewardess was thanking the passengers. She was of Indian descent, he believed and smiled politely. Sawaya who spoke Arabic had been trying to learn English over the years. He did manage to learn some phrases for him to get by.

TERROR IN THE WITCH CITY

"Have a nice day" she said, displaying a sparkling white set of teeth.

"Thank you," he replied in his best English.

*

Yassin sat in his Mercedes looking at his watch. He was less than a mile away and sat along with a dozen or so other vehicles. Passengers arriving on a flight would call for their ride to pick them up when they were curbside. Yassin was impressed with the idea of the convenience. It meant he didn't have to get into a pissing contest or get a ticket by the Massachusetts State Police that monitored Logan Airport.

He sat listening to the radio but thinking of his wife. He had not told her anything about what was going on nor would he. When they first met, he had told her that he fled Iraq as a soldier during the Gulf War in 1991. He told her that his commander had ordered his men to surrender to the Americans when they crossed the border into Kuwait. The commander did not want his men slaughtered when the tanks pushed over the border, so they surrendered to the first unit that approached.

*

Both men exited the plane and followed the signs for the luggage claim. They walked down the concourse next to each other but did not exchange a word. They looked around at all the vendors selling food, cigarettes, and coffee. Sawaya who had never traveled far in his life, was astonished by everything he could buy. The Americans had everything, especially food. No wonder they were so fat.

They took the escalator down to the ground level where their bags would arrive. After a few minutes, one of the electronic boards blinked their flight number and carrier. Sawaya was startled when he heard the beeping noise and the conveyor belt came to life. The other passengers arrived in groups and started filling in the empty place next to the machine. Abdallah hated these people already and now they crowded around him. These people had no idea what personal space was.

They waited for what seemed like an hour, but after 20 minutes they identified and took possession of their luggage. Then they proceeded to Customs Officials for processing. Abdallah headed to the farthest agent because it had the fewest people in line. He looked back to make sure Sawaya was following him. He was confident about the passport and had studied all the information. He waited patiently, pleased with the fact that the Americans were so hung up on their "civil rights" that they would go out of their way to keep from offending anyone. The Americans were such a joke. He was thankful that they were not dealing with the Israelis. He avoided traveling to Israel at all costs, not because he hated them which he did, but their efficiency. They would've grilled him until they got all the information they wanted.

The Israeli screening process was a combination of travel information, behavioral patterns, and previous intelligence. Passengers were stopped entering the parking lot and were asked certain questions. They were stopped again at the terminal and asked other personal questions. Luggage was scanned then searched by hand. Jewish passengers were processed quickly while the rest were not. At any point in the process a passenger could be taken aside for a thorough luggage and physical check to determine if they are a threat or not. The Israelis knew who the terrorists were and had no problem securing their country against them.

The liberal American media however would never allow that; so, they randomly picked a passenger to search. He knew the agents would be suspicious of him because he was an Arab, but they would not act on it.

"Good afternoon, sir," the tall blonde uniformed agent said, "Passport please?"

"Good afternoon," Abdallah said in English and handed him the forged Iraqi passport. The document was handwritten; therefore, it could not be scanned. The agent walked to a computer terminal and entered some information. Abdallah knew the name he was using was not on a watch list of any kind.

"What is the purpose of your visit?" The agent asked when he moved away from the monitor and studied Abdallah.

"Business with the Islamic Society of Boston Cultural Center," he said to the man.

The man looked at him for a minute, "Would you mind opening your briefcase?" It was not a question, it was an order.

"Not at all," Abdallah said and grabbed the briefcase.

He unlocked and unlatched it, opened it, and turned it around for the agents' inspection. The man flipped through the Arabic books and pamphlets. He looked back up at Abdallah and asked a few more questions. Then he asked him to open his suitcase, which he then checked thoroughly. The agent took the passport and stamped it.

"Have a nice visit," he said with little emotion. He stamped the passport and handed it back to Abdallah.

"Thank you," he replied, knowing what the man was really thinking.

He was pleased he had made it through customs but showed no sign of it. He put his passport in the inside jacket of his suit coat and grabbed his luggage and went through the other side of the checkpoint. Abdallah hoped that Sawaya would stick to the story and not raise any flags. He had been reminded on the plane that if he raised any attention and foiled their plan, someone would visit his wife. He knew Sawaya didn't speak English well and hoped that wouldn't raise any issues. He watched him exchange words with the same agent then passed the document. The agent returned to the computer and typed his information before he searched the suitcase methodically. They conversed again, and he watched Sawaya grab his suitcase and proceed through the checkpoint. Abdallah felt relieved and turned around. He grabbed his bags and headed for the exit door with his associate about 15 feet behind him. Abdallah took out his cell phone and dialed a number. When he heard his contact answer, he told him, "We are here," in Arabic and then hung up.

As the two men walked away, the customs supervisor walked over to the blonde-haired customs agent. He was about to inform the agent that he would be going on break soon.

"What's up?" the supervisor asked the agent, who was watching two passengers leave the terminal.

"Nothing I could put my finger on." The agent replied. "They just arrived on a flight from Frankfort."

"Drugs?" The supervisor asked.

"No, just suspicious that's all."

The supervisor stood there for a minute before he responded,

"Forward their names upstairs. Just maybe they will investigate them. After, you can take your meal break, okay?"

"Sure," he responded and went over to the computer terminal to forward their information.

TERROR IN THE WITCH CITY

*

While the agent typed his notes, Yassin was deep in thought of his limited future when the cell phone rang startling him. He answered it on the third ring, "Hello," he said in English. He listened to the man speak three words in Arabic before the connection was terminated and his heart rate quickened. The last time he was in this lot his daughters were so excited as they waited for their mother to fly in, "I got the call!" they yelled out laughing.

There was no laughter now as he started the car and put the gear selector in drive. He drove out of the lot and took a left onto Harborside Drive heading for the International terminal. Yassin had no idea what these men looked like. They would be waiting curbside at the isle for passenger pick up. He didn't know if they even knew where to stand and wait. Had they ever been to Boston before? America? He only knew their names, and they might have beards like most Arab men. They could be anywhere as he drove to the designated road. He drove slowly and scanned the crowd milling on the sidewalk. Everyone was in a rush he thought. People looking impatiently at their watch, talking on their cell phone, waiting for their rides.

He was nervous because of this something might happen to his family and his life. What kind of danger was he going put them in? He drove about half way down the waiting area when a group of passengers wheeling suitcases flooded across the marked crosswalk. He saw two men standing patiently up ahead both men were dressed nicely and looked Arabic. One was a large man who wore a suit. The other man wore dress pants and a shirt. Neither man had a tie. The larger man had a briefcase in his hand, and both had a suitcase next to them. They glanced at him as the pedestrians had finished crossing.

"That has to be them," Yassin thought. The older of the two had a look of concern on his face, while the younger man appeared confident. Yassin stopped his black Mercedes Benz and put down the passenger's window. He leaned over to speak to the younger man, "Excuse me would you be Abdallah?" he said in Arabic.

The man looked at him, and then said, "Yes, you must be Yassin."

"Yes, I am," he said and moved his vehicle ahead, then pulled closer to the curb to allow vehicles to pass.

He pushed the trunk release button as he got out of the driver's seat. He went around to the back of the vehicle to greet the men.

"I am Khalid Yassin," he said putting out his hand as he approached the older man first. He would have normally embraced them, but he did not want to attract attention. He knew there were video cameras being monitored by the State Police as he spoke.

"I am pleased to meet you, my name is Hadid Sawaya," He smiled.

"I have been looking for forward to this meeting," Yassin said with a smile.

"Me too. I am Mustafa Abdallah," the other man said and shook hands. "We will talk in the car where it is safe to do so".

"Let me get your bags," Yassin said grabbing the suitcases. "Please take a seat in the car."

Abdallah took the front seat while Sawaya went in the back. After Yassin was finished putting the suitcases in the trunk, he took his place behind the wheel.

"Welcome to America. Are you hungry?" he asked, "Let me know if you want to stop and get some food or anything else."

"No, we are all set for now, right Hadid?" Abdallah said looking over his shoulder.

"Yes, I am fine for now," he responded from the back.

Yassin followed the exit signs and drove onto Route 1A. They talked a bit about the flight and weather.

"I received your package and gathered some of the information you requested a few days ago," Yassin said, looking at Abdallah like a student trying to please his teacher.

"Excellent, but we will go over all of that later. It has been a long journey." Abdallah said. "What about a hotel?"

"I found a hotel about 10-15 minutes away from Salem, with quick access to a highway. I will take you there now," Yassin said. "I made some inquires, and there are rooms available, enough for both of you," he said as he drove past a large cross on a hill by Suffolk Down, a horse racing track.

Abdallah was looking up at the large cross on the hill and replied, "We will only need one room for me and my business associate. It is less complicated that way. If Hadid needs my help during these difficult times,

I will be available 24/7 as you Americans say. Isn't that right my brother?" he said turning to the man in the back seat.

"Yes," Sawaya answered.

Yassin looked in the rearview mirror to see Sawaya staring out the window.

"My deepest sympathy to you and your family" Yassin said looking at him through the mirror.

"Thank you" Sawaya said, looking at him through the mirror and nodded his head.

It took approximately 45 minutes to get to the hotel in Danvers. Besides the easy highway access there was a mall and several restaurants within walking distance. They circled around a 24-hour restaurant in front of the hotel and stopped at the main office that was lodged between 2 buildings.

"Drive around the buildings before I check in, please," Abdallah said to Yassin.

He drove the vehicle slowly around the driveway of the property as Abdallah scanned the area.

"I'll take care of this" Abdallah said as he hopped out of the vehicle and went into the office.

Sawaya was staring out the window into the parking lot. It was quiet in the vehicle.

"What village are you from?" Yassin asked.

"Safwan," Sawaya replied then asked, "You?"

Yassin told him where he was from then they spoke about Iraq and all that had happened. Abdallah returned to the car.

He waited until the two stopped talking before he spoke, "Room number 112 in the back. Just drop us off for tonight and come back in the morning, please. It has been a long trip and we are tired," Abdallah said.

"What about dinner tonight?" Yassin asked.

"We will go out to eat after we rest," he said. "Come back in the morning and we will go over everything. Bring all the information." As Abdallah got ready to exit the car, he added, "Oh, and we will need a car to get around. We can use your car and I will pay for your rental."

"I was going to bring you to a car rental business in the morning?" Yassin said.

TERROR IN THE WITCH CITY

"The less evidence of our existence, the better. We are not going to use your vehicle for anything illegal, I can promise that," he told him.

Yassin did not like this already, but he had to deal with him. "As you wish," he replied after a minute. "I will be back tomorrow morning around 10 a.m. If you need anything you have my number and feel free to call anytime."

"Thank you, my brother," Abdallah said and nodded to him before getting out of the vehicle.

Sawaya opened his door and looked at Yassin, "Thank you and nice to meet you."

Yassin nodded back as the back door shut. Both men retrieved their luggage from the trunk and shut the lid.

Abdallah removed the key from his pocket and unlocked the room door. He requested the room for specific reasons. It was in the back and out of sight from the main road. There were woods and brush across the parking lot just outside of the door, a good place for them to hide. If they had unexpected company, they would not be trapped like on the second floor. While he was pretty sure that Yassin would not turn him in before the mission was complete, he might try to sabotage it somehow. Yassin had to know that his family in Iraq and those here would be killed if he jeopardized the mission in any way.

Salem, MA

The contractor parked his truck and grabbed a few tools he would need for the job. He parked at the end of the road and followed the dirt path that led to the water tank. It was sunny, cool, and the smell of winter was barely noticeable. He veered off to the trail on the left at the fork and trudged up the small hill. He looked through his jumbled key ring to find the one that would unlock the gate. Once he found it, he looked up past the gate and saw the graffiti on the tank, then saw that someone had dug a trench under the fence. It had been two weeks since he was there last and knew the paint was relatively fresh. He put his keys away and took out his work phone. He pressed the contact for Salem Water.

"Bill this is Josh. I'm here at the tank and can't help but notice someone dug a trench under the fence and tagged the tank. Do you guys know about this?" Josh waited for Bill's response. "Okay I'll wait until you get here before I unlock the gate" he replied and then hung up.

The supervisor from the water department arrived 20 minutes later with his field technician. A short time later, the police arrived. They took photos of the graffiti that might match other cases.

The supervisor from the Water Department was not so much concerned about access to the water. To access the water, you would need the proper equipment to include acetylene torches. If anyone did manage to gain access to the water from the ground valve the only thing that would happen would be a few million gallons of water knocking them out due to the force of it leaving the tank.

The supervisor knew that no one could poison the water supply at least through the base tower. That would have taken barrels of regulated chemicals that were difficult to purchase. They would need access to certain equipment that was heavy and cumbersome. They would also have to have extensive knowledge of the water supply system. He was pissed that someone had circumvented the alarmed fence. He would have to give his boss a report, which would be forwarded to the Mayor. He would request that the police make extra checks of the tank.

"Kids being kids," Bill said to the contractor as he locked the gate.

"Is it possible to come back later this week?"

"This is not a good time," Josh said "but, I'll call if something breaks free."

"Thanks," he said as they shook hands.

Chapter 26

Reconnaissance

Tuesday October 27th

Endicott St., Danvers, MA

At 9:45 am, Yassin left his home in West Peabody for the hotel. He would have to tell his wife something later since he would be driving a rental. She would be suspicious, of course, and press the issue like she did about everything else. He wouldn't tell her more than he had to. Yassin knew that the two men were targeting a Salem cop who was in Iraq. The attack would happen on Halloween night, so he would have to keep his daughters from going to Salem that night as they had previously planned. He could not go to the police with this information and feared talking to anyone else.

He pulled into the lot and drove to the building in the rear. He pulled in the space in front of room number 112. He grabbed the manila envelope off the passenger's seat. He knocked on the door and was greeted with a warm smile and an embrace.

"I am sorry for my rudeness yesterday," Abdallah told him. "I was tired due to the long travel, which is no excuse."

"No apology needed. I understand you have a lot going on," Yassin said as he entered the room.

"Thank you," he responded humbly.

"Good morning," Sawaya said as he got out of his chair and shook hands. He had a genuine smile on his face.

"Did you eat breakfast this morning?" Yassin asked.

"Yes," Sawaya replied, "the food was plentiful, but the coffee was the worst I've ever had."

Abdallah nodded in agreement.

"Get used to that around here." Yassin laughed. "The Americans do not know what good coffee tastes like. There are a few places, but you have to know where to find them."

TERROR IN THE WITCH CITY

"I do like theses Cigarettes though?" Sawaya held up the pack and said, "Want one?"

"No thanks," he replied, "I had to quit for the kids' sake."

It was a lie. His wife had made him quit, but he had to save face in front of these men. They would consider him weak for obeying a woman in their culture. He took a seat at the small round table in the corner of the room and placed the envelope on the table.

"How old are your children?" Abdallah asked.

"Two teenage girls," Yassin replied.

Hopping to drop his family from the conversation.

Abdallah walked over to the table and picked up the envelope as he looked at Yassin. "Tell me about yourself and your training?" He took a seat across from the man. He picked up the pack on the table and removed a cigarette from the pack.

Yassin told him about the village he had grown up in, the elders, his schooling and the mosque. The recruiter at the mosque had inspired him and arranged everything. Yassin told him that they traveled into Syria via a smuggling route and eventually into the Bekaa Valley in Lebanon. He told him that he was trained by the Iranian Republican Guards at a training camp in Baalbeck after which he returned to Iraq.

When the first Gulf war broke out, he and several others were given uniforms and thrown in a unit that was stationed by the border. The unit was ordered to surrender to the first American unit the encountered. He was brought to Saudi Arabia and was later allowed to seek political asylum in the United States.

"Smart." Abdallah interjected.

Yassin told him that he had been provided money from a bank account until he was established. He explained that he still had the account, but it had not been used since he arrived

"What a waste." Abdallah said. "Your training sounds impressive."

"Yes, it was." Yassin replied. "How about you?"

Abdallah was waiting for this question. He didn't want to tell him how he started out in this line of work. Abdallah knew Yassin and Sawaya were Shia's whose families were originally from Iran. Abdallah, however, was a former member of the Ba'ath party and a Sunni Muslim from Iraq.

TERROR IN THE WITCH CITY

He was not sure if they knew he was a Ba'ath party member but didn't want to turn these men against him by mentioning it.

"I was trained by the Mujahedeen. I received training in the Bekaa Valley as well as you. You could say I do some freelance work for those who seek my assistance," Abdallah said, which was the truth. He had supported Al-Queda, The Muslim Brotherhood, and now Hezbollah. What he didn't tell these men that he was initially a member of the Faydeen Sadam.

The Faydeen Sadam had started out as a group of thugs and bullies and turned into a force of over 40 thousand men. The unit, which was initially ran by Sadam Hussein's son, was supposed to protect his father against domestic opponents and threats but turned into a gang that tortured enemies of the regime. Within the organization there was a special unit known as Fiday Sadam which specialized in executions. The masked men, in the unit accompanied by members of the Ba'ath party, targeted the women of families suspected of being opponents or those hostile to the regime.

While Abdallah was not a member of that specific unit, he knew people who were in it. It was rumored that the women were either raped or beheaded in front of their families in their homes or sometimes the entire village. The reason it was done in front of the village was to get the point across to those who contemplated doing the same thing. The attacks were usually done at night to avoid satellite imagery of the incident.

Tensions between Iran and Iraq began after the Shah of Iran was overthrown in 1979. Iraq accepted the Shiite religion, but Iranian leaders would have nothing to do with the Ba'ath regime which they called secular. Iranian leaders wanted to overthrow the Iraq government and replace it with a replica of the Islamic regime in Iran. In addition, three pieces of territory along the border were to be returned to Iraq due to a prior treaty that was never followed. Border clashes in 1979 and 1980 led to an invasion of Iran by Iraq.

Even though Shiites had ties to Iran most remained loyal to Iraq during the Iran-Iraq war and they suffered the most casualties. After the war the regime began a crackdown on the Shiite schools and certain religious practices in Southern Iraq.

TERROR IN THE WITCH CITY

In 1991 at the end of the first gulf war, President Bush urged the Iraqis to topple the Ba'ath party. When the US learned that Shiite rebels from Iran were pouring over the border to fight the regime, The US declined to back them due to their Iranian ties. The Shiite fighters in Southern Iraq were slaughtered by Hussein and eventually led to the creation of the no-fly zones. The Shiites also suffered the highest casualties in the first gulf war.

Abdallah knew the Shiites hated Sadam and anyone associated with the regime. He had different ties though. He was associated with some of the most feared men in the Arab world.

"Tell me about your family?' Abdallah said wanting to change topics.

Yassin didn't want to get too much into his current life. He told Abdallah that he had a wife who knew little of his past, and two children that knew nothing of his previous life, and he wanted to keep it that way. His wife would never understand that her husband was part of a sleeper cell. He explained that he was reluctant to have them over his house and that using his car would raise many questions. Abdallah nodded in agreement.

"So, what is going on that brought you here and what are you planning to do?" Yassin finally asked.

"We are here to exact revenge on the man that was responsible for the tragedy of Hadid's son and to teach the Americans a lesson about invading our country. The police officer, who you have been instructed to watch, oversaw the driver" Abdallah said.

"We will show the world on the night they celebrate Satan what Allah has in store for them," Abdallah said with a smile. "Now, tell me what you have learned about our target." He extracted the photos and documents from the envelope. He looked at several maps printed off the internet and the typed notes about the target, The Salem Police Department, and a possible vendor. "Where did you have these developed?" Abdallah asked while he looked them over.

"My home computer. Cannon makes a good product," he replied.

"This?" Abdallah asked as he held up the picture.

"The policeman lives there from what I can tell. He has a wife and two small children," Yassin said, emphasizing small children.

"Dog?"

"Not that I can tell so far," Yassin replied.

Now he knew what was going to happen, and he didn't want to take any part in attacking a family, let alone a police officer.

"Who is this?" Abdallah pointed to a name and address on the sheet of paper.

"When I went to see if I could get a vendors' license for Halloween night this man picked up his license. I found the name and address and followed him to this run-down apartment where he lives. I found out that he has a drug problem. I thought maybe we could trade some drugs for his license?" Yassin said with a smirk.

"You are devious," Abdallah said. Then he turned to Sawaya and said, "Did you hear that?"

"Yes, good idea, but how will you accomplish that?" Sawaya asked while puffing on a cigarette.

"We can continue this conversation along the way. I am hungry again, let's eat" Abdallah said.

"There is an Indian restaurant I would like to take you to. Delicious food, excellent coffee, and there is privacy as well. Please let me pay for your meals since you are my guests and going to my home would raise questions," Yassin said.

"Very well then, let's go," Abdallah said getting to his feet. "After we can hire a rental car for you, so we can be mobile, okay?" He said to Yassin.

It was not really a question, so much as a statement. He was trying to be polite.

"Of course," Yassin replied unhappily.

*

"Where do we get the explosives?" Sawaya asked from the passenger's seat car as they drove to the restaurant.

"I have that covered," Abdallah said from the back seat.

That surprised Yassin who looked at him from the rear-view mirror, "How?"

"You're not the only one supporting the cause in the area," Abdallah said with a smirk, "I made arrangements with another contact as well. Does that bother you?"

"No, of course not," Yassin responded.

The trio arrived and ate lunch at an Indian restaurant. The food was exactly as Yassin had promised and quite satisfying to the Arab men. He picked up the tab as promised, then they drove to pick up a rental. They drove to the hotel to drop off the Mercedes. Yassin insisted that Abdallah be careful with his vehicle as it was a reward for his hard work. Then they went to an electronics store, so the men could buy a GPS unit for directions.

Salem, Ma

Yassin took them on a tour of the area, so they could get accustomed to their surroundings and see where they would be operating. "First stop is the Salem Police Department which is straight ahead," he said as they drove past Steve's Market. "When anyone calls 911, it goes to that building. Then it is passed to the patrol officers, fire department, or the ambulance. I have been in there to see how easy it would be to access the 911 system."

"Impressive. The building looks a little intimidating," Abdallah said as he studied it.

"I believe it was supposed to look like a castle." Yassin said. "It would take an armed assault on the building or a car bomb to take the 911 system off line. If something happens to the system or no one responds after a certain number of rings, the calls go to another city. There are also cameras on the outside of the building that cover all avenues of approach," he finished.

"Senseless to bother then," Abdallah reasoned.

"My thoughts exactly, it would only warn them," he said.

He tuned into a parking lot to turn around. The lot was once a phone company repair facility but was now the employee parking lot for the hospital. They drove past the police station again and Abdallah looked for the cameras. Yassin followed the road to the intersection at Washington Street. He took a left and then a right onto New Derby.

"This area will be blocked off from that intersection," Yassin said, pointing back "to up the street" then pointing up Lafayette Street. "There will be a lot of police on the streets, not just Salem either. Police are brought in from all over because there are so many people," he said.

TERROR IN THE WITCH CITY

They made another left and drove past the Hawthorne Hotel around the Common and drove down Essex Street to the walking mall. Yassin pulled over to the side of the road. "Ahead is the walking mall. Most of the vendors will be set up there. Everyone passes through there. It's tight between the buildings and could be an excellent spot to yield a lot of casualties. We will walk through there later." He turned around to look at Abdallah "Okay?"

"Yes," Abdallah agreed.

Yassin pulled back onto the road and navigated the one ways and tight streets. "This is a large area to cover," he told them.

"I agree," Abdallah said.

They continued driving to Congress Street and crossed the small bridge to the point area. The vehicle took a right onto Harbor Street. Yassin had been in this area before and he knew it was a low-income working-class area. He was still amazed at how run down the area looked. Trash was strewn about, graffiti, and a general look of disorder showed who lived here.

"This is a lot different than the rest of the city, no?" Sawaya asked looking around.

"A bad neighborhood with a lot of crime. The man with the license lives there," Yassin said as he took a right onto Lafayette Street, pointing to the building.

"What is that place?" Abdallah asked.

"A tenement, rooming house, you pay weekly or monthly for a large room with a bathroom," he said as they pulled to the curb.

"How do you know this?" Abdallah asked.

"I called the number and made some inquiries," Yassin said. "I found an article about the man we want. He was arrested after stealing a ring from a jewelry store. Probably to buy drugs."

"Do you think we could pay someone to take care of his drug habit?" Abdallah asked unfamiliar with the culture.

"We do not know who his dealer is?" Yassin said as he took a right onto Peabody Street.

They continued their tour of the city by going to the residence of their target.

TERROR IN THE WITCH CITY

Yassin continued, "We will be taking a right up ahead. The street has a circle at the end by his house, it's called a cul-de-sac. His house is straight ahead, and we will act as though we are lost. Remember, once you're on the street you are trapped," He looked to Abdallah to confirm that he understood.

"I also have to tell you the other police will come after anyone who attacks one of their own. They are very protective of each other and they will not hesitate to kill whoever is responsible. All the rules get thrown out after that. They have resources that we don't," he said very seriously as he turned around in the circle.

"The Americans also hate people who hurt or kill children. I know what they can do. I have watched the news enough times," Yassin said letting it sink in for a few minutes. "Tomorrow there is a Halloween parade in Salem. It's for the children. It starts at 6:30 P.M. so we should be there," he continued.

"You mean stand in the open?" Abdallah asked.

"It's a parade. That's what people do, watch them. If we're on top of a building or hiding, we would draw attention. There is a hotel at the end of the route, but that would draw suspicion as well. After 9/11, an Arab male is suspicious," Yassin said matter-of-factly.

"You're right," Abdallah agreed.

Yassin was surprised that Sawaya had not said anything throughout the whole time they drove around. The operation was for the revenge of his child, but you would never have known it. He would have to talk with him when they were alone that was if Abdallah would ever leave them alone. He drove around for a while longer to make sure they were familiar with the streets. They drove back to Essex Street. They parked the vehicle in the parking garage across from the visitor center. As they walked down the ramp Yassin turned to them and said, "I almost forgot about this place," and pointed to the visitor center.

They crossed the street and strolled inside. They walked around feigning interest and grabbed a few fliers. Abdallah stopped at a counter and grabbed a map that was in a "free" box. He opened it up and looked through the pamphlet studying one. The other two men walked up next to him. He grabbed two more maps and handed one to each of them.

Yassin asked, "Are you ready?"

"Yes, let's go," Abdallah responded and the three proceeded to the door.

Yassin stopped by the exit door when he saw a pile of booklets that caught his attention. He bent over the thin book, "look at this," he said and handed one to Sawaya.

"Schedule of Haunted Happenings," Yassin read. "How convenient."

Abdallah moved over and grabbed his own copy. The three leafed through them as they exited the center.

"Let's walk down there. That's the walking mall that I told you about," Yassin looked around to see who was listening.

They walked about halfway down the cobble stoned street when they came upon a tourist trap that sold t-shirts, souvenirs, and ran trolley tours. They looked around but decided not to take the tour of the city and turned back.

When they were walking back to the vehicle Yassin said, "This is where the parade will go through tomorrow night."

"Where, down the street?" Abdallah asked.

"Yes" he replied.

They walked back to the vehicle and left the garage. They left downtown, and Yassin drove to a Starbucks for coffee. While it was not the best it was far better and stronger than what they had drank so far.

"Okay, if we're all set, let me drop you off at the hotel. I will be back tomorrow at 6 p.m., unless you want to eat in Salem somewhere close to the parade route. Then we can watch the parade and not look suspicious," Yassin said.

"That's a good idea," Abdallah replied.

"I will come by at 4 p.m. and then we can go over the plan," he said.

"No, we will go over it after I work out a few details. Chose a time that will have us finishing the meal as the parade starts." Abdallah said.

"I'll call you tomorrow in the afternoon, when I figure it out".

"Tell me about your business?" Abdallah asked as they drove down Route 114.

"I rent and sell movies and video games in Peabody" Yassin said not looking away from the roadway.

"Can I ask if you do well financially?" he asked.

"Yes, it provides a decent living by American standards," Yassin replied.

He then looked in the rear-view mirror to see if Sawaya was looking at him, but he was staring out the window again. He might have heard the men talking but chose to ignore it or he was just so distracted that he never heard them.

"What village are you from in Iraq?" Yassin asked.

"The one your family lives in" Abdallah lied.

Yassin turned to him and nodded in acknowledgement.

Abdallah wanted him to know who was running the operation even though he was supplying then with whatever they needed and had been an asset. Yassin had lived here long enough to know what was going on.

Abdallah was not naive to think that Yassin would not turn him over to the American FBI and cut a deal for his cooperation. Sawaya on the other hand, was useless and would only slow him down. He would have only one task and would complete it on Halloween night. Yassin would help him flee the country, so his life would be spared.

Chapter 27

Targets

Wednesday October 28th

Endicott St., Danvers, MA

Both men woke up in the hotel room early for the Fajr, the first of five prayer times or Salat's, which was practiced by Muslims before sunrise. Even though they were out of their element they still tried to fulfill their faith. They did not dare to go outside to pray toward the holiest of cities instead they prayed to Allah for his blessing and luck in carrying out their mission. Afterward they went to breakfast at the 24-hour eatery. They had gone there twice a day and had become regulars to the staff. They dropped hints to the wait staff that they were on business and staying at the hotel which would not raise suspicion. The place was convenient and less than a three-minute walk from their room.

When the men returned to their hotel, Abdallah made a call on his cell phone from the parking lot. He walked away from Sawaya, so the conversation would not be overheard. In the meantime, Sawaya unlocked the door and entered the room. He turned on the television and sat on the bed.

Abdallah came in a few minutes later and said, "grab what you need my friend. We are going to visit a mosque in Boston." He had a smile on his face. "It is actually an Islamic Cultural Center. The one I told customs I was carrying the materials for," he said.

"Do you know someone there?" Sawaya asked.

"Yes, a friend who will assist us," Abdallah said and went to his bed.

He lifted the corner of the mattress and removed a manila envelope that Yassin had brought. He opened the briefcase that contained the pamphlets and slipped the envelope inside.

"You might want to bring your Quran. We can pray amongst our people and not in hiding," Abdallah said, "We also might have a real meal there."

Sawaya grabbed his cigarettes, lighter, and holy book as he headed to the door. He went to the passenger's door of the Mercedes.

Abdallah stopped at the drivers' side door with the key in his hand and said, "This is what you wanted, right? When you approached Khalifa about revenge?"

"Yes, it is." Sawaya said.

"You have been quiet lately and it seems you are losing your desire for revenge," Abdallah said.

"I have a lot on my mind and miss my wife," Sawaya said unconvincingly.

Somerville, MA

They drove about 35 minutes to a McDonald's restaurant that was on the McGrath Highway. Abdallah pulled the Mercedes over to where a man stood not too far away from the golden arches. Abdallah rolled down the window and spoke to him briefly before he got in.

He was nicely dressed and wore a stylish watch and bracelet. He introduced himself as Ramzi Tariq to Sawaya from the backseat. They drove another 20 minutes until they reached The Islamic Society of Boston, which was both a mosque and a cultural center for Muslims. Abdallah and Sawaya both stared up at the impressive building as they passed. The Islamic center was in the Roxbury section of Boston where Tariq was a regular visitor. There was a mosque closer to where Tariq lived, but the center had everything.

They were given an extensive tour by Tariq and he introduced them to some of the staff. They stopped to have tea and talked about home and the current political situation. They went to the early afternoon prayer and met the leaders of the mosque who were present, then they enjoyed a traditional Arab meal.

After a few hours, the three left the center and maneuvered the congested roads and heavy traffic back to Somerville. Tariq guided them through the streets to an area that had several dilapidated buildings. They stopped at a building with only a number on it, #20-5. The outside had a steel door and a large garage door. There was a single window that was on the second floor. The garage door could easily accommodate a large truck.

"I will be right back," Abdallah said to Sawaya as he placed the vehicle in park and turned it off.

"It was a pleasure meeting you, my brother," Tariq said to Sawaya from the back seat as he put his hand forward to shake.

Sawaya twisted around and took the man's hand, "Nice to meet you too," he replied.

Tariq got out of the back seat and removed a set of keys from his pocket. He opened the door and held it open for Abdallah.

Tariq said, 'This way," and led him into the garage.

In the bay was an older model limousine with dark tinted windows. "I found this for sale in New Hampshire several weeks ago. I bought this for a few thousand dollars. I thought it might come in handy," he said as Abdallah walked around it.

Tariq was waiting for him to respond, hoping Abdallah would appreciate his forethought. "I thought about Salem on Halloween night and the crowds. This might be more efficient?" he asked.

Abdallah paused and massaged his bearded chin, "Yes, this might work."

"I removed the rear seats and there is plenty of space for whatever needs to be delivered" he said and pointed to a stack of cushions that were in the corner of the dark dingy garage.

Abdallah walked around and opened the rear door to look inside. "Will this be ready for Saturday?" he asked.

"I am waiting for a shipment of explosives that should be here in a few days," Tariq said while looking at him very seriously. "I don't know what your plans are, but I will have the vehicle ready for you on Saturday afternoon if you wish. I have a small crew that has worked for me for a few years now. I trust them with my life."

"Yes, call me when your shipment arrives and if there are any problems," Abdallah said.

"Do you need any hardware?" Tariq asked, "I was told that you may need one by my contact."

"I do," Abdallah said.

"Then let me get you one," he said and walked over to a duct that was against the wall. He spent a few minutes and removed a case. He placed the case on one of the work benches along the garage wall as

Abdallah walked over to him. He opened the case to reveal a 9mm Beretta with two full magazines.

"Here you go," Tariq said, "No serial numbers either, not that it would matter at this point."

"No, it wouldn't," Abdallah said and pulled the slide back to inspect it. He inserted a magazine and charged the weapon. He then placed it in one of his coat pockets. "Thank you and keep me informed of the situation."

"Of course. Does your friend need one?" Tariq asked.

"No. He wouldn't know what to do with it anyway," then Abdallah thought about it. "Yes, he would. He might kill me as I sleep." He then turned around and headed for the exit door.

West Peabody, MA

"Khalid what happened to the car?" Sarah said to her husband who was in the kitchen helping himself to coffee and looking down in his cup. "Ignition problems, it wouldn't start. I had to get it to the dealer," Yassin said without hesitation.

"Why didn't you tell me?" She asked while moving toward him.

"Were you going to fix it?" Yassin said to her with a smile. "They said it might take a few days for the parts," He kissed her on the lips as she came closer into his arms.

"Is everything all right?" She sensed some worry in him. She knew the look of concern on his face, especially after all the years they spent together.

"Business is slow and stressing me out," He lied, but it was a reasonable excuse.

"We'll manage, we always do" Sarah kissed him on the forehead.

100 Gallows Hill Rd., Salem, MA

At that very moment Blake's Saturn pulled into the driveway. He stopped the vehicle, and then placed the transmission in park. He thought it had been a good day so far. He had worked a detail this morning, which was over by 1pm. He picked up the kids, went to the playground, and visited his mother.

TERROR IN THE WITCH CITY

He opened the back door and unsnapped the seatbelt that held his daughter in the child safety seat. He helped her out and went around to the other side and took his son out of his car seat. Considering Breyden was brought into this world at over 10 lbs., it was no surprise that a year later he exceeded the weight limits of the safety seat carrier that most 18-month-old toddlers rode in. He lugged the boy and headed to the door.

"We're home," he said loudly as they entered the house.

Erin found her mother.

"What time do you have to be at work?" Kerry asked as she came around and grabbed the baby from Blake and gave him a kiss.

"Parade starts at 6:30, I have to be at the station by 5:30," Blake replied.

"Dinner will be ready before five then," she said.

"Honey you can watch a little TV after you wash up," Kerry said to Erin. "Then we will see daddy in the parade tonight".

"Yeah!" Erin ran to the bathroom.

Breyden was trying to stand on his own, leaning against the couch steadying himself.

"You can go get your stuff ready, I'll watch the baby," Kerry told Blake.

"Thanks," he said as he went upstairs.

He entered the walk-in closet in their bedroom. He pulled out his police uniform and made sure it was presentable. Blake had been wearing uniforms as part of his job for as long as he could remember. He would love to have a job where he could wear regular clothes like normal people did. Someone at work once told him that normal people wouldn't do this job after they had responded to a series of bizarre calls in one night.

One of his jobs at the Police Department was that he oversaw the honor guard. It was bestowed upon him after the retirement of a seasoned detective who had completed three combat tours in Vietnam as a Marine, whom Blake had tremendous respect for. There were two other guys in the honor guard that were also military veterans. The chief had allowed and insisted that the veterans wear the ribbons they were awarded in the military on their honor guard uniform.

TERROR IN THE WITCH CITY

There were 10 members in all who had volunteered to join the honor guard. Sometimes it was hard to get four or five members to fill in for an event. The problem was rotating schedules, vacations, illnesses, and family commitments. The officers didn't do it for the money either, the stipend they were paid came to about an extra $10 a week. It was certainly not worth the hassle considering the time they had to give, which Blake thought proved their dedication and loyalty to the department.

Blake demanded professionalism when they performed, whether it was standing still at a ceremony, or marching in a parade or a funeral. His reasoning for this was that all eyes and cameras were on them. Most people in the crowd would never pick up on an error made, but they would know. Blake went through his uniform, even making sure his shoes were spit shinned

Endicott St., Danvers, MA

While Blake contemplated what cleaned his shoes better, Abdallah had driven from Somerville back to the hotel. When he was inside the room, he scribbled some notes on a piece of paper.

"Who was that?" Sawaya asked as he sat on the bed and smoked a Cigarette.

"That man is going to help us," he motioned with his fingers to them both, "to avenge the death of your son. He is also going to provide us the means for a backup plan." He looked at Sawaya. "You were so angry when your son was killed. You sought our assistance and now we are here. It is going to happen, and nothing is going to stop it. It's too late, it really is" Abdallah waited for a response. When Sawaya didn't say anything, he continued, "Help me avenge your boy's death then we can head home, and you can be with your wife," Abdallah added sympathetically, "I am truly sorry about the loss of your son."

"Thank you," Sawaya said.

"Shall we pray to Allah that he watches over him?"

"Please" Sawaya said and knelt on the carpet.

TERROR IN THE WITCH CITY

Salem, MA

Yassin arrived in the rental and picked the two men up at about 5 p.m. He brought them to what he thought was the perfect location. It was situated along the parade route on New Derby Street. The restaurant had large windows that overlooked the street, so they would not miss anything that passed. It also had a nice selection of food and was reasonably priced. There were also generous with the portions.

Yassin knew of the Greek family who owned and operated it, because their children attended the same school functions. Yassin did not park in the lot by the restaurant, but down the street so they could leave easily. As they exited the rental, he put the digital camera in his jacket pocket in case it was needed. They were not sure what they would be looking for in the parade but came prepared.

The restaurant was run like a cafeteria. Where the customers entered there were racks that held trays and containers of silverware. Two to three cooks were behind the glass partition taking orders and then preparing the food. The menu boards hung above the cooks and daily specials were listed on a chalkboard at the front of the line. Each man had their tray on the silver rails and looked up at the board.

"The chicken kebab is excellent," Yassin said to the men who were on either side of him.

"Can I help you sir?" The olive-skinned man said from behind the counter.

All three men made their selections and proceeded down the line with plates on their tray except for one order. Abdallah ordered a Mediterranean salad that would have to be brought out to him. They passed on a cooler filled with desserts and moved closer to the cash register.

"Would you like anything to drink?" The plump woman asked from behind an industrial toaster.

They ordered their drinks then approached the register. Yassin told the woman that he would pay for all three and handed her two $20 bills.

He then led the men to the booth that had a view of New Derby Street.

"Perfect," Abdallah said as he slid across the seat that was against the wall.

Yassin and Sawaya took their plates, drinks, and silverware off the tray and placed them on the table. They set their trays on another table, so they had more room.

"This was a good idea," Abdallah said to Yassin who had suggested the parade because the police would be all over the area.

They might get a visual on Blake. They waited until Abdallah's meal arrived before they ate. Abdallah told Yassin about their visit to the Cultural Center, he didn't mention the contact they picked up nor the backup plan he had in mind. Abdallah explained to him that he needed to visit the mosque since that was the purpose of his trip to America. Sawaya just nodded in agreement.

*

"We need to get there before the lieutenant freaks out," Blake said from the back seat of the police Ford Explorer that should have been junked long ago.

The vehicle could not pass a state vehicle inspection anymore, but the police department didn't seem to be worried about it.

"Don't worry about it, we have plenty of time," Jones said as he went barreling down Peabody St.

The vehicle held five members of the honor guard, three flags and the two rifles that they would be carrying. The vehicle zoomed around the corner, and then Jones slammed on the brakes. A wooden horse was blocking Congress Street.

"What the fuck!" Blake said when he realized no one was around it.

"Relax," Jones said and hit the air horn button in the vehicle.

A moment later, the horse moved out of the way. They couldn't see who was pulling it, but they didn't care. Three minutes later, the vehicle was parked in a lot at Shetland properties, which was the beginning of the parade route.

"Cutting it close boys," the lieutenant said with just enough of a smile that they knew he wasn't pissed.

They were piling out the vehicle with all the stuff.

"Sorry, LT," Jones said, "We were practicing so hard we lost track of time."

"Yeah, I bet," he replied.

TERROR IN THE WITCH CITY

The other four started laughing.

"10 minutes," The lieutenant told Blake as he walked away.

Five minutes later, they were lined up behind the freshly washed Crown Victoria police car that would lead the way. The five members of the honor guard wore highly polished leather gun belts complete with straps that were more for decoration than necessity. They wore a special honor guard badge above the left pocket of their jacket and had a matching hat badge. The three men in the center each bore flags that had a specific order. Facing the honor guard, from left to right were the stars and stripes, flag of the Commonwealth of Massachusetts, and flag for the City of Salem. No flag was to go on the right side of the American flag. The flag for the City of Salem did not have the official seal of the city, instead it bore the famous logo of a witch on a broomstick.

The flag bearers wore a special leather carrier to support the flag. The officers on each end of the formation carried an M-14 rifle. The lead vehicle activated its lights and began proceeding down the middle of Congress Street to kick off the Haunted Happenings Grand Parade also known as the Children's Parade.

Blake watched until the vehicle was 30 to 40 feet ahead before he said loudly in a military manner, "Detail Atten-hut," He paused for a second or two, "forward march," and then they all stepped off at the same time on their left foot.

*

"That was a good meal," Abdallah said as they waited on the sidewalk in front a restaurant with hundreds of others.

"Yes, I agree," Sawaya said and took a cigarette out of the pack that was in his pocket and lit it.

A few people standing around him shot him a look of disgust as he started puffing on it right where he stood. Yassin wasn't going to give the man a lecture of the politically correct America and the witch hunt for smokers. They heard the blast of the siren before they saw the vehicle slowly take the turn. Yassin was looking at two teenage girls across the street, which reminded him of his daughters, Jannah and Sahara. He was nudged by Abdallah, who nodded his head down the street to the source of the excitement in the crowd. They saw the officers come around the corner. It took a few minutes before they would pass them. Yassin took out his camera and started taking photos of the five men as they approached.

Yassin leaned over and spoke quietly to Abdallah in Arabic. "I think the one in the middle is the one?"

Abdallah looked in the direction of the police officers," I don't know. I need to see him without the hat".

"Is that the man in the middle?" Abdallah asked Sawaya in Arabic.

"It might be, but I have to see his face," he replied.

As they got closer, Yassin snapped a few photos of the officer in the center. They had to ensure he was the man in Iraq. He couldn't live with himself if Blake was not the man they wanted. He might not live with himself after this anyway, Yassin thought.

"Would it be safe to assume his wife and kids are watching in the crowd?" Abdallah asked.

"Yes, we could follow him and see where he ends up at, but that would be extremely risky." Yassin said.

"There will be other opportunities," Sawaya said, which drew looks from both men. "Not here, too many people watching," he continued.

Neither man said anything in response. They watched the parade continue past.

＊

"Left right, left right left," Blake called cadence as he had done so many times before. "Align to the center," he said quietly enough so they could hear him, but not the spectators.

They marched down the center of the street maintaining enough distance behind the lead vehicle, so they had space in case it stopped abruptly. Blake wanted to make sure they looked good for the crowd. Their families, friends, and neighbors were in attendance, so they needed to put on a nice show. It was also a reflection of the police department. His family usually stood by the hotel at the end of the route. Once they stopped marching, he would go over to say hello, the kids loved it.

"Left right, left right left," he continued as they approached the intersection by central fire headquarters.

*

Before they left Salem, the Arab trio took another drive around the point area. It was dark, and they were hoping for another chance to see the other person they were interested in. They were also looking for a drug dealer who could fulfill their needs. As the vehicle turned right, they saw one such candidate. A Spanish man had positioned himself slightly in an alley, situated between two buildings on the right side of Peabody St. He was looking up the one-way street for possible business and probably the police.

"What about him?" Abdallah asked from the passenger seat. "Pull over," he said before Yassin could respond.

He slowed down and pulled to the right. He scanned his rearview mirror for the police car he saw slowing down on Lafayette Street.

"We will have to come back," Yassin said as he looked in the mirror, "the police are slowing down. Let me go around the block."

Abdallah saw groups of people on the corner of the intersection as they drove around. Some were kids just hanging out, maybe helping the dealers, some a little too old to be hanging out. They drove back around, but the man was gone, possibly spooked by the police or by them.

"We should leave now, we spent too much time here with this vehicle," Yassin said.

Endicott St., Danvers, MA

"We need to get a hold of that license," Abdallah said to Yassin who was seated at the roundtable in the hotel.

Sawaya moved a chair closer to them.

"How?" Yassin said.

Abdallah waited a minute or two before he said, "there is another idea."

The two men waited silently for Abdallah to continue.

"Car bomb, or vehicle born improvised explosive device as the Americans call it. It is an alternative and can easily be arranged through my other contact," he said.

"How would we get it into the crowd? Yassin asked. "The streets are blocked by police."

"That is a problem, but like I said, it is an alternative. We will have to think about it, but right now it is late, and I am tired. Call in the morning and I will let you know a good time to stop by. We have to work out these problems," Abdallah said and stood up. "Goodnight my friend," he said and put his hand out.

Yassin shook both their hands and went out into a cool night air.

Abdallah walked around the room a bit and lit a cigarette while he sat on the edge of the bed. He was not a chain smoker like his roommate. He looked down at the floor and really thought how he could resolve the problem. After a few minutes, he looked over at Sawaya.

"What?" Sawaya said.

"Grab your jacket," Abdallah said. "Are you comfortable driving?"

"Well, yes," he replied, "Where are we going?"

"I'll explain along the way," he said and took the briefcase out from the closet shelf. He put it on the bed and removed the 9mm Beretta and one magazine from the case.

Sawaya stopped in his tracks when he saw it. "Where did you get that?" he asked.

"From our other friend," Abdallah replied. He loaded a magazine in the gun, moved the slide back, and let it go forward. The round was now chambered, and he put it in the pocket of his jacket. "Come on let's go, here are the keys," he said as he passed them to Sawaya.

Abdallah was surprised that Sawaya had remembered the way back to the point area of Salem. He was nervous about being stopped by the police but had an Iraqi license and passport in case. Not his real identity of course. The license for both men had come from Nazar.

"Drive around the block, a little. He was standing by that building," Abdallah said and pointed to a three-decker brick building.

Traffic had cleared up as the parade goers headed home with their kids in tow. Sawaya drove down the tight street trying to make out the people in the shadows. They drove down Lafayette Street and turned onto Peabody Street.

"Stop, there he is," Abdallah said excitedly in Arabic.

Sawaya looked in the rear-view mirror and pulled over beyond a red work van.

"Stay here with the car," Abdallah said as he opened the door with his right hand.

"Wait, what are you going to do, kill him!"

"Yes, after I get the drugs, I need off him first."

Abdallah said so calmly it unnerved Sawaya. Then the door shut.

Peabody St., Salem, MA

Jayden Cedano saw the vehicle stop and figured that the man getting out was another customer. The stranger drove a newer, nice car and could probably afford his product and would pay a little more. He moved in the shadow of the alley, so he could see the customer to determine if he was a cop first and foremost and then to determine if he was going to be ripped off.

He knew what most of the cops looked like especially the detectives. Even if they were brought in from another department, they still had the cop look. This person didn't look like a cop. Cedano worried a little, but he still carried his product on him mostly because he didn't trust the people around him. So, he risked his freedom. He was on probation now and trying to be more careful. He hired a better lawyer too, one from Boston, but he was not cheap. Eventually, the judge would get tired of seeing him and send his ass to State Prison.

The guy walking toward him was not a cop. He wasn't like the usual customers either that ranged from teenagers to businessmen. He felt for the gun that was tucked in his rear waistband. He knew it was there but felt better when he touched it. The Glock 21 had a full magazine with one in the pipe. To the left of him a kid appeared on a bike and gave him a nod, which meant no cops were around. If one had been in the area the lookout would have peddled by and made some noise. The man walking toward him was big, dark skinned with a trimmed beard and possibly Arab or Indian.

*

Abdallah had no idea what to say. He never did this before, nor thought about it. He walked up the sidewalk and stopped right at the beginning of the alley and said in English, "I am looking to buy some heroin."

TERROR IN THE WITCH CITY

The Spanish man just stood there silently, and then as a smile crossed his face, "Are you fucking serious?" he said. "What are you a cop?" Jayden Cedano said still smiling.

Abdallah just looked at him, playing stupid.

"Well step inside here my man so we can do some business." He moved farther into the alley. *Dumb fuck* Cedano thought to himself.

The smile faded away as Abdallah shoved the man with his left hand and, with his right hand, drew the Berretta from his pocket quickly. The dealer's head smacked against the cold brick wall as he looked at Abdallah's. He thought about reaching for his gun but was inches away from the barrel of the gun Abdallah held.

"No, I am not a cop." Abdallah finally answered. "Don't reach for that gun or I will kill you. I don't want your money. I only want the heroin you have. Do you understand?" He now spoke with a slight British accent.

Cedano looked at the bearded man in surprise at his demand. Cedano was shorter and thin, wiry. He knew it was useless to try to overpower the man and run away.

"Okay, but it's tucked in the back of my pants by my ass. I need space to get it." He didn't move.

"Move for that gun in your waist and I will blow your fucking brains out of your head. Understand?" Abdallah moved the gun even closer to Cedano's face.

"Yeah, I do," he replied.

Abdallah stepped back and kept the gun pointed the gun right between Cedano's eyes. He wanted to keep the man scared but was careful to keep the gun out of reach from the dealer to grab.

*

"Control to 22," the dispatcher said on the radio. "Car 22 respond to possible gunshots on Lynch St by Congress. One call only."

"22 is on the way," the patrolman said into the microphone, then he started up the patrol car.

The officer of patrol unit #22 hit the master light switch button and drove down the street. He was on Lafayette Street when he was called, and he waited until he turned onto Peabody Street to activate the siren.

*

Abdallah who had a gun pointed at the head of the drug dealer, was no more than 10 feet away from the curb, but still tucked in the alley. The siren startled Abdallah and he looked back at the street. Cedano was also surprised by the siren and facing the street.

Sirens usually meant trouble for him. He weighed the possibility of being shot in the face. He had been dealing long enough and survived the streets to know when an opportunity was presented. The thought of disarming the man never crossed his mind; he was too big and possessed some skills. The man would have destroyed him, and Cedano was smart enough to realize that.

However, he did have a different advantage. He knew the area well, enough to run through the maze of alleys and backyards to escape death. It was no more than 20 feet to the backyard. Cedano glanced at Abdallah's head turned to the blaring sirens then he turned and ran. His sneakers pounded the cement and glided over the untrimmed grass. There was a break in the fence that led to another yard on the opposite street. Cedano leapt over the fence and disappeared into the darkness.

Once the police car shot past him, Abdallah realized that he had committed an amateur mistake that could have gotten him killed. Luckily, the dealer had chosen to run away instead of pulling his gun out. Abdallah immediately ran down the alley to the backyard and saw nothing.

"Fuck," he yelled. He realized he had just jeopardized the whole operation, *how fucking stupid*. He put the gun in his pocket and headed back to the vehicle. He opened the door and saw Sawaya who looked terrified.

"Let's go now," Abdallah said once inside.

Sawaya put the vehicle in drive looked in the rearview mirror, then began to drive. After a couple of minutes, he said, "Well?"

"The police car came around and he ran," Abdallah said.

Sawaya was surprised that Abdallah had made such a mistake but did not dare to mention it.

"Don't tell Yassin about this, understand?"

"   Of course." Sawaya replied.

Chapter 28

Horror Show

Thursday October 29th

Washington St., Salem City Hall, Salem, MA

The meeting was informal and held in the room off the council chambers. The room was used as an overflow for bigger events, media, and to store television equipment to record meetings. All the department heads, several counselors who were not busy, the clerk, and the secretary were spread around the table. Papers, folders, bottled water, and coffee cups were laid out in front of them. There were two boxes that held a few muffins that survived their first break. The two-dozen doughnuts had fared slightly better and were on the counter.

"Okay, questions, comments, concerns?" Mayor Jacob Parker said from the head of the table. "I will not take up any more of your valuable time. I appreciate the impromptu meeting, and if anything pops up that needs immediate attention, feel free to call me or my secretary," Mayor Jacob Parker said with a nod to his assistant.

He stood up as the meeting ended then went over to the clerk who was on his left

"Excuse me, Mayor?" A woman said as she moved closer, blocking his path. She was blond, and on the shorter side. She had a nice smile and was attractive.

"Yes," he replied.

"I am Rachel Logan from the Salem News. Is there any truth to the rumor of gangs from Boston coming to Salem on Halloween night, creating problems?"

The latest rumor was that several gangs from Chelsea, Revere, and neighboring Lynn were going to descend on Salem on Halloween night. It was further rumored, like it was every year that the gang initiation for the night would consist of shooting a Salem police officer. These rumors surfaced all the time during a special event or anniversary date. The police administration had to act on this and the hundreds of other rumors that circulated in the police world, even though it was all nonsense.

He smiled, "Police Chief Hampton is better suited to answer that. He is sitting right there." Parker pointed to the chief, then dismissed her and turned back to his assistant.

"I know who and where the chief is." The reported interjected and spoke louder. "I wanted to know if you are working with the Police Department."

Parker did not like her tone, but realized she was a new reporter and therefore eager and could be a pain in his ass. He didn't need to make any more enemies, especially with that shitty newspaper that would try to burn him at any chance they had. Parker looked at Hampton than back at Rachel.

"If you want to know how we are combating a potential problem, then you need to ask those specific questions." He moved towards her. "We have taken measures, or hasn't your newspaper informed you?"

Logan looked caught off guard.

"The chief and I would like to tell you exactly what we have worked out," he said with a smile and she smiled in return.

"Sit down and I'll tell you what the Chief came up with to secure the safety of the visitors, residents and businesses. Which was an excellent idea." Parker said with great confidence, as only a skilled politician could do.

Hampton looked at him and saw right through the bullshit that he just laid out to the naïve girl. He did smile dutifully at her though.

Rachel Logan didn't want to irritate the Mayor, so she gave him one of her best assets, a dazzling smile, and said, "Thank you Mayor Parker. I really appreciate this."

"Take a seat right here," Chief Hampton said while pointing to a chair. He sat down as he opened the folder. He glanced at the mayor who gave him that forced fake political smile.

TERROR IN THE WITCH CITY

Endicott St., Danvers, MA

It had hit Abdallah like a shot to the head. He grabbed the map from the table and looked at the route. They had returned from breakfast hours ago and Yassin had come over to further discuss the plan. They had been contemplating silently since then.

"Of course," Abdallah said out loud to grab Sawaya's attention.

"We will invite ourselves to the parade they are having," Abdallah said to Yassin.

"So, we call the City of Salem and tell them we are going to be in their parade? Then what?" Yassin asked him while flipping through the HBO movie guide.

"We call city officials and tell them our client wants to rejuvenate their career and needs some press. Free to the city, of course." Abdallah paced and rubbed his hands together. "Our client will arrive in a limousine and the police will need to let him through the barrier into the crowd." He smiled. "The limousine has dark tinted windows and will be loaded with explosives!"

Abdallah grabbed the movie guide from Yassin's hands and thrusted at him the 2003 official event guide of Salem's Haunted Happenings book.

"The parade of vehicles will go through the crowded streets and at a certain point the vehicle will detonate, and with Allah's hand, kill a lot of people!" Abdallah finished with his hands raised in the air.

Sawaya got off the bed with a lit cigarette in his hand. He stabbed it out in the ashtray. Sawaya looked over Yassin's shoulder. Abdallah reached for the pack of Cigarettes that were on the table, opened the top, and extracted one.

"Once we have determined a Halloween celebrity that would like to attend, we call on their behalf and make arrangements." Abdallah said grabbing a lighter. He lit the cigarette and inhaled. He liked these cigarettes, even though they were not the strong like the ones back home.

Abdallah got up and grabbed his laptop from the dresser and sat back down in his chair. Once the machine was powered up, he typed his encrypted password. He went to the search engine and typed, "Horror Stars". He went to the first title in the list, horror film stars, and scrolled down. Abdallah had known of a lot of the people on the list, because he enjoyed horror films. The infidels were the best at making movies, so it was unfortunate that those actors had all died.

At the very bottom of the list, he saw the last page was dedicated to a woman. As he searched, his business partners moved closer to see what he was looking at. He scrolled down to the woman baring her partially exposed breasts. The Muslim men stared at the pictures in silence. They would have never seen anything like that in their country.

"Who is this woman?" Abdallah asked Yassin.

"She's an American icon in horror movies." Yassin realized the word didn't translate well in Arabic. "She is a celebrity in the genre," he said.

"Would it be realistic for her to come to Salem for publicity?" Abdallah asked.

"Yes, she introduces horror movies that don't rise to greatness." Yassin said. "Do you understand?"

"Do you mean the B movies?"

"Yes, exactly."

"Find everything you can about her." Abdallah stood up and paced the room. "Find her real name and what she would be doing there. One of us will be calling the city to inform them of her desire to bless the City of Salem with her presence." Abdallah was smiling, pleased with himself.

Yassin scrolled down the page and looked at the photos of the woman. He went to the search page and pasted her screen name in the search box. He grabbed a notebook and pen from the table and wrote down the information. He then opened another screen and searched for a while before he found what he was looking for.

"There is the contact information," Yassin said as he scribbled on the paper.

Washington St., Salem City, Hall Salem, MA

Mrs. Lauren Amato was now settled back at her desk looking at the clock and thinking that the day was half over. She laid her head on her arms and wondered if she could get away with taking a quick nap. She was nodding off when the phone rang.

"Office of Tourism and Cultural Affairs, how can I help you?" Amato spoke without any enthusiasm whatsoever.

"Hello, my name is Mr. Goldman. I understand that you are hosting a parade on Halloween night. Is that correct?" Yassin tried to sound like a proper businessman.

"Yes, how can I help you?" She rolled her eyes – *another tourist*. He probably thought that witches flew in the sky on Halloween night.

"My employer would like to take part in the parade you are hosting," he said.

"Who is your employer, sir?"

"Her real name is probably not known to you. You know her as the Mistress of Darkness," he said. When Yassin heard nothing on the other side, he knew he had caught Amato's attention. He continued, "She is releasing a new movie soon and would like some background footage and media attention. I apologize for the short notice, but we were wondering if it wasn't too late?"

"No, absolutely not. Just tell me what you need, and we will get it." Amato grabbed a pen. "Could I get your name and a phone number please?"

"My boss doesn't want anyone to know beforehand. She would like to surprise the crowd at some point during the parade. Would that be all right with your office?" Yassin said.

"Yes, of course. We would love to accommodate her in any way," Amato started doodling on the paper.

"It has not been decided, but at a minimum she would like to place a non-descript limousine in the parade, free of charge, to draw some attention," he said.

"No problem at all. I will ensure there is an escort for your vehicle into the venue. All the vehicles will be lined up and proceed at a certain time," she said. "Can I have your boss's name, please?"

He waited a few seconds before he responded, "I will call you back with a person's name and number who will take care of all the details. Can I have your name?" he asked politely.

She gave him her name and her cell number just in case she could not be reached at her office. When she hung up on the phone, she made a note on the scrap paper: "Random guy calling about Mistress of Darkness?" She picked up the phone again and dialed a four-digit number.

"You will never guess who wants to come to the Halloween Parade." Amato blurted as soon as her friend answered.

Endicott St., Danvers, MA

Yassin hung up the phone. He sat by the small table that separated the two beds.

"Well?" Abdallah said. Then, not waiting for him to answer, asked, "Why didn't you give her your number?"

"We need to buy a disposable phone with the number. We don't want to seem too eager a celebrity wouldn't," Yassin said.

"You're right, very good, Mr. Goldman." Abdallah smirked.

"I will pick up a disposable phone sometime today then call back tomorrow," Yassin said matter-of-factly.

A short time later, Abdallah paced the room. He held his disposable cell phone in his hand. Finally, he dialed a number on what was described as his "burner phone".

"Yes?" Tariq answered.

"Did the delivery truck arrive?" Abdallah asked.

"No, it won't be coming."

"What?" He replied incredulously.

"The truck broke down." Tariq waited for a response. When there was none, he carefully chose his next words. "I know how it can be fixed. You will have to come over, so I can explain what the mechanics are going to do."

"Okay, we will do that," Abdallah replied.

"I need you to pick up something first."

"What?"

"We need to obtain a license plate for the delivery truck, possibly two of the same numbers. Ask your friend and he will know, okay."

"If there is a problem, I will let you know. Expect us soon," Abdallah said, sounding pissed off, then ended the conversation with the push of a button.

Abdallah turned to Yassin and said, "We are going to see the other contact right now. There is a problem that we need to fix immediately. He wants us to obtain a license plate, possibly two of the same numbers. Do you know what he is talking about?"

Yassin didn't want to go to meet the other person, but it was not a choice. "So, we need to get license plates for the limo?"

"Yes, I presume that's what they would be for." Abdallah was clearly annoyed by the question.

"There is a shopping center nearby. We need to get some tools though to steal them." Yassin stood there and thought for a minute. "Okay, there is an auto parts store down the street, we will stop there and get what we need."

Andover St., Peabody, MA

Yassin had bought one flat and one Philips head screwdriver and an adjustable wrench, all paid in cash. He had left Abdallah and Sawaya in the vehicle while he purchased the items. They drove to the North Shore Shopping Center in Peabody, where there were numerous cars for the picking. He had remembered hearing that at one time this very parking lot had the highest stolen car rate in the state.

Yassin would have preferred to do this at night, at a place that was not patrolled by security, and without video surveillance. There was no choice though, he was told to get license plates immediately. As they drove around the huge lot for the perfect vantage point, Sawaya was amazed by all the cars.

These Americans must be rich to buy these new and expensive vehicles. Yassin explained to Abdallah that the Registry of Motor Vehicles had issued one plate with green lettering but was phasing them out and would now be issuing two plates with red lettering. They found a single security vehicle on the side of the mall, assisting an elderly woman.

Yassin knew where the mall security office was and stayed clear of it. Peabody Police had a small office by a restaurant at another part of the mall. Yassin had no choice; but to do this himself. He guessed at which direction the patrol would respond if someone called security or the police. Yassin determined that they might need a distraction and used Sawaya for the task.

Sawaya would be dropped off drop in front of one of the mall entrances, where the security vehicle would most likely approach. He was instructed that if security or the police came by, he was to stop them and ask for directions to the Liberty Tree Mall.

TERROR IN THE WITCH CITY

Yassin dropped Sawaya off and then he parked the rental car in an open spot which was surrounded by other cars. He put the vehicle in park, reached down and pulled the hood release.

"What are you doing?" Abdallah asked.

"I am faking engine problems. This way it would be reasonable for me to be under the hood or looking under the car for the problem," Yassin explained. "If someone approaches, call my cell. In the meant time, I will be stealing a plate," Yassin grabbed the tools and left the vehicle.

He went around the front and put his hands in the engine compartment to free the hood. He looked around at the cars that surrounded him. The vehicle directly behind him was a Nissan Xterra. The vehicle was big enough to block him from passing vehicles and pedestrians in the other isle.

He lowered himself to the ground and checked to make sure no one was coming near. Yassin crammed the Philips head screwdriver into the bolt holding the license plate secure, and he hoped that the bolts weren't rusted on. The first one gave way and he removed it and slid it under a car on his right. He had unscrewed the second bolt, then slid it under a car on the left side of him. This was to ensure that the owner would never realize the plate had been intentionally removed. The plate clanged on the ground, and he slid it by his tools. The owner might not notice it missing for a few days, and then it would be too late.

Yassin stood up and shut the hood of his rental car, startling Abdallah. He bent down, grabbed his tools and the license plate, then went to the trunk of the rental and threw them inside. He knew that in most cases the police would not search the trunk on a traffic stop.

"One red license plate," he said to Abdallah as he entered the car. He grabbed a napkin that was stuffed in the door compartment and wiped his hands. He started the car and backed out of the parking spot.

"What about the other plate," Abdallah asked.

"I cannot get the other one right now without getting caught."

"It will have to do then I guess," Abdallah replied. "We should just go the other way and leave Sawaya behind." Abdallah laughed, trying to lighten up the situation.

"He would be fucked, wouldn't he?" Yassin said smiling as he started the car and backed up.

"Yes, he would probably cry," Abdallah said as the vehicle took a right and headed to where Sawaya stood. "I know I would," he smiled and looked at Yassin.

They pulled over, across the road and waited as Sawaya moved quickly towards the vehicle.

"He would've cried," Yassin said as he watched the panic leave Sawaya's face as he grabbed for the door handle like it was a life preserver.

"I told you," Abdallah replied as the door opened and both men smiled at each other.

"What is so funny?" Sawaya said in his loudest voice since the start of the trip. "You took forever."

The two men chuckled as Yassin accelerated the vehicle through the bustling parking lot.

Horace St., Somerville, MA

It took a little over 35 minutes to get to the warehouse. They stood outside of the large garage door. Abdallah had called ahead, but still had to knock a few times.

"How did you know it was us?" Abdallah grilled Tariq who opened the door without asking who it was first.

"I saw you on that camera over there" Tariq smiled as he pointed to the camera.

"Very good."

Tariq held the door open as the three men came in. "Anyone else here?"

"No, just as you requested."

Abdallah introduced Tariq to Yassin, and they shook hands. The men noticed the handgun in the holster attached to Tariq's belt.

"I didn't see that before; did you have that the other day?" Abdallah asked.

"I would never bring it there," he replied.

"What is it?"

"Sig Sauer," Tariq replied.

"Let's talk out back," Tariq said and led the way through the shop. "Did you get the license plates?"

"I obtained one, taking two plates was too risky," Yassin said as he handed the single plate over, "Will this do?"

"It should be sufficient," Tariq said as they moved into the area where the limo was parked.

"I hope you have a backup plan, as far as the explosives are concerned," Abdallah said.

"I do." Tariq answered. "I have an associate who is a chemist in school, MIT, one of the best schools in the country."

"MIT?" Abdallah asked.

"Massachusetts Institute of Technology," Tariq said. "We have discussed the matter and he know which materials it will take to provide the precise mixture. He has been over the vehicle. That's why everything has been removed and the windows were heavily tinted. I have a shopping list that will be filled later. All the usual precautions have been taken, so attention is not brought. He will load and prepare the materials, so the vehicle will be ready for Saturday morning, and with a few hours to spare in case problems arise."

Abdallah walked around the vehicle to inspect the changes.

Tariq looked at the other two, "I bought this vehicle in cash from an old man. I have the title, but never registered it. When the records of this vehicle are searched, if that is possible after the explosion, it will come back to an elderly man who could barely see. I wore clothing that would be impossible for him to identify me." Tariq sounded pleased. "No questions asked. The plate will be used to get to Salem from here."

"We hope," Abdallah said not smiling from the other side of the vehicle.

"All you have to do is drive slow and obey the traffic laws," Tariq said. "The plate would not be reported until after the explosion, if at all. The police will run the plate only if they pull you over. So, don't get pulled over!"

"Don't tell me, tell him," Abdallah said looking at Sawaya, "He will be driving."

The other two men looked at him uncomfortably. The garage was dead silent except for the vent system engaging. All three men stared at Yassin when his phone rang.

"It's my work." Yassin said. "They usually don't call. Excuse me?" Yassin stepped away from the men.

"Hello?" Yassin listened intently. "What? Is she all right?"

The men watched him. Yassin paced, clearly distressed. He looked up at the men who heard him say, "Yes, I am on my way. I'll be there in 30 minutes."

"Is everything all right?" Abdallah asked concerned.

"No, there was a robbery at the store. The woman who works there was brought to the hospital," Yassin said. "The police want the video surveillance and only I know how to pull it."

Yassin pulled his car keys from his pocket. "They said it was probably a junkie looking for some money. I must go. You can come with me or I will come back to pick you up." Yassin said to them.

"I will take you back" Tariq said to the other two men.

"Thank you," Yassin replied and started for the door.

"Sawaya please go with Yassin." Abdallah said. "He might need a hand." He just wanted to get rid of him.

"Okay, let's go," Sawaya said looking at Yassin.

Yassin headed to the front office and Sawaya followed him. Abdallah and Tariq walked behind them.

"If the police find out who robbed you let me know so I can kill them," Abdallah said.

Yassin believed Abdallah would do exactly that. He and Sawaya got in the car and left the garage.

Abdallah looked around and found a seat.

"Please walk me through what the chemist is going to do with the materials that will be used. I don't want you to make it too complicated." Abdallah said to Tariq.

"Come over here, and I will show you everything" Tariq said leading him over to a desk.

Chapter 29

Junk Man

Friday October 30th

Main St., Peabody, MA

Yassin and Sawaya made good time, getting back, considering it was rush hour on a Friday afternoon. They drove down Route 1 and took the Lynnfield Street exit and made it to Main Street in Peabody in record time. There was one marked and one unmarked police car. A patrolman, and a detective were in the store with a man in a suit.

As Yassin opened the door he was stopped by the patrolman.

"Mr. Yassin?" The police officer asked.

"Yes." Yassin was tense.

"Come this way, please." The officer turned around and walked up to a man wearing a dress shirt, slacks with a badge and gun affixed to his belt. "Detective, this is Mr. Yassin, the owner." The detective scribbled a few notes in his book. "Hello sir, my name is Detective Green."

"Thank you for coming," Yassin said.

Green pointed inside the store and explained to Yassin that the man in the suit was a witness. He was knocked over by the robber as he exited the store. They had a good description that they gave out on a stop and hold but needed the video for a better description and as evidence.

Detective Green knew that in a good percentage of cases, the video system was either broken or a fake because the owner was too cheap. He remembered a break to a pharmacy and learned that the cameras were not real. He also knew of a bank that had an inoperative camera system. *Unbelievable* he thought.

"My video system works, so I can show the video and give you a copy. Just give me a few minutes to get it up," Yassin said.

"That would be great," Green replied.

"How is Helen, my employee," Yassin asked. "Will she be okay?"

"The paramedics believe that she fainted, then struck her head when she landed. She should be alright." Green said. "Her family was notified. She was brought to Salem Emergency Room."

"Thank goodness."

Yassin took the detective to the office. Sawaya who came in the store beforehand, followed them both. It took about 20 minutes before a photograph of the suspect was printed and a copy of the video was made on compact disk. The tape revealed that the woman fainted, then the robber fled without taking any money.

"This is good" the detective said as he stood with the evidence in hand. "Excuse me, but I need to talk to the officer" he said and left the office.

As Yassin followed the detective to the door, Sawaya stood up to go with him.

"Stay here please while I talk to the police, okay?" Yassin said as the detective left the office.

"No, problem" Sawaya sat back down.

Yassin shut the door behind him as he left. Sawaya turned around and saw the cordless phone. He had been consumed by hate and made a bad decision with these killers. Now he would have to finish what he had started. If he did not go along with Abdallah, then his wife's life was in danger. These men were ruthless and would not hesitate in killing her to prove a point to everyone.

Sawaya would contact her and tell her to leave at night, and cross the border, and hide with relatives. He looked at the clock on the wall, 5 P.M. It was seven in the morning in Iraq. He figured it's now or never. Yassin would be busy with the police and probably would not care, if Sawaya used the phone, but he would keep it short. He picked up the phone and dialed zero.

"Operator," she said.

"Could I please have an International Operator," Sawaya waited.
*

Andrew was sitting in his room. He was 13 years old and was listing to the scanner that his uncle had given him for Christmas last year. He was supposed to be doing homework. His parents told him if it wasn't done there, would be no television tonight.

TERROR IN THE WITCH CITY

The textbook was open to the math page that required his attention, but that was it. Andrew had also done a little further research, thanks to his parents, who let him use their computer. He read an article on the internet about cordless phone frequencies and obtained their codes. He programmed the scanner with the base and headset frequencies of all the companies that he could find. Andrew was amazed that he could listen in on phone conversations that were in the area.

He figured out that he could only listen to half the conversation if the cordless caller spoke to someone on a regular phone, as he called it. He decided to start his homework because there was a playoff game tonight. Though it was not his team, it would be a good game. The Red Sox had blown it and were officially done almost a month ago, as usual. He liked the Yankees, who were playing the Florida Marlins.

He started reading the problem on the page, while listening to the scanner. He had heard the description of a robber being given about an hour earlier. Pretty exciting considering it was right down the street. Way better than the usual medical calls and motor vehicle stops that he usually listened to. He knew the interesting calls came in after he went to bed and tried to listen late at night.

Andrew heard a man speaking a foreign language and stopped reading. He pressed the button to lock the frequency. He wasn't speaking Portuguese or Greek like everyone else in the area, and it wasn't Spanish either. It sounded like those people in Iraq that he saw on the television. The man spoke to someone for a few minutes and sounded upset.

Andrew got excited when the man started speaking broken English. "I love you so much," the man said almost crying.

A robbery, now this guy, all before dinner.

"They want me to drive a car into the crowd in Salem on Halloween night and blow it up, do you understand, Ghanda?' The man was half crying, half yelling.

Andrew sat there, frozen, staring at the box. The man then switched back to his language, continuing the conversation. The call lasted a few more minutes, but the boy wasn't listening anymore. He didn't know what to do at first, but knew he had to do something. He got up from his desk and opened the door to his room.

"Mom!" He yelled at the top of the stairs.

*

Yassin came into the office and knew Sawaya had done something. He was sitting at the desk and his hands were on his forehead, his eyes were looking down. He did not say anything or move to look at Yassin. The phone was off the cradle.

"I don't know what you have done, but I have to go the hospital now to see my employee. I will drop you off at the hotel, do you have a key?" Yassin asked and grabbed the phone to replace it.

"Yes." Sawaya said his voice crackled.

"We must go now then." Yassin held the door open for Sawaya to leave.

Yassin was pissed. His business was robbed, an employee in the hospital, and he was taking part in a terrorist attack. They had traveled for a few miles and were now crawling in traffic through Wilson Square.

Yassin tried to control his anger before he turned to look at Sawaya. "Pull yourself together. Don't mention that you made a call, do you understand?"

"I will not say anything," Sawaya replied.

"Good," Yassin replied. "Did you call home and speak to your wife?"

Sawaya looked at him but was reluctant to answer.

Yassin spoke calmly. "Tell me. I won't tell that monster I am on your side."

"Yes, I called Ghanda."

"Did you warn her?"

"Yes."

"Good."

Endicott St., Danvers, MA

It was before six when Sawaya was dropped off at the hotel. He was about to enter his room when he changed his mind. He knew he would die in a few days and would soon see his son again with Allah. Sawaya felt like a certain weight had been lifted off him, that he had made peace with himself. He put the key card back in his wallet and started for the big mall across the street. He had money, so he might as well enjoy it and treat himself. Abdallah was not around and would never go looking for him.

Sawaya's wife had been warned and she would be leaving for a safe area within a few hours. He didn't want to put her in danger by turning Abdallah into the authorities right now. He had to give her a head start. If not, they would surely hunt her down and kill her. He knew her family would protect her, and she could start a new life where she was going. Sawaya believed that his wife would get over his death in due time.

He also knew that Abdallah would get caught or killed and not escape justice. He crossed the busy roadway when the lights indicated he was safe to do so. He thought about alcohol and if he should indulge, but it was still forbidden. The other hypocrites might, but he was a devout Muslim.

*

Two hours later, the vehicle pulled into the parking spot at the hotel. Traffic was light, and there was not much talk between Abdallah and Tariq on the way back.

"I will call you Saturday morning to ensure we are on schedule," Abdallah said before he opened the door.

"Not to worry. It will be taken care of," Tariq replied.

"I hope so," he said holding back what he was thinking: *for your sake it better.*

He shut the door and realized there were no lights on in the room. He opened the door with the key card and went into the darkness. *Shit*, he thought as he turned on the light, and heard the vehicle backing up. He took out his phone and dialed Yassin's cell number. After the phone rang five times, a recording came on.

He was probably at the hospital, so Abdallah didn't bother to leave a message. He thought about it for a minute then decided there was nothing he could do about Sawaya's disappearance. Sawaya didn't know anyone nor could he leave. He might have gone out to eat. He wouldn't jeopardize his wife's life and tomorrow it was all over anyway. There was no sense in showing that he had gotten the best of him. The man was going to die soon, and he might as well enjoy the last days of his life. Abdallah clicked on the remote to the television to see what rubbish the infidels were watching.

Route 128 southbound, Lynnfield, MA

Ramzi Tariq was headed south on Route 128 which was also known as Interstate 95, enjoying his BMW. He had called his associates, as he liked to call them to make sure that they did not fuck up their orders. Everyone had a separate list of items they were supposed to obtain. Neither of them knew about the other, at least he hoped.

Tariq had created a nice organization that had taken 10 years to perfect. Now he was starting to enjoy the benefits of his work, specifically the money. He always had to be careful and watch his back. Not just from the authorities, but from business associates, and friends. Even family members could not be trusted in this line of work. He had built the system so only one person had a little piece of the puzzle. Anyway, if they tried to "snitch" on him, as the Americans like to say, they could honestly give only so much information. Tariq had been fortunate up to this point and had no real dealings with the police or federal authorities, but that didn't mean that he wasn't being watched and a case against him being put together.

The pivotal point in his criminal career was when he learned of cigarette smuggling. First, he laughed at the notion and thought they were talking about drugs; but once it was explained, he took advantage of this new line of making money. He soon learned that cigarette smuggling was far more profitable than selling narcotics. It also wouldn't him thrown in jail, at least not right off the bat. Tariq never liked the idea of selling drugs that would wind up in the hands of kids. He also wanted nothing to do with hardcore drugs, he knew too many people who had screwed up their lives using heroin.

Tariq was brought in to help move some cigarettes. They bought cartons off a wholesaler, who either sold them to a distributor or sold them to the store owners themselves. The markup was incredible. Tariq and his crew initially hijacked a truck to prove their worth to the organization. It was dangerous, but well worth the risk. He assisted in the New York state area that had the highest tax rates in the country. They bought cigarettes in Georgia or Virginia, then moved them up north. Once he started expanding the business into lower New England, he found a person who could forge the cigarette tax stamp.

Tariq expanded the operation by buying cigarettes in Missouri that had the lowest tax rates and moving them into Massachusetts which had the second highest rates. He even assisted the New York market in wholesaling when they ran into problems. Now he called the shots and didn't get his hands too dirty. Tariq wasn't too keen on this latest mission, but he was paid well. It would also pay dividends down the road with further business for those organizations.

Lafayette St., Salem, MA

Officer Blake looked at the clock in the vehicle, 10:30 p.m. one hour and a half hour before he could go home. The night was dragging for a Thursday. Usually the bars were packed with college kids in session, but not tonight. He was in the parking lot at St. Joseph's Church, across from the park on Lafayette Street, monitoring traffic. Drivers would constantly blow through the blinking stoplight as they came up Washington Street, then merge onto Lafayette Street. Blake only pulled over the vehicles whose operators didn't even touch the brakes. He didn't hide the vehicle, because there was no reason to. He parked in the open and was visible to approaching traffic, and they still didn't even care.

He watched a truck blow the stop sign and was about to chase after it, when he saw Michael Mitchell cross the street and head into the park. He knew him, and thought he was cleaning up his act. He was either passing through the park or trying to score some dope. Blake sat in the car until Mitchell slowed down, then he shut the car off and left the cruiser.

Blake lowered the volume on his radio, so it didn't give away his position. He moved around to the back of the church to the other side to the driveway next to the old rectory. He watched Mitchell waiting under a tree in the middle of the park, barely noticeable. Blake moved under the cover of the tree and watched as Jayden Cedano crossed Harbor Street toward the park.

Blake keyed the mic, "Car 25, can you make your way towards Lafayette Park? No lights or siren, drug transaction about to occur."

"Copy," was the reply. "21 will head that way as well."

Blake could see the two meeting under the tree, thanks to the streetlight. He saw a hand-to-hand transaction and knew his instincts were correct, based on his training and experience as a police officer with six years on the job. He would have to write in his report that the park at this time of night was a known drug area, and Cedano had been arrested numerous times for drug dealing and a lot of other information.

"25 is on Porter Street." The radio sounded.

A minute later, the radio transmitted, "21 on Washington by Pond."

After a few minutes, both parties separated and went in opposite directions. Cedano whom Blake wanted to arrest personally, headed to Ropes Street. Mitchell headed to the Lafayette Hotel.

Blake hit the mic again. "Spanish male is moving across to Ropes. The buyer, a white male, is headed towards credit union," Blake ran across the street after Cedano.

Cedano looked back at the noise and started running. Car 25 floored it down Porter Street. Mitchell was about to run, but he stopped behind the trunk of the tree. He knew he could not outrun the police, so he decided to hide in the dark. In the commotion it might work.

Officer Kenneth Billings whom had left patrol car #21 was closest to Mitchell and did not see him hiding. However, he did see Cedano running and being chased by the other police officers. Caught in the heat of the moment and thrill of the chase Officer Billings crossed the street and began chasing Cedano as well.

*

Mitchell's heart was pounding as the cop passed within a few feet of him. He had a good size bag of heroin on him and would have been screwed if he was caught. The door of his apartment was within view. He waited until the last cop was rounding the corner onto Ropes Street then he ran as hard as he could to the door. He fought to get his key out. He knew there were more cops on the way, and he had seconds at best

*

Cedano thought he knew the streets well, and therefore he could cut through a few yards and be lost. He was about to take a right out of the driveway of the house when he heard the roar of an engine headed at him. He looked back but didn't see a car behind him as he ran down a one-way street. Suddenly, the headlights and spotlight lit him up.

"Fuck!" He realized it was a police car coming the wrong way.

He saw the lot on the left and headed that way. Unfortunately for him, the vehicle behind him took a left as well onto Porter Street then took

233

a right into the other side of the parking lot. Cedano came around the corner, disoriented and pretty much ran into the right front quarter of the police car. Officer Christina Spencer threw the vehicle in park, ran around the car and grabbed Cedano, then knocked him to the ground. His face was plastered against the pavement. He obeyed the officer's demands for his hands behind his back.

Spencer and another officer held him down as Blake handcuffed him. Cedano was then assisted in getting up, and a search was conducted. In his waistband was a handgun that somehow survived the chase. He was so pissed off at himself for not throwing away the gun.

"Look what we have here," Blake said as he grabbed the gun.

Sgt. Vincent Pelligrini had arrived just after the chase. "Okay. Search for more weapons, then do a thorough search at the station."

Cedano was transported to the Police Station in the backseat of car 25 as the other offices searched for anything that might have been thrown.

"Good job," Pelligrini said, "Go back to the station and take your time with report. If we find anything, we will let you know."
*

When Blake entered the control room he was congratulated by the lieutenant.

"Nice pinch."

"Thanks Lieutenant" he replied.

"He wants to talk to a detective and cut a deal," the dispatcher said as he filled out the booking sheet.

"I'll go back there and see if he wants to tell me anything," Blake said.

Blake was handed a set of keys and went to the detention area. Before he went inside the detention area, he withdrew his service pistol from his holster and stored it in one of the two boxes that were on the wall. He retrieved the key from the box and went into the secure area.

Cedano was in male cell number 2. There were three separate cell areas in the Salem Police Department. The female and juvenile areas each had two cells with separate doors. They were required by law to be sight and sound separate. The male prisoner area had nine cells. There was also one large holding cell by the booking desk. There were card readers at the end of the hall of each cell area. The booking officer or superior officer had to check the prisoners every so often.

The card reader would provide a timestamp of who had made a check and when. The Salem Police Department did not have a specific policy on the frequency of the prisoner checks. The unwritten rule was that the prisoners were checked before and after a change of shift. Blake whose previous employer was the Massachusetts Department of Corrections knew that they should be checked every 30 minutes. The check would ensure that there was still a living, breathing body inside the cell.

Since the building was built in 1992, the cells were modern. They were prefabbed steel and didn't have any bars. The doors were steel with a thick glass window that could not be broken. There was a small door called a food port which was used to slide food through, as well as applying handcuffs for extremely violent prisoners.

Blake stood before the door and opened the food port with the key. "What do you want?"

"I want to talk to the detectives," Cedano said.

"This isn't let's Make a Deal. I got you with a gun and a lot of heroin. What you have better be fucking incredible." Blake said.

Cedano stood there and looked at him contemplating what to say. He knew that he had to play ball with the cop who arrested him, or the detectives would never agree.

"I will share this much with you." Cedano said seriously. "A big mother fucking Arab tried to rob me of my drugs at gunpoint the other night in the point. He didn't want any money either. That ain't normal. Something going on here. I know the streets. Arab guy, big, and mean son of a bitch with a British accent."

"Criminal on the air?" Blake asked on the radio.

After a minute or so, he heard, "Criminal is on."

"Can I see you at the station please?" Blake said while leaving the cell block.

Chapter 30

Countdown Begins

Friday October 30th

Endicott St., Danvers, Ma

Yassin got to the hotel before 9 A.M. He knocked on the door and was led in by Abdallah who didn't appear to be happy and didn't say a word. *I wonder what happened last night,* Yassin thought. Sawaya was watching television smoking a cigarette.

"How is your friend, the woman?" Abdallah asked.

"Good. She was released last night." Yasin said. "Some sort of panic attack. She fainted then struck her head. She will be fine though." Yassin added, "Thank you for asking."

He took a seat and continued. "Police have the video of the attempted robbery. They think they know who he is, a local junkie."

"You need to call the city about the parade," Abdallah said, sipping a cup of coffee from a Styrofoam cup.

"That is why I bought this phone," Yassin said and pulled out a cheap looking phone. It's all set up. I wrote down what I am going to tell them. Do you want to look?" he asked.

"No need, I trust you. You have helped us more than I could have done. That's why you were sent here, right?" Abdallah asked.

"How about the policeman? Are we going to make sure he lives there so we don't attack the wrong family?" Yassin turned and asked.

"We will find out tomorrow," Abdallah replied and held the thought for a minute.

"While the family, are trick-or-treating, as you say. We will go to the house to look around and make sure there are no dogs and see how the place is laid out. We will gather facts and leave before they return. After we will go to see Tariq and pick up the vehicle."

Abdallah was pacing the room. "After the attack, while the police are surveying the carnage, we will enter his home and kill him in front of his family. Any questions?"

"Won't he be working if it's Halloween?" Sawaya asked.

Both men looked at him.

"Maybe they will give him the night off?" Yassin said.

"Maybe they won't," Abdallah said, "In any case, we will deal with that when the time comes."

He was clearly unhappy with the thought. He went to the television and shut it off then turned to Yassin and said, "Call the city now."

Yassin knew the man was serious and it was making him nervous.

"As you wish," Yassin said and looked at his script one last time.

He grabbed the phone and dialed the number. "Hello this is Mr. Goldman. I spoke to you a few days ago about the parade."

"Yes, I'm glad you called back." Lauren Amato said. "I talked to the Mayor and he is very excited about the visit."

Yassin said, "I was going to give you another contact, but we are running out of time." He was looking at Abdallah. "I will take care of the details myself," Yassin said into the phone. "What time do we need to be there and where do you want us, street name?"

"The parade will start at 10 p.m. show up at 9:45 please," she said, reading from her notes.

"Okay," he replied.

"Go to the intersection of Washington Street and New Derby Street. The police officer there will be told to let you through, I will tell them personally," she said.

"Excellent. There will be only one limo, an older model, which is what she wanted to use. At some point in the parade, she will pop out of the sunroof for the crowd. She might sign autographs and take a few photos at the end, but not before. She is very picky like that. I am sure you can understand those types," he said playing into her excitement.

"Absolutely, we have a few prima donnas here too," she said. "Okay, we will see you at 9:45 p.m. on Halloween night. Call me if there are any problems or if you need anything," Lauren said.

"I will, and we will see you then," he replied.

"Thank you," she said and hung up.

Yassin shut the phone, "Well?" He looked at them waiting for their response.

Salem Police Department, Salem, MA

Detective Nicholas Hallas went downstairs to the control room where all 911 calls made in the City of Salem were answered. He stood in front of the partition and spoke to the dispatcher.

"How many need prints?" he asked.

Every morning before court, a detective took the prints of all prisoners that were not already on file. The prints taken were entered directly into IAFIS machine (pronounced A-fis).

"Only one," the dispatcher said. "There is a note on another booking sheet that the detective on last night wanted you to speak to him about."

"Yeah, I am going to take him upstairs. I'll be all set. Can I have the keys?" he said.

He was handed the keys and walked down the hall. He stopped by the door with the sign, "detention area". He removed his short version Smith and Wesson M&P 40 from the pancake holster on his right hip and placed it inside the gun box. He continued straight until he reached the male cell area. He stood before door #2 and knocked on the thick glass. The man was wrapped in a cheap blanket that had been provided by the department. If a prisoner didn't act like an asshole, they would usually get two blankets by the booking officer.

"You want to talk?" Hallas asked.

"I spoke to someone last night," Cedano replied, barely awake and his hair a mess.

"I am Detective Hallas and my boss wants to hear what you have to say. If you want? No promises, but we will talk to the DA's office about your cooperation. Depending on what you have to say, understand?"

"Yeah," he replied.

"Then get up. We have to go upstairs to talk," he said and put the key in the lock of the cell door. He pulled the door open and waited for the prisoner to pull himself together. "Kneel on the bench so I can put the leg irons on you."

Hallas removed the leg irons he had put in his back pocket. He placed them around Cedano's ankles and double locked them with his cuff key. "Follow me."

Cedano followed the detective around the corner to a bench.

"Take a seat, I'll get your clothes," Hallas said and went to the wall of lockers and pulled out sneakers, a shirt, and sweatshirt. He placed them on the counter that separated the two.

Cedano grabbed his stuff and got dressed quickly. He followed the detective out of the detention area and up a staircase. They walked down the hall to a room with a large table, several chairs and with audio and visual equipment. There was a two-way mirror so other detectives, officers, witnesses, and lawyers could watch the interview procedure. Identifying the suspect was done differently.

"Take a seat. Do you want some water?" Hallas asked as he walked to the door on the other side of the room.

"Nah" Cedano added, "Thanks though," almost forgetting his manners.

He might have been a criminal but had remembered the manners his mother taught him. Cedano remembered that he had been in the room before trying to save his ass a different time.

Detective Sergeant Alexander Turner came in the room, "Hey Cedano, surprised to see you here," he said sarcastically.

He had a folder in his hand and took a seat across the table from him, "Okay, possession of a firearm, possession of a class A substance with intent to distribute, Heroin, also within a school zone all of this while on probation. This case is pretty rock solid, pardon the pun," he said with a snicker that Cedano did not get.

"One year hanging over your head already, right?" Turner asked.

A long moment passed before Cedano chose the right words. "This was not a normal drug rip. Something big is going on here. I've worked the streets since I was a kid and never saw any mother fucker like him."

"You were ripped off by a big guy, big fucking deal. Don't play around with me!" Turner said.

"I'm not. He was a big mother fucking Arab, looked like one, and talked with a British accent. He had a beard and everything. Put his gun right to my chest. He wasn't fucking around. Mean son of a bitch" he said with his hands moving a mile a minute.

"So, he wanted your money and drugs, come on."

"Just the drugs that's it. That shit doesn't happen like that. The guy wasn't from here and he wasn't fucking around. I was scared, and I've never been fucking scared. What the fuck is he doing here?"

Both detectives looked at each other and knew he was telling the truth.

"I don't see anything that we can work with. Maybe this guy is setting up shop himself" Turner said leaning on the table.

"No, this was different. Something going here." Cedano said.

"Where were you?" Turner asked.

"In the alley by my house where you always see me" he said with a "no shit" look on his face that caused them both to smile.

"Give me every detail and no bullshit. Your freedom is a stake. If, and only if, this leads to something then we can barter, understand?"

"I know how the game is played," Cedano said.

It took him about 30 minutes to report all the details and a few other things they asked him that were not related to the case.

"We cannot do anything about your violation, you understand that?" Turner said.

"Yeah," he replied.

"What's your probation officers name?" Turner asked and wrote it down. "I will talk to him and the prosecutor about this, if something pops up, maybe you wrap up everything as a package?"

"Ah-ight," he replied in his best street slang.

Turner stood up and said, "Detective Hallas will take you back downstairs." He put out his hand to shake.

Cedano nodded his head and shook Turner's hand. He knew Turner was a man of his word both from the streets and personally. He was brought downstairs to the booking room where Officer Brown was waiting for him behind the partition.

"Sign this?" Brown slid a form over the counter.

Cedano signed his name, which was acknowledgment that he received all his personal property after the police had taken possession. The bag that contained his property, minus his money, would be brought with Cedano by the officers who transported him. The prisoners were given their money to carry on themselves.

"Take a seat, we will be headed to court soon," he said to him.

Peabody Police Department, Peabody, MA

Officer Emanuel "Manny" Silva filled out the standard form and put an X where the reporting party needed to sign. The stolen or recovered motor vehicle (or boat) report was invalid without the party's signature. He slid the form through the slot to the other side of the bulletproof glass.

"Here you go ma'am. Just sign by the "X" and we will enter it into the computer," Silva said.

The computer was the LEAPS terminal, which stood for Law Enforcement Automated Processing System. The system was tied into at least 36 states and various queries were made, such as warrant checks, registration and license status, and missing persons.

"If anyone runs the license plate, it will come back as stolen," he said.

She signed the form and slid it back through the opening. He tore off the last copy which was pink and slid it back under.

"Contact the registry and give them a copy of your form so they can issue you a new plate."

"I honestly don't know if it fell off or was stolen," she told the police officer.

"Let your insurance company know. Maybe they will go to the registry for you. It's the least they could do for all the money you pay them."

"Yeah right? Thank you, Officer," she said, then turned around and left.

As she was walking out the door a family was walking in. Officer Silva was about to turn around when he saw the three entering the station. He pushed the button to ensure the microphone was on and he could hear them in the lobby.

"Can I help you?" he asked.

"We have a bizarre situation." The woman said. "We might be paranoid, but we need to report what my son overheard," she said.

One of these calls, he thought to himself. Normally, Silva would have found out their address and called in the area patrolman to take the report, but he decided to wait until they told the story first. He wasn't busy, and this seemed that it might be amusing.

"One minute," he said into the microphone and then came out to the lobby.

"What's going on?" he said, motioning for them to follow him to a quiet part of the lobby, where there were three chairs and a small table.

The woman began, "Well, my son was given a scanner as a Christmas gift...."

The mother did all the talking as the father just stood and watched. Silva knew who oversaw that relationship. The boy watched her talk and looked at the police officer from time to time, studying him.

"Apparently," she said, looking at the boy, "besides police and fire channels he programmed the numbers to cordless phones into the scanner."

Silva looked at the boy and wanted to smile at him, but that would not be appropriate.

She continued. "He overheard a conversation of a man, a foreigner, saying that there was going to be an attack in Salem on Halloween night."

Officer Emanuel Silva had been a police officer for over 10 years and heard some interesting things. He, like most people in his profession and experience, could judge how truthful the reporting party seemed. He had no doubt that the parents were convinced.

"When did you hear this?" Silva asked in a friendly way to the boy.

"Yesterday before dinner," the boy replied.

"Around 5 p.m.," she interjected.

He asked the boy his name and age to get a feel for him. "Tell me from the beginning what you were doing and what you heard, okay?" he asked.

The boy told him everything he knew.

"I will be right back." Silva stood up. "I would like you to talk to a detective, so they can investigate this further?"

"Sure," the mother said, and the father nodded in agreement.

"Just take a seat and someone will be down shortly," Silva said and walked away.

Silva went to the officer in charge and he explained the situation.

"Do you believe the kid and his parents?" Lieutenant Welsh asked.

"I do," he said.

TERROR IN THE WITCH CITY

He picked up the phone and dialed the extension, "This is Lieutenant Welsh, I have two parents in the lobby with their son. Long story short, the kid picked up a cordless phone call off a scanner, a foreigner, possible Middle Eastern telling someone about an attack in Salem on Halloween night." He emphasized the last two words.

He listened for a minute and looked at the monitor of the lobby. "Yeah, Officer Silva believes them. They seem pretty normal."

Due to several irate visitors and litigation, the lobby of the police department was videotaped, and conversations were always recorded. The sign in the window by the desk warned visitors of the audio and video taping.

The lieutenant hung up the phone. "Someone is coming down," he told Silva.

Ten minutes later, Detective Ronald Green, entered the lobby. He introduced himself to the family and led them to the office to take a statement. 40 minutes later, the family walked past the office that belonged to Lieutenant Welsh. The boy looked in with interest.

"Well what do you think?" The detective asked the boy when they were back in the lobby. "Do you like the place?'

"It's awesome," he replied.

Green laughed a little and then said, "Well if it's okay with your parents, you can come back for a tour. Would you like that?" He smiled.

"Yeah!" He looked to his parents.

His mother rolled her eyes and his father shrugged. Green shook the parents' hands and gave them his card. He waited until they left and headed to Lieutenant's office. Silva was sitting in one the chairs.

"Legit?" Lieutenant Welsh asked.

"Sounds it." Green leaned against the doorframe. "He might have heard an Arab male calling someone, talking about an attack in Salem on Halloween. We presume it's at night. Kid thought the guy might have been crying. We will call over there and give them heads up."

"Thanks Lieutenant" He turned and walked to the Office of Criminal Investigation.

Green who was short and stocky, had 15 years on the job. He wasn't much of a looker, but he made up for it with brains. He had the best closure rate on cases in the department, but had only been a detective for five years

Detective. Lieutenant Alfonso Diaz, of the Peabody Police Department, sat at his desk in the office of the Criminal Investigation Division. He knew he better contact Salem Police sooner rather than later. After 17 years on the job, 10 as a detective, he knew things got sidetracked in this line of work for many reasons and this information was too important to blow off.

Might as well kill two birds with one stone, he thought. He turned to Green. "How does lunch at the Salem Police Department sound?"

"Sounds wonderful, Lieutenant!" He gave a "thumbs up" signal and made his boss laugh.

Lt. Diaz grabbed the cell phone and scrolled through the contacts. He stopped and pressed the send button and waited 30 seconds until he heard, "Hello?"

"This is Al. What are you guys doing for lunch?" He used Al because he had gotten shit for his true name, Alfonso, which meant Spanish royalty, when he was younger. He replied, "Well, we received a report this morning that can't wait. If it's true, this Halloween could be a blast!"

Every officer on the Salem Police Department and any other department that worked on Halloween night held their breath until the night was over. It was in anticipation of a horrendous act that would injure or kill a lot of people during the festive night. The event was a recipe for disaster: tens of thousands of people contained within a five-block area, at night and dressed in costume, being totally anonymous and (in most cases) under the influence of drugs, or alcohol, or both. If someone had the desire and planned it properly, an attack at the right time and place would be devastating.

"Detective Green and I can pick up lunch and head to your station to discuss what we have learned," Diaz said into the phone. "Sounds good, see you then," and he ended the call.

He stood up and addressed Green. "Ready to go?"

"Yeah." Green stood and pushed his chair toward the table.

"Santoro's sound good to you?"

"No problem, boss."

They left the building and stopped at the sub shop on Main Street in downtown Peabody. Diaz ordered his favorite sub, which was a large Italian with everything, cut in half, salt and pepper and a little oil. The place had been there since he could remember, and he went there frequently. Green ordered a large roast beef sandwich, cheese and sauce, and onion rings. He would have rather stopped at Bills and Bobs in Salem, which had the best roast beef.

"Here or to go?" The man behind the counter wearing a stained t-shirt and, in a rush, asked.

"To go," Green replied.

The lunchtime rush was in full swing. Customers were coming in and the phone was ringing off the hook. They each grabbed a soda from the cooler and took a seat at the table by the counter. Neither man ever talked about a case when there were people around. They talked about the police administration, which was a better topic for eavesdroppers. Besides, they thought the police administration was fucked up and liked to bitch about it.

Their order was called. The cashier had been there for years and knew the detectives, and everyone else in Peabody for that matter. "You guys working on anything good?" Charlie asked as he put the sub bags on the counter.

Diaz grabbed a bag of chips from the rack and put them with the soda on the counter.

"No, same old shit," he replied as he dug in his pocket for his money.

"Five bucks each will cover it," Charlie said with his hands on the counter.

"You sure?"

"Yeah, you guys come in all the time, which is good for business".

"Thanks," he replied and laid a $10-dollar bill on the counter.

Green threw a few bucks in the tip can on the counter, "Thanks Charlie, have a good one" he said as he grabbed the stuff.

"Be careful guys," Charlie said as they headed to the door.

Salem Police Department, Salem, MA

15 minutes later, they were on the side of the building. They called ahead and were let in by one of the detectives. They went upstairs to the office and chatted a bit.

Detective Sergeant Turner asked, "What does the Peabody Police have for us today?"

The Lieutenant was about to answer when Captain Dennis Sutton came in the door.

Sutton exchanged pleasantries and pointed to the conference room. "Before you guys start talking, take your food in there and we can sit down and talk."

Sutton was medium built with glasses. He possessed a master's degree in criminology from Northeastern as well as two other degrees from different schools. He was intelligent and very talented at what he did for the past 25 years. He went into his office to put down his coat.

They all sat down around a conference table that was in the middle of a room which was used for everything, except interviews. There were computers, a television, maps on the wall, posters of weapons, and storage containers in the closet, along with everything else that could be stored there.

"Okay Lieutenant tell us what you have for us?" Capt. Dennis Sutton said as he opened the Styrofoam container of Chinese food.

The Lieutenant began telling him what the family had reported. Sergeant Turner and Detective Hallas looked at each other in surprise when they heard about the Arab man.

"Did I say something wrong?" Diaz asked when he caught the look.

"No, actually something right, but please continue." Turner said. "I will explain after."

The Lieutenant finished his report, then the Salem detectives told them about their conversation with Cedano. It was quiet for a few minutes as the men not only digested their food, but the information they had learned and the catastrophic results that might ensue.

"Let's run through some scenarios," Sutton said as he sipped from the soda can.

All the men discussed what they thought could and might happen.

Sutton looked at the men and nodded, thinking. "This goes no further than this room until it can be sorted. It will get passed in roll call tomorrow, Law Enforcement Information only." Sutton said then paused. "Alex, call out contact at the FBI. Let them know what we have and get their recommendations. See if they can spare an agent or two."

"Yes sir," Turner replied.

Different thoughts ran through Suttons' head as he spooned fried rice into his mouth.

Sutton looked at Diaz. "Al, can you take Alex with you to the family to see if we can narrow down the call. How far the signal reaches, suspects in the area, that sort of stuff?"

"Sure, Captain. We have already pulled it on a map, and I can show you at our office. The signal probably reaches one mile and half at most," Diaz said as he folded up the sub's wrapping paper.

"We need to see if we can narrow down the how, where, and when, but still be flexible to react to anything," Sutton said while looking down at his food. The captain continued. "We also need to get Cedano whose probably in Middleton and get a sketch of this guy and put out a bolo" Sutton said.

Bolo stood for be on the lookout which was a law enforcement flyer sent to local, state or federal governments for persons or things of interest.

Middleton, Massachusetts was location of the Essex County Sheriff's Department jail.

"I'll take care of it," Turner answered.

Five minutes later, the men stood and ended their lunch break.

Sutton turned to Turner. "Call in everyone and have them report immediately. Don't tell them why yet. Just get them here. I am going to see the chief and let him know what we have."

West Peabody, MA

"Home for Lunch?" Sarah asked as she heard the front door open and shut.

She was sitting at the kitchen table. She was eating salad and thumbing through a stack of bills. Yassin stepped through the doorway and sat at the table.

"Yes, honey."

TERROR IN THE WITCH CITY

"How is Helen doing?"

"She is back at work, actually." Yassin got up and walked to the fridge. "She was more embarrassed than anything. Thought she was a tough old woman, as she put it." he said. "Are you staying home tomorrow night?' Yassin asked while he looked through the shelves of food.

"Yes, I will be passing out candy," she replied.

"How about the girls?" He asked cautiously.

"In Salem with their friends," Sarah said looking down at the bills.

He turned around to face her and tried to conceal his reaction. "What?"

"They're teenagers, honey. They are going to Salem with their friends. They'll be home before 11 P.M. There is no school the next day and I will pick them up myself."

Yassin looked worried but said nothing and turned back to the fridge.

"What's the problem?" she asked.

"Nothing, there are a lot of weirdo's that go there. That's all" He took a package of lunchmeat from the fridge and examined it. "I would feel better if they stayed home."

"They'll be fine. We brought them up to know who to stay away from. They're good girls and have been looking forward to this," she protested. She stood up and walked over to the fridge. "What's a matter with you lately? You look so worried and stressed."

"I don't know; business I guess"

"Listen," she said with a smile on her face and putting her arms around him. "The girls won't be home for a few hours. Why don't we go upstairs so I can relieve some of that stress you have?"

He looked at her and smiled. She grabbed his hand and led him upstairs. As he climbed the stairs, he could only think that this might be the last time he got laid.

Lafayette St, Salem, MA

Steven Mears usually left work before 5 P.M. His employer was very flexible so when he needed time off to take care of something, his supervisor did not question him. He was, however, expected to make up the time somewhere. He decided he would stay late tonight since there were no plans for the evening. He needed to strip and wax the entrance hall and since it was late in the evening foot traffic was light. He had completed half the task, when a tenant came downstairs to complain about the loud TV coming from room # 705. She said it had been loud all last night and today.

"Why didn't you call the police?" He asked her.

"Because I don't want to be a rat," she said in her smart, ghetto way.

"I'll see what I can do."

She turned around and headed to the exit door. He stopped and watched the dirty whore walk out the door. Her only attribute was her nice ass. Mears wanted to keep harmony in the building. All he would have to do was knock on the door and tell the tenant to lower the TV volume. Mears took the elevator to the seventh floor and took a left down the hall. He knew the tenant and never had any problems with him. Mears knew he had some issues, like everyone else in the building. He figured he would do the guy a favor by not calling the police.

He heard the TV, but didn't think it was that loud, and knocked on the door. No one answered. He saw the light on from underneath the door and knocked again. He had spoken to the tenant before, who told him to use the master key when the knocking was unanswered. Mears knocked again, then realized the door was unlocked. He turned the knob and opened the door, slowly knocking and calling the resident's name. He saw the light on in the bathroom to the left which it was empty.

Through the crack of the bedroom door he saw the front of the bed. He walked closer and then saw the feet.

"Mitchell?" he called out.

When he moved around the corner of the wall, he knew the man was dead. Mitchell's mouth was wide open, his eyes open, he was lying on the bed, looking up at the ceiling.

"Oh my God!" Mears said and reached for his cell phone. He had the Salem Police number on speed dial due to the clientele of the building.

The dispatcher picked up on the second ring. "Salem Police this is a recorded line. What is your emergency?"

"This is Steven Mears and I am the maintenance man at 117 Lafayette St. There is a man in room #705 that appears to be dead," he said calmly. Mears had come upon a few dead bodies before in his role as building maintenance. He answered the questions the dispatcher had asked him. "Okay, I will be waiting outside the room," he said and ended the call.

As he headed to the door, he realized that he would be here a lot longer than he thought and the floor would not get waxed. He knew the police and fire department had the key for the front door, so he stayed right where he was.

Approximately three minutes later, Police, Fire, and the Ambulance crews arrived. Everyone on the scene knew Mitchell was dead, but it was not official until the emergency medical technician stated so. Officer Blake responded and took the names of everyone who had entered the apartment for the crime scene login sheet. The sergeant arrived three minutes after him. He spoke to Blake and looked around, the he called for a detective to arrive. It was obvious from the paraphernalia that it was an overdose. Blake knew Mitchell who escaped from the drug buy the night before.

"This is the guy who ran from us last night, after he bought the heroin," Blake said while looking at the body.

The sergeant stood with his hands on his hips, also looking at the body. "That was your arrest, wasn't it?"

"Yeah, but he escaped in the chaos. Too bad, he would be alive today."

"This is the path he chose."

Two detectives arrived a short time later. Blake explained what he saw when he arrived, who called it in, and what had happened the previous night. They had a camera case, and a few other items that would be used to process the crime scene.

As they started the process, Blake, looked around a bit. On the dresser were several pictures. In one photo Mitchell was standing with a nice-looking brunette and two small kids. They were all smiling, and it looked like they were in Florida or in the Caribbean somewhere. There were single shots of the children, professional type photos. There was another photo of him and the brunette who must have been his wife.

Blake picked up a lanyard that had a badge on it. It was a badge which had Mitchell's picture, name, and a number. Blake recognized it as a vendor badge for the Halloween festivities.

Blake picked it up and showed the sergeant. "What was he going to sell, dope?"

After the sergeant looked at it, he handed it to Detective Hallas. The other detective took out his Blackberry and dialed a number. He spoke for a while answering the questions and hung up.

He spoke to Detective Hallas, "45 minutes."

Massachusetts State law required all municipal police departments, except for three, to contact their respective district attorney's office in investigating a homicide or suspicious deaths. Drug overdose certainly fell into that category. It would be at least 45 minutes until the troopers from the CPAC unit, crime prevention and control, unit arrived.

"You're all set, right?" The Sergeant asked, wanting to leave.

Blake answered, "Yeah. I'll leave when the body goes or when they tell me."

Blake was stuck in the small apartment for at least two hours if not three, until either the Coroner arrived or the Funeral Home.

Chapter 31

The Waiting Game

Saturday October 31th

Halloween Night

Salem Police Department, Salem, MA 4 P.M.

The auditorium was located on the second floor of the Salem Police Department at 95 Margin Street. It was well maintained and looked new. The chairs were comfortable and had desktops for writing that were folded on the side of each seat. The seat rows were in a lecture hall that rose to a room on the top level, which was for sound and electronic controls. The Chief considered the auditorium the showpiece of the "new" police station. The building was 11 years old but was still considered new in the police world. Besides being used for training and other police functions it was used by other city agencies to accommodate large meetings. The local ambulance company, District Attorney's Office, and State Sex Offender Registry used it as well.

Chief Hampton had never seen it this full of people, with only standing room available. The captain had told him that the only people attending would be sergeants and higher ranks of the patrol sectors, downtown units and response units. That was not to say they did not want everyone there, but there was only so much room. The brief started at precisely 4 P.M. and packets were passed out to all officers in attendance.

"Before we get started, I would like to introduce Chief Charles Hampton," Captain Sutton said.

Hampton who was standing close by approached the podium. "Thank you for all coming. Usually, this is a lot lighter hearted, but based on information attained, that will not be the case." He scanned the crowd, making sure he had gained their attention. "Before we proceed, I want to personally thank you for assisting us tonight to keep the citizens of this city safe and working with the officers of the Salem Police Department."

He looked over to the corner of the room where the Mayor stood, dressed in casual clothes and looking extremely serious. The chief continued his motivational speech and then passed the floor to Captain Sutton who oversaw the event.

He placed the packet on the podium, "The packet you have outlines the chain of command, sectors, frequencies, transportation, and all pertinent information pertaining to tonight. You might want to take notes on what we are going to tell you. This information is for Law Enforcement Personnel only and will not be given to anyone else based on the sensitive nature. What I am going to tell you is not in the packet, because it has not been substantiated, and it could cause panic and chaos." He looked at the Lieutenant who stood against the wall on the wide stairs. "This is Detective Lieutenant Alfoso Diaz from the Peabody Police Department's criminal bureau."

He stepped away from the podium to make room for the man. "Lieutenant."

Diaz brought the crowd up to speed on the prior events. After he finished, Detective Sergeant Turner took his place and told the crowd about the information he had personally discovered. Next, Captain Sutton took his place back at the podium and gave an assessment of the threat.

"We have no idea if this is real or not. We don't know where or when it could occur." Sutton said. "Best guess is between 9 P.M. and until we kick people out at 11 P.M. I believe if anything occurs, it will be sometime around the parade at 10 P.M. which will be starting at Fire Headquarters. All vehicles parked downtown after 6pm will be towed. All vendors and their vehicles will be checked several times throughout the night. Concrete trash cans have been removed. Porta-johns cannot be controlled as easily, but we will work on it. Save all questions, comments, or suggestions to the end please" he said.

There was a screen behind the captain, showing a map of the area divided into sectors.

"Essex County Sheriff's Department will have their tactical response team here." Sutton pointed to their area. "NEMLEC (North Eastern Massachusetts Law Enforcement Council) will have this area" and pointed to that. "If there is an incident in either of these areas, the other team will not respond immediately. We don't want to be drawn into one area, while the attack occurs in another. The other response team will be held in reserve until a determination can be made by the senior officer on scene."

"There will be a Salem Police marked van that will be a rolling armory. It will be located behind Central Fire. It will have shotguns, M4 Carbines, AR-15 rifles, MP5 and ammo cans loaded for each weapon. There is also 9mm ammo and 40 Caliber for pistols." He added. "No forms to fill out either" which drew a few chuckles.

"The vehicle will be manned and roll to where it is needed. It will not be responding to any calls or assisting anyone." He waited a second, "All supervisors, you are to inform all of your officers of everything that is discussed here before any officer hits the street. They are to report and act on anything suspicious immediately and using their chain of command if possible. We need to use or best judgment and not overreact or let the situation get out of hand." He looked around the room.

"Also, have brought another agency into the loop. Ladies and gentlemen, this is Special Agent Roger Montgomery, from the FBI's Boston Field Office. He will be with us tonight as well as another agent." Sutton stepped back and addressed the FBI agent. "Agent Montgomery you have the floor."

Montgomery went on to explain what his office had learned, their experience with these kinds of threats, possibility of an attack, and what group of people would cause it. He gave them his best estimate and possible means, which was a vehicle borne improvised explosive device. After the agent was finished speaking, Sutton opened the room for questions and suggestions.

After all questions were answered, Captain Sutton continued his speech. "Make sure the information is passed down to everyone who is assigned to you. Also tell them that this information is sensitive and for law enforcement to know about. We do not want to cause a panic"

The Captain stated from the podium at all the officers gathered around the room. He knew they were all looking at him for answers. He hoped like hell that none of them got hurt. He hoped for the best and planed for the worst.

TERROR IN THE WITCH CITY

"Well ladies and gentlemen," Sutton concluded, "that's it. Good luck, and we will see you out there. Hopefully this will all be done for nothing, but if not, we will be prepared for terror in the witch city."

He walked down the steps to the door where they were filing out. He stood next to the chief who was shaking hands with the men and women who were responsible for the crowd control of the estimated sixty thousand revelers that would descend on downtown Salem. Slowly, the chatter died out and the room was empty.

Sutton turned to his supervisor, "That's it boss, we're doing everything we can. Now we have to wait".

Hampton looked at him with concern and nodded.

"All right. I have to go talk with the guys."

"I'll be in my office, Dennis." Hampton turned to leave. "Oh yeah. One more thing, actually two. The mayor wants the water tower covered tonight because of the vandalism. He is putting on a good show for the voters by protecting the water supply. Also, I don't want Dawson downtown tonight. I can't afford him going off. You understand?"

"Yes, I do," he replied, "I'll have Brooks send him up there. How's that?"

"Good, I appreciate that," he said as he patted Sutton on the back, and he walked away.

Sutton left the auditorium and stopped at Brooks' office. They spoke for 15 minutes, then Sutton went back to his office. After Sutton left, Brooks grabbed the radio on his desk and keyed the mic. "Officer Dawson on the air?" Brooks asked.

"Go ahead Lieutenant," Dawson responded a minute later.

"Steve come to my office please."

"Received."

Officer Steven Dawson knocked on the door frame of the office.

"Steve, come on in and take a seat," Brooks said from behind his cluttered desk.

The walls were adorned with family photos, police memorabilia and diplomas, certificates and awards. Dawson sat in the comfortable leather seat and looked around the room. He knew this wasn't going to be a good conversation.

"Do you know what's going on tonight?" Lieutenant Brooks asked.

"Yes, I heard."

"It has been decided that instead of being assigned downtown, you will be reassigned to the water tank."

Dawson stared at him with the look of disgust. He was pissed.

"I am not going to blow smoke up your ass," Brooks said before Dawson could respond. "We all know what happened, and people feel that based on your past behavior that you might get carried away tonight."

"I know that order didn't come from you," Dawson said.

"It doesn't matter where it came from," Brooks propped his elbow on the desk and let his head rest on his fist. "Steve, we have known each other for years. While I would love to have you there in case things happen, let's face it, there have been a few incidents that should not have happened. They were going to fire you for them, remember?"

Dawson stared at him but didn't respond.

"You agreed to whatever the department deemed appropriate." Brooks tried to lighten the situation. "Enjoy the peace and quiet tonight. We don't know what you're going through, but we're not your enemy," he said sympathetically.

Dawson looked at him and shook his head.

"Take a cruiser and be there by 6 p.m. If anything happens and we need you, we will give you a call. If not, you can leave at midnight. If you want to stay after, I'll buy the beers." He stood up and walked around the desk. He put out his hand for a shake.

Dawson hesitated, but finally shook Brooks' hand. He rose to his feet and gave a sigh of defeat. Brooks walked him to the door.

"I have to go now," Brooks said, and he walked away.

Dawson went to the muster room and picked up a ring of keys. They were hanging on a nail under the number 29. He found vehicle #29 parked in the lot and checked to make sure the squad car worked, which was not always the case. He made sure the rifle was in the rack above his head. The AR-15 assault military rifle was secured in all marked patrol vehicles in a rack above the cage that separated the officer's compartment from the prisoner's area of the vehicle. The AR-15 guns had replaced the shotguns that used to be in the vehicles. He onto Jefferson Avenue and headed to his apartment to grab the items that he needed to make sure his long, boring duty was more bearable.

TERROR IN THE WITCH CITY

5 P.M.

Normally on Halloween night the sergeants and lieutenants of each sector would meet the officers assigned to them in their respective areas. Instructions and assignments were given, and then everyone would roll out to their posts. However, tonight was not normal. Instead, the bosses gathered everyone in and around the police station to discuss what was going on. The briefings took longer than usual due to all the questions and anticipated scenarios being played out. Then the response teams were also briefed. Finally, the officers were given time to gather their equipment and everything else they needed.

There was less chatter and humor than usual. Once the officers ensured they were prepared, they filed out of the building alone, in pairs, and in groups. Most of them couldn't help, but wonder if the Intel was reliable, hearsay, or just bullshit.

Highland Ave, Salem, MA 5:50 P.M.

Abdallah and Sawaya sat in the parking lot of the strip mall across from the hospital. Abdallah was in the passenger's seat and looked at his watch. Yassin had just left in his Mercedes. Yassin had tried to explain the ritual of Halloween and "Trick or Treat" to him earlier, but it fell on deaf ears. Yassin told him that the City had determined that a suitable and safe time for such activity was between 6 P.M. and 8 P.M.

They had discussed it and were reasonably sure that Blake would take his kids trick-or-treating no later than 6:30 P.M. if he was not working. Yassin had insisted that Blake's address be verified, even though he had obtained it through reliable means. He wanted to physically see Blake in the neighborhood. Abdallah reasoned that Yassin was the only one who could get away with being seen in the area.

He lived locally and therefore his presence wouldn't raise any suspicion. His role was to drive to the intersection of Gallows Hill Road and Witch Way. The car would stall and break down for at least 30 minutes, or until Blake was seen. Yassin had a good vantage point to see the house and ensure that Blake lived there. While Blake and his family were out, and it was dark, Abdallah would recon the back of the house to look for an escape route.

TERROR IN THE WITCH CITY

Yassin drove down the street nearing the intersection. He placed the 5-speed transmission in neutral and intentionally stalled the vehicle. He coasted down the road and steered the vehicle slightly on the curb. When the vehicle came to a halt, he banged on the dash for theatrical purposes, in case anyone was watching. He pushed the button to activate his flashers then popped the hood.

Colby St & Hillside Ave, Salem, MA 6 P.M.

Officer Dawson parked the dark blue and gray Salem Police car at the end of the trail that led from the corner. The road was more of a trail and used by city maintenance to service the water tank. The water tank was on the top ground of a large wooded area that connected two parks by a dozen or so trails. He grabbed his bag and folding chair then headed to the tank. Dawson unlocked the gate and moved his stuff inside. After he located a nice spot to watch the area, he exited, locked the gate behind him, and did a check of the area. It was now getting dark. He checked several of the paths and found no sign of life. After he was content, he unlocked the gate and let himself back in. He was still pissed off that he was yanked from the street to watch the water tank. It was impossible to access and tamper with the water supply. There was nothing he could do about it though. No one would come up here tonight, not with a police car on the road and a cop in the fence. He looked for a place to set up his portable DVD player and thought about which movie to watch first.

    *

Yassin was starting to get nervous that someone might call the police on him because he had been there for a half hour. He had his head under the hood again and was looking down the street when he finally saw a light go on in front of Blake's house. He could see an adult with two kids. Then another adult came out and put something down on the doorstep. It must be a bowl of candy to give out to the trick-or-treaters.

Even though he could not make out his face, Yassin knew it was Blake by the way he stood. Yassin was positive that he was looking at the same person he saw in the picture from Iraq, the same person he saw in the parade. He shut the hood and went back inside the car. He turned the key and the engine came to life. He shut off the hazard lights and looked at the clock, 6:22 P.M.

He grabbed his phone and dialed a number.

"He lives there." Yassin said in Arabic into the phone. "The house is empty. They all left. Give them 10-15 minutes. I am headed back."

He ended the call. His job was done, and they would handle the rest. Yassin still didn't like this, thinking about his own children, but he was finished now.

Salem Police Department, Salem, MA 6:45 P.M.

Captain William Ross sat in the conference room that had been turned into the emergency operations center. He was hoping nothing would happen tonight since it was his last Halloween before he retired. He was just counting the days until the spring when he would hit the 32-year mark. He so looked forward to retiring down south in the Carolina's fishing whenever he wanted, instead of dealing with this shit. He knew he would be downtown later with the boss.

Tonight, there were additional dispatchers brought in to man the control room downstairs and the emergency operations center. The procedure for the night was different than usual. When a call came in that required police, fire or medical services downtown, the dispatcher would transfer the call upstairs or relay the information. The Emergency Operations Center would gather the data then forward it to a mobile command post that was parked on Lafayette Street by Fire Headquarters.

There was adequate staff to ensure the process ran smoothly. Ross was tasked with calling in everyone who was not working, which were only three officers. The other police departments were calling their own officers to request more help. Two, of the three officers were on vacation and the third was given the night off.

Those officers who wanted to take Halloween night off, so they could take their kids trick or treating were forced to take an entire rotation off. Ross found Blake's name in the computer and called his cell number first. He left a message and then dialed the home number.

The machine picked up. "Blake this is Captain Ross. Call the station immediately and ask for me." Ross hung up.

*

Sawaya dropped Abdallah off at the corner and drove out of sight. Abdallah walked to the house with a flashlight in his hand. While under normal circumstances that would be crazy, tonight it was normal. There were many adults with flashlights walking around with their children. If he needed the flashlight in the back of the house, he could use it. If someone questioned him, he could say his kid ran off and he was looking for him.

As Abdallah walked to the house, a group of kids were grabbing something out of a bucket, and then leaving the front steps. *What a bizarre ritual,* he thought as he walked in the shadows of the house. The back of the house was secluded with a hill and tower in the back.

Abdallah saw the wooden deck and the sliding glass door. He climbed the three steps. His only goal was to get a visual of the back. He was peeking into the dark house when the phone rang in the house. He froze in place. He counted five rings before it went to an answering machine. He was leaning against the door and pushed on the handle. He was surprised when he felt no tension and the door slid to the left.

Since this was not expected, he wasn't sure what to do at first. Did they have an alarm? Was there a dog? Was there a camera? He waited and listened after he opened the door, so far, no dog. He needed to make sure he kept this sneaking as short as possible and moved nothing out of place. He stepped in and shut the door behind himself. He moved slowly and tried to get a feel for the layout. He moved through the kitchen, and then into a room with kid's toys scattered about.

The street lamp shinned light through the window and the light that lit the front steps. Abdallah stopped at the staircase by the front door. He thought about going upstairs but could not risk it. He felt like he had spent too much time in the house already and needed to leave. He continued through what seemed to be the living room and back into the kitchen. He was headed toward the slider on the other side of the kitchen table when he heard a voice and froze.

"Control to Salem 23."

He looked around the empty room. He waited, afraid to make noise by moving.

"23 is on Highland Ave."

Abdallah finally saw a small light on the table.

The radio seemed very loud in the quiet house. Abdallah walked toward the radio. He saw a black Motorola Radio with "Salem Police" in white letters. There was a mic attached to a cord that must be used to fasten to a uniform shirt. He smiled and picked up the radio.

"Shoplifter at Wal-Mart in the security office, 450 Highland Ave."

The radio had two knobs. One of the knobs had numbers and the other one was blank. There was a small window on the side that he could make out.

"23 copies."

He tried the first knob slowly turning it counterclockwise until it clicked. *Hopefully, that was the power* he thought. He waited a few minutes for the radio to make noise. Since it had stayed silent, he stuffed it into the left pocket of his jacket. It didn't completely fit, but he would do his best to conceal it. He did not intend to take anything, but a police radio was too valuable to resist. Now he could monitor their response.

He made his way to the slider and went out into the cold October air. He took out his cell phone and pressed the number from speed dial and waited.

"Come get me, same place in three minutes," he said in Arabic then ended the call.

He placed the phone in his pocket, and went around the side of the house the same way he came in. He peeked around the tall bushes and saw some kids ringing the doorbell of a house on the other side of the cul-de-sac. He moved out across the lawn then onto the sidewalk. He walked at a normal pace while heading to the rendezvous point.

*

About 150 paces ahead and across the street, Erin Blake rang the doorbell of the white house.
The elderly woman who opened the door had the bowl of candy ready "Trick or Treat!"

"Oh, she's so cute," Mrs. Pelletier said as she held a few candy bars out toward the kids.

"Look at him," she said then stepped out onto the front step.

"Look at his outfit," she said, moving closer to Breyden who was in his mother's arms.

She chatted with Blake and Kerry for a few minutes as a group of parents and kids made their way up and down the street. Mrs. Pelletier knew Kevin had been away and made it a point to check on Kerry and the kids from time to time. She brought dinner over a few times and watched the kids for a few hours periodically, so Kerry could take a mental break. Both Kevin and Kerry considered Mr. and Mrs. Pelletier as grandparents even though they already had their own.

They said goodnight and went down the stairs to the next house. Their goal was to travel up one side of the street, cross over, then travel back down the other side, and back home. Kerry loved Halloween but couldn't wait to get back home and put her feet up.

*

Abdallah could see the family of four across the street and realized it was Blake's. He tried not to make eye contact, even though it was dark out, and they were 30 feet apart. He was experienced in these close contacts with his targets and had learned to relax a bit. He considered himself skilled and had operated in foreign countries and out of his element on occasion, and against far better adversaries then an American police officer. Abdallah was not too concerned about Blake nor the people he was encountering on the sidewalk but was still careful.

He passed a woman with two small kids who was too wrapped in her cell phone conversation to notice him, but the kids had. These people were Blake's neighbors. All it took was some nosy neighbor to call police or get Blake's attention. Abdallah looked straight ahead and continued walking. *The police officer in him might know something wasn't right*, he thought. Blake probably hated Arabs because of his service in Iraq. Abdallah knew Blake had some rank in the Marine Corps, so he had some years of service and experience. He was also a cop in America, which meant he had dealt with violent criminals and lowlifes, and therefore had some street smarts and not an idiot.

*

Normally Blake would look around and be aware of his surroundings, but not tonight. He was in his comfort zone. He was with his wife and children whom he had missed so much while he was away. They were out in their neighborhood, visiting their friends. He foolishly had let his guard down and would never realize the full ramifications. He heard the teenagers scream as the couple down the street had scared the older kids at their door.

Erin ran ahead of them toward the commotion.

"Not too fast honey," Blake said. Wait for us."

Blake walked along with his wife holding a plastic orange pumpkin that belonged to his son.

*

Abdallah heard the shriek and looked over. He saw the girl running. *Keep moving*, he thought, *so your father doesn't look over*. He looked straight ahead as he walked, the corner was just ahead. Two teenagers were approaching him, one dressed like a pirate and the other he could not identify. They were laughing and swinging pillowcases that held candy. They gave him a look of curiosity and continued talking. Abdallah wondered if anyone dressed up like an Arab.

He would take a left and Sawaya should be waiting a few houses ahead on the right. *He had better be there*, he thought. Abdallah was going to drive after they left Salem. He wondered if he should have waited to tell Sawaya this. Abdallah figured that they had a few hours before their work began. Maybe they would stop to eat along the way. It would be a long night after all, and Sawaya's last meal.

*

Abdallah wondered what he should do about Yassin. He may still need Yassin to help himself escape, but he hadn't planned for that yet. He did not totally trust Tariq and would only use him as a last resort. Staying in the area was suicidal, and public transportation was not an option either. He knew he had to leave the country but couldn't risk flying out. He decided that he could hide in New York City for several days and then head to Mexico. While the Canadian Border was only five hours away, Canadian Customs would scrutinize him too much. They would be more than eager to turn him over to the United States.

The Mexicans didn't feel the need to kiss the Americans asses. In fact, it was just the opposite. He could cross the Mexican border without ever having to show any identification, and then he would be home free. Abdallah decided that he would have Yassin drive him to New York City after the mission was complete. Abdallah glanced over and saw Blake and his family at another door, begging for candy. He then saw Sawaya's car

263

come down the hill and approach the stop sign. *Hopefully, this idiot wouldn't stop to pick him up right there,* Abdallah thought. It was instances like that, which blew the best-laid plans. He watched the vehicle proceed straight ahead and breathed a sigh of relief as he rounded the corner.

*

Blake turned around by the front door and waited for his wife and kids to go inside ahead of him. He was looking off to the right and saw the back of a man walking away and out of sight. Within a second the thought was out of his mind like nothing had happened.

*

Abdallah saw the vehicle on the right side of the street waiting. As he approached from the back, he saw the orange glow of the cigarette. *Enjoy your cigarette, there won't be many more he thought*. He walked around to the passenger side of the vehicle and opened the door.

7:10 P.M.

Yassin hopped in the back seat of the car that he had rented. He left his Mercedes in the parking lot of the Plaza on Route 107, which was located between the Blake's house and downtown Salem. They were headed to Cambridge to "take delivery of the package" as Abdallah had called it. They headed south to Boston. Abdallah told Yassin that they should stop to eat. Neither Yassin or Sawaya said anything.

Yassin had no appetite. Abdallah told them that he was starving, and they should enjoy their last meal together. Yassin had too much on his mind to think about eating. He thought about his daughter's going to Salem with their friends. He took comfort in the fact that they would be home when all hell broke loose.

Chapter 32

Trick or Treat

Saturday October 31st

Halloween Night

100 Gallows Hill Rd Salem, MA 7:45 P.M.

They were out a lot longer than Blake had anticipated, but he was in no rush. Neighbors and friends wanted to talk since they had not seen him in a while. Trick or treating would be over in 15 minutes. The kids were exhausted. Erin had a cloth bag that resembled a pumpkin which was half filled. Breyden's plastic pumpkin bucket was smaller and almost full of candy.

"You can have one piece of candy, then you'll have to brush your teeth," Kerry said to her Erin.

Blake was grabbing a glass from the cabinet when he saw the light blinking on the answering machine. He pressed the button.

"Blake this is Captain Ross. Call the station immediately and ask for me."

Blake looked up and saw his wife looking back at him.

"What's going on in our fair city, officer?" She smiled.

He reached for his cell phone then realized he didn't have it. *That explains not getting the call,* he thought. Blake saw the phone on the table, opened it and saw the missed call. He dialed his voice message and heard the same thing.

He dialed the work number, "Hey, this is Blake let me talk to Captain Ross," he said.

"You know what's going on?" The dispatcher said.

"No, but I was told to call the Captain."

"There's info that someone might set off a bomb downtown" The dispatcher said quietly.

"No shit, huh!" Blake replied.

"Ya, Well I'll let Ross tell you that," then the phone was on hold.

"Kevin, we need you to come in right away," Ross said.

"All right Captain. I need to change and will be there in 20 minutes," Blake then hung up after the Captain finished.

"What's going on?" Kerry asked, as the kids watched television.

Breyden was sitting on the floor with his sippy cup while Erin ate candy next to him. Charlie Brown's Halloween Special was on and the children were mesmerized. Blake knew Erin wouldn't be paying attention to the adult's conversation.

"They have some information that someone might try to set off a bomb in downtown tonight" he said.

"Oh, my God!" Kerry said in a low voice.

"Yeah, crazy, huh. I have to go in babe, duty calls. The Chief said if there was an emergency, he would call me in, I guess he wasn't joking."

"Please be careful!" she said and hugged him.

"Of course, baby. Don't worry, probably bullshit, it usually is." He kissed her.

He knew there might be some truth to it because of what Cedano had said about the Arab. Blake didn't mention it because he didn't want to upset her. He pulled back from her embrace and put a smile on his face.

"In a few hours I will be home. Maybe you should wait up in your costume," he said smiling.

"Which costume would that be?" Kerry smiled.

"The naughty wife one," he said with a smirk.

"Oh! That one. I'm pretty sure I can find that." She moved closer and kissed him passionately on the lips.

"I better go change," Kevin said and turned to the stairs.

Ten minutes later he came down the stairs in uniform. He kissed the kids' goodnight then stopped by the table and looked around.

"Did you see my radio? I thought I left it here?"

"No," she said picking up the baby.

"Probably left it at work," he said and kissed them both on the forehead.

"Goodnight Honey."

"Goodnight Daddy," Erin said and ran over to give him a kiss and hug.

He went out the front door and reached down to grab a piece of candy from the bucket on the front steps.

Salem Police Department Salem, MA 8:10 P.M.

Blake entered the conference room and saw Captain Ross scribbling some notes on a lined yellow legal pad of paper. The gray-haired man looked tired and frustrated, Blake thought. Blake knocked lightly on the doorframe.

"Hey Captain, I have to borrow a radio. I lost mine somewhere and don't have to time to look right now."

"No problem get one in the detail office then go see Lieutenant Brooks. He will tell you what is going on and where he needs you."

"Yes, Sir," Blake said and turned around leaving the chaos of the room.

"The pulse of Halloween" as someone referred to it.

Blake found Lieutenant Brooks in his office.

"I am here Lieutenant; Can I ask what's going on and where you need me?"

"There has been info to the detectives that someone might set a bomb off downtown. I didn't go to the meeting because I am stuck in here. Report to Lieutenant Hayes at Fire headquarters and he knows more than I. Sorry to drag you here. I know you had the night off, but this is unavoidable."

"No problem. I understand," he replied.

His only wish now was to go home to his wife.

Somerville, MA. 8:20 P.M.

When the vehicle pulled in front of the warehouse at 20 Horace Street, the car reeked of cigarette smoke. Abdallah, Yassin, and Sawaya agreed it was too cold outside and didn't want to put the windows down to air out the interior. They found a restaurant along the divided highway in Revere. They dined on steak and lobster. They ordered coffee to finish off the meal. Abdallah thought about alcohol, but he didn't want to cloud his judgment on a night so important. It certainly wasn't because of the religious implications nor did he care about offending the others.

Abdallah paid for the meal in cash and left a generous tip for the waiter. As soon as Sawaya was behind the wheel he took out a cigarette and lit up. He started the car and left the parking lot and headed for Cambridge. After a few minutes Abdallah produced a cigar and clipped the end with his teeth before taking a lighter to it. Feeling left out, Yassin reached over the seat for the pack and fired one up himself. It took 20 minutes to get to their destination thanks to light traffic. *The infidels were busy having their children beg for candy,* Abdallah thought.

Once they were outside of the building, Abdallah called the number and told Tariq they were waiting. He hung up abruptly. The door opened a few minutes later, "Good evening, gentlemen." Tariq said with a smile and held the door open.

After they were inside, he shut the door and engaged the 2-inch deadbolt. He knew no one was getting in that door easily, battering ram or not. "Please this way," he said and led them to the garage where the limo was parked.

The men looked at the gun in its holster attached to Tariq's waist. Yassin could see the license plate that he stole attached to the rear bumper.

"The vehicle will have devastating effects," Tariq said to Abdallah and walked toward the car.

The three stood to the side as he walked and opened the doors on the left side.

"I didn't put anything in front with the driver in case you are stopped by the police." Tariq said. "If you are stopped and they ask to search the vehicle, refuse and say nothing further. They will either let you go, or they will call for assistance. If they have you wait, kill them before backup arrives, and then leave."

"What if they look in the back with their flashlights?" Yassin asked.

"The tint is too dark, either they will give you a ticket or ask you to search the vehicle, and you know what to do." Tariq stated. "Obey the speed limit and all traffic laws, and there will be no problem."

He went to the back of the limo. "Take a look," he said to Abdallah, nodding his head like he was showing off a prize he had won.

TERROR IN THE WITCH CITY

Abdallah moved around the door and looked at all the tanks and plastic containers that held the ingredients. The rear compartment was packed and had a toxic smell. "Impressive," Abdallah said and nodded his approval.

"Yes, my crew did a great job in collecting what they needed. The chemistry professors at MIT would be proud of their student. If they only knew of course." Tariq said with a smile.

Yassin looked after Abdallah moved out of the way. Sawaya just stood there, silently watching. Tariq shut the rear door and went to the front door opening it. He reached on the dash and grabbed the set of keys. He held up the keys that had a key fob attached.

"This is the detonator switch." Tariq said. "It looks like any other key alarm, and no one would ever question it. It's simple; press any button and boom. If the police stop you and you are removed from the vehicle, do what you are told. They usually take the keys out and put them on the roof of the car. Break free, press the button, and at least one infidel dies. Understand?"

Abdallah and Yassin nodded in agreement. Sawaya only looked at him. Tariq didn't address Sawaya's blank stare. *Probably shock,* he assumed.

"That's it." Tariq said. "Do you need another gun or ammunition?"

"Let me think about it," Abdallah replied.

"When are you leaving?"

"We need to be there at 9:45 P.M. I figure 30 minutes to get there," Yassin answered.

"It's Halloween in Salem." Tariq rolled his eyes. "I would leave here at nine, the very latest. You can always park close by if you are too early."

"30 minutes then we leave," Abdallah said. He looked at his watch, then at Sawaya. "Are you ready my brother?"

"We should pray for Allah's blessing before," Sawaya said.

"Yes, that's an excellent idea." Tariq said. "You still have time. There is a clean space upstairs."

"Very well," Abdallah said hesitantly, but followed Tariq upstairs.

20 minutes later the four men walked back downstairs to the greasy, dirty garage lit by fluorescent lights. Tariq touched the shoulder of Abdallah who was ahead of him on the stairs.

"Can I talk to you in private?" Tariq asked.

"Yes," Abdallah replied and headed back upstairs and out of sight of the other two.

Tariq reached in his pocket and produced a key fob like the one on the limo key ring.

"What is that?" Abdallah asked.

"In case your man gets scared and refuses to go through with the task. You can take care of it yourself."

"An override?" Abdallah was surprised.

"Yes, you need to be close to the Limo for it to work." Tariq handed him the device.

Abdallah looked at him for a minute, "How close?"

"I have been told up to 30 feet." He pointed downstairs. "They don't know about this unless you tell them."

"That will not happen," Abdallah said. "Thank you. I expect he will not go through with this, but now I don't have to worry. Did you receive your payment?"

"Yes. It was very generous," Tariq said graciously.

"I will inform my associates of your impressive work. Hopefully they will reward you with further business." Abdallah said.

"My reward is assisting Allah in riding the world of the non-believers," Tariq said arrogantly.

Yeah right, and the check that is clearing, Abdallah thought.

Chapter 33

Showtime

Saturday October 31st

Halloween Night

20 Horace St Somerville, MA 8:55 P.M.

Abdallah and Tariq appeared by the limo while the other two men looked around the shop. Abdallah, who had hatched this plan, was pleased that it was almost complete. The fruits of his work appeared to be paying off.

Abdallah approached Sawaya and said, "It is time. Are you ready to avenge the death of your son and rejoin him in paradise with Allah?"

"No!" He looked Abdallah in the eye.

Yassin and Tariq stopped walking around.

"What!" Abdallah said, and got in Sawaya's face.

"You heard me. I will not kill innocent people for you or your warped cause."

Abdallah was stunned.

Sawaya didn't back down. He spoke loudly. "The Quran forbids what you believe are Allah's wishes. You preach and have never even looked at the holy book!"

Abdallah reached in his waistband and withdrew his 9mm Beretta and put the barrel to Sawaya's forehead.

Abdallah's teeth were clenched, and he spoke slowly. "You will drive that car to Salem or die right here and now. I will make sure your wife is beaten to death after she is raped repeatedly!"

Sawaya could smell the foul odor of the cigar on Abdallah's breath and feel the spray of his mouth as he yelled. The other men watched with their mouths open. No one moved, and it was so silent that they could hear the clock on the wall ticking away the moments.

TERROR IN THE WITCH CITY

"You cannot touch her." Sawaya rose his head higher as he spoke. "She left days ago, when I called home. You will never get away with this. They will find you and kill you. You call them Satan, but you are Satan." He took a step toward Abdallah. "You are the coward who kills innocent people and hides behind Allah and-"

Sawaya's sentence was cut off by the deafening sound of the round. Sawaya's head exploded. The bullet entered through his forehead above the bridge of his nose and spiraled through his brain. The force blew out the upper back of his head, all within less than a second. Blood, bone fragment and brain matter had sprayed against a black metal cabinet and the wall behind him. His upper torso fell back as his knees went forward. The back side of his head was almost nonexistent.

The gunshot was deafening in the garage and all their ears were ringing. Tariq and Yassin jumped when the gun went off. Abdallah turned toward them as the body fell into a pile. He lowered the gun. He opened his mouth, about to say something, but stopped and looked down at the floor for a few minutes.

Abdallah stood there thinking that this whole operation was for Sawaya. Abdallah was going through with this no matter what, he had no choice. He was approached by a member of Hezbollah to complete a mission. He was expected to carry it out no matter what occurred to Sawaya. He was also assisted by a member of Al Qaeda as well as associates of Bin Laden. Abdallah knew he would be killed if the execution of the infidel and his family was not completed.

Abdallah looked up and spoke calmly to Tariq. "Do you have anything to wrap the body in?"

It was almost a minute before he responded. "Let me check." Tariq walked to the storage area on the other side of the garage.

Yassin looked at Abdallah then looked at the gun in his hands. Abdallah saw him watching him, and their eyes finally met.

Abdallah asked, "Do you feel the same way?"

Nearly 10 seconds passed. "No."

"Good," Abdallah said then placed the gun back in the waistband of his pants.

Five minutes later, Tariq came back with a blue tarp. "This is the best I could find," he said. He had never witnessed anything like this before. "Where do we get rid of the body?" Tariq said. It was evident that he was shaken up.

Abdallah looked at him then past him to the vehicle, "In the trunk. That way you don't have to deal with the body."

Tariq looked at Yassin and said, "Give me a hand." Yassin nodded, and Tariq added, "Wait. I have a box of gloves."

Tariq went to a workbench with a toolbox on top and grabbed a handful of disposable gloves. The three men put on their gloves and laid out the tarp by the body. Yassin grabbed his feet while Abdallah bent down and grabbed the right arm. They struggled a bit, but eventually moved the body on to the tarp. Tariq folded one side of the tarp and stepped over the corpse to fold the other side.

"Just dump the body in the trunk." Abdallah said like he was talking about taking out the trash. "The explosion will take care of the rest."

Tariq retrieved the keys from the dash and opened the spacious trunk. He was going to use the trunk area for more chemicals but was advised against it by the chemist. *Now there's enough room for a headless body,* Tariq thought. The three men bent down and hoisted the body up. They moved it to the back of the vehicle and lifted it up over the lip and into the trunk. The weight of his body made a thud and the vehicle dipped a bit. They stood and stared at the lifeless body.

"Take off your gloves like this," he said and demonstrated. "Put them in with him."

The three men threw their gloves on top of the body. Tariq shut the trunk and shook his head in disbelief. *What the fuck just happened*, he thought to himself. He had never watched someone shoot anyone close like that. Tariq had been responsible for several deaths, but never carried out any himself. He never even witnessed them. He never considered himself a killer, but realized he was no different from Abdallah now.

Tariq turned to Abdallah and said, "You have to go, its 9 P.M."

He didn't care if he offended Abdallah anymore.

Abdallah looked at him, then turned to Yassin, "You will be driving."

Yassin looked at him and nodded but didn't say a word.

TERROR IN THE WITCH CITY

"Let me make sure no one is outside in the driveway." Tariq said. "I will open the garage door, so you can leave."

Yassin went to the driver's door. While he opened it, he heard Abdallah address him.

"I will follow you to Salem. I will call you with further instruction, Allah-ahckbar"

Yassin did not reply. He turned his head and looked back at Tariq, then turned around and took his place behind the wheel of the vehicle. Tariq disappeared, leaving Abdallah alone outside the car. Yassin nor Abdallah spoke as they waited for Tariq to return.

Tariq came back and said, "Okay, it's clear. Please go now so no one will see you leaving." He went to the garage door and hit the button, the garage door hummed as it raised to the ceiling.

Tariq went over to Abdallah and said, "Good luck my brother. I will watch the news." He embraced Abdallah and said, "Allah-ackbar!"

Abdallah nodded in acceptance of the blessing. "Thank you for your help," he said and hesitated for a few seconds. "Pray for him. He was haunted by his son's death."

Tariq was a surprised by the statement. He nodded then said, "I will."

Abdallah walked out the door as the limo backed out into the night. He watched the headlights disappear as the vehicle moved around the corner. He went back to the door switch and pressed the close button. The chain engaged, and the door started to lower towards the ground.

Essex St Salem, MA 9:00 P.M.

"If anything happens Jacob, it is going to be between now and 11 p.m. when we kick out everyone." Chief Hampton said. "We suspect it will be sometime during the parade."

They strolled over the cobblestones, that were on the walking mall. The area was packed with people walking around. Some were dressed in elaborate costumes and other were dressed for the cold. The smells of sausage sizzling on the grill swirled in the air along with fried dough and other foods. The vendors were doing a brisk business with long lines of cash only customers.

TERROR IN THE WITCH CITY

Ross who was in plain clothes, walked with a staffer from the mayor's office. They were several feet behind their bosses. They took a left by the empty water fountain, passing the old Daniel Low Building, then walked down Washington Street. There was a sea of people ahead of them and headlights that went on forever. Traffic that usually came up Washington was diverted to Norman Street to accommodate the throngs of visitors. Four lanes were forced into one.

Traffic was complete gridlock. The mayor and chief were greeted along their way by business owners and residents. They stopped occasionally, more out of courtesy than wanting. They eventually made their way to a parking lot that was blocked off. Two officers were standing there making sure no one moved the blue wooden horses at the entrance.

"Evening Chief, Mr. Mayor," Blake said as they approached.

"Kevin," Hampton said smiling and put his hand out. He shook Blake's hand then turned to Michael to shake his.

Hampton made introductions. "Mayor Parker, these are Officers Kevin Blake and Michael Craig. Kevin was the officer in Iraq."

"I remember," the mayor said. "Nice to have you home safe and sound. Thank you for your service," he said, shaking hands and smiling dutifully.

"Thank you, Mayor," Blake said shyly.

"Nice to meet you," Parker said to Craig and shook his hand.

"Nice to meet you. Mayor Parker," he replied.

Hampton spoke to Blake, "Sorry to have to pull you from your night off, but we might need you."

"I understand."

They spoke for a few minutes about the crowd and what was going on tonight.

"Mayor if you are ready." Hampton said, "these officers have jobs to do."

"Yes, we should go. Gentlemen it was nice meeting you both," he said to the walked away with Hampton.

"You're kissing ass again, huh?" Craig said.

"If I was, I would be a detective by now." he replied.

TERROR IN THE WITCH CITY

Route 1A, East Boston, MA 9:15 P.M.

The telephone rang, again and again. Yassin looked at the number. He pressed the button, "Yes."

"Follow the signs into Salem, you know the way. You drove us all around," Abdallah said.

"Yes, I do."

"One more thing, in case you change your mind. I have a detonator myself. Tariq gave it to me before we left. If you don't go where you are told or if you deviate from the plan, I will blow up the car. If you run from the vehicle, your family will be killed, understand?"

"I do." Yassin said then hung up.

Yassin had thought about bailing from the car but decided to wait until he got to Salem. Things were falling apart. Sawaya was dead, and Abdallah had no more help. Yassin only thought of his girls now. He looked at his cell phone and called his house.

"Hello?" Sarah answered.

"Where are the girls?"

"Where are you?"

"I can't tell you just yet, it is a long story!" Yassin yelled, "Where the fuck are the girls!"

"In Salem." Sarah answered quietly. "What's the matter?"

"Get a hold of them, now. You need to find them, pick them up and get them out of there."

"Why, what is going on?" She sounded scared.

"Listen, get a hold of them now and get them out of Salem. Immediately, do you understand? Please don't argue with me. Call me after you speak to them." He ended the call.

100 Gallows Gill Rd Salem, MA

At the same time, the cordless phone that was on the table rang. Kerry looked at the number of the incoming call. She smiled pressed the button.

"Are you coming home soon so I can be naughty?" Kerry said in her sexiest voice.

Blake hesitated before he answered. "Not yet, How's everything?"

She sensed the seriousness in his voice. "What's a matter?"

"Nothing, just making sure everything is fine," He said trying to change his tone.

"Shouldn't it be?"

"Yes honey, just making sure. Everyone is on edge here including myself and I worry about you and the kids."

"Don't worry. We survived without you all those months. Do your job, then come home, no heroics. If I am asleep wake me up anyway you want."

"Yes ma'am," he replied. "Goodnight, honey."

"Goodnight, love you."

"Love you too."

"Aww," Blake heard from behind him. "Love you too baby" Craig said, "You're so pussy whipped."

"Fuck you, you're just jealous," Blake said.

Route 1A Revere, MA 9:25 P.M.

Yassin answered the phone on the first ring. "Yes."

"I cannot get a hold of them," Sarah said frantically.

"Try again," he demanded.

"I have several times, should I go down there?"

"When were they going to leave?"

"After the parade," she said.

Yassin felt sick too his stomach. He spoke as calmly as he could. "Go to Salem and keep trying to reach them. When you find them, call me immediately!"

"Is everything all right?" She was crying now.

"No, no it is not!" Yassin hung up.

He was in Revere and about to cross the bridge into Lynn. He had lost track of everything. The ride was a blur, and he desperately wanted a cigarette. He drove down the Lynn-way with a million thoughts racing through his head. It was not even five minutes before his phone rang again. He saw the number and his heart rate quickened.

"Yes."

"I can't get a hold of them. I am on my way there." Sarah asked, "What should I do when I get there?"

"Keep trying to get through. Head to the parade area and try to find them before it starts."

"What have you done?" Sarah was crying again.

"Nothing, I have done nothing. Call me as soon as you contact them," Yassin said then ended the call.

Yassin drove for another 20 minutes until he got close to downtown Salem. Traffic had come to a dead stop on Canal Street. He tried calling his wife several times along the way, but it went to voicemail. He had made the decision a few days ago that he was not going to go through with this even before he found out his daughters would be in the target area. He was ready to attack the infidels when he first came to this country, but so much had changed. They were just people like him trying to raise their kids and live a good life. He wasn't going to be a suicide bomber.

Did Abdallah really have a remote? Who was going to help him track down his family? Would Tariq help him out now? Probably not now. Yassin would have to wait to see how things worked out once he was in position.

His cell phone rang in his hand. "Yes," he answered flatly.

"You don't sound happy?" Abdallah said with pleasure in his voice.

"What do you want?"

"Where are you supposed to meet the woman?"

"She told me to go to a parking lot on Washington Street by New Derby, where the parade begins. The police will let me in, and she will meet me there. What will you do?" Yassin asked him.

"I will watch and wait and strike when the time is right," he said with enthusiasm.

Yassin said nothing then ended the call. He thought about where Abdallah was going to park. The police weren't going to allow him through. If he did have a remote how far will it reach? Could he catch up to him on foot before he surrendered? Abdallah hadn't thought of that had he?

Yassin tried to call his wife again but had no luck. *Where are they,* he thought as he hung up? He looked at the clock as the vehicle crawled up to the flashing lights at the intersection.

Salem, MA 9:55 P.M.

Yassin grabbed the phone and scanned through the numbers dialed. He found the one he was looking for and pressed send. He waited until her heard the woman's voice.

"Hello, this is Lauren Amato. How can I help you?"

"Hello this is Mr. Goldman. How are you tonight?" He spoke calmly and politely. "Excellent," he said after he listened to her. "I am stuck in traffic by a garage and pizza shop on the corner of Canal and, I believe, Washington Street."

He waited for Amato to reply. "If it will not be problem then please go ahead. We are in an older model limousine. Tell the officer I will flash my headlights when I see him, so we don't waste any more time."

He waited for her to respond. "I will see you soon then," Yassin said, then hung up the phone.

He now realized that if he could separate himself from Abdallah, then he could warn the police. He was pretty sure that Abdallah would never get to his family. He would tell the police everything, so Abdallah would be taken down. Yassin kept thinking about his daughters, who might forgive him one day.

He dialed Abdallah's number. "I just spoke to the woman. She is sending a police officer to guide me to the staging area."

"How about me?" Abdallah asked.

"I don't know. Find a place to park. I can't tell them you're with me."

Abdallah paused for a minute, "Yes, you are correct. I should have thought about that."

"Just find a place to park," Yassin said.

Yassin knew that there was no place to park. He felt a little relieved by the change of events. Perhaps Abdallah would be too far away to detonate the bomb.

"Let me know when the parade begins and when you are in the crowd." Abdallah said.

"Of course," Yassin said and hung up, smiling.

*

Mrs. Amato approached Lieutenant Hayes who was in front of Central Fire Headquarters. She watched as he scanned the massive crowd and realized she knew him. They had run into each other as part of their jobs and in social circles and therefore, had known each other for years.

"Hi Bill," She smiled.

"Hi. How are you?" They continued talking for a several minutes.

"Bill is there any way one of your officers could bring in a limo that is struck in traffic on Canal Street by the pizza shop?"

"No problem Lauren," he told her as he looked at his watch. "It's almost 10 P.M. I have to stay here, but I have two officers watching the lot and assigned to the parade. At the staging area, go see Officer Blake, the tall guy, and Officer Craig. They are there to assist you until it's over."

"Good, okay then, I have to go, a movie star awaits," she said and walked off.

She walked down the street past the crowded bar and made her way to a parking lot. The lot had several vehicles ranging from a 1950's hot rod to a customized hearse. Both officers were talking to three girls who wore very revealing costumes. *Look at those girls dressed like whores flirting with the cops*, she thought. It was merely jealously though, and she knew it. 20 years ago, she could have pulled of that French maid outfit when she had the body. Two decades and three kids later, not so much. She still had the looks though, and a nice body. At least that's what her husband had been telling her. She wasn't exactly a m.i.l.f. she thought, but she did draw looks from both older and younger guys.

She walked up to the taller officer. "Are you Officer Blake?"

"Yes ma'am."

The girls looked at Amato; she guessed they were in college. The girls realized Amato's presence meant business. They wished the officers a safe night and giggled as they went on their way.

"I am Lauren Amato from tourism and cultural affairs?"

"Nice to meet you." Blake shook her hand. "You can call me Kevin, and this is Officer Craig."

"Michael," Craig said and shook her hand.

"Nice to meet you both." Amato tried to be nice instead of making demands; she didn't think they'd comply if they thought she was being a bitch. "Lieutenant Hayes sent me over. There is a limo waiting in traffic on the corner," she said pointing up the street.

"It is the last vehicle we are waiting for to start the parade. Is there any way one of you could bring it here?"

The officers looked up at the packed street.

"The driver will flash his lights when he sees you coming, so you know it's him," she added.

"I don't know if there is room," Blake said. "It's packed, but I'll try. Who is it?"

"It's a secret celebrity," she said smiling, proud that she was able keep a secret.

Blake sighed. "Hope they can follow directions."

"Once he flashes his lights, just guide him along." Amato insisted, "Don't waste your time talking to the driver."

"Okay." He walked toward the gridlock up ahead.

*

Lieutenant Hayes realized what he needed to make sure the parade went smoothly. He grabbed his radio and held the button down to call the EOC (Emergency Operations Center)

"Sector 3 to the EOC," Hayes said on the radio.

"EOC is on."

"Could the next available officer deliver a megaphone to Central Fire?"

"EOC has that."

A minute later Hayes heard, "Peabody Officer Silva to Lieutenant Hayes."

"Hayes is on."

"I will be leaving the station and bring that item to your position."

"Received, thanks," Hayes responded.

*

Blake moved through the stopped vehicles. *Total gridlock,* he thought. He wondered why these drivers had chosen this route despite what was going on. Were they from out of town or just ignorant? There were electronic boards at every major roadway warning drivers for the past few weeks. While the lane closest to the curb was not exactly free of vehicles, he knew he could move cars around to clear a path.

As Blake walked closer to the intersection, he saw the flash of the lights ahead. He was six or seven feet in front of the limo and motioned for it to move forward. The operator responded and the vehicle behind moved as well. Blake stopped the limo then went to the car behind making it clear to the driver that he was not to follow. Blake wondered who the big shot in the limo was. The vehicle wasn't new or even that nice, *kind of a piece of shit*, he thought. He continued to move the vehicle down the street.

Chapter 34

Right Thing

Saturday October 31st

Halloween Night

Salem, MA

Yassin had one hand on the wheel and was driving slowly behind the cop who was less than 10 feet away. He knew Abdallah was behind his car and watching. If he wanted to turn himself in, it would have to wait until he was out of sight. Yassin tried calling his wife again, but there was no response. He thought about the disaster that he helped to create. Was it his fault? His family's life was at stake, he reasoned. When he arrived in America, he was eager and willing to be the martyr, to wreak death and destruction on the infidels.

That seemed like a lifetime ago, before he fell in love and became a father. Now he needed to do the right thing. He would go to jail for a while, but he would still have his daughters alive and well. He would make the best deal he could with the FBI and tell them everything he knew. He knew a good attorney who was expensive, but effective.

The vehicle was not going any faster than 5 mph, but it was moving. He looked in the rearview mirror through the dark tinted rear window and he saw the lights of the rental car moving farther away.

*

"Testing 1,2,3 testing 1,2,3," Silva said into the red mega horn.

"You sound like a dork," Peabody Police Officer Theodore Dodek said.

"Fuck you. Are you always a smartass?"

"How long have you known?" Dodek smiled.

"Way too long."

"You're the good-looking Peabody catholic school boy, who's always followed the rules. You need a friend like me to keep you that way," Dodek said.

Silva looked at him then shook his head smiling.

They took their time strolling back downtown. They were in no rush to deal with the drunken assholes that they would encounter soon. They enjoyed the women that were wearing next to nothing though. The officers' only purpose in going back to the police Station was to use the bathroom in peace and to kill some time. Besides, it held the only clean and safe toilet they would find all night. They were on loan from a different police department known as the "away game". That meant they wouldn't get shit for going back to the station, unlike the Salem guys.

"Let's stop at Dunkin Donuts," Dodek asked.

"No, after we deliver this to the lieutenant."

"It's on the way. I'll run right in and you can wait outside, two minutes."

Instead of cutting across the old Riley Plaza to Washington Street, they walked straight up Margin St.

*

Abdallah sat and watched as the cop guided the limo through traffic. He wanted to run the cop's ass over, but they had come so far, and he wouldn't ruin the mission now. As the vehicle moved ahead, he took a right up Washington Street, as indicated by the GPS. He wanted to dump the car, but he needed it later to get to the cop's house. He drove slowly, looking for the closest place to park.

*

While Amato waited for the Limo to arrive, Officer Craig had the other drivers move onto the road outside the parking lot. She had Craig arrange them in the order that she wanted them to appear. *It would be a very short parade,* he thought.

Mrs. Lauren Amato and the City of Salem believed the parade would serve a legitimate purpose besides entertaining the crowd. It was their intention for the spectators to follow the parade, leave downtown and head toward the overpass along the North River. Shortly after, the crowd would stay to watch the fireworks. The city officials also assumed that once the fireworks had ended, everyone would just go home and not return downtown. The police administration and officers knew better, though. The crowd would not follow a few cars like the Piped Piper. Instead they would get rowdy, unruly and stay as long as they could before the police kicked them out.

Craig waited for the limo to arrive before he directed all the vehicles onto the closed street. Amato gave the drivers who were present her instructions. She was excited and could not wait to meet a celebrity. However, she would remain professional and patiently wait until after the parade to get her picture with the star.

    *

Blake approached the road where the parade vehicles waited. He turned around and gave Yassin a sign to stop the car. He turned back around and walked up to Amato. "Okay here is your limo." Blake said. "Let me know when you're ready."

"They're all lined up in order and that will be the last in the procession," she said pointing to the limo. "Can you walk along the sides of the vehicles as we go along the route?"

"Someone will get hurt that way. We will clear a path in front of the vehicles. Then we'll look back to make sure everything is going smoothly." Blake asked, "Where are you going to be?"

"I am not sure, but I'll let you know before the parade starts."

Lieutenant Hayes, who was on the other side of the wooden horses, walked up to them. He said, "Move the vehicles through and stage them in line." He looked around for the officer who was supposed to have already delivered the megaphone. "Hopefully the megaphone will be here soon," he said, a little peeved.

Two Deputies from the Essex County Sheriff's Department were ahead of the barriers. They moved the barriers aside when they heard Lieutenant Hayes. The Sheriff's Department's main job tonight was prisoner transport and traffic control.

"Move them up in line Michael," Hayes said to Craig.

Craig walked ahead of the vehicles, using his arms and shouting, to have the people clear a path. It was not easy. The lead driver wailed on the horn as they moved forward. After four vehicles were in place, Craig waited until he was told to move out. Blake had expected enough room to get the limo through, but then saw the brake light of the last vehicle. *Brain dead*, Blake thought to himself as he walked up front to where his partner was standing.

Blake said, "Hey, how about enough room for all the vehicles this time?" Then he turned and walked back.

As the limo turned right onto New Derby Street, Blake realized there was no front license plate on it. He thought that was odd. It was a commercial vehicle and required by law to have two license plates, one on the front and rear. The limousine services made sure their vehicles were properly registered and insured. It was bad business to get pulled over by the police because the vehicle was not legal. He also knew most of the limo companies had vanity plates with the company name. Blake looked at the left side of the windshield for an inspection sticker and did not see one. What kind of company was this? What celebrity was riding in that?

*

Abdallah saw the brake lights of a car on the right side of the street. Finally, a parking spot. He could not believe how many people and vehicles were here. He pulled the rental to the right, waiting on the street for the vehicle to move.

"Come on, hurry up!" He was getting pissed. He didn't know how lucky he was in finding the space so quickly. He would have to hurry down the street. He picked up the phone off the seat and pressed the number for Yassin.

The phone rang, and Yassin looked at the number. *Abdallah, fuck,* he thought to himself. He was about to answer the call when he changed his mind. He was not around and at least 10 minutes away. He looked at the phone, smiled, and then put it in his pocket.

"Fuck!" Abdallah said and banged on the steering wheel. He finally pulled into the vacant spot. He made sure he had the detonator and cell phone, then left the car. He quickly walked to the intersection where he came from. He was shocked at how the young women were barely wearing any clothes while they walked around.

*

"Let's go, what took you so long?" Silva asked.

"Relax we're here. There's the Lieutenant," Dodek said as they were less than 75 feet away.

"Hide the coffee."

They walked past the stopped traffic. As they got closer, Silva held up the megaphone.

*

Abdallah came around the corner onto Washington Street and saw the end of the limo turning onto the closed road. He smiled as he saw the vehicle cross through the police checkpoint. Everything was going according to plan. It would have been perfect, but Sawaya had screwed that up. Now he was dead, and maybe Allah would take pity on his soul and allow him into paradise with his boy. He reached into his pocket for the key fob reassuring himself that it was still there. He took out his phone and punched the number for Yassin as he continued walking toward the vehicle.

Yassin looked at the phone and decided to answer it. "Yes".

"You made it, excellent."

"Where are you?" Yassin was surprised Abdallah had found a place to park so quickly.

"I found a place to park and saw you turn."

Yassin watched as the cop started to look over the vehicle. Yassin became concerned and said. "There is a policeman who appears to be very interested in this vehicle. He is now looking at the front bumper and windshield."

"Okay relax, I will be there in a few minutes. We can't ruin this opportunity!"

*

Silva and Dodek were about 25 feet away when they saw Blake going around the back of the limo.

"Sector 3 to EOC," Blake said into the mic.

"Go ahead Sector 3."

"Run Mass registration 27JB30," Blake said.

Normally, Blake would never have done something so frivolous on Halloween night, especially downtown. There was no doubt that some of his coworkers were questioning his judgment right now. Blake knew what he was doing though. His sixth sense told him something was not right.

Silva heard the plate being run and said, "That sounds familiar."

Dodek looked at him and they both walked faster towards the wooden horses.

"Here lieutenant," Silva handed him the megaphone.

Then it struck Silva. He looked at the plate and said, "It's stolen."

Everyone looked at him.

"I took the report two days ago, stolen from the shopping center."

Hayes looked at him for a second without saying a word.

Amato was walking toward the officers gathered at the wooden horses.

Hayes shouted, "Get back now!"

She saw all four men remove their guns from the holsters. She quickly moved out of their way. The men spread out on the left side of the limo.

*

Yassin looked out the window and saw at least two pistols pointed at him through the glass. The men were shouting at him. Even though the windows were tinted, he carefully and slowly reached for the keys and shut the vehicle off. Hopefully, they would know he was cooperating, and they would not shoot him. He knew he better get out of the vehicle before Abdallah set off the explosives.

Abdallah was still a distance away when he saw two cops take something from their belts and point them in the direction of the limousine. *Shit!* he thought. He walked faster and could see the cops move around the rear of the vehicle. He could no longer see what was happening. He reached in his pocket for the device. He had no idea about the range or if this thing worked at all.

*

Craig was still in front of the vehicles when he looked back. He saw the crowd backing away and officers fanned out with guns drawn. *Fuck!* he thought and took out his own gun and moved closer.

"Take this," Hayes said to Blake handing him the megaphone.

Blake had the gun in one hand and grabbed the microphone with the other. He tried to tell Hayes something, but was cut off by the radio dispatcher.

"Sector 3 that plate is stolen," the voice said loudly.

Over the radio Hayes heard Captain Sutton said, "Lieutenant, I'm on the way."

TERROR IN THE WITCH CITY

"Response Team 1 respond immediately to New Derby and Washington Street," Sutton said as he started running from the intersection of Derby and Congress.

    *

Yassin slowly opened the door and heard the shouting. Through all the yelling, he made out the word "hands". He put his raised hands through the crack of the door as he opened it.

Yassin started shouting, "I give up, I give up!"

Hayes saw the door open and yelled, "Let's see your hands!"

Blake, who had the megaphone, grabbed the handle and said, "Get back!" The crowd had gathered around them.

Silva and Dodek moved toward the driver whose hands were visible. Blake looked around and saw the crowd was mesmerized by the drama playing out. Some people were moving closer. Craig had come around the front of the vehicle and holstered his gun. He went around the open door and grabbed an arm as Dodek was doing the same. There was little distance between the officers and the limo.

Both Officers grabbed an arm and dragged Yassin out of the vehicle. Officer Silva grabbed his shirt to assist. Yassin heard the yelling and screaming and could not process it all. He was dazed when he was slammed onto the pavement, banging his face on the cold street. He heard someone on a bullhorn.

Yassin turned his face to the left, which was plastered against the pavement and yelled to anyone who would listen, "There is a bomb in the car."

Officer Silva had his knee on Yassin's back about to handcuff him when he heard, "bomb in car". He looked up at Blake. Both Dodek and Craig grabbed Yassin's arms and dragged the man farther away, more for their safety than his. Blake realized the crowd was not moving back. A lot of people would get killed if there really was a bomb, *well fuck it,* he thought.

"Get back!" Blake yelled into the megaphone. "There is a bomb in the car!"

He knew he shouldn't cause a panic, but if not, there would be many casualties. Then he thought, *"What are they going to do fire me?"*

Hayes looked at Blake, in shock that he said "bomb". Hayes was relieved to see the crowd scatter. Now, people were running away from the area and screaming. They scattered like cockroaches in the light.

To the left, Blake saw black helmets and tactical vest clad men. Several Response Team members moved past him. If anyone was in the way, they were moved out quickly. The response team moved into place and form a perimeter around the crime scene.

*

"Oh Shit!" Sutton said as he heard what Blake had said. People were running up Lafayette Street and more were coming at him from New Derby. He saw the tactical response team members taking up positions at the intersection. He fished for his gold badge that was on the end of a chain around his neck. Sutton, who wore plain clothes, had tucked his badge under his jacket to blend in with the crowd. He knew these men would slam him to the ground if he didn't identify himself. The gold badge was worn by superior officers, sergeants and above.

He arrived at the intersection at the same time as Hampton and Ross came down Central Street. Neither of them was in uniform. Parker was running behind both men.

"They are with me," Sutton said holding up the gold badge.

"Go ahead Sir," replied the heavily armed man who was blocking the crowd.

*

Abdallah was not quite prepared for what happened next. He had the detonator in his hands when chaos erupted. It only took seconds before his plan unraveled in front of him. He saw the men draw their guns. He heard the man on the megaphone yell there was a bomb. Then hundreds of people, maybe a thousand, came running his way. He was no more than 50 feet away when they came around the corner, "like a stampede." He learned that phrase from the American Westerns he watched on Satellite TV.

He stood in the path, as the Americans would have called, "a deer in the headlights." He was unsure of where to go or what to do. He was knocked off balance by a large, drunk man running, while he held the hand of a young woman who was dressed like a whore. He saw and heard

290

the crying and screaming as the crowd just about knocked him over. The only reason he didn't fall was someone grabbed him before he went down. He looked up at the older man who helped him, then thanked him. It took a few moments before he realized that the key fob had fallen. He still had his gun though. He had no doubt the fob would be crushed in the throng of bodies running over it. He would never know if it would work at all. Abdallah surmised that Yassin would tell the police about his plan to kill Blake and his family to save his own ass.

Abdallah turned around and headed the same way he had come from. It would not be long until Blake was warned and for the police to arrive at his house to protect the family. He walked quickly back to the rental. He grabbed the phone from his pocket removed the battery and tossed it in the street. He then took the phone and threw it on the ground knowing the crowd would destroy the evidence.

*

Yassin was in pain as the right side of his head and face were pressed into the cold pavement. There were at least two knees pressed into his back with the full weight of the men on top of him. He tried to speak several times.

"Shut up!" The police kept yelling at him whenever he spoke.

He needed to tell them what was going to happen. Both of his arms were sore after being yanked and wrenched back when he was handcuffed. He heard the click of the cuffs and felt the cold steel tighten around his wrists. He did everything the police told him to do. There were men dressed in all black with helmets and machine guns. Some wore masks, including the one that rolled Yassin onto his side.

The masked man asked Yassin, "You have anything on you?"

He was scared, shaking from fear and not from the cold. "I need to," he said, before he was cut off.

"Forget it, don't say a thing!"

Yassin didn't want to piss them off and get kicked in the face. He heard stories of police brutality especially against Arabs. One man started going through his pockets, taking everything out of them. They rolled him on his other side and did the same thing. They searched his legs, groin, waistband, and everywhere. He heard several different people talking and more voices on their radios.

TERROR IN THE WITCH CITY

*

Blake never had a chance to look in the car to see if there was a bomb. Too many people had swarmed in the area and the detectives were going to make sure that no one contaminated their crime scene. This would be the biggest case of their careers. Some would gain notoriety and talk on the police training circuit. The feds would take over, but Salem police would ride this all the way.

"Great job, Kevin," Sutton said to him. "You'll need to do a report of everything that took place, when things settle down".

"Thanks Captain, I will," Blake was stunned by what had lapsed in less than 10 minutes.

The Chief walked up to him next. "Nice work Kevin. How did you know?"

"I will credit my sixth sense, boss." Blake added. "And luck."

"Good work," his boss said and patted him on the shoulders.

*

Abdallah knew not to speed or attract police attention even though they had their hands full. Many a criminal had been caught by police because of a minor traffic offense. The GPS displayed that he would reach his destination in 10 minutes. Traffic was still coming in, but that would change quickly. There were already cars racing out of the area. He was furious that Yassin had fucked up and compromised the plan. He had to complete the goal of the mission no matter what. His contributors and associates would not allow such sloppiness.

The police would be crawling all over the hotel in a little while. He was pretty sure that Yassin would sell his soul to the infidels. He would be lucky if he made to Blake's house before Yassin warned them. Abdallah stopped at the light on Loring Ave by Canal Street. He saw the blue lights approach from across the intersection. The police car slowed down as it got closer to his vehicle. Abdallah could see Yassin talking to the police, probably giving them a description of the rental car.

Abdallah felt for the gun stuffed in his waistband. He made a mental note that he had 14 more rounds left. The police car then sped up and raced past him, headed downtown. He leaned across the seat and opened the glove box. He took out the police radio, turned it on and placed it next to him on the seat. He glanced at the GPS and saw that he had seven more minutes until he got to the house.

*

Sutton had issued orders to the other tactical response team and all sectors to clear the streets immediately. Halloween Night was ending right now. Boston Police Mounted units as well as police motorcycles from NEMLEC began in the center of town to clear the area. A line of horses, motorcycles, and officers moved down the street clearing it with ease. When the crowd saw the horses moving at them, they usually got the hint. Half of the response team continued to guard the crime scene, while the other half assisted in moving out the belligerent visitors.

The prisoner was loaded in the back of a transport van of the Sheriff's Department that was assisting for the night's event. Detectives were photographing and videotaping the vehicle and scene. Special Agent Montgomery, from the FBI had summoned his agents and techs to assist. Massachusetts State Police Bomb Technicians were called to the scene immediately. Two troopers had surveyed the vehicle and wiring and disabled the configuration.

*

The crowd was pushed back. Hampton insisted that Sutton and Montgomery interview the bomber themselves once they were at the station. There was no doubt Yassin would be requesting a lawyer once they were at booking. His Miranda rights had been read on scene to ensure the case was solid.

*

Blake, Craig, and the Peabody Officers were on Washington Street. They were ordered to guard the prisoner in the van and speak to no one until they had been debriefed and their reports completed. The booking room was jammed with drunks and criminals waiting to get booked. Now, the Supervisors were scrambling to relocate them for their priority prisoner. Hampton was taking no chances on losing this to some slick lawyers trying to make a name for himself or by a legal loophole.

Blake was the closest to the back of the van and he heard some muffles and shouting from the prisoner.

"I hope they fry this fucker," Blake said to the others.

"Not in this liberal state," someone replied.

TERROR IN THE WITCH CITY

The four policemen were all on a high from the unbelievable arrest that they just stumbled upon. They had hit the proverbial police jackpot. No other case in their careers would ever come close to this one. They would ride the high for a while. Then, they would continue responding to barking dog calls, medical assists, and other routine calls that occupied their shifts. They were sure to get some serious federal court time, which meant overtime. Officer Dodek took out his cell phone, looked around, and then dialed a number.

"Are you watching the news?" Dodek spoke into the phone. "I am standing by the back of the van," he said smiling to the three others.

Chapter 35

The Bewitching Hour

Saturday October 31st

Halloween Night

Salem, MA

Abdallah wondered how he would get in the house. Maybe the rear slider was still unlocked like last time. He could not afford to draw a lot of attention from the neighbors who would call the police or come to the family's rescue. He would go to the back deck, try the slider; if not he would smash the glass. He knew he had to be quick and isolate Blake before he could respond. The kids would probably be in bed. He wanted to injure him first and then gather his family for execution. After, he would kill Blake.

Abdallah had every intention of videotaping the event, but it slipped his mind. He took the right onto the street and parked the vehicle on the right side of the circle between 2 houses. He made sure the radio was off then put it in his jacket pocket. Abdallah shut the door to the car as quietly as possible and walked on the grass between both houses.

A light was on in a bedroom upstairs and possibly another one in the living room downstairs. The side of the house had no windows. Abdallah turned the corner and stopped by the stairs that led to the deck. The light was on in the kitchen. He removed his gun slowly as he went up the stairs, hugging against the side of the house. He made his way to the top step and peeked inside through the glass. Abdallah felt relieved that he knew the layout of the first floor. He heard nothing and scanned the inside of the house that was silent. He approached the door like last time, trying not to make a sound. He grabbed the handle and slid the door slowly expecting it to stop, but it didn't. He opened the door just enough to let himself in, then closed it with as much care.

TERROR IN THE WITCH CITY

10:00 P.M.

Kerry was upstairs in the master bedroom when she thought she heard something. It might be Kevin trying to surprise her, she thought. Erin had passed out from all the excitement and the baby was sound asleep. Kerry smiled to herself and looked in the mirror to fix her long black hair. She took off her sweatshirt, then adjusted her boobs so they were hanging out of her t-shirt a little more. Her shirt would do all the talking now. She was carrying a yellow weaved basket filled with clothes in her hands and had a smirk on her face. She took one more look in the mirror, and she headed downstairs.

*

Abdallah was in the hallway that led to the front door. He heard movement on the floor above, then the footsteps going down the stairs. He leaned against the wall to create less of a silhouette. He had the gun in the low ready position. He listened for any other noise but heard nothing.

*

Kerry came down the stairs wearing a white t-shirt, gray sweat pants, and a smile for her husband. She walked off the last step, turned right around the corner, and stopped dead in her tracks. She saw the outline of a big man pointing a gun at her face.

*

"Don't scream or say a word or I will kill both of your kids." Abdallah said. "I am not here to rob or rape you. Understand?"

She did not say a word. She stared at him, shaking. Eventually, she nodded her head in understanding.

"Is your husband here? Nod yes or no."

She shook her head, "no."

"Where is he then?"

She paused for a long moment, then spoke. "They called him to work tonight because of a terrorist threat." Kerry caught on to what she had just stated. She looked toward the floor, unsure what to do next.

Abdallah nodded and smiled. "They were right. There is a terrorist threat," he said proudly. "Put down the basket and stay quiet." He put his gun to her chest. "Go back up the stairs."

"Don't hurt my babies." She started to cry.

TERROR IN THE WITCH CITY

"I want to make sure your husband is not upstairs," he nudged her with the gun, "but any stupid move gets the kids killed."

She turned around and walked upstairs. He was a few steps behind her with the gun pointed to her back. She went in the room where the light was already on. He looked around and nodded to her. Abdallah pulled out the radio and turned it on. He attached the mic to the zipper of his jacket. He turned the volume up high. She looked at the radio then looked at him.

"What do you want?" She asked nervously, and tears started flowing down her cheeks.

"I need to check the other rooms," he said.

Kerry stood looking at him.

"Now move!" he said.

They moved down the hall to the end. Abdallah looked at her for a minute without saying anything. She stayed silent, still crying and shivering too. They were standing in front of two closed doors.

"Open the door to the kid's room so I can see he is not here," he said.

She looked at him now with growing hatred. She wanted to hit him, to run, to scream to the kids and tell them to escape. She knew every plan that flashed through her mind was crazy. There was nothing she could do to fight a man with a gun.

"Open the door or I will!" he said louder.

She opened the door on the left side of the hall and walked in. She waited for Abdallah to enter the room. He looked in, took a small step inside, nodded, then stepped out. She moved across the hall to the opposite side and opened the door. Abdallah followed her in, looked at the crib and the shadows around the room. He stepped out of the room and waited for her. He saw more tears running down her cheek.

"How old?" He asked.

"18 months." She replied, not looking at him.

Abdallah was not sure he could hurt a baby. He would be thought of as a monster. What would the western media say about that? He knew that the longer he waited, the more likely his plan would fail.

"Get her out of bed!" He nodded to the door opposite of them.

"What?" Kerry challenged him.

"Get your daughter out of bed and downstairs with you."

TERROR IN THE WITCH CITY

She was sobbing, "No!"

"Then I will," he said moving to the door.

"No, you won't!" She stood in his way and put up her hands to stop him.

He slapped her in the face so hard that it caused her to sway and almost lose her balance.

He shouted in her face. "Don't ever touch me!"

Kerry was not crying anymore, she was pissed. Abdallah knew that even though he had size and strength, a protective mother was unpredictable. Kerry entered the room and went to the bed, the she pulled back the covers. She bent down and picked her daughter up, carefully putting Erin's head on her left shoulder. Kerry turned around and walked past Abdallah, eyeballing him as she went down the stairs. He followed her to the living room. Kerry sat on the couch in the dark room, holding Erin tightly. Abdallah looked at her and saw pure hatred. He grabbed for the microphone.

     *

Blake was leaning against the van waiting with the three guys. Dodek was telling them a funny story when he was interrupted by a call on the radio. The speaker did not sound like anyone he knew. "Officer Blake are you there?" A man with an Arab accent sounded through the radio.

Blake stood up straight and said, "Who the fuck is that?"

The voice of the dispatcher interjected the conversation on the radio. "This is the EOC you are on a police emergency frequency. Please identifying yourself?"

"My name is not important," Abdallah said. "but what I am doing is."

"Please terminate transmission." The dispatcher repeated, "You are on an active police frequency."

"Officer Blake, I am at your house at 100 Gallows Hill Road, and I am going to kill your wife and daughter," Abdallah keyed the mic and placed it by Kerry and Erin.

Blake heard his wife and child crying in the background. He turned around and looked at Capt. Sutton, who was staring at him in shock. Blake looked around the area and saw Detective Alexander Salas leaning against the unmarked Crown Victoria with the lights on and engine running. Sutton followed his gaze to the car. Blake sprinted to the vehicle.

Sutton watched him and yelled to Detective Salas, "Go with him!"

"By the time you get here Officer Blake it will too late," Abdallah said on the radio.

Sutton knew that any officer who had been listening to the radio were already on their way to Blake's house. He felt useless, but he had to do something. He keyed his mic, "All units, 100 Gallows Hill Road immediately!"

Someone, please be close, he thought.
*

Abdallah who never used a police radio before, was pissed that his transmission was cut off. He didn't know they had the power to override him. He took his anger out on the hostages.

He pointed the gun at Kerry. "Get up!"

Kerry was crying and pushing herself up, trying to stand tall in front of her child, hoping her courage would make Erin feel protected. "Please don't hurt her!" Kerry cried.

Erin was awake and looking around, clinging to her mother's neck. As she made eye contact with Abdallah, she began to cry harder and held her mother tighter.
*

Dawson stopped talking on his cell phone when he heard Blake's address through his radio. He remembered that Blake's house was on the other side of the tank. He quickly stood up from the chair and ran to the gate. Then he thought, *do I need, the pistol or rifle?* He needed to get back to the car for the rifle. While he was running, he thought about the terrain. The tank was on a hill behind Blake's house. There were no paths or trails, just thickets and brush. The back of the house and deck were at the bottom of the hill. *How the fuck do I get close without giving myself away,* he wondered?

The rifle had a long distance, but it was dark out and had no night sights. The pistol was good for no more than 25 yards and had no night sights either. Dawson unlocked the car door and put the keys in the ignition and pressed the Aux1 button. The button unlocked the solenoid that released the gun lock. There were guns stored in every patrol vehicle.

TERROR IN THE WITCH CITY

Dawson heard the click and reached up and pulled the metal plate which held the AR-15. There was a full magazine in the well, and all he needed to do was pull the charging handle back and release the bolt. He left the keys in the ignition and ran as fast as he could down the dirt path.

    *

Blake opened the car door and reached down for the keys to start the vehicle, even though it was running. He put his foot on the brake and shoved the gear selector into drive as he shut the door. Blake looked over as Detective Salas jumped in and shut the door.

Blake hit the siren and slammed the gas as the vehicle immediately bogged down, "Fucking piece of shit!" Blake yelled.

    *

"Your people will never make it in time." He watched his hostages as he spoke into the mic. "I am here to exact revenge on you the man responsible for the death of a small child in Iraq."

Kerry was looking at him now.

"To the back deck." He ordered her.

He continued using the radio. "United Sates Marines, being supervised by Officer Blake, drove over an innocent boy and killed him. Now I am here on behalf of that family to take your family."

Abdallah opened the glass door to the deck and motioned for Kerry to go outside. The he continued, "Blake, your wife, and child will die at my hands; just like the child was killed at your hands as the whole village watched."

Abdallah was standing in the house, his gun pointed at the back of the mother and her child. Kerry stared at the stars, as if some angel would swoop down to save them. Erin stared over her mother's shoulder at Abdallah. He was smiling.

The statement stunned everyone who was listening. No less than 10 vehicles were driving frantically to the residence. Every man wondered who would arrive first, who would put the bullet through the terrorist's skull.

    *

Blake was on Jackson Street heading for Highland Avenue, going as fast as the vehicle would go. He had driven in the other lane and even on a sidewalk at one point. His passenger was holding on for dear life to anything that he could grab. Blake barely missed a Honda CRV, the horn wailing as Blake blew through the light at the intersection.

    *

    Dawson ran on the existing trail until it ended. He passed the tank, then he started making his way through the brush carefully and quietly. It was dark out which would hide him until he entered the back yard. Dawson knew he would have to quickly acquire his target before taking him down. It would be his pleasure, though. These people had killed Dawson's wife on that plane and now they were going to kill Blake's family.

    *

    "Hurry up!" Abdallah yelled.

    He grabbed Kerry and shoved her through the open glass door. She was holding Erin, both were crying and screaming. Erin clung to her mother but watched Abdallah as he pushed them.

    "We are going outside," Abdallah pushed her. "Your husband killed a child and now you and your daughter will pay."

    *

    At the top of Cherry Hill Road, the man behind the wheel of the white pickup had worked hard since six in the morning. Carlos had been a landscaper since he arrived in America from Guatemala two years prior. He was lucky to be employed and didn't have to hang out in the Home Depot parking lot. He knew other immigrants waited there, hoping for a stranger to offer them an odd job. He despised being a day laborer and waiting for some white asshole to pull up, pay shit and insult him all day long. They treated him like a slave. He had advanced from that though and now worked for a nice guy out of Swampscott. Carlos' only worry was his boss finding out that he did not have a driver's license and fire him.

    He had been given his own crew earlier in the week and decided to reward himself and bond with his guys over a few Coronas. That was hours ago. Now, he was headed home to his wife and kids, with a nice paycheck given in cash and the last Corona between his legs. His truck went down the steep hill that curved a bit. When he turned the wheel to the right, the beer slid out and fell on the floor. Carlos corrected the vehicle and looked down on the floor to find the bottle. As he did this the light at the intersection ahead had changed to red.

He found the bottle that he was looking for. When he looked up, he saw the red light. Since he had been drinking for several hours, his reaction time was slow. Then he was distracted by the blue swirl of lights and the siren.

*

Blake saw the light turn green. The right turn was just ahead after the light, three more minutes and he would be home. Something to the right caught his attention, then he saw lights and movement. He also heard Salas yell something. His brain was trying to process everything. The last thing he could remember was the white front fender of a vehicle. His memory went black when the unmarked Crown Victoria was struck violently on the right side.

*

Dawson, who was making his way through the thorn bushes, was trying to be quiet. He stopped when he heard the crying and yelling as the glass slider opened. He saw the man with Blake's wife and child. He saw the outline of a gun in Abdallah's hand, as he dragged the woman outside. Dawson froze in the shadows; he was still a distance away. He knew he could not be seen from this position but would if he moved closer.

Thankfully he had charged the weapon as he ran, or he would have been heard. *Fuck,* he said to himself, knowing he would have to take the shot now. He assumed a tight kneeling position and was working on his sight picture and alignment. There was not enough light to get a good shot. He could not risk shooting the woman even though she was going to die if he did nothing. He didn't need a scope for the distance. He had trained in the Marine Corps shooting at 100, 200 and 500 yards without any mechanical sight assistance. He had trained at night before, but with a night sight.

*

Blake woke up a few minutes later and didn't know where he was or what had happened. Salas was knocked out, and there was blood all over the interior of the vehicle. It took a little bit before Blake remembered that he had to get home to save his family. He reached for the mic that was clipped on the dashboard. He winced at the severe pain he felt.

TERROR IN THE WITCH CITY

He wondered how the mic had stayed in place. The windows were smashed, glass was everywhere, the car was crumbled; but the mic stayed in place on the dashboard. He didn't have the strength to remove it from the holder.

Blake reached over and keyed the mic, "We have been hit by a car. I cannot make it." He managed to get through the pain. "I love you both," he stammered, then he cried.

*

Abdallah heard the transmission and smiled. Kerry and Erin heard the radio and started bawling. The smile disappeared when Abdallah heard the sirens getting closer. He had no more than a few minutes. He knew he would not get a chance to kill Blake. He would kill his wife and daughter, though, and be a martyr, an honored soldier of Allah.

Abdallah held the button on the mic. "Officer Blake, since you cannot be here to watch, I'll tell you what I am going to do to them."

*

Dawson moved closer and could hear Abdallah. Blake was out of commission, and the cruisers would not make it in time. He had to stop this lunatic himself. He watched the man and he inched closer. He knew the crying would mask the noise, so he could move again to get a better shot.

*

Both girls were sobbing uncontrollably. Erin was still in the house, clinging to the frame of the glass door, while Kerry stood just outside.

"Get her out now!" Abdallah shouted to Kerry.

He keyed the mic and put it close to them for a few seconds. "You hear that? None of you can do anything about it. You are weak and defenseless. Where are you now U.S. Marine! I am going to kill them on the radio!"

The siren grew louder.

He grabbed Kerry and yelled, "Move over here now!"

*

Dawson was still in the bushes but had moved as close as he could. He lined the rifle up on the target. He moved the front sight post on the silhouette of the man, using the rear sight aperture. He needed light but went off the mantra he knew so well; adapt, improvise and overcome.

TERROR IN THE WITCH CITY

He knelt again, assuming a tight kneeling position. His left elbow rested forward of his left knee. His right ass cheek rested on the heel of his right foot. The butt stock of the rifle was nestled tight in the crease of his right shoulder. Dawson breathed out slowly, shut his mouth and inhaled through his nose. He shut his left eye and aligned the sights. He adjusted his right foot slightly. His breathing slowed down as he concentrated.

*

"Get over here!" Abdallah said and yanked Kerry away from Erin, to the middle of the deck.

Erin still clung to the frame. She was so scared. Then she remembered something her father told her the night he left for Iraq.

*

Abdallah stepped back and keyed the mic, "Blake say goodbye to your wife first. I will let you listen to me shoot her."

Abdallah was three feet away from her. She stood facing him, but looked over his shoulder, into Erin's eyes. He raised his gun.

*

Erin remembered her father's words, "If you are ever scared turn on the light," That night he held her hand and stayed with her until she fell asleep. In the morning when she woke up, he had already left for Iraq. Now, Erin took her father's advice. She felt for the light switch and flipped it up.

*

Abdallah looked over at her when the light went on. He knew it didn't matter no one could save them. He turned his gaze back to Kerry and raised the gun to her face.

*

Dawson was surprised to see the light on inside the house. He had been almost perfectly aligned on the bad guy. He moved slightly to the left for a perfect headshot. The pad of his first finger applied an even slight pressure to the trigger of the rifle as he held his breath.

*

Abdallah's brain never registered that a shot had been fired. The 5.56 millimeter round entered his head at 3200 feet per second, slamming him into the glass door. Blood and brain matter smeared along the glass and the siding as his body collapsed onto the deck. Kerry screamed hysterically and ran to her daughter.

Abdallah's hand was still on the microphone when the shot rang out. Everyone listening on the radio heard the shot then silence.

*

Officer Steven Dawson reached down and turned his radio on with his left hand. His right hand still held the rifle. He reached for the mic. "Officer Dawson to Salem control and all units, I have one terrorist down. Both hostages appear unharmed. Roll rescue this way." He waited a few seconds when no one responded. "Do you copy, Salem?"

There was silence on the air.

"This is Chief Hampton. I copy your transmission. Thank you, thank you very much."

There was another moment of silence before another officer responded. "Thank you, Steve, thank you," said a man who was crying.

*

It was a little before lunchtime the next day when the patrolman removed the yellow crime scene tape. Detectives from Salem Police, troopers from the Mass State Police CPAC unit, and agents from the FBI had all come and gone. The rental car driven by Abdallah was towed back to the Salem Police Department for processing.

Reporters from several news services had been in the area all night long and into the morning; they were talking to neighbors and trying to speak to police. They were told to attend the press conference later; no information was to be released until then.

Kerry and Erin were taken to the hospital and checked out for any physical injuries which were minor scrapes and cuts. There real injuries were psychological in nature and would take years to treat. Kerry's parents were brought to the hospital to be with their daughter, son-in-law and grandkids.

Blake and Salas were in a guarded hospital room and would be for a few more days. Detective Salas had taken the brunt of the accident. He suffered a concussion, broken arm, and leg injuries. Blake fared much better, but was ordered by doctors, his wife, and Chief Hampton to stay another night to avoid the media circus.

TERROR IN THE WITCH CITY

The drunk driver was treated for injuries and brought to the police department for booking. He went to court in the morning and released before the ink was dry, which was, usually the case. He nearly killed two policemen and barley got a slap on the wrist.

Breyden was the only one who was rested that night. He had slept peacefully in his crib as all hell broke loose on the other side of the house.

36592728R00187

Made in the USA
Middletown, DE
15 February 2019